P9-CAM-382

UNDER A CRESCENT MOON ...

Protected from the ocean by an arc of lava rock, the warm water in the cove barely moved around his legs as his eyes drifted over her alluring body. The soft moonlight played across Lucky's skin and emphasized the black bathing suit.

The halter top covered her breasts, making them seem even fuller, then it nipped in at her waist, playing up its smallness and showing off the provocative curve of her hips. The effect was simple, conservative, breathtaking.

Until she turned her back. Man, oh, man. What had he gotten himself into? Her suit didn't *have* a back. It was bare to the waist, a thousand times sexier than any skimpy bikini.

His gaze kept returning to her expressive face. She couldn't seem to look away from him either. The magnetism she generated was almost a tangible thing. He imagined making love to her in the water, a whirlpool of stars overhead.

"Lucky," he said, putting his hand on her waist.

"Don't," she warned, but she didn't try to pull away.

"Don't what?" He couldn't resist teasing her. She was so cute, so enthusiastic about life despite all that had happened to her.

"You're thinking about kissing me," she replied.

He openly studied her mouth, its full lower lip irresistible. "What makes you say that?"

"I can tell what's on that naughty mind of yours."

"Trust me, angel, kissing you wasn't what I was thinking about."

PRAISE FOR MERYL SAWYER

LAST NIGHT

"Bold drama, sensational suspense and riveting sexual tension . . ."
—*Romantic Times* [4½ stars]

"Her best romantic suspense ever, a searing tale of deceit and greed filled with snappy prose and riveting sexual tension."
—Ft. Lauderdale Sun-Sentinel

"The author expertly keeps the story moving . . . style and verve hold the whole together and will have readers looking for more."
—*Publishers Weekly*

"Ms. Sawyer is an extremely resourceful and talented author with a knack for throwing curves into her stories that keep the reader breathlessly waiting for the climactic ending. Combine this with emotional intensity, sensuality and sumptuous characters, and you have a splendid reading experience."
—*Rendezvous*

A KISS IN THE DARK

"A finely crafted, engaging read."
—*Publishers Weekly*

"All the hallmarks of this award-winning author's works are present in this intensely emotional, complex and riveting tale." [4½ stars]
—*Romantic Times*

"Recommended by word of mouth—A KISS IN THE DARK is a romance with surprising plot twists as well as a mystery with ardent overtones."
—*Library Journal*

PROMISE ME ANYTHING

"A really good book impressively delivered."
—*Los Angeles Daily News*

"Meryl Sawyer has produced another sparkling gem of a book. . . . showcases her talent for delivering complex, intriguing and fast paced tales of greed, betrayal and love. An intense and spellbinding read."
—*Romantic Times* [4½ stars]

NEVER KISS A STRANGER

"An entertaining read."
—Publishers Weekly

"You will love it!"
—*Rendezvous*

UNFORGETTABLE

Meryl Sawyer

Zebra Books
Kensington Publishing Corp.
http://www.zebrabooks.com

ZEBRA BOOKS are published by

Kensington Publishing Corp.
850 Third Avenue
New York, NY 10022

Copyright © 1997 by M. Sawyer-Unickel

All rights reserved. No part of this book may be reproduced
in any form or by any means without the prior written consent
of the Publisher, excepting brief quotes used in reviews.

If you purchased this book without a cover, you should be
aware that this book is stolen property. It was reported as
"unsold and destroyed" to the Publisher and neither the Author
nor the Publisher has received any payment for this "stripped
book."

Zebra and the Z logo Reg. U.S. Pat. & TM Off.

First Printing: January, 1997
10 9 8 7 6 5 4 3 2 1

Printed in the United States of America

*To the courageous Search and Rescue Teams in our country.
This book is dedicated to the men and women and all the
fine dogs who are there when we need them.*

The best way to love anything is as if it might be lost.
—G.K. Chesterton

Chapter 1

The bleached-white skull of a moon shot out from between the clouds, lancing the night sky with a single beam of light. The sudden brightness revealed a man squatting on his haunches, a dog at his side. They had been on the rocky ledge overlooking the ocean for more than two hours.

The rain lashed the wind-sculpted bluffs as it had all evening, a storm with blinding bolts of lightning followed by earthshaking thunder. Neither man nor dog even flinched. They possessed the gift of supreme concentration, the ability to focus on their task regardless of the conditions. The man came by it naturally, calling on some inner source of strength that had always been a mystery to others.

He had trained the dog to home in on his objective and ignore everything around him. Now they were out for the ultimate test.

Thunder boomed an ominous warning, and with a final flash of light on the turbulent sea and its scudding whitecaps, the moon disappeared behind a bank of churning clouds. The wind rose, howling along the volcanic cliffs and valleys. Chain lightning arced across the sky and seared the tops of the wind-whipped palms.

"There for a second, I thought it was going to clear," Greg Braxton said to the greyhound at his side. "That would have ruined all our fun."

Dodger gazed at his master through the pelting rain. His fawn-colored coat was soaked to a deep mahogany. Rivulets of water cascaded off his ears and sluiced down his sleek back to pool around his haunches.

"It's not going to get much rougher," Greg told the dog. "We might as well go for it."

Though his legs ached from being in one position for so long, Greg instructed his mind to ignore the pain. With a flick of his wrist, he signaled for Dodger to rise. The greyhound shifted to his feet, steadier on all four than Greg was on two. Still, it had to be hard on the dog. This was by far the most difficult exercise he'd put him through, but it was necessary. Soon they would fly to the mainland for certification. Before Dodger could qualify as a disaster dog, he'd have to pass a grueling test that even the most highly trained dogs often failed.

"Search," Greg commanded, turning up his palm.

Like an eagle, Dodger soared off the cornice and landed on the boulder below. He pivoted, whirling to the right, then bounded effortlessly over jagged rocks and loose slag. One misstep and Dodger would plummet to the base of the cliff, where the savage riptide would drag him out to sea.

Greg followed, lightning—nature's flashlight—guiding him. Scrambling to keep up with the dog, he hobbled over the rough boulders, scythes of wind-driven rain slashing at him. Despite the rocky terrain, leafy ferns had taken root, making the rocks dangerously slippery.

"Dodger! Where are you going?"

The dog veered sharply to the left, not to the right where Greg had planted the vial. It was hidden so carefully in a lava rock crevice that he doubted he could find it again. The vial of scent had been distilled from a cadaver and was used to train disaster dogs.

Pseudo-corpse was expensive as hell. So what does Dodger do? Runs away from the "body in a bottle." Greg took a second to catch his breath. Okay, this is what happens when you let a dog's mournful eyes get to you. Dodger had been born to race—and trained like a robot to chase a mechanical rabbit. Maybe the greyhound couldn't be retrained.

Greg turned to go back to the camp. Three sharp barks pierced the air, all but lost to the wind and the rain.

"What in hell was that? Couldn't be a signal!" Above the drumbeat of the rain and the wind scouring the volcanic ridges, three sharp barks rang out again. "Christ! It *is* a signal."

Greg sprinted across the jumbled remnants of the age-old lava flow. The rain flew sideways in the wind, blasting his face like bullets and funneling down his chin into his slicker. He finally found Dodger. "What do you see, boy?"

The dog peered down the sheer drop, one foot raised, pointing like a retriever. Good, Greg thought, at least he had learned to point out targets even if he couldn't locate the vial of pseudo-corpse. Lightning flashed, momentarily flooding the area with an eerie violet-white glow.

"No way!" Greg muttered, spotting the car at the base of the cliff.

His mind must be playing a trick on him. It was too much like another night when he'd looked down from a road and had seen a car at the bottom of an embankment. Of course, it hadn't been raining that night, and he hadn't been alone. The Maui Search and Rescue Team had been with him. But they'd been too late.

Greg mentally gave himself a hard shake. That was then and this is now. He yanked out the flashlight fastened to his belt and concentrated the beam on the rocky beach below. The tunnel of light stabbed through the darkness and hit a white Toyota.

"Where'n hell did it come from?"

Greg had chosen this remote spot because the road ended a mile behind him. The Hana side of Maui was rain forest, and what passed for a road washed out whenever the Pineapple Express blew in and drenched the Hawaiian Islands. The road had been impassable for the better part of the day, but some fool had ventured out. Was the fool still alive?

He put his finger in the air and twirled it as if starting the Indy. Dodger responded to the signal and sprinted down the steep ravine. As the dog vaulted over the rocks, Greg calculated his chances of bringing anyone up the embankment. He had some gear back at the camp, but not nearly enough.

Summoning help was out of the question. The crack rescue team in Kihei would need a helicopter to get to this remote site. Sure as hell, the chopper would be grounded by the weather. There was a police substation back in Hana, but the road had been closed by the storm.

Dodger was almost near enough now to determine if the person inside was alive or dead. Greg couldn't help thinking this was a good test. Part of the canine certification exam would be to find a body underwater. Body gases lifted off the water at the spot where a person went down. One whiff and a trained dog could pinpoint the location and determine if the victim was dead or alive.

Tonight there's more than enough water to call this an aquatic test. He shielded his brow from the rain and squinted into the tunnel of light. Dodger barked once, then waited exactly five heartbeats before barking again.

''How could anyone have survived that fall?''

Greg charged over the rocks, leaping across several small boulders until he reached the pup tent where he'd set up camp earlier. Inside was a small emergency kit, a length of rope, and heavy-duty gloves. The bare essentials were all he'd been able to bring on his motorcycle. He brought them out of habit, never expecting to need them.

''Let's hope this rope is long enough,'' he mumbled to himself as he dashed back to the bluff. "Or else you're a dead man."

He secured the rope around the largest boulder he could find. He yanked on his gloves and repelled down the treacherous embankment much faster than was safe. His boots slammed down on the boulder at the base of the steep ravine. Waves that usually rolled onto the peaceful shore now pummeled the beach, blasting the rocks with blinding clouds of spray and flinging chains of seaweed into the air.

"Good work, boy," he yelled to Dodger over the thunderous roar.

As he opened the door, he saw the interior of the car was dry and dark, but a flare of lightning revealed a woman slumped sideways from the driver's seat to the passenger side of the car. She was slight with a wild mane of blonde corkscrew curls that hung to her shoulders. He reached for her wrist and immediately found a strong pulse.

Greg pulled out his flashlight to determine the extent of her injuries and didn't see anything more serious than a few bruises. She'd collapsed facedown, and in the clusters of wild curls he saw a little blood seeping from the back of her head.

"A head injury," he said over his shoulder to Dodger. "Doesn't look bad, though."

He stood there a moment, the rain drumming across his back and splashing into the car. The storm was moving inland; he imagined the thunderheads stacked like pyramids against the buttress of Haleakala. The dormant volcano blocked tropical storms, making this side of the island a rain forest.

Great. He could count on this ravine being under water when the runoff from Haleakala became a flash flood. How long did he have? Not more than a few minutes, half an hour at most.

"We don't have any choice," he said to himself, but Dodger answered with a sympathetic whine. "We have to move her."

He gently turned the woman to face him, then checked again to see if she had any serious injuries. She might have internal injuries, but he doubted it. How lucky could someone get? It was a one in a million chance that anyone could survive a crash like this.

He took a closer look at her face. An angel in a whore's makeup. Her heart-shaped face, framed by wild bleached blonde curls, sported cherry-pink lipstick and eyelashes with enough mascara and shadow to have wiped out an entire cosmetic counter.

The tiger-print dress she wore was just as cheap. It had a short skirt that skimmed the tops of her thighs and a halter top too small for her breasts. Sexy as hell, though, if she was your type.

"Hardly the girl next door," he said to himself. An image of Jessica appeared out of nowhere. During the last two years Greg had willed himself never to think about his dead wife—and he'd succeeded—until now. Jessica had appeared as wholesome as if she had just baked cookies. Maybe it was better when they looked like this woman. At least you knew you were dealing with a tramp.

Greg stumbled toward his tent, not certain if he could make the last few steps without dropping the woman. He elbowed the flap open and laid her on the air mattress. He collapsed beside her, breathing like a racehorse. She wasn't heavy, but the trip up the ravine had been brutal. If he hadn't been in Olympic shape, he would never have been able to carry her.

A whine caught his attention. "Come in, Dodger," Greg called. "I don't have the strength to dry you."

The dog nosed his way in, then shook, spraying the inside of the tent with water. Greg almost laughed. He'd purposely brought the tent so they could be dry after the test. Between Dodger and their rain-soaked clothes, it was as wet inside as it was outside.

Dodger settled at his feet while Greg hung the flashlight from its noose at the top of the tent, then reached for the Mylar blanket he kept with his emergency supplies. He unfolded the long foil sheet from a small pouch. The storm had brought a damp chill to the warm tropical air that wouldn't be good for someone in shock.

"Doesn't look like the same person, does it?" he asked Dodger.

The grueling climb up the ravine in the pouring rain had washed away the woman's garish makeup and soaked her wiry curls so that they hung in limp strands to her shoulders. The rain had plastered her dress to her body, outlining her slim hips. The halter top seemed even smaller now, the sheer fabric revealing the fullness of her breasts.

"I'm losing it," he muttered as he wrapped the blanket around her. Not only was he talking to his dog more than usual, but now the woman was beginning to seem attractive. "Okay, so go out and get laid."

He could think of a half-dozen women who'd let him know that they'd be thrilled to accommodate him, but after Jessica's death, none of them held any appeal. He secured the blanket around the woman's torso, concealing her provocative breasts, then worked his way down to her feet.

"She's damn lucky," he said, nose to nose with Dodger in a tent designed for one person. "She might have a slight concussion, that's all."

Dodger wagged his tail, fanning the moist air that was musky with the smell of rain-soaked clothes, wet dog, and body heat. Greg pulled off one of her tennis shoes, thinking it was a weird choice of shoes considering the sexy dress. He was working on the laces of the other shoe when he realized they didn't match.

"What's this?" He held them up to the dim light shining from overhead. One shoe was a size six with red corkscrew shoelaces, while the other was a size seven and had ordinary laces. "Why's she wearing a size six?" he asked, and Dodger cocked his head. "Her toes had to be doubled over."

He inspected her feet, the light even dimmer now, the flashlight sure to conk out at any moment. Her toes were painted the same cherry-pink as the lipstick she'd been wearing. The skin on her right foot was scored with indentations from the smaller shoe.

"Ooookay. It takes all kinds." He tucked the Mylar around her feet. Then he shucked his slicker, tossed it into the corner, and shrugged out of his shirt.

Greg heard the crackle of the foil blanket. He spun around and saw the woman was sitting up, the Mylar barely covering her breasts, her eyes open. When he'd checked her pupils, he'd noticed that her eyes were green, but now as she stared at him, he saw they were kelly green with gloss-brown lashes and delicate brows that flared upward. Her eyes were so astonishing that he sucked in his breath.

"How are you feeling?" he asked.

She mumbled something that sounded like *"thrill,"* although he couldn't be certain. Wisps of hair had dried around her temples, but the rest was still wet and appeared almost brown. The color offset her eyes far better than the bleached blonde, he decided.

A moment passed and she spoke again, but he couldn't tell if she was saying "Thrill me" or "Don't thrill me." What did she mean? She sounded upset, desperate.

"You'd better lie down," he said. "You're in shock. It'll be morning before I can get you to a hospital. The storm washed out the road."

She stared at him—or through him—with glazed, intense eyes roiling with emotions he didn't understand. Instinctively Greg was shaken in a way he'd never been before. His breath stalled in his throat; he couldn't move. The flashlight emitted nothing more than a faint glow now. But it was enough. Her breasts swayed slightly, the nipples pouting seductively at him through the wet fabric. Slow heat unfurled in the pit of his stomach, then centered in his groin.

Again she whispered something about "thrill." Jesus! Had he rescued a two-bit hooker? "You're in shock," he repeated. "You'd better rest."

She moved toward him, closing the small space between them until Greg could feel the heat of her body, could see the drops of moisture on her lashes. "Give me a chance," she said. Despite the intimate pitch of her voice, he sensed something was terribly wrong. "I can make you love me."

Sweat peppered the top of his lip. He swiped at it with the back of his hand. The world was filled with all types of women. He'd spent time with more than a few, but he was out of his league here.

"Forget about love," he tried to joke. "A simple thanks for rescuing you and a box of chocolate chip cookies will do."

"Love," she whispered, her mesmerizing eyes never leaving his as she kept inching nearer, until she was so close that his uneven breath ruffled the wisps of hair framing her face. He caught the heady scent of cheap perfume as she edged closer and one pert breast brushed the damp hair on his chest. He jerked back and hit the side of the small tent.

He realized that she had yet to blink. Uneasiness prickled across the back of his neck, raising the fine hairs and making him wonder what in hell was wrong with her. He waved his hand in front of her nose. Nothing. Not even the flicker of an eyelash.

"She's in a trance or something." His words bounced off the walls of the tent.

With a whimper that might have been a cry of pain or longing, she threw her arms around him. "I can make you love me. Please. Let me show you."

He had no doubt she could do it. The soft mounds of her breasts molded against his torso. Through the fabric he felt the heat of her body and the throb of her pulse in her taut nipples. Her eyes were incandescent, riveting. Her lips, so temptingly close to his, were slightly parted, revealing the pink tip of her tongue. The warmth of her body seeped through his, tiptoeing through his veins and trembling through his chest as erotic as jungle drums at midnight.

She tugged his hand to her breast and coasted it along her

chest until his warm palm was centered on her tightly spiraled nipple. He tried, he honestly did, but couldn't resist cradling her softness in his palm, testing the weight of her breast with a slight rise of his wrist, exploring the pliant fullness with his fingertips, then brushing the peak with his thumb.

What was he doing? This woman must be on drugs—or *lolo*—crazy. She needed help—not sex. He eased her back onto the mattress.

She bucked, thrusting her hips against his, sending an upward surge of heat through his groin. He slung one leg across the tops of her thighs, anchoring her in place. The fight went out of her as he lay beside her, his body half covering hers. The rapid tempo of his own breathing startled him, yet she didn't seem the least bit agitated. If anything, she seemed detached, on another plane entirely. This was just too friggin' weird.

"Don't do this to me," she whispered, desperation in her voice. "I can make you love me."

Her hand glided across his torso, tracing the contours of his chest, her eyes on his. They had a haunted quality as if she were seeing something, experiencing something that he couldn't.

Her hands. Oh, Christ . . . her hands were in his pants. Faster than a bolt of lightning, one hand shot inside his underwear. She touched him lightly with her fingertips, a low moan rising from her throat, her eyes narrowing slightly.

"Don't!" he said, pulling her hand away.

He sucked in a gulp of air, amazed to discover he was hot and achingly hard. Squeezing his eyes shut, he called on the reservoir of strength he had used so successfully to cauterize his feelings during the past two years.

It took a full minute for his breathing to return to normal and for the pressure building in his chest to diminish and erase the lingering imprint of her hand. Then he eased his eyes open, almost afraid of what he might see.

Her head was resting against his shoulder. She was still staring at him, a sheen of tears glazing her eyes. She'd aroused him, true, and part of him hated her for it, but she was scaring him now. Something was terribly wrong with her.

He told her what he thought she wanted to hear. "I love you."

She moaned, a plaintive sound that bordered on a sob, a cry so piercing it vibrated through his bones. Her eyes had that faraway look, yet they bored into his, seeming to speak to him alone. "Please, don't hurt me."

"I'll never hurt you," he said, feeling *lolo*—crazy—himself for talking to someone who didn't even know he existed.

Her tense body relaxed, becoming soft and pliant in his arms. He released her hand and, with a sigh, her eyes closed. She went utterly still just as the light went out, leaving them in complete darkness.

Chapter 2

She awoke by degrees, drifting upward through cushioning layers of sleep, dimly aware of a buzz in her head. She tried to open her eyes, but they were too heavy. Her whole head seemed unnaturally large and noisy, the drone of a million hornets filling her ears.

"Breathe deeply," she told herself.

She sucked in air so hot and so thick that it was like breathing through a wet blanket. The smell filling her nostrils made her gag. Was she in a kennel? The odor of wet dog and something equally musky had ripened in the oppressive heat.

She managed to force one eye open. "Oh, my God!"

A Day-Glo orange sky greeted her. Where was she? Jerking upright, she tried to remember. Both eyes were open now, pinwheels of light whirling in front of her, backlit by the dreadful tangerine sky.

She covered her eyes with both hands and tried to swallow, but her mouth was dry; her tongue felt like sandpaper. For a second she thought she might be ill, but the surge of nausea passed, and she eased her eyes open. Her head was a dead weight, and the hum in her ears made it hard to think. It took several seconds to realize that she was in a small tent.

"Funny, I don't remember going camping."

She glanced around and spotted her tennis shoes. The first shoe went on easily. The other one belonged to someone else. Not only was it too small, the curly red shoe laces didn't match. She checked but didn't see her other shoe.

A yellow slicker was heaped in the corner with a shirt. Picking it up, she saw the blue polo shirt was a man's XXL. What was she doing in this small tent with a man? A very large man at that. Who?

Her muzzy brain didn't have an answer. All it kept saying was *It's hot. Get out of here.* She started to jam her foot into the mismatched shoe, then noticed the horrid pink nail polish on her toes and fingers. Yuck! Why would she use such an ugly color? And what was she doing in a cheap tiger-print dress?

She forced her foot into the shoe and scrambled on all fours toward the closed flap of the tent. Another wave of nausea urged the bile up from the pit of her stomach. She closed her eyes, hugging her shaking body, and her head fell forward. Her hair tumbled across her face, tickling her nose. She looped the long strands behind each ear before daring to open her eyes again.

Feeling better, she nudged the tent flap aside and crawled out. She gulped in air that was only slightly cooler than it was inside the tent. Moist plumes of heat shimmered up from the rocky ground in a vaporous mist that brought with it the earthy scent of rain. She rose to her feet and saw an endless expanse of azure sea that blended with the sky at the horizon. A flock of tiny birds rose off the water and floated like a cloud, skimming just above the breakers.

"Where am I?" she asked aloud.

The rugged coastline was austerely beautiful, yet somehow lonely. Frightening. Stately palms stood like sentinels guarding the deserted beach. Gazing at the ocean, she stood there, trying to recall what she was doing here until she realized someone was watching her.

She turned slowly, to keep her stomach on an even keel, telling herself to stay calm. A few feet away in a shadowy bower of ferns, a man was sitting on a rock, shaded by enormous tree ferns, a mug in his hands. His deep blue eyes pierced her with a physical force she felt all the way to her toes.

His eyes weren't Santa Claus blue, all twinkly and merry. No. These eyes were as cold as the gleaming blade of the knife hanging from his side. Tall, big-boned with formidable shoulders, he could snap her in two with one hand, and right now he looked as if there was nothing he'd like better.

She glanced around quickly, her wariness mounting. She was alone with this man in the middle of what appeared to be nowhere. He hadn't done anything; he hadn't even spoken, yet she was on the verge of panic.

He looked like someone you wouldn't want to meet in a dark alley—or even in a church. Not only was he big, he looked just plain mean. Several days' worth of dark beard stubbled a square jaw and shadowed an upper lip crimped over a slightly fuller, yet no more friendly, lower lip.

They were at the beach but he was dressed for the mountains in khaki shorts and sturdy hiking books. A faded navy tank top stretched across his tanned shoulders and pitched low over his chest, revealing a wealth of dark hair. A scarred leather belt rode low on his narrow hips, holding the knife that she had noticed earlier, a canteen and a flashlight.

Her head hurt so much, her heart was racing so fast that she couldn't concentrate, yet she knew he didn't like her. Dozens of thoughts whirled through her mind like dervishes. Who was he? Why didn't he like her?

He wiped his forehead with the back of his hand, lifting the midnight black hair that rippled across his brow. "How are you feeling?"

The voice was rich and deep, yet totally devoid of emotion, scarier somehow than if he'd shouted. She managed to croak out a few words between parched lips. "Fine. A little headache, that's all."

"You sure?" he asked.

A subliminal flash of intuition told her that he'd been prepared for something terrible. What had he expected her to do? He controlled his expression, remaining very still, as if unaccustomed to sharing his thoughts with anyone. But his hands gave him away. They were splayed across his bent knees, the fingers digging into his skin even though both kneecaps were scraped raw. His legs had multiple cuts and livid bruises. What on earth had he been doing?

"I'm fine. Honest." It was all she could do not to bolt up the rocky hillside, but she didn't move. Where should she go? Which way would she find help?

Without another word, he extended his arm, offering her a cup of coffee. She moved closer, walking stiffly like an old lady with crippling arthritis. She accepted the cup and took a sip, conscious of him studying her intently. The warm liquid ran down her throat and hit her stomach. Instantly, the caffeine shot through her veins, giving her a much needed boost.

She ran her tongue over her dry lips and said, "Thanks."

He lowered his hand to pat the dog crouching in the shadows beside him. Until that second she hadn't noticed the animal, but the coffee seemed to have cleared her head a little. Well, how bad could this man really be? He had a dog and he'd made no move to hurt her. Maybe if they talked a bit, she would remember who he was.

"Your dog's a greyhound, isn't he?"

"Yeah."

Sheesh. He was some conversationalist. She drank more coffee, hoping to rid her brain of the incessant buzz and remember what on earth she was doing here. "If he's a greyhound, why is he tan?"

"They come in all colors."

"Do you race him?" This was an inane conversation, but she didn't know what else to say. It seemed idiotic to confess she'd forgotten who he was. Talking—or the coffee—had calmed her nerves a bit. Any second she'd remember what she was doing out here.

"Nope. Dodger's a hunter."

There was something about the way he shifted on the rock, folding his bare arms across his chest and flexing the muscles visible beneath the tank top that frightened her. Or maybe it was the word *hunter*. There was something lethally quiet about him that seemed unnatural. "What does Dodger hunt?"

"He's a search and rescue dog."

"Really?" That explained the man's hiking clothes, as well as the knife and other gadgets hanging from his belt. He must be part of some rescue team. "Someone's lost?"

"Nope." He was studying her as if her brain was the size of a pea. "You were in an accident. How's your head?"

"Accident?" She reached back and touched the base of her skull through hair like a bramble bush. Ooow. The huge lump had a small cut on it. No wonder she had the mother of all headaches.

"Don't you remember the accident?"

"No," she conceded. "What happened?"

He tilted his head toward the stony outcropping of rock nearby. "You drove off the road."

"I did?" she asked as he rose and walked toward her. She resisted the urge to back up, reminding herself that he didn't mean her any harm.

"Keep your eye on my finger," he said.

Greg moved his index finger toward the tip of her nose. She concentrated on his finger, realizing that his arms were as cut and as bruised as his legs. Had that happened when he had rescued her?

"Hmmm," he grunted, apparently satisfied with the way her eyes followed his finger until they almost crossed. The exercise made her feel nauseous again, but she didn't mention it. "Suck in your breath."

She inhaled sharply, aware of his steady, inquisitive stare.

"Any sharp pains?" he asked, and she shook her head. "You're damn lucky. No broken bones. Probably no broken ribs either."

"I was in an accident," she repeated, trying to make sense of her situation.

He pointed to the rocky cornice a short distance away. "Your car went off the road over there."

She picked her way over the rocks to see her car, barely conscious of the man and his dog following at her heels. She must have a mild concussion, she decided. That was why her head ached and her ears rang. Come to think of it, her whole body was painfully sore.

At the edge of the overhang, she stopped and gasped. "Oh, my God!" It wasn't just an outcropping of rock that gently tumbled to the sea as it had appeared from the camp. No wonder she hadn't noticed it. The volcanic formation twisted sharply to one side, concealing the steep drop into a ravine where a white car lay mangled on the rocks.

"I was in that car?"

He came up beside her. "Don't you remember?"

"No." It seemed pointless now to conceal the fact that she didn't remember what happened. Judging by the condition of the car, it was a miracle she'd survived. Obviously the trauma had caused her to block out the accident. "Where are we?"

"You're on the Hana side of Maui about two miles from Lindbergh's grave."

The way he said it, she should know who Lindbergh was, but the name didn't sound familiar. "Lindbergh?"

Again he looked at her strangely. "You know, the first man to fly solo across the Atlantic. The Lone Eagle."

"Oh," she responded, still not remembering Lindbergh. "What was I doing out here?"

"You tell me."

She shrugged, puzzled about why she was here. If only she could get rid of this killer headache, she would remember what had happened.

"I found you when I was training Dodger"—he halted, then smacked his thigh with his hand—"Son of a bitch!"

The smile that lit his face stunned her with its intensity. She was positive this man rarely smiled, but now the genuine warmth was unmistakable. He dropped to his knees and put his arm around the dog.

"You knew the difference between body A and body B, didn't you, Dodger?" he asked, and the greyhound responded with a happy swish of his tail.

"Body A and body B?" she repeated, looking down at the car. She clutched the hem of the tiger-print dress to keep her hands from trembling. *My God, she had almost died.*

"Are you sure you're okay?" He studied her with an unwavering stare.

She nodded. It was a miracle that she was alive. What was a little headache? "How did you happen to find me?"

"You have Dodger to thank. I never would have found you." Greg gave the dog an affectionate pat. "Let me show you something." He turned his palm to the clear blue sky. "Search," he told the dog.

Dodger vaulted over the embankment and was airborne for a moment. She gasped out loud. It was such a long way down. He landed, surefooted, on a rough-hewn rock, swiveled to the right, and disappeared from view.

"If an explosion levels a building, who do you want to find first?" the man asked.

"Anyone who's alive."

"Right," he replied, a smile shadowing his lips. It wasn't for her, though. He was gazing at the spot where the dog had disappeared. "That's body A. The person who's alive. Body B is someone who's dead. Last night we were looking for body B."

"You mean there's someone dead down there?" *Please, God, don't let me have been the driver. I can't face being responsible for someone's death.*

"No, there isn't anyone else in the car." He smiled again

as Dodger reappeared and bounded up the steep slope. His jaws were open slightly, but she couldn't see what he had in his mouth. The dog halted in front of the man. He reached out, removed a small vial from Dodger's mouth, and passed it to her. "Take a whiff."

She inspected the rubber stopper and saw a pinpoint hole in the top. She sniffed but couldn't smell anything except the briny tang of the sea. With a twist of her hand she removed the stopper. The stench hit her nostrils and her stomach heaved, bringing the coffee up into her throat.

"Careful," he said, taking the god-awful vial from her before she dropped it. "Body in a bottle—the smell of death—body B. In the old days we had to hide parts of dead bodies to practice for search and rescue. Now we use pseudo-corpse. It's distilled from a cadaver."

She had to swallow hard to keep the coffee where it belonged. It took several gulps of sea air to banish the noxious odor. "What Dodger smells is coming through the pinhole? His nose is that good?"

The man capped the vial and stuffed it into his pocket. "Dodger has a great nose, and he runs like the wind."

The unmistakable pride in his voice told her just how wrong she had been. This man meant her no harm. She'd overreacted to his rough appearance.

It was an astounding miracle they'd been here to save her. She looked more closely at the embankment. Dodger had managed it with ease, but she couldn't believe one man had been able to bring her up the slope. "How did you get me up here?"

He shrugged, his eyes now on the ocean. "Carried you."

He made it sound easy. Granted, he was strong, but the face of the ravine was littered with boulders and loose rocks. She ventured a look at him, again noticing the cuts and livid bruises. He'd risked his own life to help her, and she was acting like an idiot, thinking he was a killer or something. She turned to him, wondering how you could ever really thank someone for saving your life. She reached out to touch his arm, but he quickly moved away.

"It must have been murder getting me up the embankment," she said, flustered by his reaction. She had the distinct impression that he didn't like her. "I don't know what to say. What can I do to thank you?"

He took another step away from her. "Don't thank me."

"You saved my life and I don't even know your name."

"I'm Greg Braxton."

Greg. It fit him perfectly. It was solid and abrupt sounding, yet craggy like the rocks nearby. Suddenly, she couldn't help wishing he liked her. She risked another look into his intense blue eyes and saw him staring at her expectantly, obviously waiting for her to tell him her name.

"I'm . . ." Her name was on the tip of her tongue. It just wouldn't come out. She tried again. "I'm . . ." She closed her eyes for a second. *Come on, you know your name. Come on.* "I have a little headache. It's got me really confused. I can't seem to remember my own name. Or what I was doing here . . . or anything."

"Don't worry about it." There was a low, hard edge to his voice that disturbed her. "Sometimes people have trouble remembering things after an accident. It'll come back to you. Until it does, let's call you Lucky. After all, you are lucky to be alive. Damn lucky."

She stared at the beach. Waves pummeled the rocks with awesome force, shooting skyward in billowing clouds of spray that coated rocks halfway up the bluff with glistening foam. That he had managed to bring her up the steep face of the ravine was nothing short of a miracle.

Lucky. It sounded so simple. A toss of the dice. A winning lottery number. A player who draws an ace. But she had been luckier than anyone could imagine. She had survived a sure-death crash.

"Are you positive you're all right?" Greg asked again, and

she suddenly realized that she had no idea how long she had been staring down at what was left of the car.

"I'm fine. It's nothing but a tiny lump on my head with a small cut that's giving me a little headache."

He frowned, obviously not believing her. "I'll go into Hana and get an ambulance. You rest over there in the shade. Don't be surprised if it takes a while. After last night's rain, the road's going to be washed out in places."

She choked back a sob, panicking at the thought of being left alone. "Let me come with you."

He shook his head, ruffling the glossy black hair that fell across his forehead. "I'm on a motorcycle."

"Please. My headache isn't that bad." The thought of being left behind was far worse than the monotonous hum in her ears or the killer headache. She touched Greg's arm, her fingers curling around his biceps. "Please. You could take me right to a doctor."

A full second passed as he gazed down at her hand. Finally, he said, "Okay, Lucky. Maybe that's best." He kept looking at her hand and frowning. She pulled it away.

When they reached the tent, he yanked a piece of orange nylon out of a backpack and shook it out. The black letters on it read "Disaster Dog Trainee."

"What's that for?" she asked, watching him use Velcro strips to fasten it on Dodger's back.

"Like a guide dog, a disaster dog can go into buildings where other animals aren't allowed. This will get Dodger into the clinic at Hana."

He motioned for her to follow him, and they picked their way up the slope. Raindrops still clung to the fragrant grasses and the wildflowers that sprouted from between the rocks. Rivulets of water trickled from the crevices, wending their way to the sea. They reached a muddy road that was nothing more than dirt ruts and bits of crushed lava. Parked at one side was a huge motorcycle wrapped in plastic sheeting.

Stately trees bordered the side of the road opposite the ocean.

Lush banks of ferns, some almost as tall as the trees, others so wispy they might float away, sheltered sprays of orchids no larger than thimbles. The lilting calls of birds rode the rain-scented air. From deep in the foliage she heard the rush of water. A stream or perhaps a waterfall. She wasn't certain; the buzz in her head still had her off-kilter.

Greg pulled the plastic off the Harley, then slung one power-ful leg over the machine. It roared to life, a deafening sound that masked the ungodly noise in her head. She tried to gauge what he was thinking as he looked at her, but his eyes were as blue as the sea and just as unreadable.

"Get on." Greg pulled a pair of aviator sunglasses off the handlebar and cleaned them with his shirt.

Lucky climbed behind him and the motorcycle shot forward, mud flying up and splattering her bare legs. She threw her arms around his waist. Trees rushed by, ferns whipped past in a gust of wind that sent her hair streaming behind her like a banner. They passed one waterfall that cascaded down over huge boul-ders covered with ferns, and minutes later another. She couldn't hear the water above the noise of the bike, but the fine spray misted her skin.

He swerved constantly to avoid rain-filled potholes, making her stomach churn. Dodger wasn't having any problem though. He loped along beside them so gracefully that she would have smiled except her head ached too much.

She rested her cheek against the solid wall of Greg's back and closed her eyes, barely aware that her body was fused against his. It felt reassuring to be so close to someone, to rely on his strength for a moment. Greg was lean, yet ridged with muscles. Beneath her arms his body tightened, and she realized how hard she was squeezing him. She relaxed, her head still against his powerful torso and listened to the thud-thud of his heart.

Her stomach had settled and she was thinking more clearly. She needed sleep, then she'd remember who she was and what she was doing in the middle of nowhere. She kept her eyes closed, her head pressed against Greg's shoulder blades, and let the drone of the motorcycle block any conscious thought.

Lucky wasn't sure how long they had been traveling when Greg slowed down. Opening her eyes, she saw a cluster of palms bent sideways in the breeze, their fronds sounding like flags whipping in the wind. A sign nearby read "Hotel Hana Maui."

"I'll bet you're staying here," Greg said over his shoulder.

"Why?" The bungalows facing the tranquil cove and the green expanse of hillside where cattle were grazing could have sold a million rolls of Kodak. But it didn't look the least bit familiar, nor did the wooden cross on the hill facing the sea. Surely if she'd seen a cross without a church or a graveyard nearby, she would have remembered it.

"You were driving a car with a rental sticker. Just about the only place to stay around here is this hotel. Do you feel well enough to stop and see if we can find your friends? They might want to fly you directly to Honolulu to see a doctor. The clinic here's pretty small."

"Oh, yes. Let's find them." She could stand this miserable headache a bit longer if she could find her friends. Anything was better than not knowing her own name and feeling so alone.

Greg brought the Harley to a stop, then helped her off. She walked beside him with Dodger at her heels. Dark splotches danced across her field of vision, zooming forward until the tranquil cove disappeared, then retreating until they were nothing more than dark pinpricks. Suddenly the spots were back—larger and darker than before. She reached for Greg's arm to steady herself.

"You okay?"

"Yes," she managed to answer.

The open-air lobby was strewn with palm fronds blown in by the storm. A maid was mopping puddles off the slate floor. Nearby a crimson parrot swung on his perch, chanting, "Heavenly Hana, heavenly Hana, heavenly Hana."

The woman at the reception desk had an orchid behind one ear, a swath of jet-black hair that hung over one shoulder like a panel of silk, and a warm smile for Greg. *"Pehea oe.* Some storm, wasn't it?"

Pehea oe? Lucky wondered if her brain had scrambled the word. It sounded like a greeting, but she didn't recognize it.

"Yeah, a killer storm," Greg replied. "Any of your guests missing?"

"Not that I've heard. Why?"

Greg turned to Lucky, and she realized that she was clutching his arm so hard that her nails were biting into his skin. "She was in an accident out past Lindbergh's grave."

The receptionist looked at her as if she'd been born without the most critical part of her anatomy—her brain. "What was she doing way out there?"

The conversation was taking place as if she were a deaf mute. She wanted to speak, but her aching head prevented her. Not only was there a roar in her ears like the rush of the ocean, the room was spinning, the slate floor tilting upward. She needed all her energy just to stand upright and listen.

"I don't know why she drove out there. Is she one of your guests?"

"No." The woman shook her head. "I've never seen her."

The phone rang and the receptionist moved to answer it. Behind the bamboo counter was a matching bamboo-framed mirror that captured Greg's reflection. She must be getting used to him, Lucky decided. He was beginning to look better, not scary at all.

She noticed another woman had come up to the counter and was standing next to Greg. The woman was a hard, wild-looking person with frizzy blonde hair and a tiger-print dress. Who would bleach her hair platinum like that?

Lucky squinted, taking a closer look. She shuddered, her entire body quaking. *Couldn't be.* A sob lodged in her throat. She shook Greg's arm, still staring at the mean, hideous woman in the mirror.

"That's not me!" She pointed to her reflection. "I swear, that's not me!"

Greg put his hands on her shoulders. She knew she was screaming now, her cries ricocheting through the lobby, but she couldn't stop. "That's not me! That's somebody else! You've got to believe me!"

A wave of dizziness crashed over her. The world pitched precariously from side to side like a ship in a hurricane. Then everything skidded to a halt. Her breathing stopped; her heart no longer pounded in her ears. All sound ceased. For a moment she was conscious of Greg's lips moving and knew he was speaking to her, but the pain in her head blocked his voice.

Darkness enveloped her like a vision of hell.

Chapter 3

Cody Braxton looked up from the duty roster as someone knocked on his office door. His dispatcher stood at the threshold, frowning.

"Chief, the Hana Clinic just called for the S and R chopper."

Cody nodded, wondering why he'd bothered to tell him. Technically, Search and Rescue was part of the Maui Police Department. They were required to report their operations to him, but the unit was staffed by trained volunteers who knew exactly what they were doing. The police merely filled out incident reports.

"Have a car meet the helicopter at the hospital and get the details." He knew he sounded impatient, but he had the twins' soccer game in an hour and he still had a mountain of paperwork to process. That's what being chief of police on Maui amounted to—paper pushing.

The dispatcher cleared his throat. "It's your brother, chief. He rescued the victim last night."

The dispatcher walked away, leaving Cody to stare at his back. So that's why he'd been told. Everyone knew Greg hadn't spoken to him in over two years. Once they'd been inseparable, and Cody missed his older brother more than he ever could have imagined.

Cody rarely wrote up S and R reports, but he realized if he took this one, he would see his brother again. He checked his watch. If he met the helicopter and wrote up the IR, he would miss the soccer game. He hated not seeing his boys play. He hated missing an opportunity to talk to Greg even more.

Without thinking, he lifted the receiver and called Sarah. He always let her know if he was going to be late. She answered after several rings, the twins shouting in the background. He imagined Sarah in the kitchen, the baby crawling across the floor, the boys squabbling as usual.

"Greg rescued some woman last night near Hana."

"Search and Rescue had to go out in that terrible storm?"

"I'm not sure." Cody glanced up at the wall map of Maui. The big green dot was the central police station in Kahului, where he worked. Two small blue dots marked the substations in Lahaina and Hana. Whenever S and R went out, the dispatcher was required to post a flag, but there was no red flag on the Hana side of the island.

It was rarely necessary for the police to assist the S and R unit. Most calls pertained to tourists lost in the rain forest or hikers injured while climbing Haleakala. But last night's electrical storm had been highly unusual for the tropics where lightning was rare. None of the rescue choppers would have flown teams to the treacherous back side of the island in such a storm.

"I guess it wasn't an official Search and Rescue operation."

"Greg was out there alone, wasn't he?"

"Probably." More and more lately, Cody had heard reports that Greg was wandering the wilderness that made up much of the island. He still headed the Marine Research Institute, of course, but he seemed to have lost his enthusiasm for the job. For life. "I have to see him."

"I understand," Sarah replied. "I'll tell the twins you'll be late for the game."

He hung up, saying, "I love you." He made certain to tell Sarah that at least once each day. He wouldn't chance losing her a second time.

Cody drove through the busy streets of Lehui. The flip side of paradise, he thought. Commercial laundries. Uniform shops. Honeycombs of low-end housing. He could have been any-where in Kansas, not within a mile of the beach. Some people would have found the town depressing, but not Cody. This was his town, his island. He'd tried living on the mainland, and he had hated it. Give him the flip side of paradise any day.

He pulled into the Lehui Hospital parking lot and was waiting out back when the S and R helicopter touched down. No one was surprised to see him. Being chief of police wasn't much more than a title. He still went out on calls like the rest of the men.

A greyhound wearing an orange disaster vest was the first one off the chopper. The tan-colored dog hopped out and stood at attention. That had to be Greg's dog, the one he'd heard so much about. His brother had always been good with animals. It was people who gave him trouble. Cody supposed it all went back to Aunt Sis. If only she hadn't been so hard on Greg. If only Greg had been less stubborn.

You couldn't change the past. That was for sure. You had to live with it.

Two Med Techs removed a gurney, then Greg climbed out. Something in Cody's gut clenched, and he felt the dampness under his armpits. Two years; not one word. Greg couldn't refuse to talk to him now. He was too much of a professional not to give the police a full report.

Cody hung back, concealed by the crimson bougainvillea, the warm, never ceasing trade winds rippling through the leaves, watching his brother. Greg still had that solid running back's build, all lethal force and speed even though he would be thirty-seven in another month. He still had the gloss black hair that reminded Cody of their mother. He still had that stern, uncompromising expression—thanks to Aunt Sis.

Greg bent to say something to the woman on the gurney. Cody was too far away to hear what they were saying, but Greg's expression softened for a moment. Then he looked up and spotted Cody.

The men rolled the gurney toward the emergency entrance, and Cody greeted them, smiling as he always did, asking about their families. Greg kept walking behind the men wheeling in a blonde with a mane of wild curls. He didn't bother to give Cody a second glance.

They shouldered their way through the double doors two steps behind the gurney. The ER had the usual assortment of broken bones, stomach aches, and *mokes,* island toughs, who'd consumed too much *okolehao* last night. No doubt the home brew made from ti roots had given them whopping headaches and alarming heart palpitations. Maybe they'd learn a lesson.

"What happened to her?" Cody asked Greg as they stopped at the registration desk with the gurney.

Greg's eyes never left the woman, and for a moment, Cody thought he wasn't going to answer. "Last night her car went off the road out beyond Lindbergh's grave. I found her."

"Christ! In that killer storm?"

Greg nodded and looked him directly in the eye. It took all Cody's willpower not to back away. Even at the funeral Greg hadn't spared him one glance. Two years hadn't changed his brother's eyes, though. They were still searing blue, all hellfire and brimstone.

"Better send the chopper back to the beach and lower one of the guys to check the rental car for her purse," Greg told him.

"Lower?" he echoed, feeling the fool for not having read between the lines. When his brother said "off the road," Cody had envisioned the woman's car in one of the dozens of creeks that made the Hana road famous. Now he knew better. The blonde's car had gone off one of the treacherous cliffs the islanders called *palis.*

Greg had brought her up alone, and it hadn't been easy, judging by the cuts and bruises on his body. *I'll be damned.* He didn't know why he was so surprised. Greg often managed to do the impossible.

"I never should have moved her," Greg said, and Cody could see his brother was more than a little shaken. He had to be; he was talking to him as if the past had never happened. "With the storm, I couldn't get anyone out there to help. I thought a flash flood would rip through that ravine and drown her."

"Those ravines are usually death traps in a storm."

"Not this time. The water went around the car." Greg glanced at the woman who was still waiting to be admitted. "I think I made her injuries worse. She can't remember a damn thing—not even her name. You should have seen her at the Hana Maui Hotel. She went ballistic when she saw her reflection. She doesn't even recognize her own face."

"Look. It was a judgment call. You did the best you could." Cody tried his winning smile, but Greg didn't respond.

"Shit, no. I screwed up big time. She said she was okay, and I let her ride into Hana with me. I thought all she had was a bump on the head and a small cut." Greg shook his head derisively. "Take a few pictures of her. You may have to show them around."

Cody didn't agree, figuring the woman was a tourist. She was probably vacationing with someone who would call the police station any minute, frantic.

Still, he went out to get the Polaroid every island cop kept in the trunk. The last time he'd used the camera, he'd taken a picture of the damage Mrs. Grohe's goat had done to her neighbor's onion patch. The animal had broken through the fence and eaten dozens of expensive Maui onions being raised for shipment to the mainland. That was life in paradise. Nothing much more exciting than goats with onion breath ever happened here.

He went back inside and found Greg following the gurney down the corridor to the x-ray unit, talking to the blonde. Cody stopped the attendants and hurriedly snapped a few shots. Despite the cheap dress and mud-splattered legs, the woman wasn't bad looking. Great eyes. Killer body. Tangled blonde hair styled like a Brillo pad in a wind tunnel. One thing was for sure: Anyone who had seen this woman would remember her.

Lucky awoke slowly and moved her head, noticing she was in a hospital room. The skull-splitting headache was gone, replaced by a dull throb at the base of her skull. Now she was more aware of her body. It ached as if she'd gone over Niagara in a barrel. No doubt being poked and prodded hadn't helped. Blood samples. X-rays. An EEG. A Cat scan. The MRI. They'd shaved a patch on the back of her head, and it had taken two stitches to close the small cut.

Finally, they'd let her go to sleep. How long had she been out? She sucked in a calming breath. It was dark inside the room; she must have been asleep for hours. You're better, she told herself. The headache is gone. Now, what's your name?

Something stirred in her brain, something so elusive that it vanished in an instant. It was there, though. Her name was there, locked inside her head. She beat her fist against the mattress. Why? *Why?* Why couldn't she remember?

Never forget. I love you.

The words came out of nowhere like a hushed whisper on the wind. For a moment she thought she had actually heard something, then she realized the message had come from that dark void of nothingness inside her head. Still, it was a comforting thought. Somebody loved her.

She checked her hand for a ring. Nothing.

She must have a family, friends. A boyfriend. Someone

would miss her, and when they did, they'd come for her. She'd be kissed and hugged and cried over. Then she remembered that horrid-looking woman standing beside Greg Braxton. *Oh, Lord! That can't be me.*

But if that wasn't her, who was it?

She squeezed her eyes shut, willing an image of herself, of how she really looked, to present itself. Nothing appeared except utter darkness. A shiver rippled through her, followed by a disturbing thought. Something terrible had happened to her.

Tears seeped from between her lashes. "Don't you dare," she said out loud, willing herself not to cry. "Don't . . . you . . . dare."

"Dare what?" The voice came out of the dark.

Her eyes flew open. "Greg?" She fluttered her lashes to get rid of the tears.

"Yes. You're awake." He flicked on the light. He'd been sitting so still she hadn't realized anyone was in the room.

He came up to the bed and she almost gasped. He had shaved and was wearing a clean shirt and cotton slacks with a stiletto-sharp crease. From his square jaw to his high, tanned cheekbones to the intriguing cleft in his chin, Greg Braxton was awesomely male. Big. Rugged.

Here was a man accustomed to giving orders, to being in charge. Judging from the way he'd behaved when she'd fainted in the hotel lobby, then come to a few minutes later, he expected people to do what he told them. She doubted anyone on earth could have gotten her to this hospital any faster.

She recalled the ugly tramp she'd seen in the mirror, the reflection that had sent her into a tailspin. Oh, God, she didn't want to be that woman and have Greg look at her.

"Feeling better, Lucky?"

"I'm okay," she responded, ashamed of all the trouble she'd caused him. She wanted him to go home. He'd done more than enough. "Shouldn't you be with your family?"

He shook his head; his gleaming black hair shifted across his forehead. "Dodger's the only family I have."

"What about that policeman with the camera? One of the nurses said he was your brother."

Dodger's cool nose nudged her hand. She hadn't noticed him before, but now his soulful eyes gazed at her, silently asking if she was all right. Tears flooded her eyes. A man and his dog had risked their lives to save hers.

She stroked Dodger's head. "How can I ever repay you two?"

Greg's eyes met hers. "It isn't necessary. It's what we do."

She reached out and took his hand. For an instant he appeared startled, then quickly regained his usual composure. She traced the back of his hand with her thumb, hating the gaudy pink polish. Hating whoever she was. "I'm sorry for all the trouble I caused."

"It's okay," he said, then awkwardly shifted his stance and changed the subject. "You've been asleep for more than twenty hours."

"That long? Nobody's come for me?" The apprehension she'd felt earlier returned. Something *was* terribly wrong.

His hand closed around hers, his long fingers wrapping around her smaller hand. "Most of the people on Maui are tourists traveling with family or friends. Someone will turn up."

He slowly withdrew his hand and she resisted the urge to grab it again, to keep that human connection. The strength in his touch made her believe her fears were just her imagination and everything was going to be all right.

"My brother's chief of police. He sent a crew to check the car for your purse, but they didn't find it. He's contacting the rental car companies. They'll have a record of who rented your car and where they're staying."

"Good," she said, unable to take her eyes off his, wishing she were herself, not some hard, cheap blonde. She wanted to be someone special, someone worth saving.

"There's a conference of neurosurgeons at the Four Seasons Hotel. Dr. Hamalae is consulting with several of them right now. They're going over your test results. They should have a report soon." Greg reached down and petted Dodger, fondling the greyhound's ears. "Remember your name yet?"

"No. It's on the tip of my tongue, but it just won't come out. I guess you'll have to call me Lucky a while longer."

He nodded, and she was grateful that he didn't ask the same litany of questions everyone else had. If she couldn't remember her name, how could she tell them her address or her phone number?

"Is there anything I can get you?"

My memory. Get me my memory, she wanted to scream. Instead, she replied, "I'd like a rubber band to get this hair off my face."

Greg left the room with Dodger faithfully following, and Lucky stared at the ceiling, asking her mind to cooperate. All she wanted was her real name. She was sure the rest would come later, after the shock of the accident wore off.

She heard a noise and looked up, expecting to see Greg. It was his brother. The family resemblance was evident in the angular jawline and distinctive cleft chin. This man's hair was lighter than Greg's, and his eyes were a warmer blue. She had the impression he was a lot happier than Greg.

He walked into the room and stopped beside her bed. "Remember your name yet?"

His tone reflected total skepticism. Obviously, he didn't believe she could not remember her name. After the ordeal of tests and being forced to answer the same barrage of questions over and over, she snapped, "No."

"Well, then, I guess you're Jane Doe." He pulled out a wallet with a badge and identification that said he was Cody William Braxton, Chief of Police. "You're under arrest."

Chapter 4

Where the hell was Cody? Greg stood at the counter, trying to be patient while a nurse rummaged through a drawer looking for a rubber band. The team Cody had sent yesterday to search the car hadn't found Lucky's purse or the rental contract that was supposed to be kept in the glove compartment. That meant the police would have to check every car rental company on the island.

Would that have taken all day? Maybe. He knew the primary agencies were at the airport, but dozens were located at hotels and the handful of towns on the island. At each location the police would have to compare the license number of the car with the numbers on the rental contracts.

He supposed Cody was busting his butt on this one. He'd gone out of his way to have the crew who searched the car bring back Greg's things from the campsite and pick up his Harley at the clinic, saving him another trip to Hana. Cody wanted forgiveness. What a crock! He wouldn't even be talking to his brother now if he hadn't found Lucky.

Lucky wasn't what he expected, Greg decided, determined

not to think about his brother. The morning after the crash, she seemed totally different. She didn't pull any of that sex crap. Okay, she'd held on a little too tight on the ride into Hana, pressing her breasts against his back. That was nothing, though, compared to the night before, when she'd put her hands in his pants. He couldn't look at her hands without remembering.

He swore under his breath. Lucky had gotten to him—big time. Desire, hot and demanding, had surged through him, mocking his usual self-control. He was so disturbed by his reaction that he hadn't mentioned the incident to anyone.

"Here you go." The nurse interrupted his thoughts, giving him a rubber band.

"Mahalo." He thanked her over his shoulder, already turning to go back to Lucky's room. What was he going to say to her? Aw, hell, just seeing her in bed, the hospital gown barely concealing sensuous curves and full breasts, had conjured up centerfold images.

"Son of a bitch!" he muttered, disturbingly aware of the tension in his body, a heightened sense of physical need that he had suppressed for years. Why now? Why with this woman? Any fool could see that she was nothing more than a slut. Hadn't he learned his lesson with Jessica?

He paused a moment to pet Dodger, thinking that the faster he got away from Lucky the better. "Good boy. You ready to leave tonight for the certification test?"

Dodger wagged his tail enthusiastically. One good thing had come out of that miserable experience on the cliff: Dodger had proved himself. When they went for his certification, Greg was certain his dog would pass.

He wandered down the long corridor and halted outside Lucky's room, startled to hear his brother's voice. "You have the right to remain silent—"

Greg rushed inside. "What in hell's going on?"

Lucky's eyes were wide with disbelief and Cody was standing, feet apart, his belligerent stance.

Cody turned to Greg. "The rental car was stolen. She claims

she doesn't remember her name. Real convenient when you're guilty of grand theft.''

Greg handed Lucky the rubber band with what he hoped was a reassuring smile. ''Stay with her, Dodger. We'll be right back.''

Out in the hall, it was difficult to resist hitting his brother. He'd wanted to deck Cody for the past two years. He sucked in his breath and reminded himself not to give Cody the satisfaction of seeing him lose control.

''I thought you were a good detective.'' Greg couldn't keep the caustic tone out of his voice. ''If you'd bothered to check with Dr. Hamalae, he would have told you that Lucky could have been a vegetable. Her head injury was so unusual that Hamalae consulted with two doctors from the mainland who're here for a conference. They've been going over the test results since noon.''

''The nurse said all she needed was a couple of stitches.''

''Apparently there's been internal bleeding. Hell, I'm no doctor—''

''Don't you care that she was driving a stolen car?''

He remembered the way she'd been dressed and the mismatched shoes. Put that together with the way she'd acted in the tent and . . . man, oh, man . . . who knew what she'd done. Still, he'd be damned before he'd concede that Cody was right.

''Someone else might have stolen the car.''

Cody slammed the heel of his palm against his forehead, a gesture that reminded Greg of their father even though Cody had only been four when their parents were killed. He couldn't possibly remember the way Dad would hit his forehead when he was angry, yet Cody always did the same thing.

''Something's mighty fishy here. That car has been missing for over a year. For months we had that license number posted on our dashboards,'' Cody said and Greg could tell he was making a supreme effort to be patient, to breach the chasm between them. ''We never saw that car—not once.''

Greg knew his brother was justifiably proud of himself.

Crime was almost nonexistent on the island. If a car had been
stolen, it would have killed Cody not to recover it. Few cars
ever left the island, and it was easy enough to prevent one from
leaving by having the port authority watch for it. The rental
car had been here all the time, yet the police had missed it.

"If you were so on top of things, why didn't you recognize
the license number?" Greg realized his voice was more than
bitter now, but he couldn't help it. He was so damn mad at
Cody, even after all this time, that he couldn't help himself.

Cody hesitated, visibly upset, yet when he spoke, his tone
was level. "I didn't actually see the car myself. I sent a team
there to search for the woman's purse, remember? When I saw
their report, I recognized the license number immediately. I
spent all day showing the blonde's picture around at the hotels
so I could ID her."

"What did you find out?"

"Nothing. No one recognized her. That's why I'm here to
look at her clothes. It's a long shot but perhaps there's a label
or something that'll give us a clue."

"Aren't you missing the obvious?" There was venom in
Greg's tone. Cody assumed that belligerent stance again, but
Greg kept talking, his voice no less antagonistic. "She had to
be staying on the Hana side up in those hills somewhere."

Greg knew it would take days to search the area. Roughly
a thousand people lived on the far side of paradise, thriving on
the isolation. Around Hana you could find everything from
rock stars' estates to middle aged hippies living in old school
buses. Most of them shunned the tourist side of Maui and
guarded their privacy like pit bulls.

"You're probably right," Cody admitted. "I have to arrest
her, though. The blonde—"

"Lucky," Greg interrupted. "Call her Lucky."

"Lucky," Cody said the name as if he was chewing tin foil,
"was driving a Traylor rental car."

Tony Traylor was head of the joint council, the group representing the towns on the island, in effect, Cody's boss. Three

hundred pounds of blubber in a Hawaiian shirt, Tony was an arrogant loudmouth who lived to throw his weight around. Undoubtedly, Cody had taken heat for months when one of Tony's cars had been stolen and not recovered.

"Cody, my man, you swim through political crap like a shark. Tell Traylor you won't arrest her until you've checked those hills to see if she was living there. Anyway, I doubt Dr. Hamalae will release Lucky for a few days. By then I'll have gone to San Francisco to certify Dodger and be back."

"Stay out of this," Cody warned. "I smell trouble—big trouble. Lucky isn't a dog left to die in a swamp. She's more like one of the alligators that were ready to eat Dodger."

Greg had to bite the inside of his lip to keep from whacking his brother. He resented Cody keeping track of what he did. Okay, so Dodger had been among a pack of dogs dumped in the Everglades when he washed out on the Florida racetrack circuit. Greg had been in Miami at the time, concluding a deal to buy a German shepherd to train for S and R, when he'd heard about the one dog who'd survived the ordeal in the swamp. He couldn't resist going to see Dodger. The dog's eyes had gotten to him, so loving and trustful despite the cruelty he had endured.

"She didn't steal the car," Greg said. It was a gut reaction like taking Dodger home.

Lucky peered into the mirror in the small bathroom attached to her hospital room. Ugly. Hard as nails. The cheap blonde with tumbleweed hair glared defiantly back at her. "I don't know you."

The lips moved, but that didn't make the face staring at her any more familiar. She edged closer, aware of Dodger at her side, and inspected the horrid reflection carefully. *Couldn't be me!* Surely you would recognize your own face, wouldn't you?

She gripped the rim of the sink with both hands to steady her shaking body. Was it possible she had stolen that car?

When she heard the charge, she'd been so certain that she couldn't have done it. Now, looking in the mirror, she wondered.

This strange woman might have done anything.

"Oh, God, please tell me it isn't true."

But God didn't answer. Instead the stranger in the mirror stared back at her, daring her to prove she wasn't a thief. It was possible, she supposed, quaking. She was living a nightmare. *Anything* was possible.

Dodger licked her hand and she slowly sank to her knees, her sore body protesting every inch of the way. On eye level with Dodger now, she petted him and gazed into his soulful eyes. She had the uncanny feeling that the dog understood her pain.

Never forget. I love you.

The haunting words came from the dark void where her memory should have been. It was a comforting thought; someone cared. Surely someone would show up and straighten out this mess. Suddenly, she had the unsettling feeling that her mother was searching for her.

"Mom," she whispered, "I'm here in Hawaii. Please come get me before they throw me in jail."

Dodger responded with a sympathetic swipe of his tongue on her cheek, and she couldn't help smiling. She was a grown woman. Thirty-something, judging by what she'd seen in the mirror. Why was she crying for her mother?

"When things get rough, there's nobody like your mother, is there?" she asked Dodger as she slowly rose. But her mother wasn't here, and she had the disturbing suspicion she might never see her again.

She was alone.

The reflection in the mirror mocked her. She leaned nearer, more than a little afraid of the stranger, taking a closer look. The eyes seemed . . . right. Deep green with minute stitches of gold. The nose was canted just slightly to the left, yet it, too, seemed to go with the eyes. Her lips were familiar as well, full and soft and ready to smile.

"So what's wrong, Dodger?"

As the dog wagged his tail it dawned on her why the face in the mirror was throwing her—totally throwing her. It was the god-awful hair. A cheap frizzy permanent had kinked the shoulder-length hair so much that she doubted a comb could get through it. The hair had been bleached a baby-white blonde that contrasted sharply with her dark eyebrows.

She finger-combed the hair as best she could, then tugged it back into a ponytail and secured it with the rubber band Greg had brought her. The hair covered the patch on the back of her head where they'd shaved her scalp to stitch the cut. "Better, huh?"

Dodger wagged his tail just as someone called hello from the other room. It wasn't Greg's voice. A surge of excitement sent her heartbeat into double-time. Someone's come to get me, she thought.

One hand clutching the hospital gown that gaped open at the back, she emerged, Dodger at her heels. Anticipation turned to apprehension in a heartbeat that felt like an explosion inside her chest. It was Dr. Hamalae and two other men in lab coats. They must be the doctors he'd consulted. Behind them stood Greg Braxton.

"We have your test results," Dr. Hamalae said. "Why don't you sit down while we explain them to you?"

She sat on the bed and covered her short gown with the sheet. Dodger deserted her, trotting over to Greg, and she realized he was going to leave. "Greg, please stay," she pleaded before she could stop herself.

She could tell Greg's smile was forced, but she didn't care. At least he was staying with her. She silently willed him to come stand near her. Instead, he leaned against the wall, Dodger at his side.

"This is Dr. Klingman from the Stanford Medical Center,"

Dr. Hamalae said and a man with a full head of dark hair brindled with gray shook her hand.

"I'm Kurt Jorgen from the Sloan Kettering Institute in New York," a second man greeted her, and she instantly liked him even though he was younger and less imposing than the other doctor.

"They're at the Four Seasons for a conference on neurology," Dr. Hamalae explained. "That's fortunate. We didn't have to fly you to the mainland for an accurate diagnosis."

"What's wrong with me?" she asked, and Dr. Hamalae looked at Dr. Klingman, then at Greg. She sensed that something terrible *was* wrong; this wasn't just a simple concussion.

Dr. Klingman cleared his throat. "The electroencephalograph indicates abnormal brain waves. This is confirmed by Dr. Jorgen's detailed examination of the MRI. A portion of your substantia nigra cells have been destroyed, abbreviating certain cognitive capacities. It's called Hoyt-Mellenberger syndrome."

"Exactly what does this mean?"

Dr. Klingman smiled at her as if she were a young child incapable of intellectually grasping what he was saying. "The accident damaged part of your brain."

"All I have is a little cut on the back of my head," she protested.

"You suffered a blow that caused a hairline fracture, which resulted in internal bleeding. The bleeding stopped, but not without destroying a number of cells."

"I feel fine," she insisted. "Really, I do."

Dr. Klingman studied her for a moment. "I'm sure you *feel* well, but what do you remember about the past?"

"Nothing . . . yet. But it's right there. I can feel it."

The doctor shook his head. "I'm afraid you will never be able to remember everything."

What did he mean? she wondered with a grim sense of foreboding. Wasn't she going to remember her own name? She looked at Greg to see what he thought and saw he was frowning at Dr. Klingman.

"Just what won't she be able to remember?" Greg walked over and stood beside her. She reached out and touched his hand. He hesitated for a fraction of a second, then his strong fingers curled around hers.

"The accident could have left her paralyzed or wiped out her entire memory bank, not just part of it." The doctor turned to her. "Then you would have had to relearn everything again as if you were a baby. Walking, talking—everything."

Her breath solidified in her chest, becoming a dead weight, as she realized what he was saying. No, she wanted to scream. It couldn't be true. She glanced at Greg and saw her knuckles were ridges of bone. She had a death grip on his hand. She let go and clutched the sheet instead.

"Am I going to remember my name?"

Dr. Jorgen smiled encouragingly. "You'll remember your name as soon as the shock of the accident wears off because you've undoubtedly said it and written it thousands of times. It's stored in the part of your brain with the rest of the information you've learned by rote."

She felt as if a noose were circling her throat, choking her. This could *not* be happening. Surely, this was a dream and she would wake up. She gasped for air and realized she'd been holding her breath. Greg reached for her, hesitating a moment before his hand settled on her shoulder, steadying her trembling body.

"I'm not going to remember *anything* about my life?"

"I'm afraid not." Dr. Klingman smiled that indulgent smile again, and she battled the urge to scream. This was her life, not some textbook curiosity. "You see, there are three types of memory systems. Semantic, or learned memory, is what we've consciously studied and mastered like mathematical equations or a foreign language. The second type of memory is procedural. If you do something often enough, you learn what to expect. A baby learns that fire is hot and won't stick his hand into the flames.''

"What about my past? Things that happened to me?" She heard the threat of panic in her voice and knew Greg heard it, too. He comforted her with the pressure of his hand.

"That's episodic memory. It's the collection of events, feelings, and thoughts we accumulate over time." He shook his head sadly. "That's the memory system you've lost."

Her heartbeat jarred her chest as the full impact of the doctor's words hit her. "Lost?"

"It could be worse," Dr. Klingman said. "You still have your sense of smell."

"What's that got to do with it?" The irritation in Greg's voice was unmistakable. Evidently, he found this as perplexing as she did.

Dr. Hamalae spoke up. "For some reason memory and the sense of smell are centered in the same area in the brain. When smell is wiped out, the memory systems collapse. All you have then is short term memory. You can't remember anything for longer than—say—ten or fifteen minutes."

"Oh, my God!" She was truly lost and having them tell her that it could have been much worse didn't make her feel "lucky." It terrified her. She imagined being tossed overboard into a fathomless sea with no hope of reaching shore.

"Don't worry," Dr. Jorgen assured her with a warm smile. "Your family will tell you all about your past. They'll have photographs maybe even home movies. The mind is a funny thing. Give it enough information and it'll fill in the blanks."

She understood that Dr. Jorgen was trying to make her feel better. But she wasn't buying it. He didn't know what it was like to encounter a black void when you asked yourself what you looked like. "You're telling me the past is gone," she heard the anger in her voice and paused to temper it. "All I'll have is what other people tell me. I won't know how I used to feel."

None of the doctors denied it. She didn't know whether to

cry or to scream. If she did either, she probably wouldn't be able to stop. Greg gently squeezed her shoulder, but even his reassurance didn't help.

"Let me get this straight," Greg said. "She's going to remember how to drive a car, yet she won't remember the plot of a book she read once."

"Right," Dr. Klingman agreed. Now he looked positively bored.

"What does *Gone With the Wind* mean to you?" Dr. Jorgen asked.

She realized it was a loaded question; she *should* know what the term meant. "Something blew away in the wind. That's all."

"It's a famous book that was made into a movie. Undoubtedly you read it or saw the movie. Probably both." Dr. Jorgen's eyes were filled with compassion. Unlike the other doctor, he at least cared. "You'll get the chance to experience a great many things again like rereading *Gone With the Wind.*"

Screams of frustration and denial rose to her throat. She clamped her lips shut, telling herself they'd taken time from their conference to study her case and blaming them was infantile. Still, anger burned inside her, and it was all she could do to control herself.

"I've never heard of Hoyt-Mellenberger syndrome," Greg said.

"It's extremely rare," Dr. Klingman explained. "Usually the entire memory bank is destroyed, and the person simply has to relearn everything."

The doctors talked, discussing memory loss and using terms like *temporal lobe* and *right brain* and *left brain.* None of it made much sense to her. All she understood was that her sense of desolation, of being alone in the world was a permanent condition. She *was* lost. And even when her family managed to find her, her life was never going to be the same.

Never forget. I love you. The words she couldn't get out of her mind had a bittersweet ring to them now. If someone did love her, she wasn't going to remember him. He would be a stranger just the way her own reflection was.

She tried to tell herself that she was fortunate to be alive. Lucky. Everyone kept tossing the word around, but she didn't feel the least bit lucky. The truth was her life had vanished. Gone with the wind, she thought, wondering if that so famous book/movie was about someone whose memory had disappeared. It seemed to fit perfectly.

She barely realized the doctors were leaving. Dr. Hamalae said he would see her in the morning while Dr. Jorgen offered to return and show her the tests so she could see for herself where the damage had occurred. She muttered her thanks, doing her best to sound sincere.

Greg sat down on the bed beside her, and gazed at her, his blue eyes as intense as ever, yet there was a flicker of compassion or—oh, God, maybe it was pity. She hated that thought. The only person on this earth she truly knew was Greg Braxton. More than anything she wanted him to like her, not pity her.

"You're lucky to be alive," he said, and she had the distinct impression that he was at a loss for words.

"Yes, just call me Lucky." She tried not to sound sarcastic. After all, Greg was her only friend. He'd risked his own life to save hers—or what was left of hers. "I realize I could have died or have been left a vegetable. I must focus on the positive." She touched his arm and he glanced down at her hand. Why did he keep looking at her hands? It must be the horrid nail polish. "I don't want you to think that I'm not grateful to you for saving my life. I truly am. It's just that this is such a shock."

His eyes met hers and he nodded slowly. She couldn't help wondering what he was really thinking. "I'm supposed to leave in few minutes," he announced. "Dodger and I are flying to San Francisco. . . ."

Greg paused, and she decided he was wondering if she knew where San Francisco was. "San Francisco: a city in northern California. A huge bay. The Golden Gate Bridge. Cable cars," she said, the words spewing out as if a robot were speaking.

She stopped for breath, realizing for the first time that there were things she knew and others, like *Gone With the Wind*, that she would have to relearn. "I'll ask if I don't understand something. I'm going to deal with this memory thing openly."

He nodded his approval and checked his watch. "I have to leave right now if I'm going to catch the last flight to San Francisco. Dodger is scheduled to take the certification test so he can be registered as a disaster dog. We don't have to go. If you need me to stay, I will."

She almost hugged him. Including the day of the accident, she had been missing three days. Where were her friends and her family? Gone with the wind, apparently. All she had was Greg Braxton, and just the thought of him leaving brought the sting of tears to her eyes. Of course, she wanted him to stay, but she had no right to ask.

She reached down and petted the dog's sleek head. "No. It's important that Dodger be certified. After all, we know he's the best, don't we? I'll be fine . . . honest."

"You sure?" he asked, and she managed a confident nod. "My brother's not going to arrest you until he does a little more checking. I'll bet he finds out you didn't steal that car."

She opened her mouth to assure him that she wasn't a thief. Suddenly, she recalled the weird-looking woman in the mirror. *Who knew what she might have done?*

It was after midnight by the time Cody left work and was driving along the moonlit road toward his home in the up-country. He didn't live close to the station, preferring the cooler hills at the base of Haleakala. The dormant volcano was Maui's crowning glory, and along its slopes was fertile ranch land. If it hadn't been for the ocean glimmering in the distance, the up-country could be mistaken for Tennessee.

But it wasn't the lush green grass or the whitewashed fences that attracted Cody to the up-country. He'd moved here, stretching his finances to the limit to keep his family away from the tourist area. Here his boys could ride their horses when they weren't playing soccer, and Sarah could have a garden. If they lived closer to the beach, they would be stuck in some tiny condo surrounded by tourists who threw their money around like confetti, and his children wouldn't have a sense of value.

He pulled into the driveway of the dilapidated home that he and Sarah were still restoring and parked the Bronco. The breeze, always cooler here than on the coast, was moist against his face and filled with the fragrant scent of plumeria, as he strode up the walk. The house was dark except for the light in their bedroom. Sarah was waiting up for him the way she always did. He entered through the back door, taking care not to make noise and wake the baby.

He tiptoed into the twins' room. Phew! The place smelled of gym socks and looked as if there had been a preemptive strike on a sporting goods store. Although they were just eleven, his sons lived for sports. He and Greg hadn't been much different, he thought, stepping over the bat that lay in the middle of the floor.

"Sleep tight." He kissed each boy on the cheek, saddened that they were at the age where they no longer wanted him to kiss them. Let them know you love them, he told himself. It's the most important gift you can give a child.

Dodging the clutter, he left the room, thinking of his own childhood. The only person who had loved him had been his brother. After their parents had been killed, Cody and Greg had been sent to Hawaii to live with Aunt Sis. It would never have occurred to the old bag to kiss them. She was too busy yelling at them, finding fault with everything they did.

Greg had received the brunt of Aunt Sis's anger, shielding Cody whenever he could. Sometimes Greg had even lied and taken the blame for something Cody had done. Through it all, though, Greg had loved his brother in a way that he'd never been able to love anyone else, even his wife, Jessica.

Greg simply refused to open himself to others. Sure, he was good with animals. He was the most skilled volunteer in the

S and R unit, and he had a stellar reputation for his work with whales at the Marine Research Institute. Yet when it came to people—especially women—Greg gave only so much. With Jessica, it wasn't enough.

You can't change the past, Cody reminded himself, feeling the too familiar depression returning. He missed his brother so much that at times he actually felt physical pain. At least they were talking now, but he doubted Greg would ever forgive him.

He ventured into his daughter's room, taking extra care not to make any noise. If Molly woke up, they would pay hell getting her to sleep again. She was curled up, her plump little arm circling the one-eared stuffed elephant that she dragged everywhere. He bent low and brushed a kiss across her cheek. Her body was warm, her breathing too soft to hear, and she smelled of baby powder.

He tiptoed out of the room and went down the hall. Sarah was sitting up in bed reading a mystery, her thick black hair falling over her shoulders. She set the book on the nightstand, then put out her arms to hug him. His spirits lifted a little. Having her love almost made up for losing Greg's.

"Rough day?" she asked after he'd bear-hugged her and kissed her twice.

"Yeah." He pulled off his holster and opened the safe in the nightstand. Once the gun was inside, he spun the dial and locked it away from the children. "Greg's going to get mixed up with that woman. I can feel it."

Sarah's dark eyes widened. "The one who stole the car?"

"Right. Greg's calling her Lucky. The doctors say Lucky should remember her name, but she claims she can't." He sat on the edge of the bed and pulled off his shoes.

"You know what the *Tattler*'s saying, don't you?"

He shook his head. The *Maui Tattler* was the island's biweekly newspaper. It had an appalling similarity to mainland tabloids. Elvis sightings. Aliens with heads like lightbulbs zipping around the up-country in spaceships and hovering over the beaches, bent on abducting tourists.

"They're calling her Pele's ghost. She was found along the side of the road, and no one seems to know who she is. It's romantic."

"That's *lolo*. The woman's a car thief."

When he'd called home to say he would be late, Cody had brought Sarah up-to-date on the case. He was surprised that she saw anything romantic in this, but then, she could "talk story" in the Hawaiian tradition, retelling island lore over and over and over. One of the most popular myths was that Pele, the volcano goddess who had given birth to the islands, often appeared at the side of the road as a young woman needing help. It was considered bad luck not to help her. No matter what you did, the ghost disappeared as unexpectedly as she had appeared. "I don't want Greg mixed up with that weird blonde."

"She reminds you of Jessica, doesn't she?" Sarah asked, more than a trace of bitterness in her voice.

Jessica. The word hung in the air like a poisonous gas. Since Jessica's funeral, neither of them had mentioned her name. He met Sarah's steady gaze and saw how much she loved him. And how much he'd hurt her. Honest to God, he didn't deserve her.

"Yeah," he finally said. "This isn't Pele's ghost. It's Jessica in another woman's body."

"The *Tattler*'s going to love that one. Invasion of the body snatchers."

He knew Sarah was trying to joke, but there wasn't anything humorous about Greg's dead wife. Jessica had deliberately tried to wreck all their lives. And she'd almost succeeded.

"Yes, Greg has a way of spotting the walking wounded. Then he doesn't know what to do with them." Cody unbuttoned his shirt, wondering if there was any way he could help his brother.

"Nobody could have saved Jessica."

So true. Jessica had been beyond redemption. Cody had been an idiot to have had an affair with his own brother's wife. He could still see the shocked look on Greg's face as he'd come down the embankment with the search and rescue team after the accident. The last thing Greg had expected to find that night, when Jessica had told him she had gone to the mainland, was Cody with his wife. It was the last thing Sarah had expected, too. If she hadn't been pregnant, she might have left him. The baby—and the twins they already had—had earned him a second chance.

Of course, there had been no second chance with Greg.

"No one could have saved Jessica," Sarah repeated, bitterness underscoring every word. "She was a lost soul."

"No one can help this woman, either," Cody said, determined to change the subject. There was no way he could explain betraying both his wife and his brother. "Remember I said I was going to be late because I'd found something when I checked Lucky's clothes?"

"You said her shoes didn't match."

He shrugged out of his shirt. "I thought the one with the curly red laces looked familiar. I took it to the evidence locker. It matched a shoe we had from another case."

Sarah straightened, bringing her knees up to her chest and locking her tanned arms around her legs. "Really? What case?"

He couldn't help smiling. Sarah loved a mystery; she read them constantly. Well, this case was a real lulu. If Greg weren't involved, he'd actually enjoy it. Most of the police work he did gave new meaning to the word *boring*.

"About a year ago, a hiker fell off a trail not too far from the Iao Needle. By the time someone spotted her body, it was badly decomposed. She had only one shoe on. We figured the other was lost in the brush nearby. It wasn't worth looking for."

"You're kidding!" Sarah's eyes were wide. "Lucky was wearing the mate. How do you suppose she got the dead woman's shoe?"

Chapter 5

The sun stalked across the horizon, blasting the Gold Coast's private beach with morning light and bouncing off the high-rise office buildings in the distance. The breeze barely ruffled the water now, but later the wind would rise and whitecaps would stud the sea. The perfect time of day he thought as he finished his morning jog. The only footprints in the sand were his, as if he owned the whole cove, not just the biggest estate on the beach.

Like a miser with a nugget of gold, he valued his privacy. So what if his neighbors didn't know he was one of the wealthiest men in the world? It gave him a perverse sense of pleasure. Not only was he fabulously wealthy, he could find out anything about his neighbors—and secretly impact their lives in a thousand different ways without them ever being aware of his existence. Once someone had called him the Orchid King because one of his businesses involved exporting orchids. It was just a front, of course, a means of concealing his real business, but he adored its cache.

Orchid King. The name rolled off his tongue like French

wine. The title suited his vision of the modern world. There were still kingdoms to rule, people to conquer. Only the methods had changed. Pomp and circumstance were out. Computers had become the modern weapons of war.

He slowed his pace, cooling down, and trotted barefoot through the iceplant bordering the sand onto the dichondra. He walked up the marble steps to the terrace, noting with approval the maid had already changed the flowers. He hated seeing the same floral arrangements two days in a row.

His partner was seated at the table on the open-air terrace facing the sea, intently studying the morning paper. "Check this." The man pointed to a small article in the lower corner of one of the back pages. "Of all the fucking luck!"

The Orchid King reached for the pitcher of ice water the maid always had waiting and poured himself a glass before reading the article. "Luck is my middle name," he said with a laugh. He'd been joking a lot more than usual lately, trying to lift his spirits.

His partner scowled. "Your luck just ran out."

The king's pulse kicked up a notch. Most of the time his partner—his closest friend, almost a brother—was usually easygoing and upbeat. Something really was wrong. The caption of the short article caught his eye. "Mystery Woman Survives Crash." He sank into the chair and read it word for word.

"She's alive," his partner muttered, shaking his head incredulously.

The king stared at the picture, breathing like a marathon runner, but it wasn't from jogging. He was so relieved that she was alive that he thought he might hyperventilate. Get a grip, he told himself.

Thank God. She is alive. He should be even angrier than his partner, but a part of him was secretly thrilled that she had survived the crash. It was hard to imagine living the rest of his life without knowing she was somewhere on earth. Laughing. Smiling. Breathing.

"No doubt about it," the king said with a laugh. "She has nine lives."

"Do you have to joke about everything?"

He ignored his partner and studied the grainy photograph. No one would recognize her with that tangled mane of hair so heavily bleached that it looked white. She stared out from the newsprint with wild, unfocused eyes that reminded him of a rabid dog. Usually those eyes were a compelling, seductive green fringed with gloss-brown lashes.

And a body that wouldn't quit. She'd captivated them both—especially his partner who was easy to manipulate.

"It says here that she has permanent amnesia," he said softly.

"Pure shit!" His partner jumped up and walked to the edge of the terrace. "I've got to go to Chinatown for a meeting. While I'm gone, you do some checking. I'll bet that bitch is up to her old tricks."

The king couldn't disagree. She'd come to them, literally out of cyberspace, a woman without a past—or so she claimed. There had always been a part of her, a secret self she had never shared with anyone. Who knew what she had been hiding? Who knew what secrets lurked in her past?

His partner threw the paper aside. "Amnesia, my ass. She's lying."

The king wasn't certain when he'd fallen in love with her. It had probably started on-line when he'd read her intriguing posts on his computer screen. It had been a game then, but later, when she walked into their lives and became more than just an image from cyberspace, he'd truly fallen in love.

They had both fallen for her, but, the king prided himself on his ability to be objective. *To do what had to be done.* He didn't trust her any more than his partner did. She'd already proved she couldn't be trusted.

"They're calling her Pele's ghost," the king said. "What a hoot."

"You may think this is funny, but I'm telling you—"

"It's the shoe I'm worried about," the king interrupted, his tone deadly serious. "That screwup could lead the police back to us."

Greg eased his foot off the gas pedal and downshifted, turning into the police station parking lot. "What in hell's going on?"

In the seat next to him, Dodger cocked his head. There were so many cars in the lot that Greg had to drive to the back to find a parking place. They'd been on the mainland for almost a week, and Dodger had passed the certification test. Greg had been tempted to call about Lucky but had resisted, thinking it was best to distance himself from the woman. Now that he was back, the urge to know what had happened to her had gotten the better of him.

He still remembered the look on Lucky's face when the doctors told her she would never recall her past. The memory triggered a raw ache, and his gut twisted. Her expressive green eyes had darkened with disbelief, then fear. In spite of his doubts about her, he'd been shaken all right, more than shaken. He'd even volunteered to stay with her.

Christ! What had he been thinking? That weird syndrome had wiped out Lucky's episodic memory, but she should be able to tell them her name. He had watched her carefully while the doctors explained her condition, remembering how her body had trembled. It would take a world-class actress to be so convincing, wouldn't it?

Greg got out of the car and Dodger leaped out behind him. Cody would know what had happened to her. As much as he hated talking to his brother, it was better to see him than to face Lucky again, assuming she was still around. He had a weakness for her that disgusted him. He held the station's door open and let Dodger in. A blast of arctic air greeted them.

"Is the chief in?"

"Nah," the desk officer responded. "He's in Honolulu. Comes back this afternoon."

Great, he thought. He could get the information he wanted without facing Cody. "What happened to the woman whose car went off the cliff?"

"She's over yonder"—he cocked his head to the side—"in jail."

Greg stormed out the door and around to the side of the building, Dodger trotting at his heels. "That lying son of a bitch! He put her in jail."

Evidently, no one had identified Lucky and posted her bail, or she wouldn't still be here. It had been a week since the accident. Where was her family? Or her boyfriend? She was cheap-looking—definitely not his type—but he would bet anything there was at least one man in her life, probably more.

A line of people two-deep led into the small jail. Christ! The place had exactly four cells, two for men and two for women. And a drunk tank. This was a lifetime's worth of visitors.

"What's going on?" he asked the last person in line, a plump woman in a fuchsia muumuu.

"We're waiting to see Pele's ghost," she informed him.

"What?" he asked, then it dawned on him. The legend about young women being found along the side of the road. They must be waiting to see Lucky.

He barged through the door, ignoring the woman who was yelling for him to wait his turn. Inside, people were milling around, filling the reception area with a steady drone of noise and the rank odor of bodies that had been waiting too long in the tropical sun. He angled his shoulders sideways and strode through the crowd into the interrogation room.

"Where's the jailer?" he demanded.

"On the other side of the door takin' money," a man answered.

"Shit!" The island had more legends and goddamned superstitions than any place on earth, but this sideshow was unbelievable. So what if seeing Pele's ghost was supposed to bring you good luck? How could anyone treat another human being like this? Greg worked his way to the door, set to let the jailer have it. He was a head taller than everyone else, so he could see over them into the cell block.

Look at her! Christ! Lucky must have flipped out or something. She was pacing the tiny cell. Three steps and turn, three steps and turn, three steps and turn. Her wild mop of platinum hair swished across her shoulders, a stark contrast to her baggy orange prison jumpsuit.

Her eyes stopped him cold. Even at this distance, they were astonishingly green. Striking. But her fixed stare chilled him. She looked exactly the way she had that night in the tent. Dozens of people were gazing at her as if she were a circus attraction, yet she apparently didn't know they were there.

"Ain't she something?" the woman beside him said.

Damn Cody. How could he let this happen? Everyone was making fun of Lucky, circling the cell and laughing like hyenas celebrating a fresh kill. To them she wasn't a woman alone in the world with no one to help her. She was nothing more than a sideshow freak.

"You should see her at night," commented someone behind Greg. "She sleeps under the bed."

Under the cot? The thought of her huddled on the cold cement like an animal while people watched—for luck—did something to him. He shoved his way toward the man taking the money. He clenched his fists, then took a deep breath. It was all he could do not to take a swing at the jailer.

Silence fell over the crowd, like the eerie hush between a blinding bolt of lightning and the roar of thunder sure to follow. He looked toward the tiny cell and saw that Lucky had dropped to her knees. Her tormented expression had been replaced by a smile. For Dodger. Somehow the dog had slipped through the crowd and stuck his head between the bars. Had he ever seen a woman that happy, that thrilled to see someone?

Dodger's tail was going a hundred miles an hour. Lucky reached out to pet him and he licked her hand. Amazing. Dodger had been bred to run and subjected to ruthless training. He simply had not been allowed to show affection. An electric shock with a cattle prod would have been his punishment had he even tried. Greg encouraged him to show his emotions, but all he got was a cold nose on his hand, never a warm lick, the canine expression of love.

"Pele adored animals," someone said, "especially sharks."

Lucky was petting Dodger now, stroking his silky ears, but her smile had vanished, replaced by a tight frown. What was she thinking?

A long-buried memory returned with startling clarity. Suddenly, he was a heartsick seven-year-old again, standing at the Humane Society with tears in his eyes. His parents had been killed in a car crash. He and Cody were going to live with their aunt. Muffin couldn't come. He was too old to survive the six-month quarantine in Hawaii, Aunt Sis claimed.

Some nice family would adopt Muffin, she insisted when Greg had refused to part with the dog his father had given him. He knew a lie when he heard one—especially from Aunt Sis. People wanted cute puppies, not stick-ugly mutts with gray muzzles.

At that moment, he'd needed his dog so much. Nothing could erase the pain of his parents' sudden death, but holding Muffin, having his dog sleeping beside his bed eased his heartache. He didn't want to leave him like this.

He stood in front of the cage and said a prayer, begging the Lord to have mercy, to send Muffin to some nice family, to give him another boy who would love him with all his heart.

Although dozens of years had passed, Muffin's face still haunted him. Black nose between the bars. Tail wagging hopefully. Soulful eyes pleading: *Don't leave me.* Muffin had been put to sleep, alone and forsaken, believing Greg had deserted him.

That's what the woman was feeling. Abandoned. Hopeless. For one shining moment, Dodger had lifted her spirits.

Lucky abruptly stopped patting Dodger. She rose, regarding the silent crowd with a stare that seemed to go right through them, a look that made them all seem like the sleazy voyeurs they were. She turned away, now regarding them with something that bordered on disdain. It was an imperious gesture, and it took everyone, including Greg, by surprise. Until he realized Lucky had lost everything on earth—except her pride.

The crowd watched as regally she sat on the bed, turning her back on them. Aloof, she put her head in the corner. Her riot of curls tumbled forward, shielding the sides of her face from the mob and revealing the small shaved patch on the back of her head.

Primal rage shot through him. He grabbed the jailer by the throat, yelling, "All of you—get the hell out of here."

Why couldn't they leave her in peace? Lucky wondered. She should be used to the gawking, the snickering. Being treated like a lower life form incapable of feelings. She tried to concentrate on counting her footsteps as she paced the cell, blocking out the people watching her.

But she couldn't ignore Greg. Seeing Dodger had filled her with such happiness. At last someone—even if it was a dog— was glad to see her. Then it had dawned on her that Greg must be somewhere nearby.

His voice had ripped through the crowd as sharp as a new razor. Right now she could hear the shuffling of feet. People were leaving. *Please, God, make Greg go too. Don't let him see me like this.*

She wasn't anyone worth saving. This single thought had haunted her these past days. No one had come forward to identify her. Adding to her misery, the owner of the car rental agency was pressing charges. The public defender representing her was convinced she would be convicted.

Just when she thought she'd hit bottom, Cody Braxton had informed her that she had been wearing a dead woman's tennis shoe. She had racked her brain for some plausible explanation, her stomach churning at the macabre thought. She remembered putting on the shoe and knowing it wasn't hers. But how had she gotten it?

A variety of scenarios flashed through her mind. All of them seemed to indicate that she was involved in something criminal. The police chief certainly thought so. He had reopened the investigation into the hiker's death. Could she be a thief, or worse? She just didn't know anymore. She hated herself. Hated what she saw in the mirror. Hated not being able to remember her own name. Hated having Greg Braxton pity her.

Lucky kept her forehead braced against the cold concrete, thankful for the silence. Evidently everyone had left. She closed her eyes, telling herself to rest. She was so tired that she was shaky. The crying made it impossible to sleep at night. The first time she had heard it, a few minutes passed before she realized no one was actually crying.

It was all in her head.

She was alone in a prison cell. But the sobs had seemed so real. So hopeless. Each time she tried to sleep the same sound whispered through the empty corridors of her brain until it became a keening wail.

The clanging of the cell door startled her, and she realized she must have dozed off. It was probably lunch. What had the woman who had been in the other cell called it? Blowup. The soy-based protein expanded in the stomach and felt like cement.

"You're outta here," the matron informed her.

"Someone's posted bail?" She hadn't remembered how bail worked, but the public defender had explained it. The matron nodded, glaring at her as if she were public enemy number one.

Once freedom would have filled her with hope, but not any longer. If her family hadn't come for her by now, they never would. Greg Braxton must have posted the bail. She swung around and faced the wall. "Tell him to save his money. I'm not budging."

"Suit yourself." The woman left with a belittling huff of disgust.

Didn't Greg have any sense? Couldn't he see she wasn't worth his trouble?

Never forget. I love you.

"Stop it!" In sheer frustration, she banged her head against the wall before she remembered the doctor's warning that another blow to the head might cause even more damage. "Why are those words imprinted in my brain?"

Last week the words had comforted her. That was before she'd been imprisoned. She'd spent only three days in jail, but it seemed like a lifetime. If somebody had once loved her, they'd deserted her now.

Something cold touched her arm and she whirled around. Dodger stood beside her, his soulful eyes on her, his tail wagging. In spite of herself, she smiled. Then she saw Greg standing in the open door, his six-foot-plus frame dwarfing the tiny cell.

"Come on." Greg's quietly spoken words ricocheted off the walls.

Something tightened in her chest, hurting a bit, yet giving her a curiously weightless feeling. A combination of pure joy and loneliness, a bittersweet ache that she had never before experienced.

Smothering a sob, she bit down on the inside of her cheek. Like a swift-rising tide, hope welled up inside her, taking her by surprise. The cinch around her chest tightened again, and the bittersweet ache intensified. Until this second she had no idea how alone she'd been. Now here was the one person she truly knew. Someone who was, in an unexplainable, frightening way, part of her.

Greg drove down the road with Lucky at his side and Dodger in the backseat. Unfuckingbelievable! What had possessed him? He had posted bail, putting up the one thing of any value he owned—his home.

Why? To have Lucky stare out the window, her head averted, clinging to the door like a limpet. She hadn't said a damn thing.

He'd led her out of the cell, gotten her a lab coat to wear instead of the prison jumpsuit, and taken her to his car.

"Want a baseball cap?" he asked as he stopped to let a truck loaded with sugar cane pass. He didn't know what else to say. He reached into the backseat and snatched his cap off the seat beside Dodger.

Without looking at him, she took it and pulled her unruly hair through the opening in the back of the cap. He stared at the bushy ponytail. Evidently she had no idea what he'd risked to help her. All she offered him was the back of her head.

What did he expect? Gratitude. No way. Like Jessica, women were users. Or, like Aunt Sis, they hated men. Hell, Lucky was happier to see Dodger than she was to see him. He'd let her get to him. Again.

He gazed through the windshield up at Haleakala. The dormant volcano was sporting its usual troop of clouds, shielding the top of the peak from view. It was raining on the upper slopes, making the hiking trails along "house of the sun" treacherous. He looked down and checked his beeper; search and rescue was on twenty-four-hour call.

When he'd posted Lucky's bail, he hadn't stopped to consider what would happen if he had to leave her for a rescue operation. Could he trust her not to take off? He wasn't sure. It wasn't like him to waffle, but she had him confused as hell. One minute he believed her, the next he wasn't so sure.

"Where are we going?" she asked, but she didn't look at him.

"To Kmart. You need some clothes."

There was a moment of silence, then Lucky spoke, still turned away from him. "Attention Kmart shoppers! Attention Kmart shoppers!" She finally faced him and beamed a smile that could melt your heart. "I've been in Kmart. I know I have."

He grinned at her childlike enthusiasm. Okay, so she'd been in a Kmart and relished the memory. How many times could she have heard that Kmart slogan? Surely not more times than she'd heard her own name. Then why couldn't she remember it?

Was he risking everything he had for a woman who could be a talented liar? A thief? A woman who would disappear—like Pele's ghost—as unexpectedly as she had appeared?

Chapter 6

He was smiling—or trying to—but Lucky knew that he was thinking she was a thief. That she really knew her name. Her own smile crumpled. Why had he bailed her out if he didn't believe her?

"Let me tell you. I'm a real college of knowledge," she said, unable to keep the bitterness out of her voice. "I know Jupiter is the fifth planet out from the sun. Khartoum is the capital of the Sudan. There are two varieties of Scotch: Highland malts and island malts. Why, I can even spell *verisimilitude*. But I don't know my own name."

Greg stared at her in that disturbing, intense way of his. "Your name will come to you . . . probably when you least expect it."

"That's what the doctors told me," she said as he drove into the Kmart lot. "Someone will ask me my name, and without thinking, I'll say it. The name will just pop out from wherever it's been hiding."

He pulled into a parking place. She couldn't tell what he

was thinking now. He had a way of closing himself off that upset her.

"Why didn't you just leave me in jail?"

Greg turned off the engine and yanked the keys out of the ignition, then he gripped the steering wheel with both hands, staring straight ahead. "Everyone deserves a break. They were ganging up on you, not giving you a fair chance."

So, he had fought for the underdog. That explained a lot. To her, he was special, the only person she really knew. The best man in the world, someone who had saved her life. To him she was a cause. There was nothing personal in this. She might be an endangered species or a rain forest.

She closed her eyes for a second. Right now she wished she were a rain forest. It sounded cool and green and quiet. And very far away. She let her mind drift for a moment, pretending she were somewhere else.

A rush of warm air enveloped her and she opened her eyes, realizing they'd been closed for a few moments. Greg had opened her door and was waiting for her to get out, Dodger at his side.

Inside Kmart it was cool, the smell of new clothes and popcorn in the air. Children were laughing, running up and down the aisles. It was comfortingly familiar. She had been in Kmart before, but she had never been in jail. Everything about that experience had been terrifyingly new.

"*No ka oi!* Wow! Look at those!"

Two teenage girls were pointing at her shoes. The vinyl slippers had Maui PD stamped across them. Greg had been able to rustle up a lab coat that could pass for a dress, but she'd had to borrow the shoes.

"Waaay cooool!" they cooed as Greg guided her down the aisle.

She supposed she should be thankful that the girls hadn't recognized her and called her Pele's ghost. And laughed at her. The baseball cap probably helped by hiding most of her hideous hair and shadowing her face.

Dodger sprinted ahead of them, then stopped with one paw raised, pointing to the panty hose display that consisted of two cabinets pushed together.

"What's the matter, boy?" Greg halted beside the dog. "Is someone under there?" He held up one finger, but Dodger didn't respond. Then he held up two fingers. Dodger barked once, twice, three times.

"Body A!" She couldn't keep the excitement out of her voice. "It's alive!" But how big could it be? It was probably a rat or a mouse.

Dodger barked three more times. A few shoppers stopped to watch. A damp patch of moisture formed on the back of her neck and she moved closer to Greg. After her experience in jail, she was positive if more than three people were near her, she'd reach critical mass and run. But these people weren't interested in her; Dodger had their attention.

A man elbowed his way through the group. His "Welcome to Kmart" badge said his name was Hank and he was assistant manager. "What's going on? Dogs aren't allowed in the store."

His officious tone didn't faze Greg. "You've got a problem here."

Greg shoved the cabinets apart. A small gray animal with a bushy plume of a tail blinked at them. Obviously, they'd awakened the poor thing. But what was it? Not a rat. Not a squirrel either.

The animal quickly regained its wits, took one look at the people and bolted, scurrying down the aisle at astonishing speed. Greg snapped his fingers and Dodger was racing after the animal. The crowd followed, led by Greg.

She trailed along behind. The good old college of knowledge had severe gaps. She didn't have the vaguest idea what kind of animal that was. Like a dying heartbeat, the secure feeling of being in a Kmart—a place she remembered—vanished. What she didn't know, what she would have to relearn was overwhelming.

Dodger had the creature cornered in the garden department.

The little beast was up on its hind legs, teeth bared, claws out. The animal was much smaller than Dodger, but it looked vicious. One swipe of its claws and Dodger could lose an eye.

"Stand back," Greg ordered and everyone obeyed.

He leaned down and grabbed the animal. There was a lot of hissing and flailing claws, but Greg had it by the scruff of the neck. He walked toward the plant arcade, holding the squirming animal away from his body.

"Get that dog out of the store," the manager told her as soon as Greg had disappeared from sight.

"Dodger's a special dog," she informed everyone with pride, repeating what Greg had told her while he was getting her out of jail. "See that?" She pointed to the gleaming chrome badge on the back of his collar. "It means he can go anywhere, just like a Seeing Eye dog. He's a registered disaster dog."

She was about to subject the uppity runt of an assistant manager to the biggest piece of her mind she could spare, when she spotted a woman staring at her intently. If the slim brunette had been in a grass skirt instead of a buttercup yellow halter dress, she would have been perfect for a travel poster. Something about her expression told Lucky that the woman thought she was Pele's ghost. If the woman said anything, the crowd would taunt her the way they had in jail.

"Come, Dodger." Lucky snapped her fingers the way Greg did, and Dodger trotted off with her, leaving the amazed crowd and the beautiful brunette behind. She led Dodger into the lingerie department, confident that Greg would find her when he returned. She stopped between two racks of bras and matching panties.

Dodger licked her hand, a quick flick of the tongue. She petted him the way Greg had that day when Dodger had found the vial, jostling his ears.

"You're good at what you do, Dodger. The best." She kneeled beside him and gazed into his eyes. She couldn't resist giving him a hug. The dog stiffened as her arms wrapped around him. Evidently, Greg didn't hug him often. A few seconds passed as she murmured what a good dog he was, and Dodger's taut body relaxed. He licked her cheek, just another quick swipe of his tongue, but it made her happy. She kept hugging him, wishing she had someone to hug her.

Greg walked back into Kmart and didn't see Lucky and Dodger. He told himself not to worry. Dodger was too well trained to go off with anyone. He stopped in his tracks and scanned the store. Nothing. No sign of a woman in a baseball cap with wild blonde hair streaming out the back. No dog in sight either.

Well, hell, where would she go? His gut instinct said she hadn't run out on him, but his brain said she might have. She was weird. Who knew what she might have done? He'd been so pissed at how Lucky was being treated that he'd ignored the inner voice warning him not to get involved with her.

Suddenly, the image of Aunt Sis's scowling face intruded. *You're too stubborn fer your own good, sonny. It'll get you in a peck of trouble.*

As much as Greg hated to admit the old biddy could possibly have been right, he had to concede that she was. He always had been incurably stubborn. Now that character flaw could cost him his house. He should have left Lucky in jail; cleared out the gawkers, sure, but he should have known better than to risk everything he owned for her.

He quickly walked into the women's department. A few women were mauling the racks for bargains. No sign of Lucky or Dodger. He heard a soft voice and edged his way through an armada of racks laden with frilly lingerie. Jesus! Who bought this stuff? He peered over a rounder of bras and saw Lucky sitting on the floor, hugging Dodger. He almost heard his own sigh of relief.

"You're both good at what you do," Lucky was saying to Dodger. "Really good. The way Greg handled that—that animal was marvelous."

He couldn't help smiling. Capturing a mongoose could be tricky, but he'd done it in seconds—like a pro—then released it.

Lucky was fondling Dodger's ears now. "I'm in good hands with you two. I know I am. I'm just a cause to Greg like a white rhino or a jaguar, but that's okay. I don't mind. At least Greg's willing to help me. You see, he's all I have."

All I have. The words echoed through his mind. What would it be like to be alone? To recognize no one except the stranger who'd rescued you? He couldn't imagine it.

Despite his suspicions—and he had them in spades—he felt a powerful bond with Lucky. That night in the tent, she had touched him, reaching a dark, unexplored part of his psyche. It was a feeling he'd shared once with his brother—years ago when their parents had been killed and they'd had no one but each other. Now Lucky had no one but him.

"Greg's wonderful, isn't he?" Lucky asked Dodger.

He couldn't handle it, had never been able to accept praise. He'd only been doing his job. He turned to walk away, but her next words halted him.

"Why couldn't I be a nuclear physicist or someone like that? Someone worth saving?"

Her voice was low, her attention solely on the dog, yet without even looking at him, she triggered feelings he'd never realized he had. Aw, hell. Before he knew it, Greg was sitting beside her. "Lucky—"

She turned away, focusing on Dodger, her face shadowed by the cap. "Greg, what kind of animal was that? A ferret? I can't exactly remember what a ferret looks like."

He gave her credit for trying to be upbeat, for hoping he hadn't overheard her heartfelt conversation with a dog. He went along, pretending he hadn't overheard her, trying to ignore the quickening in his nerves and the tension in every muscle.

"That was a mongoose. Years ago someone decided to bring them to Hawaii to control the rats that live in the cane fields," he explained with more detail than necessary, not knowing what else to say. "Too bad no one bothered to check that the mongoose hunts by day while rats are nocturnal. Now they both live side by side in the cane fields." She rewarded him with a suggestion of a smile, which kicked up his pulse another notch. "I let the mongoose loose in the field next to the parking lot."

"There's a lot that I'm not going to remember like the mongoose."

There was something vulnerable and imploring in her tone, but she didn't lift her head to look at him.

"I want to thank you," Lucky said, "for getting me out of that awful jail."

"Then why won't you look at me?"

Lucky pushed the bill of the baseball cap to the top of her forehead, revealing eyes that were wide and green and filled with raw emotion. "I want to be someone worth rescuing. I don't want to be a criminal."

Man, oh, man, were those tears in her eyes? He had never been able to handle tears. Jessica had used them constantly, crying whenever she didn't get her way. Granted, Lucky had every reason to cry, but he couldn't stand it. He started to reach out to her, intending to put his arm around her, but stopped himself in time, remembering how she'd behaved in the tent.

Too late. She moved toward him with a sound that could have been a sigh or a sob. He had no choice but to put his arm around her. That's all he meant to do. She needed someone besides a dog to comfort her.

She touched his arm, barely making contact, her hand coasting upward, her eyes never leaving his. He held himself stiffly, trying not to let her touch him, but it was impossible. Her soft breasts melded against his torso. She wasn't doing anything— exactly—just letting him comfort her.

"I appreciate all you've done for me," she whispered, her breath soft and warm against his neck.

Christ! He gazed up at the rounder of bras dangling overhead, striving to control the treacherous warmth thrumming through his veins. With a quick intake of breath followed by a soft sigh, she hugged him. A charged silence arced between them, and for several heavy heartbeats neither moved. He sucked in a deep breath to relieve the pressure building in his chest.

She kissed his cheek, nothing more than a brush of her lips, but before he could stop himself, both his arms were around her. He intended to give her a quick, reassuring hug—nothing more. But suddenly he was kissing her, cradling her in his arms and pressing the hard contour of his chest against the lush fullness of hers.

He steeled himself, half expecting her to pull something the way she had that night in the tent. Her lips were soft and pliant beneath his and unexpectedly tentative as if the last thing in the world that she had expected was to be kissed. Her lips parted, welcoming him with another little sigh, then his tongue brushed hers. The contact sent a fierce jolt of longing surging through him. He knew she felt it, too. She went utterly still, then her tongue daintily caressed his.

The hesitant way she moved, the way she clung to him had an unexpected sweetness about it. He thrust deeper and she arched against him, triggering a low growl deep in his throat. Jesus! What this woman could do to him without half trying.

Every muscle in his body was taut with need, making it impossible to think of anything but what it would be like to kiss his way down her neck until he reached those enticing breasts. He imagined his tongue teasing a nipple, sucking gently while his hand explored the softness of her inner thighs and the moist heat waiting there.

He pulled back a fraction of an inch, a noise nearby disturbing him, making him angry. He looked up and saw a woman watching them.

Aw, shit! Here he was sitting on the floor, bras brushing his head, kissing a woman who had become the island laughing-stock until he had a world class hard-on and who shows up? His sister-in-law. But Sarah Braxton wasn't paying any attention to him. She was staring with unabashed curiosity at Lucky.

Chapter 7

Lucky gazed out the car window at the ocean. The last rays of the sun gilded the water, turning it a burnished gold. They had driven through the greenbelt of hotels and luxury homes in Wailea and were now on a less-traveled road marked Makena Beach. The land here was arid, its volcanic history more evident than in the lushly landscaped Wailea.

She wanted to ask where they were going, but didn't. Greg had been strangely silent since Sarah Braxton had appeared. His beautiful sister-in-law was the same woman Lucky had noticed earlier. Sarah had been wonderful, helping Lucky choose enough clothes to last until the trial.

While they had shopped, Greg waited at the register. He'd barely thanked Sarah as he paid for Lucky's clothes. Sarah had been gracious, ignoring his rudeness—or perhaps she was used to it. Lucky remembered Greg insisting he had no family, yet she learned that he had two nephews and a niece. Sarah had proudly told Lucky about her children as she helped her, but she never mentioned a rift between her family and Greg.

Lucky didn't say anything about the tension. This could be

like the mongoose—a gap in her memory. Maybe there was some clue as to what was going on here, and she just didn't understand.

She ventured a look at Greg. His eyes were on the single-lane road that was little more than dirt tracks now. Here the houses were spaced far apart and separated by black rock beaches. She wondered where they were going but assumed he was driving her to his home.

Why wasn't he talking to her? He hadn't said two words since Sarah had appeared. Why had he kissed her? He hadn't wanted to. She'd made the first move, overwhelmed by the need to be held and comforted.

A hot flush of shame inched up her neck the way it had in jail when she'd discovered that she was the local freak. The memory ate at her like a corrosive acid. She'd tried to maintain her dignity, but it had been such a degrading experience, one she knew she'd never forget.

"Do you know what happens if you don't appear in court next week?" Greg asked unexpectedly.

She faced him with a surge of relief. At last he was talking, but what was he getting at? Was this something else that she didn't understand? "I'll be there. Sarah helped me select a dress."

Greg kept staring straight ahead, concentrating on the rutted road. "If you don't show, I forfeit your bail. I'll lose my house."

It took her a second to realize that he thought she was going to run out on him. She didn't understand him—not for one second. One minute he was acting as if she was special, and the next she was a criminal. Obviously, the man couldn't make up his mind.

"I'm not going to run away," she said, anger reflected in each word. "I'll be there. By then your brother should have found out who I am. I'm certain that my family will explain that I didn't steal that car. You'll be off the hook. They'll repay you for the clothes." She held up the receipt that she'd been clutching in her hand. "I'll see that you get back every penny. I swear."

Greg cocked his head to the side and studied her for a moment, but he didn't say anything.

She realized her tone had been too sharp. Where did such anger come from? Why was she alienating the only person who'd helped her? He had even put up his home so she could get out of jail. Who could blame him for being concerned that she would run out?

"You've done so much for me," she said, emotion breaking in her voice. "Thank you for buying me clothes and posting bail. You've been so wonderful. I would never run out on you."

"I didn't think you would. I just wanted you to know what's at stake."

He was staring at her so intently that she wondered again if she was missing something. "My life's at stake. If I can't prove I didn't steal that car, I'm going to prison. That's a three-year minimum sentence. But I wouldn't do anything to hurt you."

Greg nodded slowly but didn't say anything more. Lucky sensed that he was a man unaccustomed to showing his emotions. He didn't like her to touch him; she'd already noticed that. When she'd put her arms around him in Kmart, it had been like hugging a cement block. He'd quickly changed, of course, but she suspected it was against his better judgment.

"I'm going to get you the best lawyer in the islands."

"I'm sure the public defender will be just fine. He—"

"Forget it." Greg cut her off with a wave of his hand. "Tony Traylor controls Maui. He's head of the joint council. That's like being a mayor, only more powerful. You're accused of stealing one of his rental cars. He's not going to let the DA cop a plea for a lesser charge. You'll get the max unless we hire a big gun."

His support brought tears to her eyes. She gazed out the open window at the turquoise sea, blinking rapidly. Greg might yo-yo, believing her one minute and doubting her the next, but she knew that he was going to stand by her. To him she wasn't a freak—Pele's ghost—to be ridiculed and humiliated. She was a person who deserved a chance.

One day, she'd be able to repay him.

A jumble of confused thoughts and feelings assailed her. In so many ways, she felt close to Greg Braxton, but in reality, she must have been this close to another man. A husband? A lover? Wasn't there someone, somewhere, who cared about her at least as much as this stranger?

There had to be, she reasoned, yet she had no memory of another man. There was only Greg. She might have been held and kissed by someone else, but she would never remember it. The thought generated a gnawing ache deep inside where her memory should have been. She tamped down the painful longing. That part of her life was gone.

The kiss in Kmart was really her first kiss, Greg the first man to hold her. To care about her. It was impossible for her to imagine feeling this strongly about another man. A crucial part of her that she hadn't known was lost had been found. No, she thought, *discovered* was a better word. There was amazing physical pleasure in being kissed.

Lucky ventured a glance at Greg, wondering what he thought about the kiss. His jaw was set like a steel trap, and he was staring straight ahead. Obviously, he'd overheard her talking to Dodger and had felt the need to comfort her. It wasn't his first kiss; it hadn't been that special.

Pull yourself together, whispered a voice in her head. You've got to be strong to face the ordeal ahead. Stop crybabying to the dog and expecting Greg to hold you.

Greg slowed the car and turned onto a drive that led down to the water. On the point, surrounded by a black volcanic rock beach, stood a house. The thoroughly modern glass-walled home seemed lonely, isolated. How far away was the nearest house? Half a mile at least, she judged.

"You aren't bothered by neighbors, are you?" she asked.

"There's a building moratorium. If they lift it, you can expect hotels with flocks of tourists frying their bodies, sipping Mai Tais, and bitching about taxes.''

''That would be a shame,'' she said, looking around. There was just enough light seeping over the horizon from the setting sun to see the tiers of hills that stretched up from the beach to the mountain dominating the skyline: Haleakala. Close to the house the terrain was volcanic, with tufts of wild grass and white ginger bringing color to the dark rocks. Higher up were acres of pineapples and cane fields that swayed in the wind, reminding her of spring corn.

''What's that?'' Lucky pointed to a horseshoe-shaped out-cropping of rock that rose from the ocean not far from shore.

''That's the Molokini Crater. It's a cone of an extinct volcano. Like Haleakala, only smaller. It's a dive site these days.''

She started to say something but stopped, spotting the car as they rounded the bend. The small white Bronco was marked Maui Police Department.

It was so quiet in their car that Lucky could hear her heart beating in double-time. Oh, no! They'd come for her. They couldn't arrest her, though, could they? She was out on bail. Maybe there was a new charge. Maybe they'd found out something about the hiker.

Get a grip, she told herself. Don't panic.

''It's my brother.'' Greg pressed the opener and the garage door slowly rose. ''You take Dodger inside while I talk to him.''

Leaning against the squad car, Cody waited for Greg to come out of the garage. He had been back on the island for only an hour, and all hell had broken loose. At headquarters, he'd gotten word that Greg had posted Lucky's bail. Minutes later, Sarah had called. What on earth had Greg been doing sitting on the floor of Kmart kissing that weirdo?

The island was a small place, really tiny when you subtracted all the tourists. It was a working stiff's idea of paradise. Great climate, chamber of commerce views. And sky-high prices that came with a tourist economy. The locals shopped at Kmart.

What had happened in the store would be around the island in a heartbeat. Not that he cared about gossip—he'd been the center of the juiciest scandal to hit the island in a decade. But he didn't want his brother to lose everything because of this woman. Who knew what Lucky was up to?

This was one helluva case. It had all the earmarks of an aberration in paradise—a real crime. He would have enjoyed every second of the investigation if Greg hadn't been involved.

Cody shook his head, his eyes on the isolated house. Out here Cody felt cut off from the rest of the world. How did Greg stand it? It was lonely and desolate. The wildness of it, the loneliness suited his brother in a way that Cody would never understand. Give him the up-country, with its grassy meadows and cowboys and farmers. People. Give him people, not a house at road's end, facing the sea, its back toward civilization.

Greg stalked out of the garage, a sullen expression on his face. Cody inhaled sharply, anxious to avoid a confrontation.

"I hear you posted Lucky's bail."

"So?" Greg challenged him.

Cody realized his brother wasn't going to make this easy. Did he ever? "Are you sure you know what you're doing?"

"Your jailer was letting half the island in to get a peek at Lucky and charging them five bucks a crack."

"I heard about it when I got back. I've taken care of him."

"Lucky could file a suit for violating her civil rights and bankrupt this island."

Cody mopped his brow with the back of his hand. Already Tony Traylor was screaming to the heavens about his brother springing Pele's ghost. Like a snake, Traylor had slithered into the political arena, shedding his morals early on. He'd sacrifice Cody rather than lose one vote.

"Stay out of this, Greg. She's nothing but trouble."

"Lucky has amnesia. She needs help. Treating her like a criminal is the worst thing for her."

"There's some controversy about her diagnosis," Cody began, and was rewarded with a slight uplifting of Greg's brow. "She still has her sense of smell."

"What the hell does that have to do with it?"

"I was just in Honolulu. The doctors there sent her test results to several university hospitals and got mixed opinions. Some agree with the neurosurgeons who examined Lucky here, but others felt the Hoyt-Mellenberger syndrome doesn't apply. They say with true memory loss, your sense of smell goes. When they tested Lucky, she could still smell things."

Silence followed his announcement. The only noise was the rush of the surf against the rocky beach. Greg always had been a lone wolf, a man with a wild streak, but tonight he seemed different. Cody couldn't quite put his finger on the change.

"It could be a fluke," Cody admitted, feeling the need to fill the silence. "Hoyt-Mellenberger is rare, and no two cases are alike, but the shoe makes—"

"What shoe?"

Didn't Greg know about the hiker? He must have left to certify Dodger before the story broke. It was dark now, only the light of the rising moon illuminating the darkness. It was difficult to tell what Greg was thinking as Cody told him about the dead hiker and the shoe that had suddenly turned up a year later.

"There's probably a reasonable explanation," Greg said when Cody finished.

"Really?" Cody told himself to be patient, quickly counted to three, then continued. "That hiker fell from the trail near the Iao Needle. She wasn't trotting around up there wearing one shoe. And she had some weird bugs in her hair."

"Bugs?"

"Yeah, bugs, like dead bodies. It was just that no one had seen those kind before." Cody shook his head. "Know what I think? Someone drove her up to the trail head, carried her up a ways, and threw her over. It was supposed to look like an accident."

"Lucky isn't strong enough to carry anyone up that trail," Greg insisted with characteristic stubbornness.

"I didn't say she did it, but I do think she knows something she isn't telling. I've sent her prints to the FBI. Let's see what comes back from their new database." He opened the car door, saying over his shoulder, "I've posted Lucky's picture at the airport and with the harbor masters. She can't get off the island."

"She hasn't got any money to buy a ticket," Greg responded, but he didn't sound nearly as confident as he had earlier.

Cody turned the key in the ignition. "Lucky's *lolo*—a mental case. Say the word, and I'll take her back to jail."

Greg didn't hesitate. "No way."

"Be careful. Lock up any weapons you have around. I don't want another dead body on my hands." Cody paused, suddenly aware of how callous he sounded. "Seriously, I'm worried about you. I know you still blame me for Jessica's death. I can't change the past. I made a mistake that I'll never be able to make right. But I don't want anything to happen to you."

The emotion in Cody's voice was still ringing in Greg's ears as his brother drove away. Forgive Cody? Hell, no. Some wounds never healed; they just festered. The painful memory of the night he'd discovered his wife with his brother still brought a gut-wrenching stab of pain—if he allowed himself to think about it.

"Spaghetti okay?" Lucky asked when Greg walked into the kitchen a few minutes later.

"Sure," he replied as he studied her. She was flitting around Jessica's kitchen, seeming completely at home. He hadn't forgiven Cody, but he'd be a fool not to heed his brother's warning. Any jerk could see that this wasn't a simple auto accident. A lot more was going on here, and Lucky was at the center of it.

"What does Dodger eat?" she asked.

He noticed she hadn't asked what Cody had wanted. "I'll feed him." Greg walked into the pantry and scooped four cups of kibble into Dodger's bowl. The dog sat obediently at his side, waiting for the "eat" command. Greg snapped his fingers and pointed to the bowl. Dodger dove in.

"He's incredibly well trained." Lucky was standing in the doorway, surprising him. He hadn't heard her walk up.

"He's a great dog." Greg gave Dodger a quick pat. "Let me show you the guest room."

He walked through the kitchen and down the hall. Jessica had decorated the room with care, insisting her parents would visit often. Of course, they hadn't. The only times he'd seen them had been at the wedding and at Jessica's funeral.

On a raised dais was a platform bed swathed in expensive silk, which Jessica had insisted on calling café au lait even though anyone else would have called it tan. A black lacquer headboard shaped like a swan's wings and black accents completed the decor, which Greg had found austere even for his taste.

"Oh, my." Lucky put her hand on his arm.

He quickly pulled away. After that kiss the last thing he needed was for her to touch him. He refused to let Lucky get to him again.

"Here's the closet." He opened the door to the closet. There were plenty of hangers for the few clothes Lucky had bought.

He left her to put away her things while he sorted through his mail. Even when she returned to the kitchen to toss the spaghetti in the boiling water, he ignored her. Look too deeply into those green eyes, examine too closely those provocative curves, and it wouldn't be hard to imagine her flat on her back with those sexy breasts offered to him, those slender legs locked around his hips, those hands touching him, guiding him into her.

Christ! How was he going to spend the night under the same roof with this woman? If he hadn't kissed her, he wouldn't have known how soft she felt or how hot she could get him.

He forced himself to sort through his mail, managing to steer his thoughts away from her.

"Isn't it any good?" she asked when they sat down to dinner, and he barely touched his spaghetti.

"It's great," he answered truthfully. It was excellent spaghetti sauce. He had no idea how she'd managed it in such a short time. Jessica would have spent hours in the kitchen, using every pot, consulting some expensive cookbook, and coming up with only a mediocre sauce. But then, Jessica's interest in cooking had never really gone beyond having every gourmet gadget available and an impressive cookbook collection.

"I'm just too tired to be hungry. I'm on mainland time, you know. To me it's the middle of the night."

"Go to bed. I'll clean up and turn out the lights."

"Okay." Greg rose and gave Dodger the stay command. "I'll leave Dodger with you. Let him out just before you go to bed. He'll be fine until morning."

Lucky smiled, obviously thrilled to have Dodger's company, and Greg walked up the hall, confident that if Lucky ran away Dodger would come get him. He stripped down to his shorts and stretched out across the bed. The sliding door was open, bringing in the smell of the sea and the lulling sound of the surf on the rocky beach. Overhead the soft swish of the ceiling fan could be heard in the moonlit room.

He loved this place. Loved the wildness of the ocean surrounding the point. Loved the way the endless sea flowed into the horizon. Loved the way the wind and surf lashed the rocks, sculpting them little by little over eons. The timelessness of the sea and the shore awed him as much as its beauty. Here his troubles seemed unimportant—a mere blip in nature's grand scheme.

The thoroughly domestic sound of pots and pans coming from the kitchen broke into his thoughts. Until now he'd never realized how quiet the house had been the past two years. When

Jessica died, the house went with her. But not tonight; now the house had new life. Lucky. He could hear the low murmur of her voice and knew she was talking to Dodger.

Once again desire surged through him, making him furious with himself. But that didn't make it go away. What was wrong with him? It wasn't as if he couldn't get laid. All he had to do was hang around one of the hotel bars and pick up a woman. Tourists were quick to hop in the sack. Best of all they soon went home.

Having Lucky here was different. Since Jessica's death he'd never brought a woman home. Casual sex in hotel rooms protected him from the complications of a relationship. Now he'd gone over the edge without even realizing that he wasn't just bringing Lucky home. He'd brought her into his life.

Suddenly, he recalled the serious expression on Cody's face as he'd talked about Lucky. Psychopaths could be charming even sexy, he reminded himself. But for the life of him, he couldn't envision Lucky as dangerous.

As a precaution he slipped out of bed and took the car keys from his pants pocket, and hid them under the mattress. Then he flopped down on the bed again. Rolling over, Greg tried to forget about Lucky and to concentrate on the mess he'd find at work after being away from the institute for a week. Someone had brought in a wounded shark even though they weren't equipped to treat it.

The institute studied humpback whales and monk seals—period. There wasn't enough money for those projects, but you couldn't explain that to the volunteers who made up the majority of the center's staff. They loved the sea and every creature in it. Greg had learned a long time ago that you couldn't save them all.

Sometimes it was all you could do to save yourself.

His thoughts drifted and he closed his eyes, listening to the surf and the muffled sound of Lucky's voice. He saw himself with Cody on one of the rain forest trails. They were hunting the wild pigs that roamed the area. How long ago had that been? He couldn't quite remember. A long time ago. Before Jessica had died.

A child's sobbing harrowed the silence, startling him. Greg bolted upright, with a neck-wrenching jolt, realizing he must have fallen asleep. The air was heavy as a blanket in the dark room. The ceiling fan had conked out again. The house was still; the luminous dial on the clock read 2:14. He'd been asleep for hours.

Obviously, he hadn't heard a child's cry. It must have been the fan squeaking to a halt. Still, the haunting memory left him shaken. It seemed so real, the way dreams often did.

He stroked the midnight stubble along his jaw, then slowly sank back down on the pillow again, closing his eyes and telling himself to go back to sleep. His bedroom door creaked and he squinted across the moonlit room. He'd left the door ajar, so Dodger could summon him if Lucky left. The door inched open and he waited, half expecting a tall figure to loom in the shadows. Instead, Dodger trotted in, and Greg jumped to his feet. The dog's appearance could mean only one thing: Lucky was gone!

Chapter 8

Greg stormed down the hall, Dodger beside him, cursing Lucky for skipping out on him. The guest room door was open. In the moonlight Greg could see the platform bed had been slept in, the top sheet pulled from its moorings as if Lucky had been extremely restless. An open book lay on the nightstand, but there was no sign of her.

"Christ!" Greg couldn't remember the last time he had been this pissed. *I wouldn't do anything to hurt you.* What a crock! She'd lied to him, disarming him with that wounded-doe expression.

He flicked on the light switch. Nothing. Great! The power was out again. Or Lucky had tripped a breaker.

"Why 'n hell would she do that?" he muttered as he hurried back to his room. Why would she want the house dark? He scrambled into shorts without bothering with a shirt or shoes. It took him a minute to find the car keys hidden under the mattress.

"Come on, Dodger. She couldn't have gotten far."

He was halfway across the house before he realized Dodger

wasn't with him. The last time he'd seen him had been in the guest room. He called again, louder this time, "Dodger. Dodger."

But Dodger didn't respond. Greg slipped into the kitchen, alert for any sound or motion. His sixth sense had kicked in, telling him Lucky might still be in the house. He crossed the small room and opened the knife drawer. Moonlight from the window illuminated the gleaming blades. The largest knife was missing from its slot.

"Aw, shit! What's she up to?"

Cody's words came back to him: *Lucky's* lolo—*a mental case. I don't want another dead body on my hands.*

Find her, get the knife away from her, then take her back to jail. From now on he would mind his own business, Greg promised himself. He would return to work and forget about the past. And Lucky. To hell with the whole damn mess.

Greg crossed the living room, the moonlight sufficient to assure him that Lucky wasn't hiding there. And there was no sign of Dodger, either. He didn't know what Lucky was up to, but when he found her he wasn't falling for any of her lines. She could just rot in jail for all he cared.

The house had never been so quiet. The only noise was the ever-present rush of the surf on the rocky beach. Then a plaintive whine cut through the stillness.

Dodger! What had she done to him? He barged into the room, primed to disable Lucky with a flying tackle but wary of the knife. Halfway across the threshold, he spotted Dodger. What in hell was he doing?

The dog was standing, pointing like a retriever at the closed door to the closet. Lucky must be hiding in there, but why hadn't Dodger barked? That, not whining, was the signal. Unless Dodger sensed danger and this was his way of warning him.

He motioned for Dodger to move back, and the dog retreated to the doorway. Greg quickly assessed his options, confident that the survival training he'd had with S and R was enough to overpower one slight blonde, even if she was armed with a butcher's knife. When she lunged out of the closet with the deadly knife, he would restrain her with a hammerlock.

He flattened himself against the wall and grabbed the lever handle. The door flew open. Greg waited and waited, every muscle tense. A rivulet of sweat trickled down between his bare shoulder blades. He edged forward a fraction of an inch.

The moonlight hit Lucky's toes, spotlighting the ugly pink polish. Greg jerked back. Then the odd angle of her foot registered. He peeked around the corner again.

Lucky was asleep on the closet floor, curled into a fetal position, her head resting on a pillow. From under the white linen the blade of the knife caught a moonbeam. There was just enough light to see the glistening tear tracks on her cheeks and wet lashes.

It slowly dawned on him that the noise that had awakened him had been Lucky crying. He remembered what the people had said about Lucky sleeping under the cot in jail and realized she wasn't trying to get the jump on him. She'd deliberately taken a pillow and gone to sleep in the closet.

He hated to admit it, but his brother was right. Lucky must know more than she was telling. Why else would she be hiding with a knife for protection?

Lucky stirred, stretching slender, bare legs across the closet floor, the nightgown she wore shifting to the tops of her thighs. She'd washed her hair and had pulled it off her face in a French braid that was still damp. She whimpered, a disturbing sound that reminded him of the cry that had awakened him.

He sank to his knees and touched her cheek. "Lucky, wake up."

Her lashes fluttered open, and she gazed back at him. She looked disoriented and half wild, the way she had that night in the tent. He kept the knife in sight, not knowing what to expect.

"Greg," she whispered, the threat of tears in her voice. "You found me."

Had she been hiding from him? The idea was so astonishing that he concentrated on her and took his eye off the knife.

"I didn't want you to see me like this." She sat upright, the nightgown clinging to her full breasts. "I didn't want you to think I'm crazy."

He didn't think it. Hell, he was *convinced* that she was a world-class loony tune. But there was also something about her that called to him. She seemed lost, alone, yet she had a sensuality that was very appealing. His reaction to her disturbed him, making him angry with himself and irritable.

"What are you doing in the closet?" Greg asked, more sharply than he'd intended.

"I can't explain ... exactly. When I fall asleep, I hear a child crying."

"There's no child within miles of here."

"I know." There was something wounded and imploring in her eyes. "It's in my head. And I get this scary feeling that something terrible—really terrible—is going to happen to me."

Aw, hell, he didn't know what to say. She was hearing voices but not realizing that she was actually making those sounds. What was wrong with her? How could he help her?

"I had this irresistible urge to get under the bed the way I did in jail, but of course I couldn't get under there"—she pointed to the platform bed. "I don't dare sleep unless I'm hiding."

Jesus! This was just too friggin' weird.

"It doesn't make any sense, does it, Greg?"

Of course it didn't, but he kept hearing a keening cry that sounded like a child's terrified sob. A cry for help. A cry Lucky thought was only in her head.

"Try to understand," she pleaded, her anguish evident. Her slender fingers tugged at the hem of her nightgown. "I have to sleep. I'm so exhausted, I'm punchy. I haven't been able to sleep since I left the hospital, and they stopped giving me medication to help me sleep. Shut the closet door and let me stay here. I'll be all right. I promise."

What in hell could he say? He couldn't leave her on the closet floor. He didn't have a choice. Greg rose and pulled her to her feet. "Get in bed. I'll sit with you until you fall asleep."

"Please, I don't want to bother you."

He put his arm around her and guided her to the bed. "It's okay. Dodger and I will watch over you. Just get some sleep."

He made himself look the other way while Lucky lay down and pulled the sheet up over her breasts. Sitting beside her, his shoulders propped up against the headboard, he stretched his legs out on the bed and clicked his fingers for Dodger. The dog came up beside them and gave Lucky a quick lick on the hand.

"I'm safe," Lucky said to the dog. "There's no reason to hide."

"We won't let anything happen to you," Greg assured her.

Gazing out the window, he waited for her to fall asleep. The guest room faced Haleakala, and in the full moon the towering volcano was a specter against the starry sky. A wedge of bats flew by the window, creating a riffling ghost of a shadow below them as they left the refuge of their treetop homes to forage. Normally, Mother Nature at work soothed him, assuring him the world was still in balance.

Not tonight.

Tonight his whole world was off-kilter. He didn't know what in hell to do about it. Greg waited, hoping that with the light of dawn would come an answer. Lucky was breathing evenly now, and he expelled a sigh of relief. A few minutes passed before he allowed his eyes to close.

Shaking awakened him, and for a moment he couldn't imagine where he was. Then it all came back with startling clarity. The closet. The knife. Lucky was beside him, trembling violently. He slid down next to her and scooted close, until the hard wall of his chest touched the curve of her back. "Lucky, I'm here. You're all right."

A soft whimper escaped her lips. Her hands were clutching the sheet now, twisting it convulsively. He cradled her in his

arms and manacled both her wrists with one hand. "Lucky."
Again he tried to awaken her. "I'm here with you."

He repeated the calming words until she relaxed. Her head
stopped thrashing and her body softened, melding against his.
She released her death grip on the sheet, and he let go of her
wrists. Although her body was still, her heartbeat thudded,
strong and heavy, against him.

Lucky turned her head to face him. Until that moment he
hadn't realized he had moved onto the pillow beside her. "Oh,
Greg, I'm so frightened."

He moved back, deliberately putting more distance between
them, aware of his body once again reacting to hers. "What
are you afraid of?"

"I . . . don't know exactly. I was having some sort of dream.
It seemed real. You know how dreams are. I was hiding in a
closet and someone was coming to get me."

"Who?"

"I don't know . . . really, I don't." She moved slightly, the
fullness of her breast pressing against his arm. "Where's the
knife?"

"In the closet."

"I'd feel better if I had it."

"You don't need it," he responded, wondering what she
was hiding from. "You're safe."

She snuggled closer, telling him without speaking that she
was afraid. The warmth of her body crept through his, the clean
smell of shampoo filling his nostrils. Her head was light against
his shoulder, her hair damp. Her lips were dangerously close.
A kissable mouth—most definitely a kissable mouth.

For the love of God, get up, get out of here.

Her hand began to move, skimming across his bare chest in
lazy circles, teasing his taut muscles. A fraction of an inch at
a time, the tips of her fingers furrowed through the dense hair
on his chest, and he automatically tightened his groin muscles.
Every increased tempo of his pulse reminded him that her hands
were on him, prowling with agonizing slowness across his

heated skin. Her body was flush with his, so close that he could feel the rapid thump of her heart where her breasts were pillowed against him.

Swear to God, she had him upside down and backward. He didn't know what to make of her. He reminded himself that she was probably a slut—possibly worse. Another woman very much like her had ruined his life. But his body just didn't give a damn.

"Lucky," he said, his voice a shade shy of a whisper, and she looked up. In the moonlight her eyes were almost black, with only a thin hoop of green, but it was a very luminous green. Unbelievably sexy.

She made the first move, touching her lips to his with a measure of shyness that surprised him. He nudged into the moist chamber of her mouth as he pulled her closer, his tongue mimicking what his body longed to do. There was no artistry to the kiss. Hell, no. It was hot and hard and totally carnal.

The dark undertow of desire surged through him. In an instant he had her exactly where he'd pictured her so many times that he'd lost count. Flat on her back. Like liquid heat his body spread over hers, his leg coming up to cover hers, his sex nestling into the cleft between her thighs. He changed the angle of his head, slanting it to one side so he could thrust his tongue deeper as he languidly moved his hips against hers.

Man, oh, man she felt so good that he thought he was going to lose it like a horny kid in the backseat of a Chevy. Had he ever been this aroused? No, he silently conceded, striving to maintain control. He pulled back, sucked in a stabilizing breath and was astonished by the reverent expression on her face. If he didn't know better, he would have thought she was in love with him.

"Don't stop," she whispered.

"The thought hadn't crossed my mind."

With those words unbridled passion took over, urging him to rip away the silly little bow holding the top of her gown together. Her breasts spilled free, the nipples large and taut and thrusting up at him, beckoning him. He shoved the fabric aside, then cradled the fullness in his hands, fondling those pert nipples with the rough pad of his thumb.

"Oh, Greg, I had no idea—"

He buried his face between her soft breasts and inhaled the delicate scent of soap and woman. Angling his head to one side he blazed a trail of moist kisses until he found a tight nipple. Between his lips it felt like a small rosebud and he sucked on it until she arched up against him, offering him even more.

Her hands were on his back now, her short nails digging in, which only aroused him to a frenzy. He ground his hips against her, his erection, thick and achingly hard until she moaned, scratching his back in frantic pleasure. He shifted his head and took care of the other breast, aware that he wasn't going to last much longer. His burgeoning erection was pressing against his zipper, screaming for relief.

Some distant bell rang, telling him that he needed protection. Aw, crap! The only box of condoms he had was in the glove compartment of his car because he always went to the woman's bed, never bringing her to his. That realization brought a tiny ray of sanity to a brain hijacked by his libido. This woman wanted him to have sex with her—another tie that would bind him to her. She was counting on him not being able to resist her.

So far it was working. Every chance he'd had, he'd been all over her. And taking her once wouldn't be enough. That much he could tell by the little he'd already sampled. Then she would have a hold over him. He would be damned before he'd be led around by his cock.

Take control. The idea was startlingly simple and unbearably erotic. Yeah, take charge. Of course, he would have blue balls for a week, but he would have the satisfaction of not allowing another woman to manipulate him.

With the moist tip of his tongue, he scorched a path of kisses down the flat plane of her belly, shoving aside the nightgown as he went. The sweet delicious scent of her skin became sexier when he reached the dark patch of silky curls, which made him shudder with anticipation. It was all he could do to control his own body.

His fingers skimmed through the slick curls. "You're so wet," he said and she responded with a low moan. "So sweet."

He eased his finger inside her, surprised at how tight she was even though she was more than ready. With his tongue he found the right spot and stroked the supersensitive skin.

"What are you doing?" she asked with a gasp.

"Panning for gold." He almost laughed at the stupid joke, but he was so close to losing it that he needed to divert his attention. She was driving him crazy, but he'd be damned before he would let her know.

It only took a few seconds—she was easier than he'd antici-pated—and she began to shudder from within.

"Oh, my," she cried. "Help me."

Greg rolled onto his back, huffing like a racehorse. Okay, so there was a stick of dynamite in his pants and a willing woman beside him. He could get through this, he assured him-self, resisting the temptation to roll over and bury himself to the hilt inside her.

As it turned out, there wasn't any temptation to resist. The even cadence of Lucky's breath, and the rise and fall of her breasts told him she'd fallen asleep. He was left staring at her gorgeous body, wondering if she'd gotten the message: No woman was going to manipulate him.

"Someone named Greg Braxton posted her bail," the Orchid King informed his partner.

"What do we know about him?"

His partner hunched forward, concentrating on the computer screen that was tracking orchid shipments out of Singapore. There was only a trace of concern in his partner's voice, but the king knew better. His partner was upset she had found another man. With a man to help her—she was dangerous . . . if she remembered what had happened.

"Braxton is the man who found her," the king explained. "He's a volunteer with the local search and rescue unit, but he works at the Marine Institute."

His partner turned to him. "Is Braxton married?"

"No. His wife died in an accident over two years ago."

"So Miz Nine Lives sucked him in, huh?"

"Looks like it," the king admitted. "Wonder what she's up to. Maybe she really doesn't remember."

"She's fakin' it. The only reason she hasn't exposed us is that I have the ace."

A few minutes later the king was walking up the path to his home, still concerned about the whole situation. He knew his partner was right, though. The ace was the key.

Greg Braxton was the wild card. The name alone conjured up an image of a tough guy. And a smart one. The data banks the king had accessed—and he'd hit every one—told troublingly little about the man. MIT on a scholarship. Worked full time throughout college. Afterward he'd received a grant to do research at the marine facility at Woods Hole, then he'd returned to Hawaii.

The king didn't like not knowing more. Most people left tracks that could easily—and anonymously—be traced through the Internet. But not Braxton.

Worse, he could imagine the woman he loved in Braxton's arms. It made him want to kill them both.

Lucky gazed out the kitchen window. The sun glistened on the waves like a thousand fallen stars. *It feels so good to be alive.* The world seemed beautiful and new and full of promise. The opposite of last night, when she had hidden in the closet.

She returned to the macadamia nut pancake batter and wondered how she would face Greg when he awoke. The memory of what he'd done made her ache with pleasure, but obviously the man had problems. He seemed virile and totally capable of making love to her the way she instinctively knew he should. But he hadn't.

It was probably a physical thing. No, that didn't seem right. He'd been erect, yet he hadn't made love to her properly. What was wrong with him? Maybe it was something that she was supposed to do or know—like the mongoose.

Lucky felt Dodger's cold nose at the hem of her shorts and knew Greg must be up. As she reached down to pat the dog, she heard him walk into the kitchen.

"Been up long?" he asked.

She turned to him with a smile. "A couple of hours. Long enough to make coffee and start on pancakes."

He poured himself a mug of coffee. He was still wearing the shorts he'd had on last night and his hair was mussed, giving her a hint of how he must have looked as a boy. Greg turned, and his eyes met hers over the rim of the cup.

The hot flush of humiliation that she'd felt so often surged through her once more. "I'm sorry about last night. The closet part, I mean."

He shrugged it off, but she wondered what he was really thinking.

"I feel so much better now." She tried for a light tone. "It's amazing what a few hours' sleep can do." Greg sat at the table without responding, making her want to fill the uncomfortable silence. "I've been thinking," she continued, quickly turning away from his questioning eyes.

Actually, she had been doing more than just thinking, Lucky acknowledged as she ladled a dollop of batter onto the griddle. She had been up for hours and had made a call, learning no one had come forth to identify her. She couldn't continue to impose on Greg; she had to take action.

"I've been thinking," she repeated, facing him again. "There's no medical reason I shouldn't remember my name. Yet I can't. I honestly can't. But what if I were hypnotized?

I'd say my name just like that''—she snapped her fingers. ''Right?''

Greg stared at her, his face expressionless, but she sensed that he thought this was a wild idea. Lucky turned away, inspected the air bubbles in the batter, and flipped the pancake.

''I think Cody could locate a psychologist who uses hypnotherapy,'' he finally responded.

''Thanks,'' she said, but she barely had the word out when the crunch of tires sounded on the lava rock lane that led up to the house. It was a police Bronco. Suddenly, she was afraid, yet unexpected anger surged through her, eclipsing her fears. Why couldn't the police just leave her alone?

Chapter 9

The minute Cody walked through the door and saw Greg at the kitchen table, an intense surge of relief swept through him. His brother was safe, alive. And as sullen as ever.

"What brings you out here?" Greg's tone could have frozen vodka.

Rather than admit how worried he'd been, Cody slid into a seat and began to explain. "I thought that you might want to know what the FBI fingerprint search revealed."

"No, you didn't." Lucky gave Greg a plate of pancakes that made Cody's stomach growl. "You were worried that I'd killed Greg, weren't you?"

Cody met her furious gaze, then he turned to his brother. Greg was staring at him, waiting to hear why he'd driven all this way when he could just as easily have used the phone. "I was at the station when Lucky called. She asked if she'd been identified yet. The duty officer called me over, and I told her that she wasn't in the FBI's computer. Then I asked to speak to you, but she wouldn't—"

"Greg needed his sleep," Lucky interrupted as she handed Cody a cup of coffee. "I didn't want to disturb him."

"What were you doing at the station on Sunday morning?" Greg asked.

"A meeting." Cody shrugged as if it hadn't been important. He didn't want to tell Greg how hard Tony Traylor was pressing him to make a case against Lucky. As head of the joint council, Traylor packed a political wallop that would make most mainland politicians green with envy.

"The hiker's been dead for over a year, but her remains are going to be exhumed and sent to the FBI facility in Quantico for analysis." He didn't add that Traylor had insisted on this. Cody had resisted; no policeman wanted the Feebies horning in on their territory telling them how to do their jobs.

Greg said, "You must have some theory about this case."

"Lucky's fingerprints aren't in the police computers or the DMV data banks in any of the larger states. Could be she's from a small state that hasn't computerized yet."

"What do you *really* think?" Lucky asked.

Cody realized that she was far too perceptive. He'd thought she would be easy to ID, but that hadn't proved to be the case. He'd developed another theory.

"I think that you were here with a married man. You had a fight with him . . . or something. When you ended up in the hospital, he couldn't come forward without exposing his illicit affair."

"You're saying I'm someone's mistress." Lucky slowly sank into the chair, her expression grim.

"That doesn't explain why she was wearing a dead woman's shoe," Greg interjected.

"My theory doesn't cover everything." Cody took a swig of coffee. "Someone knows who Lucky is. They must have a good reason for not coming forward."

"What are you going to do now?" Greg wanted to know.

"I'm sending her prints to the DMVs in smaller states to be hand-checked. It'll take time, but it yields results."

"Don't waste the taxpayers' money." Lucky stood, then walked over to the stove. "Find someone to hypnotize me. Then I'll be able to tell you my name."

"Great idea. Why didn't I think of that?"

"I have no idea," Greg replied, his voice laced with sarcasm. "I'll go back to the station and check our records. Seems to me there's a list of all kinds of reputable therapists."

Cody sipped his coffee, conscious of the tension in the air. At first he assumed it was a time bomb of anger that had ticked inside Greg since Jessica's death, threatening to explode. But as they discussed contacting the hypnotherapist, he realized that the tension was between Greg and Lucky. She seemed to be subtly trying to please him, handing him more of those mouth-watering pancakes and refilling his coffee. His brother never spared her a glance, refusing to look directly at her—until she turned away. Then he tracked her every movement. Uh-oh. He's falling for her.

Not that he could blame his brother. Lucky had sex appeal in spades. A dynamite figure. A pretty face with unusual green eyes. With that bleached hair pulled into a braid and the tan shorts, she almost looked like a model for L.L. Bean. But Cody kept seeing her on the gurney in that too-tight, cheap dress with her wild hair. No. There was nothing wholesome about Lucky.

She was intelligent, though. He would grant her that. You could see it in the way she sized up a situation and came up with solutions, like being hypnotized. He sensed the chip on her shoulder and the conniving attitude.

He'd bet a year's salary that under hypnosis Lucky still wouldn't remember her name. It was just a ploy to make Greg believe in her. No doubt Lucky had her own reasons for not wanting to be identified.

Greg silently followed Cody out to his car. For a moment, while they'd been sitting in the kitchen eating, it had seemed like old times. Cody dropping by, hanging around for a third cup of coffee.

But everything had changed.

Greg wanted to ask about Cody's boys and about the baby he'd never even seen. But he'd be damned before he would give in to the urge. He refused to be dragged back into his brother's life again.

"You'll find someone to hypnotize her, won't you?"

"I'll get on it right away," Cody promised as he opened the Bronco's door. "You agree with me, don't you? Lucky's someone's mistress. She wasn't here alone."

Greg shrugged, remembering how Lucky had looked when he'd first seen her. Mistress was far too glamorous. A two-bit hooker was more like it.

Cody leaned against the open door, his arm casually draped over it. "Lucky's just like Jessica. Can't you see that?"

Greg gazed past Cody at the wind-ruffled water, striving to maintain his control. Just hearing his brother say Jessica's name made him want to hit something. Yet he knew Cody was right. Why in hell was he destined to become involved with tramps?

"Lucky was afraid to go to sleep last night. She hid in the closet with a knife to protect her. I think someone's after her, but she doesn't remember."

Cody listened with a knowing nod. "Maybe it's not a married man. Maybe she's up to her pretty little eyeballs in some drug deal that went sour. Remember, she crashed on the remotest part of this island, not far from where the Feds caught the *hui*—the Hawaiian mafia—sub last winter."

Greg couldn't argue. Running a small submarine that usually took tourists around the coral reefs, the *hui* had been stopped by federal agents. A cache of pricey "Maui Wowie" from marijuana plants in the rain forest had been aboard.

Drugs were a possible explanation, but there was still a seed of doubt in his mind. That cry in the night and Lucky's face when he'd awakened her disturbed him. A piece of the puzzle was missing, yet Greg didn't have a clue as to what it was.

"Guess I was wrong," Cody said, climbing into the car. "I thought for sure she'd have you in the sack by now." The door closed with a heavy thud and Cody leaned out the window. "That's what she'll try to do, you know. Women often use sex to get what they want."

The Bronco shot forward, spraying bits of crushed lava and leaving Greg standing there, itching to haul into Cody with both clenched fists. He watched the car until it was out of sight, then slowly walked around the house to the rocky beach. Usually, the sea calmed him, easing his tensions and making him forget the past. He watched the undulating waves for some time, but it didn't help.

The anger he'd suppressed for so long had eaten away at him, changing him. He could live with that change and pretend the past never happened until now. Until Lucky. She was forcing him to deal with his brother. And with the anger that still burned white-hot like the core of a flame.

The flame burned even hotter because Cody was absolutely right. Jessica had used sex to get what she wanted. When he didn't pay enough attention to her, Jessica would have an affair. Nothing serious, she would say, crying and claiming to love him—just a "fling."

The first time he'd forgiven her, but the second time, he asked for a divorce. And Jessica had tried to kill herself. He'd taken her back, truly believing she was sorry and knowing her lifelong battle with depression meant she often thought about killing herself. For a while things had improved then he realized she was involved with someone. It had never occurred to Greg that it was his own brother.

"Stop thinking about it," he said out loud. He couldn't do a goddamned thing about the past, but he could prevent Lucky from manipulating him the way Jessica had. The sooner they identified her and she was out of his life, the happier he would be.

After what he had gone through last night, he'd have aching balls for a week, but at least he had shown her who was in charge. Tonight she could just sleep in the damn closet for all he cared. He wasn't taking her into his bed and giving her another opportunity to seduce him.

"What do you think he's doing out there?" Lucky asked Dodger. She had been watching Greg from the kitchen for the last fifteen minutes. He was still sitting on a chunk of lava rock and staring out at the sea. "Come on, Dodger. Let's see if he wants company."

Outside, the sky was so clear and blue it made her want to skip. With Dodger at her heels, Lucky crossed the small grassy area to the glistening ribbon of sand that wound between the dark lava rocks and the shimmering water. Garlands of deep green seaweed were being nudged ashore by a never-ending troop of waves pebbled with whitecaps. When she reached Greg he didn't turn around, even though he must have heard her approaching.

"Greg." She touched his shoulder with her hand. The warmth of his body, its solidness and the security he represented, caused a sudden tightness in her chest. He pulled away with a quick flex of his shoulder. "What's wrong?"

"Sit down," he told Lucky without looking at her.

She sat on a small rock nearby, bracing herself for what could only be more bad news. Dodger settled himself at Greg's feet, leaving her alone. Greg was silent and avoided looking at her, the same way he had all morning. Lucky gazed out at the sea that stretched in one magnificent aquamarine sweep to the horizon. It seemed so vast and empty, echoing the loneliness she felt.

"We need to talk," Greg said, finally turning to face her.

Clear and startlingly blue, his eyes gazed into hers with disturbing intensity. In that instant, she was again lost to a feeling that was quickly becoming too familiar. She wanted this man to believe in her, to care about her. It took her a second to remind herself that this was just wishful thinking, and that the longer she indulged in it the harder it would be to accept the truth: Greg didn't care about her the way she longed for him to do.

"What do you want to talk about?"

"Someone is after you. That's why you were hiding in the closet. Why don't you tell me about it?"

There. He had stopped waffling and made his decision. He didn't believe her. As much as she might have wished otherwise, she'd known all along how he felt. Lucky had no idea why it was so terribly important that Greg believe in her, but it was.

"You know I can't remember the past. The doctors say I have Hoyt-Mellenberger syndrome—"

"True, but there seems to be some dispute about how much someone remembers when they still have their sense of smell."

"Really? Why didn't anyone tell me this?"

He shrugged and looked away, as if the gulls squabbling over a small fish in the tide pool nearby were more important than she. His reaction triggered a wellspring of anger that surfaced with unexpected suddenness. I have a quick temper, she realized.

"I didn't tell the police everything," he continued, taking her by surprise. He turned to her, his expression deadly serious, and she knew she didn't want to hear this. "The night I found you in the car you were wearing lots of makeup. The way you were dressed in an outfit that was indecently short and too tight across your breasts made me think that you were . . . a hooker."

In that instant, she somehow knew that he had more to say, and she shuddered inwardly. "What else? I might as well know everything."

"You were in some sort of trance or something." He shifted uncomfortably, but his gaze remained steady. "You couldn't keep your hands off me. In two seconds you had my zipper down—"

"No way!" She jumped to her feet, furious. "You're wrong!"

Why are you yelling at him? asked a little voice inside her

head. Greg's an earnest, honorable man. He saved your life. Control your stupid temper.

"I unzipped your pants?" she asked, her voice low, and he nodded.

Oh, God, it couldn't be. But she remembered the gaudy pink polish and the wild-looking woman in the mirror. She also remembered . . . last night. She hadn't been able to resist the urge to touch him and she had kissed him, starting everything.

Dear Lord, could she actually be the woman in the mirror?

Chapter 10

Greg drove along the frontage road to the Kehei Marina, where the Marine Research Institute was located, with Lucky beside him and Dodger in the backseat. Since he'd confronted Lucky she'd been very quiet, answering him in monosyllables. Her anger didn't surprise him. She could deny it all she wanted, but she must know more than she was telling.

"The institute is open around the clock," Greg explained. "Even on Sunday there are seals to feed, and someone brought in a shark."

Lucky didn't answer, and Greg stole a glance in her direction. Her hair hung down her back in a thick braid, but it was so crimped that it looked like a gnarled branch. He sure as hell wasn't an expert on women's hairstyles, yet he knew a cheap bleach job and home permanent when he saw one. What kind of woman would deliberately make herself look so trampy?

Lucky was wearing conservative tan shorts and a sleeveless lavender blouse that deepened the green of her eyes. She hadn't purchased any makeup, so she didn't look at all like the woman he'd pulled out of the car. Still, she looked sexy as hell. No doubt the volunteers who staffed the institute would be coming on to her.

He pulled into his parking place. "Nomo's in charge of volunteers. He'll find something for you to do, like feeding the monk seals or preparing their food."

Lucky climbed out of the car without a word and followed him up the path, her eyes narrowing obstinately as she walked beside him. Yeah, she was pissed big time that he hadn't fallen for her little act.

The institute was a concrete bunker just steps from the ocean. The lower floor of the building was a laboratory with very modern facilities, considering their tight budget. The upper floor, where Greg had his office, overlooked the two pools in which the injured and sick animals were treated. Under a cluster of palms stood a bamboo annex—not much more than a shed— where dive equipment was stored and volunteers changed clothes.

Another group of date palms shaded the pools, which were separated from the beach by a low wall of reddish-black lava rocks. Huddled in groups, some gulls were perched on the wall while others patrolled the shore, plunging headfirst into the waves to catch a fish, then returning to the sky with their prize. On the other side of the wall was a short stretch of crystalline sand where the waves tumbled onto the shore, leaving a tide line marked by seashells. Two dive boats with the Marine Institute logo of a whale's flukes were moored just offshore.

"Hey, *aikane!* Look who's back," yelled Nomo.

Body like a tombstone, with graying black hair that toppled over his broad forehead and a toothy grin, Nomo had been in charge of the volunteers for three decades. Greg had first met him when he'd gotten into trouble for joyriding in the principal's new car and the juvenile authorities had sent him to volunteer at the institute. The facilities had changed a lot since then, but Nomo was the same, still using Hawaiian words like *aikane*— buddy.

Greg greeted the older man with an affectionate slap on the

back. "This is Lucky. Think you can find something for her to do?"

Nomo turned his megawatt smile on Lucky and clutched her hand in his usual bone-crushing handshake. "Get outta here. We don't have *anything* for her to do."

Lucky smiled, proving no one could resist Nomo's charm. "What's a monk seal?"

Greg studied her, thinking that he'd mentioned the Hawaiian seals during the ride here, but she'd been too angry with him to ask. S'okay. The less talking they did the better.

"It's just a special type of seal found only in the islands," Nomo explained as he led them toward the largest pool. "We've got a half dozen who are too old to survive on their own and three pups who've lost their mothers." He turned toward Greg. "The big news is the tiger shark."

Nomo stopped in front of the saltwater pool and pointed to the diver walking in slow circles, holding a young tiger shark under his arm.

"Why's he carrying a shark?" Lucky seemed so intrigued by the unusual sight that she forgot she wasn't speaking to him.

"Sharks have to keep moving to keep water passing through their gills, or they'll die. When they're sick, there's no choice but to walk them twenty-four hours a day." He turned to Nomo. "You know we can't save him. Let him go."

"He'll die, *aikane*. You know that."

Lucky squatted to get a better look at the shark, Dodger at her side. "What's wrong with the shark?"

"Some fisherman tried to cut off his fins to sell for shark fin soup," Nomo replied, "but they botched the job. Cut the fins with . . . looks like a machete, but didn't get them off. Somehow the shark got away. One of the dive boats coming back from the Molokini Crater found him and brought him here."

"Shark fin soup. You're kidding." Lucky looked so upset that Greg was tempted to put his arm around her.

"It's no joke," Nomo assured her. "It's a delicacy in Japan. Trouble is, they butcher the shark just for the fins, then leave it to die."

Lucky gasped. "That's unbelievably cruel."

"There's nothing we can do to save him," Greg said. "We have no way of reattaching his fins. We're just wasting our time."

"You have to try," Lucky pleaded, making him feel guilty.

"The kids here on summer internships feel the same way," Nomo said. "It's better if he dies here, and everyone knows we tried."

Greg realized Nomo was right. Summer interns were mostly pain-in-the-ass rich kids looking for an excuse to spend the summer in Hawaii, but they went back home and convinced their parents to donate to the institute. Without those funds, the institute's projects with the monk seals and humpback whales would be in jeopardy.

"Okay, keep walking him," he said and Lucky rewarded him with a smile.

He left Lucky with Dodger and Nomo and went upstairs, dreading the avalanche of paperwork that he knew was waiting on his desk. At the top of the stairs he found Rachel Convey gazing out the office window at Lucky and Nomo, who were still watching the shark. Rachel had a doctorate in marine biology and was the foremost expert on the humpback whales who wintered each year in Hawaii. For the past three years she and Greg had been working on a joint project, decoding the sounds whales made underwater.

"Pele's ghost, right? She doesn't belong here. She'll only cause trouble." Rachel's voice was low and matter-of-fact, but she failed to conceal an undertone of bitterness. Greg would have to be brain dead not to know Rachel had a thing for him. He had never encouraged her, striving to keep their relationship professional.

"Her name's Lucky. She's volunteered to help with the seals," Greg said, stretching the truth. He'd dragged Lucky along because he needed to keep an eye on her. She hadn't run away last night, but who knew what she might pull. "Nomo will take care of her."

"I ran the stats on those high frequency sounds the whales make," Rachel told him, moving away from the window. "They're on your desk."

So was half the world. There were stacks of unopened envelopes, invoices, and requisitions to sign. It was hard to believe he was really a scientist, Greg spent more than half his time balancing the books. He might as well have had a degree in business for all the financial crap he did. It would be days before he could analyze the stats on the high frequency sounds they'd recorded last winter when the whales were offshore.

He was halfway through the first stack of letters when the phone rang. The institute was too strapped for cash to have a secretary, so he answered it. Cody was on the line.

"It's all set up. I had to make several calls to Honolulu, but finally this Dr. Forenksi called me back. She's flying in tomorrow afternoon to see Lucky. Have her at the Up-country Clinic at four."

"I'll have Nomo drive her—"

"No, Greg. I want you to be with her. If you find out her name, call me. I'll take it from there." Cody paused, and Greg heard the squawk of the police radio in the background. "There was a reporter here a few minutes ago. Says he's with the *Star Investigator.*"

"That's like the *Maui Tattler,* only worse, right?"

"Yeah, junk food journalism. Aliens. The diet to end all diets. A story on Pele's ghost is perfect. Fenton Bewley knows you posted bail. I couldn't keep that from him. It's public record, but I didn't tell him where she's staying. Watch for him. Mid-fifties, bald, big black mustache."

Every protective instinct Greg had fired at once. He needed to get rid of Lucky as quickly as possible—for his own peace of mind—but he'd be damned if he'd allow anyone to humiliate her. The scene in the jail replayed in his mind and he tightened his grip on the receiver.

"Cody, thanks. I owe you one."

Greg dropped the receiver in the cradle. *I owe you one.* He and his brother used to say that to each other all the time. He hadn't heard the words in over two years—and he certainly hadn't said them.

He kept staring at the photograph of Jessica that he still kept on his desk to remind him just how treacherous women could be. The all-consuming rage he usually felt when he thought about his wife in Cody's arms just wasn't there. Okay, it still hurt, but not as much.

I owe you one. Cody was still smiling an hour later. How long had it been since he'd heard Greg say that? He missed his brother, and seeing him, talking to him, made Cody miss Greg all the more.

"Chief," said one of his officers. "Tony Traylor's here."

"Again?" Cody couldn't believe it. Traylor had called a meeting first thing that morning. Sunday. Unbelievable. The entire point of the meeting had been to bully Cody about Lucky. Cody checked his watch, knowing he would never make it to the church picnic now. He quickly called and left a message on the machine so Sarah wouldn't worry.

"Arrest Pele's ghost for possession of stolen property," Tony Traylor demanded without preamble as he lumbered into Cody's office, followed by two *mokes*. The island tough guys didn't intimidate Cody. Their brains would fit in a thimble. As usual, Traylor was giving orders and expecting them to be followed.

Fat with swarthy skin that looked as if it had been sand-blasted, Traylor was dressed in his trademark Hawaiian print shirt, the loud kind that had gone out of style in the sixties. His sharklike eyes zeroed in on Cody as he sat behind his desk, bracing himself for a confrontation.

"My lawyer says we can get that bitch on possession of stolen property even if we can't prove grand theft." Tony collapsed into the chair opposite Cody's desk, and the *mokes* stood behind him.

"I don't want to harass Lucky," Cody replied, his tone firm. Why was this so important to Traylor? he asked himself. "Your cousin—you remember, the one you insisted I hire as a jailer— well, he was letting anyone with five bucks in to see Lucky. She's considering a civil rights suit that could bankrupt the state."

That stopped him. Traylor swiped with the back of his beefy hand at the sweat that peppered his brow. "Who the fuck's her lawyer? I'll fix his ass."

Cody couldn't resist. "Some hotshot from the mainland probably."

Traylor hesitated; his influence didn't extend to the mainland. "Where's she staying? I'll knock some sense into that bitch."

"Hey, Tony, it was only a car. What's the big deal? I'm building a case against her."

Traylor shifted in his seat and the chair groaned. Undoubtedly the springs would be shot, and there wasn't any money in the budget to replace the chair. "The bitch had my car for over a year. If she gets away with fucking me around, everyone will want a piece of my ass."

There would be plenty to go around, Cody thought, struggling not to grin. "Let me take care of her. That's my job."

With a grunt, Tony heaved himself to his feet and sauntered out of the office without saying goodbye, the *mokes* obediently trailing in his wake. Cody rocked back in his chair, wondering if that was the real reason Traylor wanted Lucky in jail. Maybe, the man had an ego the size of the Hindenburg.

But Cody wondered. He suspected that Traylor was behind the "Maui Wowie" business. High in the inaccessible rain forest, the islanders grew premium marijuana to be sent to the mainland. Twice a year the Feds came in with helicopters and pulled up the plants. Somehow, new plants had reappeared by the next time the Feebies did a flyover.

Very little happened on the outer islands that Tony didn't know about. Not for the first time, Cody wondered if he was part of the *hui*. The Hawaiian mafia was notorious for its ruthlessness and its code of silence. Even if Traylor wasn't a member of the gang, Cody would bet his next paycheck—if it hadn't already been spoken for—that Traylor knew exactly what went on in the remote reaches of the island where Lucky had been found.

Three hours later Greg had cleared most of his desk and set aside the less urgent mail and messages. He told himself that he was just going to take a walk around the compound to see what had happened in his absence. He'd only thought about Lucky once or twice since sitting down. All right, more than that. He'd analyzed his response to her from every angle, then reexamined the details, but he couldn't make sense of his reaction to this mysterious woman.

Outside the air-conditioned office, the late afternoon air hit him like a blast furnace and sweat prickled across his neck. The heat brought out the loamy smell of the tropical soil and the sweet scent of wild ginger and plumeria. He didn't see Lucky but he knew where she was, because Dodger was beside the pool with the shark.

"Nomo!" Greg yelled.

Lucky was in full diving gear at the bottom of the tank, walking the shark in endless circles. Dodger kept pacing, more concerned than Greg had ever seen him, staring down into the water at Lucky. He wasn't the only one. Nearby stood a group of gawking summer interns—all male.

"Yeah, boss?" Nomo said, trotting over from the sheds.

"What's Lucky doing in there?"

"She wanted to help the shark." Nomo checked his watch. "It's time for her to come out." He leaned down and tapped twice on the side of the pool to get Lucky's attention, then motioned for one of the volunteers to take her place.

"How is it that she remembers how to dive but doesn't know her name?" Rachel asked.

Greg hadn't noticed Rachel come up beside him because he had been watching Lucky. It was hard to tell what was going on through the water, which distorted the two bodies exchanging the shark, but it was taking a helluva lot longer than it should have. He imagined the kid with his hands all over Lucky.

He forced himself to face Rachel. "Memorizing dive tables is a learned activity, like studying a foreign language. Lucky still has those memories. What's missing is the episodic memory bank ... the recall of single events from the past."

Rachel stared at him, her brown eyes filled with some emotion that defied description. "I'm going out on the *Atlantis*," she said quietly.

The *Atlantis* was a glass bottom boat that took tourists over the magnificent coral beds where tropical fish gathered along the reefs. Once a week someone from the institute, usually Rachel, went out and gave a lecture. It helped raise funds to keep the institute's projects going. Greg watched her walk away, asking himself why couldn't he fall for her, a good woman, someone who shared his interests. But the feeling just wasn't there, and wishing wasn't going to make it happen.

He turned just in time to see Lucky wading toward the shallow end of the pool. Aw, shit. The standard-issue black tank suit they kept around for volunteers didn't begin to fit her properly. It was two sizes too small on top and the wet fabric clung to every provocative curve. Water sluiced off her shoulders, running in steady rivulets down the slope of her breasts and across her erect nipples. A half-dozen leering summer interns were waiting, anxious to help Lucky remove her air tank.

Even Nomo was standing by with a towel for Lucky. In four angry strides, Greg was at the shallow end, and he yanked the towel from the older man's hand. He had it around Lucky two seconds after she handed her tank to a guy who couldn't keep his eyes off her cleavage.

Lucky was oblivious to the men, gazing at Greg with those alluring green eyes. "The shark's name is Rudy," she informed him with the most adorable smile he'd ever seen. "He was swimming along the reef with his mother when he was caught."

Astonished silence greeted this announcement. Christ, the woman was a menace to society. Now all those snot-nosed interns would be worrying even more about a shark who was nothing more than an eating machine.

He hustled her to the bamboo annex that housed the changing rooms. Lucky stopped at the freshwater shower. She tossed him the towel, then turned on the water. Man, oh, man. He tried to look away, he honestly did, but Greg kept remembering the previous night and her gorgeous body trembling with need—for him.

"You know, Rudy's given up hope," Lucky said from under the spray. "He doesn't think he'll ever find his family."

"That so?" he managed to say. The guys by the pool might find her damned near irresistible, but all he saw was . . . trouble. Especially since she kept lifting her face to the fine spray, thrusting her breasts upward until they threatened to spill out of the suit.

"That's enough." With an angry twist of his hand, he turned off the water.

"Okay." Lucky gave him an impish little smile, and Greg suspected she knew all about the traitorous throb in his groin. She swung her sopping wet braid over her shoulder and wrung it out. "I have an idea."

So did he, but he doubted they were on the same wavelength. In that suit, she might as well be buck naked. Who did she think he was—the Pope?

"Don't you want to hear my idea?"

He jammed his fists in his pockets to keep himself from hauling her into the darkness of the shed and taking her standing up. "Get dressed and come up to my office. I want to talk to you."

Greg was halfway to the stairs when Nomo stopped him. "Pele was always good with animals—especially sharks."

"You can't believe that crap," Greg told him. Pele was the goddess of fire who had given birth to the islands, and according to legend, her brother was a shark. Nomo reminded him of his sister-in-law, Sarah. Both were native Hawaiians, and both loved island lore and could "talk story" by the hour, retelling age-old tales. What a crock!

"Get outta here," Nomo said. "Can't you see that Lucky's a natural with sharks—just like Pele."

"She's nothing but trouble." The sooner he dumped her on someone else, the happier he would be.

Chapter 11

"Yo, Nomo, there's some reporter out front asking questions about Lucky," called one of the volunteers.

"Let me handle him," Greg told the older man. "You get Lucky up to my office where that bastard can't find her."

Greg recognized Fenton Bewley immediately from Cody's description. And hated him on sight. Bewley was lolling against the hibiscus planter in front of the building, a toothpick between his teeth.

"You Greg Braxton?" Fenton asked without removing the toothpick, and Greg nodded. "Any relation to the chief of police?"

"Who's asking?"

Bewley pulled a tattered press card out of his wallet, and Greg inspected it. "I heard you posted bail for Pele's ghost. Know where I can find her?"

"She'll be in court next week for her trial."

Bewley's eyes narrowed, and he worked the toothpick back and forth beneath a mustache that was as stiff as a whisk broom. "How much is this gonna cost me?"

Pocketbook journalism. Greg hated it, but he knew that was how the tabloids worked. "You haven't got enough money. If I catch you trespassing on the institute's property again, I'll have you arrested."

"I can find her," Bewley said. "I can find anyone."

Greg had no doubt he could do it and cursed the smallness of the island, where everyone knew each other's business. He didn't want Bewley to plaster Lucky's picture beside yet another grainy photo of an alien who'd abducted some female and had his way with her extraterrestrial style, cashing in on America's libido.

Lucky was waiting in his office, wearing the shorts again—thank God. The conservative outfit emphasized a body that wouldn't quit, but it wasn't as revealing as the skimpy swimsuit.

"Want to hear my idea?" she asked before he could warn her about Bewley.

"I'm dying to hear it." He sat at his desk and shuffled the papers he'd already sorted. Common sense said not looking at her was his best bet. "Shoot."

"The institute doesn't work with sharks, right? Well, somewhere in the world someone does, and they'll know how to help Rudy. All we have to do is get on the Internet and ask."

"It's not that simple. You have to know what you're doing. Most people are roadkill on the information superhighway."

"Let me try." The enthusiasm in her voice forced him to look up. She was sitting at Rachel's computer. "Don't touch a thing! Jesus H. Christ! You could delete months of research if you're not careful."

Wide-eyed, she gazed at him. "I'll be careful, Greg. You've got to let me try. Rudy is counting on me."

Wow! She was a world-class fruitcake. He'd never met anyone like her, and if his luck held, he never would again.

"You think I'm crazy, don't you?"

"Now that you mention it, yes."

His sarcastic tone didn't faze her. "The Internet will come through for me, you'll see. Let me use your computer." She was across the room and pulling a chair up to his computer before he could tell her to stay away from him. "What's the password?"

"Knom. Monk spelled backward, for the monk seals we're researching," he answered, watching to see if she actually knew what she was doing.

She did. Minutes later she was wailing on the Web, surfing through cyberspace. He relied on *Internet for Dummies* to help him negotiate the net, but not Lucky.

"I'll be damned," he said, watching her out of the corner of his eye while he stroked Dodger's head and prioritized requisitions, knowing the budget couldn't fund them all. Dodger responded by putting his head on Greg's knee. His eyes were on Lucky as she typed with the kind of speed that came only from spending hours at a keyboard. "What's missing from this picture?"

Unless prostitution had gone high-tech, hookers did not wail on the Web. Okay, so maybe he'd been too quick to evaluate Lucky. Perhaps *hooker* had been a bit harsh. Could be she was just a "free spirit," like Jessica. The way Lucky had come on to him that night in the tent had led him to believe she was a pro.

"I've got someone on the scene," the Orchid King informed his partner as they sat at the bank of computers in their office. "We'll find out what she's up to."

"You sent someone to Maui?"

"Sure. Money talks. I hired the best. Don't worry."

"I would feel better if we just tracked her with a computer."

The Orchid King frowned at him. "Even I can't find out what we need to know with a computer. Someone has to go there. It can't be either of us, now, can it?"

He tried to joke, but it feel flat. Lately he hadn't been able to make his partner crack up or even smile. How could he think of anything funny when he kept seeing the woman he loved in Greg Braxton's arms? He knew his partner was thinking the same thing, too.

"We're going to have to start warehousing orchids here," his partner said, abruptly changing the subject. "I've found several buildings that will work. They're all in Chinatown, near the docks. Why don't you come with me so we can make a decision?"

"I don't like having the orchids so close to home. It's too risky."

"It's a foolproof plan. If we're going to move into the big leagues, we have to do it now. Do you want the gangs from Hong Kong horning in on our territory?"

"You're right. Let's go for it," the king said with more enthusiasm than he felt. He followed his partner out of the office and down the stairs. "What are we going to do if we find out she doesn't remember a thing?"

"Leave her with that Braxton guy. See if he can handle her."

"That's not an option, and you know it."

"So then we'll play the ace, right?"

Yes, play the ace.

The next morning Greg sat in his office, conscious of the tension pulsing through the room. Lucky was beside him at his computer, poring over the responses to Rudy's condition that had come in from experts all over the world. Rachel was at her desk, tabulating another set of high frequency sounds, her back rigid.

To say Rachel resented having Lucky on her turf was like saying the Pope would be thrilled to share his pulpit with Satan. Rachel was so angry that Greg was concerned she might quit. It was a miracle she hadn't done so already. With her credentials, she could get a job at a dozen facilities for a much higher salary. She stayed here, he had told himself, because their research on whales was different, important. Now he suspected she had other reasons for remaining.

The sooner he was rid of Lucky the better. How many times had he uttered those words? Too many. He smiled inwardly, finding some satisfaction in recalling that last night he had been able to ignore her. After dinner he'd gone to his bedroom and locked the door. It had been harder than hell to sleep, but he'd finally managed. And nothing had awakened him. No crying.

Where Lucky had spent the night he could only guess. She had certainly *looked* rested, her eyes clear and bright as she scrolled through the messages from other marine facilities more experienced in dealing with sharks. He was probably the one who looked like a piece of shit after a rainstorm, having spent most of the night tossing.

"This is it!" Lucky cried. "A researcher in Australia has the solution to Rudy's problem."

Greg ignored Rachel's dismissive sniff and leaned toward Lucky. "Okay, I give up. What should we be doing with . . . Rudy?"

She turned to him, her green eyes fired with such enthusiasm that it took a supreme effort not to respond. "We take a staple gun—you know, the kind surgeons use—and reattach his fins. By the time the tissue mends, the staples will dissolve and Rudy will be able to swim on his own."

"That's ridiculous!" Rachel vaulted to her feet. If looks could have killed, Lucky would be pushing up daisies. "A shark's skin is cartilage. It doesn't mend the same way a human's does."

Lucky responded to Rachel's attack with a thoughtful nod. "Yes, I know, but a shark's cartilage may be different."

Rachel rolled her eyeballs, then looked at Greg. "Pul-eeze. Cartilage is cartilage. It doesn't regenerate like skin."

"There's a lot we don't know about sharks," Lucky argued. "There's no explanation for why sharks don't get cancer like other living creatures, but they don't."

For a moment, the only sound was the whir of the air conditioner and the chink-chink of Dodger's collar as he nuzzled Lucky's hand.

"You picked that up off the Internet?" Greg asked. The cancer angle was one of the newer developments in marine studies, one that had generated enviable amounts of research funding.

"No. I just knew it. I'm not sure how. Is it important?"

"Not really." But it was. Lucky knew too much, remembered too much. He had the disturbing feeling that Cody would be proven right again. Lucky would go to the hypnotist but conveniently not remember her name. He would never get rid of her. Greg seriously doubted he could make it through another night with her just down the hall.

"Can we try it?" Lucky wanted to know.

Her expression was so earnest, so adorable, that he had to steel himself against it. Rachel chose this moment to stomp out of the office, which brought him back to his senses.

"Look, Rudy is a tiger shark. He may look docile, but in an instant those teeth can tear you in half." He paused for a breath, seeing he hadn't changed her mind. "Walking him isn't risky, but holding him and positioning the fin to staple it is another thing. All he has to do is get pissed off, and one of us is without a hand—or worse."

"Rudy would never hurt me."

"You've flipped! Sharks don't think like people. He doesn't know you're trying to help him." Greg stood up and turned off his computer. "Let's go. It'll take twenty minutes or so to get to the clinic. Since Dr. Forenski has made a special trip to see you, we don't want to be late."

Lucky rode through the peaceful countryside filled with a sense of anticipation. In an hour or so she would know her name. Maybe then she could prove to Greg that she was telling the truth. So far her past had been a mirage, shimmering in the distance, out of focus. Out of reach.

Never forget. I love you. Those words kept echoing through the empty corridors of her mind, but she had no idea who might have said them. Had there been another man before Greg? Someone who had loved her? An ache of loneliness constantly bombarded her, an ache so intense she would gladly have traded it for physical pain.

"Good boy," Lucky said as Dodger leaned over from the backseat and put his muzzle on her shoulder. She ventured a glance at Greg. He was staring at the road, his elbow resting on the open window ledge, his wrist casually draped over the steering wheel. He downshifted to let a truck loaded with sugar cane cross the road.

"This is the up-country," Greg explained without looking at her. "Farming, ranching. Few tourists make it to this part of the island."

"It's beautiful," she said, truly meaning it. In every direction were fields of sugar cane that looked a lot like corn, their stalks rustling in the trade winds, and miles of terraced red earth spiked with the bright green tops of young pineapples. Along the road were clumps of wild ginger dancing on the breeze like graceful ballerinas.

They drove on, climbing higher on the Haleakala highway until the cane and pineapple fields became lush green pastures bordered by whitewashed fences. Cattle and horses grazed on the dense grass, oblivious to the sun-dappled sea visible like a mirage on the distant horizon. Thickets of ferns banked the road at times, shielding the pastures from her view. Above, towering over the island like a godfather, was Haleakala, its summit obscured by a skirt of clouds.

They pulled into a town with wooden sidewalks, hitching posts, and water troughs. They drove past Hibner's Livery and Yamaguchi's General Store, stopping for a trio of horsemen who crossed the road, laughing and waving cowboy hats with flower *leis* on the crown. Something wasn't right.

"It's the mongoose."

"What?" Greg asked.

"There's something I don't understand. This place looks familiar, but it doesn't look anything like Hawaii—"

"This is Makawao. Cowboy country Hawaiian style. It looks a lot like Texas, doesn't it?"

Lucky realized he was trying to trap her, and she didn't know how to respond. Somehow she had known this place was different from the rest of the island. Yet she couldn't have come up with Texas if her life depended on it.

On that skeptical note, they pulled into the Up-country Clinic, which looked like a mountain chalet of some kind. They parked and walked silently across a lot filled with pickup trucks and Jeeps, Dodger at their heels. The receptionist led them to a private office.

Dr. Forenski was waiting for them. Petite, almost fragile looking, with short-cropped white hair and a face weathered by the sun and time, the doctor stood and offered Lucky her hand.

"Well, you've been through a terrible ordeal," Dr. Forenski said, motioning for Lucky and Greg to have a seat.

The sympathy in the doctor's tone was echoed in her eyes, and Lucky liked her immediately. Too often people looked at her with suspicion, never thinking how she had suffered.

"When Chief Braxton contacted me, he told me what happened," she continued. "I've read the papers—which, of course, can't be trusted—and I have your test results, but I would like to hear the details from you two."

Greg began first, relating how Dodger had found the car. Then Lucky explained how she'd awakened with no memory of the past, having not a clue as to where she was or how she'd gotten there. Dr. Forenski listened silently, nodding sympathetically and putting Lucky at ease.

"You didn't recognize yourself in the mirror and became . . upset," the doctor said. "Do you know yourself now?"

Lucky shrugged. "I guess. My reflection seems more like me without my hair frizzled around my face like—" she searched for the word for a second before it popped into her mind, "like a tumbleweed."

"Interesting. You don't recognize your face and you don't remember your name. You should, because you would have looked in the mirror thousands of times and used your name repeatedly. That should imprint them in your mind, unlike the material that's a one-time image that is filed in your episodic memory bank." Dr. Forenski studied Lucky thoughtfully, evidently believing her and searching for an explanation. "I wonder why it isn't working."

"Could it have something to do with the fact that Lucky still has her sense of smell?" Greg asked.

"Possibly," Dr. Forenski admitted. "I saw that on her charts and immediately called a colleague of my late husband, who is on staff at Harvard Medical School. Dr. Robinson's done a lot of research on Hoyt-Mellenberger syndrome. Since it's so rare there isn't much data, but he did know of one case where the sense of smell was still intact."

"Is it important?" Lucky asked. "I just want to be hypnotized so I can find out my name."

The doctor smiled reassuringly. "It's important only because the sense of smell and episodic memory are located at almost the same place in the brain. That's why the most vivid memories we have come to us when we smell something. One whiff of apple pie baking and poof"—she snapped her fingers—"I'm six years old again, sitting in my grandmother's kitchen."

"I would give anything if I could just remember my grandmother," Lucky said. Dodger must have sensed her anguish, for he trotted over and gave her a quick swipe with his tongue.

Dr. Forenski leaned forward and touched her arm. "The nice thing about our brain is its amazing ability to recover. You know, there are people out there functioning—literally—with half a brain. Many others have been in worse accidents than you and have gone on to lead normal lives. When we find your family, they'll tell you all about the past, and your brain will process the information until you will almost believe that you do remember the past.''

The other doctors had told her the same thing, but somehow hearing it from this woman comforted Lucky. Cody Braxton might despise her, but he'd found someone who truly wanted to help her.

"Are you ready to get started?" Dr. Forenski asked.

"Yes," Lucky replied. "May Greg and Dodger stay?"

"If you like."

Lucky nodded and looked at Greg. If he was surprised by the request, he didn't show it. The doctor glanced quickly at them both. No matter what they learned, no matter how bad the news, Lucky wanted Greg to know the truth and to hear it firsthand.

Chapter 12

Greg watched as Dr. Forenski settled Lucky onto a chaise, half tempted to slip out of the room. Why had Lucky asked him to stay? He just wanted her to tell them her name so he could get rid of her.

"There's nothing to be concerned about," the doctor said as she pulled her chair next to the chaise where Lucky was reclining, then motioned for Greg to move closer. "Under hypnosis, people don't do anything they wouldn't do in normal circumstances."

"I understand," Lucky responded, and Greg decided he really liked this doctor. She was taking time to put Lucky at ease and she seemed to genuinely care about this case, unlike the doctors who had originally diagnosed Lucky.

"I want you to look directly at the clock on the wall," Dr. Forenski told Lucky. "Concentrate on it and slowly count backward from one hundred."

"One hundred ... ninety-nine ... ninety-eight ... ninety-seven ... ninety-six ..."

Greg studied Lucky as she counted, thinking how vulnerable she looked. For a moment, he almost believed her.

"You're beginning to feel very comfortable . . . very relaxed, aren't you?"

Lucky nodded. "Seventy . . . sixty-nine . . . sixty-eight . . ."

"I want you to close your eyes and relax even more."

With a sigh, her lids fluttered shut. "Sixty-seven . . . sixty-six . . ."

"You're beginning to feel very tired, very sleepy, aren't you?"

Again Lucky nodded and Greg watched her closely, looking for any sign that she was faking. Beneath the pale blue shirtwaist her breasts rose evenly, as if she were already asleep.

"You may stop counting when you are fully asleep," the doctor instructed, then waited until Lucky mumbled the number forty-seven and stopped there.

"How do you know she's really under?" Greg asked. He couldn't help being skeptical, remembering how Lucky had behaved that night in the closet. He still couldn't decide if she had been telling the truth or if she had been acting.

"Are you having a problem with this?" Dr. Forenski asked.

He suspected she could see straight through him, could see through most people, actually. "I don't really believe in hypnotism," Greg admitted.

"Lucky, you can hear me, can't you?"

"Yes," came Lucky's soft reply, as if she were far away.

"I want you to open your eyes and stand up."

Lucky swung her slender legs to the floor and rose, her eyes opening. The dusky sweep of her lashes, shadowing her eyes, and her slightly parted lips were sexy as hell, but was this just an act? If so, what in hell was she trying to prove?

"Please stand on one foot with the other leg straight out behind," the doctor said and Lucky balanced herself on one foot. "Good. Now put all your weight on the ball of your foot and stretch out your arms."

It looked like a ballet position to Greg as Lucky balanced on tiptoe, one leg raised, her arms out like wings.

"Perfect," said Dr. Forenski. "Hold it right there. Don't move."

Dodger rose to his feet from his crouch beside Greg, his eyes trained on Lucky. She stood stock-still, perfectly balanced like a statue, not a real person. Greg became increasingly intrigued as the seconds passed, wondering how she managed it.

"She knows we're here, don't you, Lucky?"

"Yes, you and Greg and Dodger are sitting there watching me." Her lips moved as she spoke, but her body never wavered.

"Only the most highly trained dancer is capable of holding such a position," the doctor informed him. "Yet under hypnosis anyone can do it, because their mind is in an altered state, unencumbered by the usual distractions around them. They have total control over their bodies and, more important, over their minds."

"Her eyes are glazed over," Greg said. "That's how she looked the night I found her, except that she was babbling and acting weird, too. I kept talking to her, but she didn't seem to hear me."

"She was probably reliving the events just prior to the crash. It's a fairly common reaction."

He remembered Lucky's hands in his pants and his own unwilling response. If she'd been reliving something that had just happened, she had been with her lover. The thought caused a twinge beneath his breastbone that he refused to call jealousy. Greg barely heard the doctor tell Lucky to go back to the chaise and close her eyes.

"Can you hear me?" she asked, and Lucky replied that she could. "Good. Now I want you to tell us your name."

"They call me Lucky."

"What do you call yourself?"

"Lucky Braxton," she answered immediately.

The intimate pitch of her voice brought him up short. Lucky

Braxton. The name sounded so . . . right. Uhh-ooh. What in hell was he thinking?

"Is that your real name?" the doctor asked, and Lucky admitted it wasn't. "Why do you call yourself that?"

"Greg started calling me Lucky because I was so lucky to survive the crash. I added Braxton because it's really scary not to have a last name. Anyway, I feel I belong with Greg. He found me . . . and saved me when I was in jail . . . and I'm staying with him."

A constricting knot of tenderness tightened in his throat, and it was all he could do to swallow. She really, truly appreciated all he'd done for her. He was touched in a way that he could never have verbalized.

"I understand, but do you know your real name?"

"No, I honestly wish I did . . . but I don't."

Greg let his hand drop to stroke Dodger's head, expelling his breath in relief. *She didn't remember.* The thought hammered through his head. Clearly, Lucky was hypnotized, and all she could think was that she belonged to him. She had been telling the truth. What about the closet? She must have been leveling with him then, too. She had been afraid but didn't know why.

"All right, now I want you to go back in time. Let your mind slowly drift backward to the day of the accident. Tell me what you see."

"See? I can't see anything except . . . well, these waving bands of light, like I'm in a fog. No, not fog. It's more like water."

"Is it rain you're seeing?"

Lucky hesitated, and Greg thought that perhaps she was remembering the storm that had pummeled the coast the night he'd found her. "No, it's water. It's like I'm in the ocean, under the water. All I see are these shifting bands of light, filtering down from above where the sun must be."

Dr. Forenski leaned toward Greg and spoke in an undertone. "This is the way most amnesia patients describe the past when it isn't there. You'd think they would see nothing but darkness.

They don't. Most report some sort of light, but they can't see anything because there is nothing there to see.''

Greg couldn't take his eyes off Lucky. Her lower lip was caught between her teeth, the way it often was when she was at the computer concentrating on what was on the screen. She was trying desperately to see the past, but it wasn't there. His heart went out to her, the way it had the day he'd found her in jail with people gawking at her, making fun of her.

"Lucky, let's go back even farther. Let yourself slip back in time now. It's summer of 1990. Can you tell us where you are?''

Two beats of silence, then, "No. I can see there's light but it's distorted, like a cheap prism. I have no idea where I am.''

Greg listened, convinced that Lucky had told him the truth, as the doctor regressed Lucky to earlier and earlier periods of time. And she never saw anything except gauzy light.

Finally, Dr. Forenski turned to him. "It's clear to me that her memory bank has been entirely erased, which is consistent with Hoyt-Mellenberger syndrome, but it doesn't explain why she cannot remember her own name.''

"Isn't there anything else you can do?'' The last thing Greg wanted was to be right back where they started. Not only would he have to face his skeptical brother, but he would have to spend yet another tortured night under the same roof as this woman who thought she belonged to him.

Dr. Forenski considered the situation for a moment, running buffed fingernails through the short hair at her temples. "I could try to take her back before her fourth birthday. Most people can't recall this time period. They think they do, but studies have proven they're injecting memories from other sources.

"Different kinds of memory are stored in different parts of the brain. It's possible that Lucky is among the rare few who can recall this period in their life. Even if she does remember, though, she may not know her last name at such a young age, or if it's an unusual name, she won't be able to spell it.''

"It's worth a shot." He kept hearing Lucky saying she belonged to him. If she didn't remember anything at all—even from her earliest childhood—she *would* belong to him, at least until someone claimed her. This thought filled him with an unexpected sense of elation.

"Lucky, I want you to go back even farther in time . . . way, way back. You're very young, very little. You haven't been walking long or talking much. Go back . . . back to those days when you were a toddler."

Lucky's teeth released her full lower lip and a subtle change came over her face. She cocked her head to one side as if listening. Dodger rose to his feet, his body trembling beneath Greg's hand. Lucky seemed so . . . different. Instinctively, he knew she wasn't acting.

"Lucky, tell us what you see."

"It's dawrk," she said with the voice of a very young child.

One by one, the fine hairs along his nape stood at attention. Dodger stopped quivering, his sleek body now rigid beneath Greg's palm.

"What did you say?"

"Dawrk. Dawrk."

"Is it dark where you are?" The doctor slanted a glance at him. "Do you see any light at all?"

"Unda the door."

"There's light coming from under the door?" Greg spoke for the doctor, who obviously hadn't a clue.

"Umm-hmm."

Her response was childlike, and something else that he couldn't quite put his finger on for the moment. Then it hit him. It was the threat of tears in her voice—the voice of a child. Either she was about to cry or had been crying. Man, oh, man. What next?

"Do you know where you are?"

Lucky turned her head away from them, burrowing into the chair, but not before Greg saw the tears seeping from between her closed eyelashes. "Inna closet."

"A closet!" The words shot out of him as he recalled the child's cries that had awakened him. Aw, hell. Couldn't be! Yet he knew it was.

Dr. Forenski put a finger to pursed lips to silence him. "You're in a closet?" she asked, and Lucky nodded, turning back to them, tears silently tumbling down her cheeks. "What are you doing in a closet?"

"Hidin'."

The word came out, followed by little hiccuping sounds that resembled a sobbing child. It triggered a chain reaction of raw emotion. For a second he wanted to take her into his arms as if she were still a small child, then he was angry, furious that someone would abuse a child. He tamped down his feelings and the rational world returned, reminding him there wasn't one damn thing he could do. She was reliving an event from her past.

Dr. Forenski looked concerned, but she didn't know the half of it. In discussing the case, they had concentrated on the night Greg had found Lucky. They hadn't mentioned Lucky hiding in the closet with a butcher knife for protection.

"Who are you hiding from?"

She opened her mouth, struggling to speak, but nothing came out. Then she gasped and shuddered. "Mom-m-my."

Greg's gut twisted, a juggernaut of painful memories returning with startling clarity. But when he'd done battle with Aunt Sis—forced into hiding more than a few times himself—he'd been a lot older, better able to defend himself.

"Why is your mommy upset with you?" Dr. Forenski asked.

Greg wanted to scream, Don't you get it? But he could see that she did indeed suspect something. The doctor was just trying to draw it out of Lucky as she huddled in the chair, a traumatized child, reliving the past.

Lucky balled up one fist and rubbed her eyes, a childish mannerism that made his throat tighten even more. Dodger echoed his feelings with a low whine and an imploring look that seemed to say "Stop this."

"I be bad. Berry, berry bad."

It was all Greg could do not to yell at the doctor to stop. With each word Lucky's face contorted even more, until it was obvious she was in pain. Having suffered so many beatings himself, he knew that she must have been beaten severely.

"What did you do that was so bad?"

"Me drinked the las' of the milk."

Aw shit. He saw himself with Cody, making macaroni and cheese from a box for the fifth or sixth night in a row, thinking they were deprived because Aunt Sis had nothing else in the house. She would spend every dime at the bingo parlor before she would worry about what they ate. This was even worse. Lucky had been so much younger, unable to protect herself.

"What will happen when your mommy finds you?" the doctor asked, and Greg had to resist the urge to strangle the woman. Didn't she know what happened to children who were raised by psychos?

"Mom-m-my will burr me."

"Burp you?"

"Burn her," Greg hissed into the doctor's ear. Didn't the woman's IQ hit double digits?

"Burn? Hot?" Dr. Forenski asked, a tight frown creating a cross web of lines on her already-furrowed brow.

"Uh-huh," Lucky confirmed. Her knees were now up to her chest in a fetal position that wasn't much different from the position he'd found her in that night in the closet.

What had happened last night? Greg wondered. He'd been too damn horny to trust himself to go check on her. How had she managed to go to sleep without making a sound?

"What's your name?" Dr. Forenski asked, obviously reluctant to ask any more questions about Lucky's troubled childhood. "Can you tell us?"

"Sh-ud-up."

"What was that, honey? Tell us your name again."

Greg had the sickening feeling he knew what Lucky was saying.

"Sh-ud-up."

The doctor looked at Greg with wide, disbelieving eyes. This time she got it. "Shut up. Is that your name?" the doctor asked, and Greg braced himself for the answer.

"Uh-huh." Lucky was a tight ball, so turned into herself it seemed impossible for anyone to contort into such a position.

"Do you know your last name?"

"Wasa las' name?"

"Do you know where you live?"

"Inna closet."

Not even when his wife had been killed and his brother severely injured in an accident had Greg broken down and cried, but now a convulsive sob—one he barely silenced—racked his body. He knew what Lucky had been through because he'd faced a similar demon. But he'd been older, more capable of bearing the assault. Not Lucky. She'd been younger. And alone.

"Do you know the names of any of your mommy's friends?" the doctor questioned, evidently unwilling to give up what Greg already knew was a lost cause. Lucky, the child, remembered nothing that could help them identify her now.

"No," she responded in a plaintive voice.

"Stop it!" Greg vaulted to his feet. "This isn't getting us anywhere. You're just torturing her."

He barely heard Dr. Forenski tell Lucky to sleep for a few minutes, that when she awoke she would remember what she had said but wouldn't feel any of the pain. All Greg could think about was how she must have suffered. Sure, his childhood had been hell, but he'd had Cody. Lucky had been alone.

Dr. Forenski rose and motioned for him to follow her out of the room while Lucky slept. Greg snapped his fingers, but Dodger refused to budge.

"Okay, boy. Stay with her."

Dr. Forenski led him down the hall, saying, "I believe I know why Lucky can't remember her name. It's obvious that she was an abused child, not just physically, but mentally as well.''

"Her bitch of a mother told her to shut up so often that she thought 'shut up' was her name.'' Greg followed the doctor into a small office that looked out onto the parking lot. "Now she can't sleep at night unless she hides in the closet.''

"Really," she Dr. Forenski remarked, sitting at the desk. "Tell me about it.''

Greg explained how he'd found Lucky in the closet. "She was afraid, but she didn't exactly know of what. She never mentioned her mother, so I assumed she was afraid of someone in the present.''

"She may not consciously realize what's frightening her. While we're sleeping, the mind is playing, tossing memories and experiences around. Lucky's brain doesn't have much left to work with. It is not surprising that it focuses on this traumatic incident, because her brain doesn't have anything else to use. In time, she'll dream about it less and less. The brain will have newer experiences to focus on.''

"Is there anything I can do to help her?''

"You must understand how important you've become to her. Until she finds her family—if she has one to find—you are the most important person in her life. It's clear to me that she's in love with you.''

Greg jumped up and strode over to the window that faced the parking lot. "I don't want her to love me.''

"Don't you?''

He didn't answer, because he honestly didn't know how he felt about Lucky now. He'd gone into the session telling himself that he wanted to be rid of her. Then he'd seen a different side of Lucky. She'd moved him, touching an inner place he hadn't known existed.

The doctor continued, tactfully dropping the matter about Greg's feelings for Lucky. "Abused children often become runaways. Life on the streets is harsh, but it's better than what they had at home. Many runaways are forced to drugs or prostitution to survive. Didn't you say that Lucky was dressed like a prostitute?''

"Yeah." Greg turned to face her, leaning against the window ledge. "She acted like one, too."

"Those women often change their names. Perhaps Lucky has used so many names that recalling the name on her birth certificate isn't possible with her condition."

A cold knot formed in his gut. He managed to nod as if he didn't give a damn. But he did. Lucky was a bizarre amalgam of innocence and sexuality. Common sense said that she had been with other men, yet he didn't want it to be true.

"You know, this may be a blessing in disguise," the doctor told him. "Traumatic head injuries often radically change a patient's personality. Considering what Lucky's life seems to have been, this could give her the chance to start over."

Chapter 13

Lucky ventured a glance in Greg's direction. They'd left the clinic a few minutes ago, after a long discussion with Dr. Forenski. Greg had been strangely silent, his face a study in self-control. Had he been a professional card shark, no one would have known whether he held a winning or a losing hand.

She turned away from Greg, telling herself it didn't matter what he thought. Every instinct for self-preservation warned her to look forward, not back, and to rely on herself. The session had been both draining and discouraging. Not only hadn't she learned her name, but she had discovered her mother hadn't loved her, hadn't wanted her.

An indescribable emptiness overwhelmed her, a void she knew couldn't be filled. She kept hearing a voice. *Never forget. I love you.* Who loved her? Where was he when she so desperately needed him?

Forget it. Concentrate on the future.

"Dr. Forenski believes I was an abused child who ran away and then became involved in drugs or . . . something."

She couldn't bring herself to say prostitution, determined

not to think of herself that way even though she believed it could be true. Given what Greg had told her about the night he'd found her and the way she'd acted when she was near him, it seemed to be the only explanation. Still, it wasn't the way she wanted him—or anyone—to think of her.

"Her explanation's better than anything anyone's come up with. You can't tell us your name because you've used more than one."

Was that why she'd said that she wished her last name was Braxton? And that she belonged to him? What made her say those things when she knew perfectly well he did not want her? Even though she'd been hypnotized, Lucky had been aware of her surroundings and had known that Greg was there. Her thoughts came out, though, and she'd been powerless to stop them.

Greg pulled to the side of the road and parked the car, then led her to the edge of the bluff overlooking the island. From this elevation, the world was either blue or green. The endless blue sweep of the sea blended with the sky at the horizon, but the land was a mosaic of greens, from the green of the cane fields to the deeper green of the mature pineapples to the bright spring green of the wild ferns. Symbolizing it all was the mossy green crest of Haleakala silhouetted against the blue-blue sky.

Greg was silent for a moment, staring across the multitiered fields. "I didn't hear you crying last night. Were you able to sleep in the bed?"

Lucky considered lying but stopped herself, thinking about what the doctor had said. Whoever she'd been before the accident, whatever she'd done, it didn't matter now. This was a chance to start over. Good people did not lie, particularly to someone trying to help them.

"No. I slept in the closet." She gazed into his eyes and saw something she hoped wasn't pity. "I shouldn't have that problem tonight. After my session I know exactly what I'm afraid of—something that happened when I was a child. It can't hurt me now. There's no reason to hide."

"If you went into the closet last night, you must have cried."

She quickly looked away. Did she have to tell him everything? Keeping some things to herself wasn't exactly lying.

He caught her arm and gently turned her to face him. "You were crying again, weren't you?" She nodded. "Why didn't I hear it? Hell, I was awake the whole night."

Lucky gazed down at his strong hand clasping her arm and remembered how she'd clutched it that day in the hospital. "I made a gag out of a blouse so I wouldn't disturb you."

"Oh, Christ! You didn't."

Greg swung her into the circle of his arms, gently cradling her against his chest. The elusive scent she recalled from the night she'd slept with him enveloped her. His closeness was so male, so powerful, that a familiar shiver of awareness crept through her.

"I'm sorry. I should have checked on you," he whispered, his breath warm against her cheek.

"I didn't want to bother you." A white lie, she quickly assured herself. She had wanted him to take her into his bed again but she'd known he didn't want her. Gagging herself had been the only option.

He looked into her eyes, his expression earnest, concerned. "Promise me you won't do it again. Come to me if you need me."

"You do believe me." She touched the back of her head where the thick braid covered the shaved patch. The lump was still there, tender and ridged with stitches. "You know I'm not pretending."

"Yeah, I know. That's what my gut instinct told me when I saw you in jail. It's just ... well, you seemed like such a different woman the night I found you."

She buried her face against his chest. How could she explain what she didn't understand herself? Her behavior had been so ... crude. "I'm sorry—"

"Don't be. Let's forget all about it."

His voice had taken on a strange, harsh quality. Not wanting to break the spell, she didn't look up. Lucky sensed he wanted to comfort her yet was holding back as usual, keeping a safe distance between them. She tamped down the reckless urge to touch her lips to his and breach the barrier. Each time she'd been the one to initiate things, however; this time she wouldn't.

He touched her face and she trembled slightly, his fingers sliding across her cheek and gently lifting until her lips were a scant inch from his, forcing her to look into his eyes. Their gazes fused, his filled with a dangerous sensuality.

Greg angled his head so his mouth covered hers and he kissed her, slowly, deeply. Lucky willingly gave herself to the kiss, opening her mouth and leaning into him to savor the hard contours of his body. Hot and demanding, his tongue mated with hers. She teased it with darting little caresses of her own.

As they kissed, his hands explored the plane of her back, then coasted lower and lower, until he'd skimmed across the curve of her hips to cradle her buttocks with both hands. Her pulse throbbed, kicking into high gear, and a low moan built in her throat. She arched against him, unable to resist moving her hips while he plundered her mouth with his tongue, letting her anticipate how it would be to make love to him.

Take no prisoners.

He would be that masculine, that demanding, expecting her to give herself fully and completely. In return he would give her just as much. Here was a man who rarely gave up control, but when he did . . . oh, my.

Unexpectedly, he pulled away, as if struck by lightning. "Great timing. S and R is beeping me." Greg grabbed the beeper he always wore on his belt and tilted the face so he could read it.

Lucky longed to tell him to ignore it and continue kissing her, but she knew it wouldn't do any good. Greg's sense of duty was too strong.

"A 7–13. *Seven* means they need a dog, and *thirteen* means the Iao Valley State Park. It's probably a hiker lost near the Iao Needle."

"That's where the hiker with the missing shoe was found, right?" she asked as he guided her back to the car, his arm still around her. "What is the Iao Needle?"

"It's a basalt rock pillar that's over two thousand feet high. In ancient times the *alii*—Hawaiian royalty—buried their dead in the caves that are all over the Iao Valley. There are lots of legends about ghosts and hauntings. You know how people love that stuff, so it draws tourists who rarely hike. At least once a week one of them wanders off a trail and gets lost."

Greg opened the car door and Dodger hopped in the backseat, then Lucky got in. "I need to get to the command station as soon as I can. It'll be dark in a couple of hours—that's when people who are lost panic. They go deeper into the rain forest and are harder to find. If you're ever lost, just stay put."

She couldn't help smiling to herself, feeling proud. Greg was so competent, so dependable. Whoever was lost didn't have a clue as to how lucky they were.

"I'm going to swing by Cody's house. I'm sure Sarah is home. I'll use the phone there to tell S and R that we're on the way."

Home. Unless you can never return home, never see your family again, you will never really appreciate what the word *home* means, Lucky thought. You have to lose everything to understand.

She forced her mind away from thoughts that could only make her miserable, determined not to feel sorry for herself. "Too bad you don't have a car phone."

"It wouldn't do any good. The only cellular station on the islands is in Honolulu."

How did she know about car phones? she wondered. She hadn't seen one—that she could remember—yet the word had just popped into her head. Her brain was amazing. Sometimes it knew so much, guiding her through cyberspace on auto pilot, yet at other times it stalled on an ordinary word.

They drove down a country lane banked by tall ferns shading clusters of orchids whose blossoms were no larger than a penny.

The air was cooler in the up-country, fragrant with the scent of meadow grass and the earthy ripeness of the tropics. Overhead swooped a flock of birds, soaring high and free, leaving a riffling wedge of a shadow on the land below.

Cody's home was a rambling ranch built on a raised platform and shaded by stately eucalyptus trees. Off to one side was a garden and beyond it was a pasture, where two horses were grazing near a frisky colt with legs too long for its body. A goat roamed the side yard, the bell around its neck tinkling, while two mutts stood on the porch, barking furiously at the approaching car.

Sarah came out the front door, a toddler balanced on one hip. She was obviously surprised to see them, but waved and smiled. Lucky was unexpectedly glad to see her. During this terrible ordeal, few people had been as kind and as understanding as Sarah.

"The baby must be Molly," Greg said. "She looks just like Sarah."

"You've never seen your niece?" Lucky couldn't believe it. Judging by the look on his face, she'd hit a raw nerve. The mongoose again. There was something going on here that she didn't understand. How could her brain come through for her one minute, telling her about car phones, yet not let her pick up on what was going on with the Braxtons?

"Mind if I use the phone?" Greg called through the open window when they pulled to a stop. "There's an S and R emergency."

"Sure," Sarah replied, and he climbed out of the car and hurried inside, while she walked over to the passenger side. "How are you doing?"

"Fine, thanks." Lucky had the urge to tell Sarah everything, but then she suspected most people did. Sarah was one of those people whom it was difficult not to like. She was very pretty, with brown eyes and long silky hair several shades darker, and she had a cheerful openness about her that put Lucky at ease.

"Ma-ma, Ma-ma," cooed the little girl in Sarah's arms.

"Molly," Sarah said, pointing to Lucky, "this is Lucky. Can you say *Lucky?*"

"Yuc-ky. Yucky," Molly responded, and Sarah and Lucky both laughed.

"Great! Now I've been called everything," Lucky said.

Sarah's smile vanished. "Don't let the *Tattler* article bother you. It's nothing but a cheap tabloid."

Warning spasms of alarm erupted inside her. Oddly enough, what she'd learned under hypnosis had calmed her fears, giving her a sense of self, but now her anxiety returned. "What did the article say?"

Sarah didn't meet her inquiring gaze. "Nothing really. It showed a picture of you being wheeled into the hospital and another taken while you were helping the shark."

"That doesn't sound so bad," Lucky observed, before she deciphered Sarah's troubled expression and knew that somehow it spelled more bad news.

"Yucky, Yucky," cried Molly, stretching her little arms toward Lucky.

Lucky got out of the car and reached for the child. Molly smiled Sarah's open, friendly smile and eagerly came into Lucky's arms. "Sarah, I don't understand what's going on," Lucky said as Molly played with her braid, slapping it on Lucky's shoulder.

"Come inside. I'll show you the article."

Carrying Molly, Lucky followed Sarah into the house. The wood floor in the living room was covered by a sisal area rug and thick bamboo furniture. An old Hawaiian quilt with star bursts and bright yellow pineapples hung on one wall. Lucky immediately understood that the furniture was functional, inexpensive, and that the quilt—safely away from the children on the wall—was the prize possession.

Greg's raised voice came from the nearby kitchen, where she could see him talking on the telephone. "I'm telling you, Cody, she's not faking it. Lucky isn't ever going to be able to tell us her name."

"I hate to have them fighting over me," she whispered to Sarah.

"At least they're talking," Sarah said as Greg slammed down the receiver. "I'll explain it to you later."

Greg rushed out of the kitchen and came to a halt when he saw Lucky holding Molly.

Lucky pointed to Greg. "That's your Uncle Greg. Can you say *Greg?*"

Wide-eyed the child stared at Greg for a long moment, then she beamed at him and reached out her chubby little arms. "Gra-a-a."

"This is Molly," Lucky said, offering him the chance to hold the child.

He tried to move away, but Molly shrieked, "Gra-a-a."

He swung her into his arms, then gave her a little bounce that made Molly squeal with glee. There was something natural in the way Greg handled the child that told Lucky that he had experience with children, or maybe he was just comfortable with them, the way he was with animals.

"Let me drive Lucky back to your place," Sarah suggested. "That way you can go right to the rescue site."

"Good idea," Greg replied as he passed Molly back to her mother. He pulled a money clip out of his pocket and took out several bills. "Could you run Lucky by Kmart and get her a one-piece suit that's . . . you know, decent?"

Lucky opened her mouth to say she could darn well pick out her own suit, but he was out the door before she had the chance. Anger erupted inside her, but she mastered it, wondering yet again about the source of her hostility. He was only trying to help her. She turned and saw Sarah smiling like a miser who suddenly discovered gold.

"Well, I'll be. Greg's finally getting over the bit—" Sarah stopped abruptly, then said, "Little ones tend to pick up all those naughty words."

Sarah had been about to say *bitch*, Lucky thought as she followed her into the kitchen. Did she mean Jessica Braxton had been a bitch? It didn't seem likely. "Greg still has Jessica's picture on his desk."

Sarah put Molly on the floor and the child toddled across the room, swaying from side to side like a drunken sailor. "On his desk, huh? I'm not surprised. He's too stubborn to admit he made a mistake."

She gestured for Lucky to take a seat at the butcher-block table. Sitting, Lucky glanced around the kitchen, which opened onto a family room that faced the rolling hills stair-stepping down to the sea, a mere sliver on the horizon. The walls were covered with sports awards of all sorts, from certificates and plaques to trophies that gleamed in the late afternoon light. Magnets plastered a soccer schedule to the refrigerator, and beside it was a finger painting that Molly must have done.

Sarah handed Lucky a glass of lemonade. "You're good for Greg."

"I've been nothing but trouble since he found me. You see how he fights with Cody."

Sarah turned to check on Molly, who was pulling Tupperware out of the cabinet. "They're talking again, and if Greg can vent enough of his anger, maybe he'll listen to reason."

"About what?" Lucky couldn't help but ask, realizing she wanted to know as much about Greg as possible.

She sipped the lemonade and listened with growing alarm as Sarah told her about the fatal accident that had exposed the affair between Cody and Jessica. Lucky was stunned to learn Greg hadn't spoken to anyone in his brother's family since the accident. How could he cut himself off? She would forgive anyone in her family—even her mother—just to have a family to call her own.

Sarah leaned across the table. "I knew the second I met Jessica that she was trouble. She was one of those crisis-oriented people. Everything was a big deal, a trauma. She just wanted attention, and she never got enough of it from Greg.

"You see what he's like. He has his hands full at the institute, then he's the ace on the search and rescue team. He needed to marry someone a little more independent. Jessica cheated on him right from the first. She did it to get his attention, and when that didn't work anymore, she went after his brother.''

"I can't imagine Greg putting up with it."

Sarah shrugged. "I guess he loved her—at least at first—but she suffered from depression and threatened to kill herself if he divorced her.''

Lucky couldn't imagine anyone treating Greg like that, but obviously she'd been wrong. It was becoming clearer to her with each day that she didn't have the proper emotional perspective on life. She didn't quite know how to read people.

"Threatening to kill yourself is emotional blackmail. It's not playing fair." Sarah watched Molly, who was now surrounded by an armada of Tupperware. The child was beating on a plastic bowl with a wooden spoon. "You must have been very strong to have forgiven Cody.''

"What choice did I have? Face it, men are weak. Their brains are in their jockstraps. I love Cody. If I didn't forgive him, I would only be hurting myself . . . and my family. It's been two years. I know I did the right thing.''

"I'm sure you did, but Greg still hasn't forgiven Cody. Do you think he ever will?''

"Maybe, now that you're here."

"Me? What do I have to do with it?''

"Greg's interested in you—as a woman. You're forcing him to deal with his feelings about you, about Cody . . . about lots of things.''

"He just feels responsible for me because—''

"Don't you get it? Greg wants you to wear a swimsuit that covers every inch of your sexy figure, so other men can't see you. Believe me, if he didn't care about you, he'd never think about what kind of suit you wear." Sarah rose and picked up a paper from the counter. "He'll go ballistic when he sees this.''

Lucky took it and saw the dreadful image that had replayed in her mind dozens of times—the face she'd seen in the mirror and failed to recognize as her own. The headline read "Pele's Ghost Finds Brother." There was a long article covering most of the front page and another grainy photograph that must have been taken with a telephoto lens. It showed her emerging from the pool, dive tank on her back, wearing a bathing suit that made her look like a cheap slut.

"Oh, my God, no wonder Greg wants me to get another suit. I look disgusting." She read the headline again. "The article is just plain stupid. Rudy isn't my brother." She pushed the paper aside.

"According to Hawaiian legend, Pele, the goddess of fire, created these islands. She was the number one, most important god . . . a woman." Sarah grinned and winked. "I like that part. Kuhaimoana, her brother, the next most powerful god, was a shark. The paper says you plunged into the water the first chance you got and talked to a shark."

"That's ridiculous! Rudy's part of an institute project. . . ." Lucky stopped, realizing she had been talking to a shark. He hadn't talked back, of course, but his name had come to her suddenly.

"The legend about Pele says she often appears at the side of the road with a dog," Sarah went on. "You weren't with a dog, but Dodger did find you. It's the kind of story islanders love because it ties in with the history of the island."

"I'd rather be a ghost than a car thief," Lucky tried to joke.

"Forget it. That's just how the *Tattler* makes money." She opened the refrigerator and found a bag of carrots. "It's time to feed the horses. Watch Molly for me while I put out their hay."

They went down the slope to the pasture, where the colt and two other horses were romping through the grass, walking slowly to allow Molly to toddle along ahead of them. Birds trilled in the distance, flittering on bright wings through the skein of vines that grew wild, hanging from the trees in garlands that brushed the ground.

While Sarah forked hay into the manger in the nearby corral,

Lucky stood at the fence, helping Molly feed carrots to the horses who were jostling for treats. The shy colt's eyes shifted warily, but encouraged by the others, he reached out his velvety muzzle and plucked a carrot from Molly's chubby hand.

Sarah finished and opened the gate with a click, which was as good as a dinner bell, sending the horses trotting across the pasture and into the corral. Lucky lifted Molly off the top rail and put her on the grass. The child immediately grabbed a stick and lurched off after a butterfly.

"Isn't she something?" Sarah asked. "Perpetual motion. At the same age, though, the twins were worse. Boys are double trouble."

They sat on a flat rock, watching the horses swish their tails as they ate to ward off the bevy of bluebottles that had appeared. Both women kept an eye on Molly as she explored the meadow where the rippling breeze combed the grass, parting it and making the sprigs of white ginger sway. Lucky decided that this was as good as life gets. But she couldn't help wondering if there had been another time, another place, where she'd sat quietly enjoying Mother Nature's gifts.

With someone she would never remember.

"Oh-oh, oh-oh," came the call of a bird on the rain-scented wind that promised the usual late afternoon shower.

"Hear that?" Sarah jumped up and sprinted over to her daughter, who was nearby. "Honey, listen." She cupped her ear and little Molly cocked her head.

"Oh-oh, oh-oh," the bird repeated, louder this time.

Molly's eyes grew wide, and she called, "Oh-oh, oh-oh."

"It's an O'o bird," Sarah told them. "They mate for life, and when one mate loses the other, they call until they find each other again. When I was a child, you used to hear them all the time. Now they're almost extinct."

"Stink." Molly struggled with the word.

"Extinct. It means there aren't many left. Someday there won't be any."

They listened as the O'o pleaded for its mate to return.

Sadness welled up inside Lucky like a swift-rising tide. Why wasn't there someone out there looking for her, missing her?

They listened, hoping to hear the rare bird again, but the only sound was the rising breeze fluttering through the branches, bringing with it a heaviness in the air that heralded a tropical shower. Molly became distracted by a cat stalking its way through the tall grass, its tail an orange plume in the lush greenness. She ambled after it, giggling as she went.

Lucky couldn't help thinking she'd love to have a child. Greg's child. But until she found out who she was and her future was settled, she didn't dare dream.

Sarah returned to the rock where Lucky was sitting. "Tell me about your session with the psychologist."

Lucky didn't need any encouragement to talk to Sarah. Although this was just the second time they'd been together, it seemed as if they were old friends. She told her about being regressed to the point that she was only a bit older than Molly, and how she'd been hiding in the closet. Sarah didn't say anything but she kept her eyes on her daughter, frowning as she listened. Sarah was a model mother, having held her family together through its crisis, and Lucky knew she couldn't imagine mistreating a child.

"I feel better now," Lucky concluded. "I honestly do. I had no idea why I had the overwhelming urge to get in the closet, and now I understand. Dr. Forenski says I'll get over it, and that's a relief."

"She thought you might have run away as a teen, then turned to a life on the . . . ah . . . streets."

"It's okay, Sarah. You can say it. I may very well have been a prostitute or dealing drugs." She looked into Sarah's warm brown eyes and saw a friend. "I think I was a prostitute."

"No. I don't believe that."

Lucky told her about what she'd done to Greg that night in the tent, things Greg had not mentioned to Cody. Sarah slanted a quick glance at her daughter, who was now pulling up clumps of ginger with both hands, then she looked back at Lucky.

"Greg thinks I'm a hooker. He told me so."

"Oh, Lucky, no wonder he's having such a hard time. Jessica behaved just like some—" Sarah tossed her hair over shoulder, obviously annoyed with her choice of words. "It would have been nice if you were the girl next door, but then some man would probably have come for you, and Greg wouldn't be fighting his attraction, would he?"

"No," Lucky admitted. "Dr. Forenski says even a minor head injury can change someone's personality. I might not be *anything* like the person I was before the accident. She told me to start over and be whatever I want to be."

"And what do you want to be?"

"Not a hooker, that's for sure. I want Greg to respect me. I want to do something worthwhile, like saving Rudy, but I'm not going to get the chance. Next week is the trial. Unless someone miraculously comes forward to explain what I was doing with a stolen car, I'm going to prison." Lucky sucked in a calming breath, remembering her terrifying experience in jail. "Sarah, I have an idea. Please help me. . . ."

Chapter 14

"Chief, there's someone here to see you." The duty officer rolled his eyeballs and Cody looked past him, half expecting to see Tony Traylor. The jerk had already called three times today to see if they had anything new on Lucky. But it wasn't Traylor. This man had gray hair parted and swept to the side like British royalty, and he was wearing a suit and a tie. In the islands, no one dressed like that except when he was in a casket.

"Dr. Carlton Summerville," the man said, extending a hand with a gold watch that would have cost Cody a year's salary.

Cody shook his hand, mentally betting that this had to do with Lucky. He only hoped that this clotheshorse had come to ID the blonde. After his fight on the phone with Greg, nothing would make him happier than getting rid of Lucky. Just as he thought, she'd managed to convince Greg that she didn't remember a thing.

"I'm doing research on Hoyt-Mellenberger syndrome," Summerville informed him in a tone that implied his study was akin to discovering the cure for cancer. "I want to interview the Jane Doe you arrested."

"She's out on bail. I don't know where she is." He was stretching the truth, not lying. Cody glanced up at the wall map and saw the flag near the Iao Needle. He knew Greg and Dodger were up there, but Lucky wouldn't be with the S and R unit.

"I understand your brother posted bail," the doctor said.

The best defense was usually a good offense. "That's right. What medical school are you with?"

"I'm not. I'm doing research for a private group, the Wakefield Foundation. They fund a number of research projects. Most of them deal with cranial injuries."

The answer was smooth, stated in simplistic terms that even Quasimodo would understand, but Cody's sixth sense went on alert. What did this man really want?

"I'm the foremost expert on Hoyt-Mellenberger. I often use hypnosis."

"That so?" Cody had discussed the disease with doctors in Honolulu. Most were surprised Lucky couldn't remember her name, but none of them had mentioned hypnosis. That had been Lucky's idea, and he'd had a difficult time locating a doctor to do it. He'd met Dr. Forenski earlier in the day and had discussed Lucky's condition with the hypnotherapist. "Why is hypnosis important?"

"It's complicated," Dr. Summerville responded, implying Cody was just a dump cop. "Now, if I could see this woman, I could evaluate her suitability for my research."

"She's due to be in court next week. That's all I can tell you."

"I can make it worth your while . . ." The doctor reached for his wallet.

"Forget it." Cody watched the doctor leave, his tasseled loafers clicking on the floor. Interesting, no one had come forward to identify Lucky, but two different men had appeared willing to put up cash just to see her.

"Okano," he yelled to the only detective on his force. "Let's run a background check on Fenton Bewley. Start with UPI.

Then try the AMA for Dr. Carlton Summerville. Let me know what you come up with.''

His phone rang and it was Sarah, which was unusual. She rarely called him, so Cody prepared himself for a problem with one of the children. Last time Jason had slid into home plate and had broken his arm.

"I told Lucky she could waive time and get her trial postponed for a few weeks, right?'' Sarah said.

"Yeah.'' A defendant could waive his or her right to a speedy trial and the court date would be set for later. "What are you doing with Lucky?''

Cody listened with growing irritation as Sarah explained that Lucky needed more time to remember her name. It was bad enough having his brother involved with this weirdo, but now Sarah was on her side. When Sarah made up her mind about something, you could move heaven and earth, but you couldn't budge her. That's why he loved Sarah. She'd stuck by him when most other women would have walked out the door.

"Tony Traylor will put pressure on the judge to refuse Lucky's request,'' Cody said, hoping to discourage Sarah.

"I'm contacting Garth Bradford in Honolulu. I'm certain he'll help Lucky.''

"You're probably right.'' Bradford was the best criminal attorney in the islands. As a young man he'd been a good-looking jock, but an auto accident had left him paralyzed and confined to a wheelchair. If you were rich, his fees hit the stratosphere, but he took many cases of clients who couldn't afford to pay him. "One of Bradford's stares could back down a pit bull. Then he'll throw out enough legal bullshit to bury the island. There isn't a judge around here willing to tangle with him.''

"Exactly, especially since the *Tattler* has made Pele's ghost an island sensation.'' Sarah laughed and Cody couldn't help smiling, thinking how much he loved her. "I have a great idea about how to help Lucky.''

Uh-oh. Now what? He braced himself, listening carefully.

"She went on-line last night," the Orchid King told his partner. "She surfed into a marine biology Web site and asked about reattaching a shark's fins."

"She knows exactly who she is."

"I've downloaded all the research on Hoyt-Mellenberger syndrome. If she really has it, she's lost the ability to recall events in the past. But things she's done over and over, like going on-line, will still be in her brain. It's called procedural memory."

They were walking along the beach, where a glowing crimson sun was melting into the sea, painting the sky cerise and mauve. Like holiday bunting, garlands of seaweed decorated the beach as the tide retreated, leaving a cache of shells. In the distance, the city's high-rises stood out like grim reapers against the darkening sky.

"Have you heard anything from our source on Maui?" the king asked.

His partner stopped to examine a rare checkered cowrie shell that had washed up onshore. "We planted a bug in the police chief's office."

"Perfect. Now we'll find out everything the police know immediately."

His partner tossed the shell aside and it skipped across the wet sand into the surf. "They're trying to get Lucky on *Missing*."

"Unfuckingbelievable! The show's at the top of the rating charts. If they blast her picture across every boob tube in America, there's a good chance someone will recognize her. We can't let that happen."

"Why not? You said you went into every data base and erased all traces of her existence using the computer."

"True, but what about her past?" the king asked. "Do you really believe she didn't have a family or friends when she came here? She must have been hiding something."

His partner shrugged it off. "So let the skeletons fly out of her closet. What do we care as long as no one can trace her back to us?''

The king cared . . . more than he wanted his partner to know. He didn't have any right to love this woman, but he couldn't help himself. ''She's up to something. I can feel it.''

''She was hypnotized today.''

''What did she tell the shrink?''

''I don't know yet.''

''She goes to trial next week. Maybe they'll jail her and that'll be the end of it.'' The king liked that idea better than having her family claim her or letting her stay with that prick Braxton.

''They've called in Garth Bradford, and they're going for a postponement.''

''Bradford? Shit!'' A rogue wave breached the tide line, halting inches from his feet, showering his bare legs with a fine mist, making him even angrier. ''He's the best. He'll get her off.''

''Forget her,'' his partner said. ''I have.''

The king knew a lie when he heard one, but he understood. His partner loved this woman as much, maybe more, than he did.

''Concentrate on a warehouse full of rare orchids,'' his partner continued quietly.

They had rented a warehouse on the fringe of Chinatown, near the docks. The first shipments of orchids from the golden triangle were due in at the end of the week. It gave the Orchid King a deep sense of pleasure to know many of the orchids were so exceedingly rare. A single plant could bring thousands of dollars from collectors. Since China had opened to the West, it was now possible to send in smugglers to strip the rain forest of its rarest treasures. And bring them to him.

''What are you thinking about?'' his partner asked.

''Orchids, of course, and how to strip the last of those phalaenopsis orchids from the rain forest on Maui without getting caught.'' It was a lie: He couldn't keep his mind off a woman who was as unusual as the rarest orchid.

It was almost ten o'clock by the time Greg drove down his driveway with Dodger in the backseat. Ahead his house was all lit up, the first time in over two years that he hadn't returned to a dark home. He was stunned by how pleased he was. Okay, blown away. But then everything he'd learned about Lucky today had thrown him.

What he'd seen in the doctor's office had profoundly upset him. She truly remembered nothing about her past and never would. He'd vacillated about her so much, unwilling to believe her yet not quite willing to say she was a liar. Then he'd discovered they had more in common than he ever would have suspected.

He could still feel the lash of the belt as Aunt Sis lit into him yet again. But it was nothing compared to burning a young child, traumatizing her so much that she didn't even know her own name. *Shuddup.* Son of a bitch! Who could be so cruel?

Lucky didn't *seem* upset by what she'd learned. The doctor's hypnotic suggestion that she not be bothered by what she'd discovered apparently had worked. Lucky was grateful to know the truth and concerned about whether he believed her. Once her preoccupation with what he thought would have annoyed him. But not anymore. Now Greg found it unexpectedly touching.

''What in hell am I going to say to her?'' he asked Dodger.

Talk? Hell. It was the last thing he wanted to do. He wanted to kiss her, to make love to her. That was the only way he knew how to comfort her. He was hopelessly lost at expressing himself. Except in bed.

He pulled into the garage and turned off the ignition. Phew! Greg swiped at his gritty forehead with the back of his hand. His entire body was coated with sweat and dirt from climbing around in the bush, and he smelled like two-day-old roadkill.

"Okay, Dodger, let's hit the shower." He opened the door for the dog.

Greg walked into the house and stopped, his stomach rumbling. The aroma of something delicious was coming out of the kitchen. She'd made him something special and was waiting for him. How many times had he wished Jessica would do that? Of course, she never had. If he was late for dinner, he could just fix himself something while she sulked.

"We're back," he yelled.

"Great," she called from the kitchen. "Did you find the hiker?"

"Yeah," he said, walking into the room. "The kid had fallen down a—" Greg stopped dead in his tracks. "Lucky?"

Only the eyes were familiar. Wide and green and rimmed by dark wispy lashes. Okay, the sexy bod was familiar, too.

"What happened to your hair?"

"Do you like it?" she asked, her voice unsteady.

Christ! This was a new woman. The frizzy blond hair was gone, dyed a warm chestnut brown with reddish highlights. It had been cut short into windblown curls that tumbled naturally around her cheeks.

Silence charged the air like a tropical storm. Her eager, excited expression touched him in an unfamiliar way. She could completely undo him with that look. Loneliness lurked behind those intense green eyes, along with a raw pain that he understood perfectly.

"You don't like it," she said, disappointment underscoring every word.

Then he realized that he'd been too stunned to say a word. "Like it? Hell, I love it." He grinned at her and she rewarded him with an adorable smile. "You look great."

"I told Sarah to do it." Lucky patted the back of her head. "I have to comb the back into a ducktail and spray it so the shaved spot won't show, but it's a lot better than long, kinky hair."

"Do you recognize yourself now?"

She shook her head. "No, not really. This isn't me. I like it, though." She grabbed a bag off the counter. "Look at this." Lucky pulled out a black one-piece suit. "What do you think?"

Greg nodded, not trusting himself to tell her what he really thought. She was so damn cute, with those provocative green eyes and a body that wouldn't quit. "Great suit," he mumbled, turning to go. "I'd better get in the shower."

It didn't help. The water sluiced over him, cascading in rivulets over his chest and down his hips to his legs, but the telltale throb in his groin was still there.

How long had it been since he'd had a woman? Not long really. He seemed to remember a redhead from Tulsa who'd been staying at the Four Seasons last month. Or had it been the Texan with the wraparound legs staying at the Hyatt? Obviously, it had been too long, Greg thought, soaping himself thoroughly.

He grabbed the bottle of Avoderm that he kept in the shower for Dodger and bent over to shampoo him. The greyhound obediently stood at attention while Greg worked the dirt out of his coat and tried to forget Lucky for a few minutes. Unfortunately, the dog wasn't the only thing standing at attention. His cock was responding the way it did whenever Lucky was around, only now it was worse. All it took was thinking about her, and then even a cold shower couldn't help.

He turned off the water and threw a towel over Dodger before he shook and splattered the mirrors with water. When Greg finished drying Dodger, the dog trotted off toward the kitchen, obviously expecting Lucky to feed him. How quickly she fit into their lives.

He toweled his hair, then left it half dry and peered into the mirror. Dark bristles stubbled his cheeks, but he didn't want to take the time to shave. In the hamper he found some cutoffs that weren't too raunchy and put them on. Zipping invited self-castration, but he managed. Then he pulled on a T-shirt and didn't tuck it in, hoping it concealed his condition.

Lucky was in the kitchen, humming softly as she huddled

over the stove. "It's beef Stroganoff and crème brûlée," she announced.

Christ! He'd been so busy lusting after her that it hadn't dawned on him that she was an excellent cook. Greg glanced around the kitchen. No cookbook. A gourmet who surfed the Internet. Not your basic hooker profile. Go figure.

Tonight Lucky looked like a sexy version of the girl next door, not like a hooker. He'd spent plenty of time asking himself why he was resisting her and, for the life of him, couldn't come up with one good reason. He remembered the way she'd felt beneath him, the way she'd responded to him. He wanted more, wanted everything. Tonight.

"Here you go." The minute he sat down, Lucky served him.

She smiled across the table. It was difficult to believe she was the same hard-edged woman who'd gone for his cock that night in the tent. Of course, if she went for it now, he wouldn't back off.

"Delicious," he said, wolfing down a forkful. The last thing on his mind was eating, but she'd gone to so much trouble that he couldn't disappoint her.

"Tell me about the rescue operation."

She sat opposite him, her expression so earnest he stopped chewing for a moment, thinking how Jessica had never been interested in him. After a long day, she would want him to listen to her problems, most of which didn't amount to anything. Lucky, on the other hand, had troubles up the wazoo, but she wasn't dwelling on them.

"It was easy," he said. "I gave Dodger the search command the way I showed you, and he found the boy."

"Dodger, you're so smart." Lucky leaned over to pet the dog, and Greg noticed Dodger was sitting right next to her. So much for loyalty. "How does he do it? Does he follow a trail like a bloodhound?"

"No, because we don't usually have the victim's clothes to give him the scent. He patrols a given area until he picks up a human odor."

"Do we smell that different from other animals?"

"Absolutely. Humans have the most distinctive smell of all the animals," Greg explained, and she looked so intrigued that he couldn't help smiling. "We stink, and when we die, it's even worse."

"Really? What if the person had just died that second?" Lucky asked.

Greg wished she'd hurry up and finish her dinner. He enjoyed talking about his work, but right now he had other things on his mind. "The minute you die, the body begins to give off gases. A human nose can't detect them for hours, but a dog can."

"What about people Dodger knows? Could he pick me out of a crowd?"

"Remember when you were in jail? He found you in a few seconds, didn't he? Dodger could probably smell you half a mile away."

"What a great nose, Dodger." Lucky gave him yet another pat, and the greyhound responded with two quick swipes of his tongue on her hand.

Something about the scene made him feel funny inside. Warm and mellow, yet tense. His home. His dog. He told himself to hold it right there, but the thought came anyway. His woman.

His feelings for her were too complex to analyze. From the first night, she'd gotten to him in a way that no woman ever had. It was like trying to put your finger on quicksilver. The minute he thought he had her figured out, she changed.

He watched her eat, dainty little bites, cooing to Dodger, who was lapping up the affection with a flavor straw. The throb in his cutoffs intensified and he shifted in his chair, his pulse accelerating. He sucked in a breath that seemed to vibrate through his whole body.

Lucky popped up and took her dishes to the sink. "Let's go for a swim. I want to try out my new suit."

"Swim?" he repeated, as if it were a foreign word.

"Sure. The ocean's right out your door. Don't you make the most of it?"

She looked so happy and full of life that he couldn't say no. He kept remembering her childlike voice saying: Shuddup.

"Meet you at the beach," he said, trying to inject a note of enthusiasm into his voice.

"Aren't you going to put on your suit?"

"Nah," Greg replied as he turned away from her and shucked his T-shirt, tossing it over a chair. "Hurry up."

Sex on the beach was out of the question, he decided, following the footpath between the rocks that littered the shore, leaving nothing but a thin ribbon of sand along the water's edge Okay, a quick dip, then they could spend the night in his bed.

He kicked off his shoes and walked into the welcoming warmth of the tropical surf in his cutoffs, inhaling the bracing scent of the sea. Protected from the ocean by an arc of lava rock, the water in the cove barely moved, its waves lulling and seductive against his skin. Above a crescent moon, sharp as a rapier, gilded the dark water with threads of light.

Lucky picked her way along the trail, Dodger at her heels. The moonlight played across her bare skin and emphasized the stark black suit. The halter top covered her breasts all right, making them seem even fuller, then it nipped in at her waist, playing up its smallness and showing off the provocative flare of her hips. The effect was simple, conservative. Breathtaking.

Until she turned her back to kick off her sandals. The damn suit didn't *have* a back. A swatch of black fabric covered her cute little ass. But that was it.

"Come here," he said, standing in water up to his waist.

Chapter 15

His eyes drifted over her alluring body as the warm water lapped around her thighs, but his gaze kept coming back to her lips. She couldn't seem to look away from him either. The magnetism she generated was almost a tangible thing. He imagined making love to her in the water, a whirlpool of stars overhead.

Lucky came closer, moving the water aside with her arms. Her eyes glinted in the moonlight, the irises wide and banded by hoops of silvery-green. Waiting in slightly deeper water, he studied her mouth, its full lower lip irresistible. Even now he could feel the imprint of those lips on his skin.

She stopped an arm's length away with a mischievous smile. Desire coursed through him, hot and deep and astonishingly primitive. He reached out to haul her into his arms but she jackknifed into the water, cleanly splitting the surface. She arched upward like a water sprite, gracefully rotating her arms in a circular motion and kicking her feet in perfect time.

"The butterfly?"

Surprised, he had no choice but to swim after her, thinking

that she must have been on a swim team or something. A quantum leap from the dog paddle, the butterfly was rarely used except by competitive swimmers. Greg had always been a strong swimmer, his job requiring hours in the water weighted down by' an air tank, so he pulled up beside her with a few powerful strokes.

"Amazing," she said as she stopped and treaded water. "I just have no idea what I can do. My brain said 'butterfly' and I did it. I wonder what else I can do."

He had some pretty good ideas about what else she could do, but he didn't verbalize them. "Why are you so surprised? You jumped in the tank with the shark."

"That was only walking around. This is different." There was that adorable smile again. "I wonder what else I know."

Before he could offer one really interesting suggestion, she flipped over and backstroked toward the shore where Dodger was waiting, impatiently patrolling the rocky beach. In the shallower water she stopped and stood up, tossing her short hair back and flinging a cobweblike skein of water that shimmered in the moonlight.

With her hair short and slicked back, Lucky looked young, vulnerable, and light years away from the woman he'd found in the car. Greg swam up beside her and stood, letting the water sluice off him, unable to ignore the hot undertow of desire. He'd had all the fun he could stand.

"Lucky," he said, putting his hand on her arm and gripping her waist to counter the surge of the ocean.

"Don't," she warned, but she didn't try to pull away.

"Don't what?" He couldn't resist teasing her. She was so cute, so proud of her short hair, so enthusiastic about life despite all that had happened to her.

"You're thinking about kissing me. I can tell."

He grinned. "Trust me, sweetheart, kissing wasn't what I was thinking about, but it's a start."

Her eyes widened, her gaze traveling across the broad planes of his chest and trailing down to his waist, where the dark water concealed the erection beneath his cutoffs. Two could play this game, he decided. He examined every inch of her face from those wide, expressive eyes to the delicate slope of her cheek to the lower lip he always found so provocative. Then his eyes dropped to her shoulders following the wide straps of her sheer suit to the lush fullness of her breasts. And the taut nipples beneath the wet fabric.

He glanced up, meeting green eyes staring at him with a look charged with emotion. He had the unsettling feeling her mind was not on making love. Remembering all she'd been through today, he ran his fingers into the cluster of wet curls framing her face, wanting to say something comforting but not finding the words.

"Oh, Greg." Lucky turned her head to the side and brushed her lips across his wrist in a fleeting hint of a kiss that was as soft and as warm as the night air. And unexpectedly tender.

His fingers sifted through her hair and found the bald patch at the back of her head. The hair was beginning to grow back now, short and prickly. He traced the spot with the tip of his finger while he drew her closer with his other hand.

"Greg, I need to explain something."

"We're way past talking, sweetheart."

Parting her lips, she raised her head, inviting his kiss. He reveled in the warmth of her mouth, his tongue tracing the moist interior. Her arms curled around his neck, her fingers finding the sensitive spot at the nape and caressing it, fueling the aching need building in him by the second. His tongue grew more insistent, conducting a mating dance with hers.

The water was warm, the tropical night even warmer, but her body was hot. Its heat enveloped him, coiling around his belly and thighs, unfurling rapidly where her chest was pillowed against his torso. He wanted to see those breasts again, touch them, brand every luscious inch with his mouth.

For now he satisfied himself with running his hands over her bare back, roving lower and lower and lower until he was just below her waist where the back of the suit began. In a heartbeat, his hand was under the fabric and splayed across her cute bottom. Her lower lip trembled as she drew in a startled breath.

But she didn't pull away. Not at all. Her legs tangled with his, encouraging him to take her weight as they rode the gentle surge of the ocean, the water swirling seductively around them.

The blood throbbed in his veins and his breathing was harsh as he pulled her closer, his hands still on her bare skin, angling her body so it was flush against his erection. Lucky shuddered, her fingers digging into his shoulders. Greg moved against her, his jutting hardness teasing the softness between her thighs. The sensation was so arousing that he couldn't help groaning out loud. When was the last time he'd wanted a woman this much?

Her hips snug against his, her lips on his, he inched his hand between their bodies and cupped her breast. Soft and pliant, its plumpness eluded the breadth of his fingers, the tightly spiraled nipple an erotic bead in the heart of his palm. His pulse skyrocketed and his cock swelled with anticipation. Christ! What this woman could do to him without half trying!

He lifted his hand, aroused by the weight of her breast as he stroked the nipple with his thumb. "Still want to talk?" he managed to ask.

Her answer was a sigh of pleasure that filled him with masculine pride. He had her now. No, make that *again,* Greg thought, remembering the other night. This time he intended to sheathe the iron heat of his sex as deep inside her as he could. And stay there.

The slow undulating waltz of the sea caused them to sway slightly, drifting with the current, the sand shifting beneath his feet. He clutched her tighter, supporting her weight, savoring the dark, sultry embrace of the night. And the woman.

Unexpectedly Lucky dropped her arms and let go of his legs. She sank back in the water, then righted herself mumbling, "I— I can't do this. I'm a new person now."

"What in hell does that mean?"

She gazed at him, her eyes reflecting desire and a tremendous strength of will. "Whatever I was in the past doesn't matter anymore. I've been given an opportunity to start over. This time I'm not going to be a whore."

Trying to conceal his frustration, he silently began to count, intending to go to twenty but getting only as far as seven. "I'd hardly call this being a whore."

"What would you call it?"

That got him. Greg had no idea how to respond. He was royally pissed at himself, at her. Still, she had a point. He did think she was easy, and he wanted her just the way she'd been the other night. Beneath him, wearing nothing but goose bumps.

"You want me. I want you. It's simple."

"I don't want this." She took two steps backward. "I'm going to be a better person."

"No?" He pointed to her chest where her nipples raised the wet fabric. "Every time you're near me, your body sends you a message. Right?"

She set her jaw like a mule ready to plant one in his chops and gave a little shake of the head that shimmied her breasts seductively, making him even more furious. "I can be strong. I don't have to revert to my old ways. Besides your . . . physical disorder—"

"What?" He advanced on her, fully intending to haul her into his arms and kiss her until she came to her senses.

She stumbled onto the rocky shore, the surf foaming around her ankles, and Dodger trotted up to meet her. "You know, the other night—"

"I didn't see you complaining," he shot back as it dawned on him what she thought.

"No," she conceded, "but you couldn't perform. It wasn't the—the real thing."

He stomped up to her, splashing as he went. "You want the real thing, huh?" He grabbed her hand, shoving it over his bulging crotch. "What's this? Soda pop?"

"Oh, my," she whispered.

Her fingers coiled around him, then tightened, and he struggled to maintain control. He hadn't gone off since he was a horny teenager, but he was damn close now. A low growl built deep in his throat, and it was all he could do not to moan out loud.

She yanked her hand away. "Not many people get a second chance at life. This time I'm going to be a better person." Lucky turned then and headed up the trail, Dodger at her heels.

Cody sat in Greg's office the morning after Sarah had convinced him to contact the producers of the popular television program *Missing!* He resented the way Lucky had wormed her way into Sarah's heart, but unquestionably she had. His wife had taken Lucky on as a cause just as she had the Nene— the endangered Hawaiian goose—several years ago. And once Sarah made up her mind, there was nothing anyone could do to stop her.

He'd gone along with Sarah's suggestion, not only because he wanted to please her, trying as usual to make up for the past, but also because it gave him another excuse to see his brother. The blonde had obviously sucked Greg in with whatever stunt she'd pulled during the session with the hypnotherapist. Cody cursed himself for contacting the doctor in the first place. He'd known Lucky wasn't revealing her true name.

"Where's Lucky?" Cody asked, glancing around the room and seeing only Rachel hunkered over her computer as usual.

"She's in the pool with the shark," Greg answered, his tone almost civil, and Cody couldn't help thinking that he looked exhausted.

"Rudy, huh? I read about him in the *Tattler*."

"Yeah . . . well, don't believe everything you read." Greg rocked back in his chair and Cody braced himself for some cutting remark, but it didn't come. "So what are you doing to ID Lucky now?"

It dawned on Cody that Lucky must not have explained

Sarah's plans. He took a few minutes, drawing out the story so he could spend more time with Greg, and told him about Garth Bradford and the TV program.

"Garth Bradford agreed to take Lucky's case?"

"Yep. You know how convincing Sarah can be. It took her one minute to persuade him. Bradford will appear before Judge Nagata next Thursday and waive time. Looks like you'll have Lucky around for at least another month or so. Think you can handle her, or do you want me to make other arrangements?"

Greg's shrug said "Who cares," but Cody had more than a sneaking suspicion his brother cared very much. "I can handle her," Greg responded quietly.

"I spoke personally with the producer of *Missing!* and he sounded really interested. I sent him the police report and the picture I took of Lucky when they brought her into the hospital. I'm betting they go for it. A woman with amnesia found wearing a shoe belonging to a woman who had mysteriously died a year earlier. Then the whole Pele's ghost angle. It's a one-in-a-million story."

"Lucky can't go there to film. It would violate the terms of her bail."

"Haven't you seen the program?" Cody asked, and Greg shook his head. "Lucky won't have to do a thing. Actors recreate the incident with the usual dramatic crap that Hollywood comes up with, then at the end of the program they show pictures of the missing person and give a toll-free number for tips. They've found hundreds of missing people."

"I see," Greg commented, as if they were discussing the weather.

The more Greg displayed his indifference, the more Cody became convinced that it was all an act. Great! He hadn't fallen for Lucky, had he? Didn't he ever learn?

Almost as if Greg had read Cody's mind, he retreated into belligerent silence. Cody understood. Greg had been deeply wounded when Cody and Jessica had betrayed him. His pain forced him to lash out, to be cruel.

"I've sent Lucky's prints to the states that don't have computerized print records. It'll take time, but we should find out something if the TV program doesn't turn up someone who can ID Lucky."

"Have you seen Lucky since Sarah fixed her hair?"

Greg's question caught Cody totally off guard. He'd been expecting a scathing remark directed at him. Maybe he wasn't reading his brother as well as he thought.

"No, I came right upstairs, but Sarah told me about the new hairdo."

Greg got to his feet. "Come on. She's feeding the seals."

Cody followed his brother downstairs, walking beside him as they crossed the yard, passing the pool where a volunteer was walking the shark that Lucky had named Rudy. Behind the screen of oleander bushes was the area where the orphaned seals were kept. Nomo saw them from across the pool and waved. The woman beside him, with Dodger at her elbow, paused as she scooped a mackerel from the bucket, frowning when she spotted Cody.

"Shit! Lucky doesn't look like the same person, does she?"

"Nope," Greg responded. "And she doesn't act anything like the woman I rescued, either."

Cody studied Lucky as she fed the rambunctious seal pups, while Greg told him about her computer skills and her swimming ability. "Something's funny here. The last thing she seems like is a two-bit hooker."

Cody couldn't disagree. Right now Lucky looked so wholesome and natural, sitting on the side of the pool, her long legs dangling in the water as she fed a particularly friendly pup. It wasn't hard to see why his brother had fallen for her.

"I like my drug theory," Cody said. "You found her in the twilight zone of Hana. Who knows what goes on back there?"

"I'll bet Tony Traylor knows exactly what goes on back there."

Again, Cody couldn't disagree.

* * *

It was late in the afternoon by the time Lucky finished her turn walking Rudy around the pool. The young shark was more despondent than he'd been the first day, and she knew that he was losing the will to live. But he was still friendly with her, rubbing up against her and letting her put her hand in his mouth. That's when she'd discovered the loose teeth, and one sharp fang had come out in her hand.

The tooth was a triangle serrated on two sides. About two inches long, it appeared to have broken off at the base. She couldn't figure out how Rudy, still so young that his dark tiger stripes had yet to fade into the more muted gray of an adult, had lost a tooth and had several others that were loose.

Greg would know, Lucky decided as she climbed out of the pool and handed Nomo her air tank. She paused to give Dodger a quick pat. Since the scene on the beach last night, Greg had been polite, speaking to her only when necessary. The minute they'd arrived at the institute, he'd dumped her on Nomo.

She dried off and changed clothes in the annex adjacent to the pools, carefully setting aside Rudy's tooth. From now on she intended to dress more carefully and behave herself. She was justifiably proud of the way she'd resisted temptation last night. It would have been easy—and heavenly—to have given into Greg. But she didn't want him to think she was nothing but a tramp. She wanted to be someone special, and yearned for Greg to realize this with a desperation that actually frightened her.

Greg wasn't upstairs in his office when Lucky entered with Dodger at her heels, but Rachel was there. She was gathering up her things, apparently leaving for her late afternoon excursion on the research boat *Atlantis*. Lucky ignored Rachel's scathing glare and went over to Greg's computer terminal.

Rachel came up behind her, and Lucky tensed, running her fingers through her damp hair, nervously making certain the bald patch was covered. Rachel reached past Lucky and picked up the photograph of Jessica.

"Greg was crazy about her—absolutely crazy. He still loves Jessica. That's why he keeps her picture on his desk. No one will ever take her place."

She put the photo back with a thunk and left. Lucky got the message. She was not replacing his wife. "I'm not trying to take her place," she told Dodger. "I want to be better than she was."

It took her a few minutes to log on and read her messages. The researcher in Australia had suggested she try putting her hand in Rudy's mouth as a preliminary test of how likely he would be to let her use the surgical staple gun on him. She reported her success, and just in case Greg didn't know the reason, told the Aussie about Rudy's teeth.

Greg appeared some time later. "Good boy," he said to Dodger, then sat down without a word to Lucky.

She was less than a foot from him, so close she could see the pinpricks of moisture across his brow from the grilling sunshine outside. But she might as well have been on another planet. When she finished on-line, she shut down the system and began to speak. "Greg, I—"

"Why didn't you tell me about Garth Bradford?" he cut her off.

A swift shadow of anger swept across his face, then vanished, his usual unreadable expression returning. But she sensed the dark undercurrent of anger moving through him like a subterranean stream. He was definitely making an effort to hold his anger in check.

"I meant to but . . . things got out of hand and you swam away. Where did you go? I was worried."

"Don't ever worry about me. I can take care of myself. I don't need anyone fussing over me." His eyes warned her not to mother him, to mind her own business. "I swam around to the point and back. When I got home the house was dark. You couldn't have been too worried."

She didn't tell him that she'd waited to hear his return before allowing herself to fall asleep, realizing he might resent her even more. Instead, she briefly explained what she and Sarah had done. He didn't seem particularly pleased, and she wondered if anything she did could please him except sex. He certainly didn't have a sense of humor. When she'd tried to tease him about not performing, he'd taken it wrong and had gotten all huffy.

"If *Missing!* airs my story, I think someone will know me, don't you?"

"Probably," he replied grudgingly. "I thought you wanted to be a new person."

"I do, but I have to know if I have a family." Lucky knew better than to say she would never turn her back on her family the way he had. "It's like Rudy looking for his mother."

"Do you know what you're doing? You're projecting. That's a psychological term meaning you're taking your feelings, your fears, and transferring them to someone else. In this case, Rudy. Believe me, that shark's mother couldn't care less. They're not like whales who live in pods and take care of each other."

Lucky knew he was mistaken about Rudy, but Greg was on a roll now and waiting him out seemed prudent.

"A shark travels alone. He's nothing more than an eating machine. Tiger sharks are the worst. They're one of the few sharks who eat other sharks. Rudy probably ate his mother."

"That's ridiculous," she snapped. "Rudy wouldn't do that. Nomo spotted a shark in the bay yesterday. I'll bet it's Rudy's mother."

"This is Hawaii. Shark stories make up half the island's lore. That's because we have so damn many sharks. If there's one in the bay, it isn't Rudy's mother."

"Maybe you're right," she hedged, unwilling to concede but knowing she sounded nutty because she *felt* Rudy telling her things. "No matter how bad the news, I want to know who I am. I have to find my family, and I can't help believing Rudy does, too."

This time he didn't argue with her. If anything, his gaze softened as he slowly nodded. Greg turned to resume his work, but Lucky stopped him.

"Look at this" In her palm was Rudy's tooth, gleaming like polished ivory. "I put my hand in Rudy's mouth and discovered several of his teeth are loose. This one fell out."

"Why in hell would you put your hand in a shark's mouth?"

"The researcher in Australia said it's a good way to test Rudy's suitability for the staple gun."

"I risk my ass to save your life, and you try to give it back by putting your hand in a shark's mouth!" He was furious now, making her sorry she'd shown him the tooth.

"I didn't mean to seem ungrateful, but I thought it best to prep Rudy for the staple procedure."

"There isn't going to be any procedure. Fire a staple gun, and that shark will go ballistic. We'll have to fish out what's left—if there's anything left—with a leaf net."

"But Rudy didn't even flinch when I tested the rest of his teeth to see if any others were loose."

He grimaced as if he were actually in pain. "You tested *all* his teeth?"

"Yes," Lucky replied, proud that Rudy trusted her enough to let her wiggle all his teeth. "He has razor-sharp teeth."

"All the better to eat you with."

She didn't respond. He was so furious now that she had no idea how to deal with him.

"All the better to eat you with," he repeated. "Sound familiar?"

She shook her head, knowing this must be a mongoose thing again.

It was frightening to realize how many things she didn't know.

"'All the better to eat you with' is from *Little Red Riding Hood,* a well-known fairy tale."

"I don't know it, but I'm imagining a small car with a red

hood, probably a convertible, riding through the cane fields. Close?''

Greg actually smiled, shaking his head, and she couldn't help smiling back. There was so much she'd have to relearn. If he'd be patient, she'd love to have him teach her.

''Why are Rudy's teeth loose? Is there something wrong with him?''

Two beats of silence. No doubt he was counting his blessings, and she with all her dumb questions wasn't among them. But if she didn't ask, she would never learn.

''Rudy's lucky to be alive.'' His blue eyes had become sharper, and she could almost hear his mind going click-click-click, thinking but not revealing everything. Bad news, no doubt about it.

''That's what everyone said about me, too. Lucky. Lucky. Lucky. I'm sick to death of hearing that.'' She tried to temper the sarcasm in her tone, but it was difficult. Anger often seemed to erupt from some hidden depths, making her sound shrewish and ungrateful. ''Please tell me what's wrong with Rudy.''

''Fishermen always keep baseball bats on their boats.''

The ache in her chest swelled, until it was a sob lodged in her throat.

He hesitated, then explained, ''They club the fish until it's unconscious, so they can fillet it or, in this case, slice off the fins.''

She couldn't help the tears that welled in her eyes, so she gazed down at the broken tooth to avoid Greg's probing stare. She could almost feel Rudy's pain. And she realized that in an uncharted part of her brain was the irretrievable memory of facing death the way Rudy had. Lucky looked up at Greg and saw the last thing she expected from him: tenderness and compassion.

''Angel, keep Rudy's tooth for good luck.''

Her heart lurched, echoing in her voice in a quaver. ''How can suffering bring luck?''

His hand closed over hers, the fingers strong, and she remembered the other times his strength had seen her through a crisis. "In ancient Hawaii, there was no metal. Shark's teeth were made into spears and knives—weapons, that are still called *leiomano,* meaning made from shark teeth." He squeezed her hand, his fingers twining through hers. "It's only natural that a tooth is considered a good luck charm, like a rabbit's foot."

She gagged, imagining a bunny's bloody paw. "A rabbit's foot is good luck?"

Greg smiled, his teeth white against his tanned skin, and she couldn't help thinking how truly lucky she was to have him helping her. "Don't worry. Rudy will grow another tooth just like people do."

Lucky didn't want to admit she had no idea people grew a new tooth when they lost one. Shuddering inwardly, she was overwhelmed by what she didn't know. "Rudy's going to die if I don't help him," she said, forcing her thoughts away from her troubles.

"The institute studies monk seals, who are so rare the state established a wildlife refuge to protect them. Tiger sharks like Rudy are their number one enemy." Greg ripped out the words, his impatience reflected in every syllable.

"He's injured. He deserves a chance to live. I'm going to staple his fins back on. I checked with Dr. Hamalae and he has stainless steel staples that don't dissolve. Then if Rudy's cartilage doesn't regenerate, his fins will still be attached."

"Look, a tiger shark is nothing more than a vicious killer. Only the great white shark kills more people. Fire that staple gun underwater and that shark will eat you alive—before any of us can save you."

"But—"

"You're not going to do it, understand?"

She gazed down at the serrated tooth in the palm of her hand, thinking about baseball bats, rabbit's feet, and luck. Bad luck.

Chapter 16

"It's for the good of society," Dr. Carlton Summerville explained to Lucky as they stood beside the shark pool the next day. "The more we know about Hoyt-Mellenberger syndrome, the easier it'll be to help people like yourself."

Lucky had no idea how the doctor had gotten inside the institute's gates, which had been locked to keep out reporters like Fenton Bewley, but she suspected Rachel had let him in. There was something odd about the doctor. Lucky had disliked him the moment he'd introduced himself. She'd seen enough doctors, answered enough questions, to last a lifetime.

"I'm sure Dr. Forenski would be willing to lend you the tape she made."

"I tried to contact her, but she must have an unlisted number."

"Ask Cody Braxton. He must know how to contact Dr. Forenski. He found her."

"I plan to do that, but I thought—"

"Get the reports from the doctors at the hospital. There were three of them, you know. That should be all you'll need."

Lucky stepped around him, determined to get into the pool with Rudy before Greg returned. She had the surgical staple gun in her satchel, and she intended to reattach Rudy's fins before Greg could stop her.

"You're being selfish," he called after her. "Think of the other people with head injuries. They'll suffer needlessly because of you."

She stopped and swung around to face him. "All right! I'll talk to you, but not now."

"When?"

"Call me." She hurried toward the annex to change into her suit, cursing herself for allowing the obnoxious man to persuade her, yet feeling guilty at the same time. She wouldn't want to put another living soul through this nightmare if she could help in any way.

Wearing the black suit and dive tank, her mask high on her forehead, Lucky made her way to the pool with the staple gun in the dive pouch at her waist. Looped over her arm was the special flotation device she'd designed for Rudy. Nomo and Dodger were waiting for her at the shallow end.

"Did you remember to shower thoroughly?" Nomo asked.

Lucky nodded, touched by his fatherly concern. Nomo had reminded her repeatedly about sharks' acute sense of smell. They might react adversely to perfume or shampoo they found noxious smelling.

They also smelled fear. The Australian researcher cautioned her to have no one in the pool who was afraid of Rudy. The body secreted a slight odor when someone became anxious. Sharks easily picked up the scent because two thirds of their brain was devoted to the sense of smell.

"Want some help?" asked one of the cute male interns from the marine research center in Woods Hole.

Of all the people to go into the pool with her, he would have been the best choice. But she couldn't risk anyone else's life. She had to go in alone.

"No, thanks. Just wish me luck."

Lucky gave Dodger a quick pat, knowing he would be pacing along the perimeter of the pool, the way he always did, until she resurfaced. Waving with one hand to the group of volunteers who had gathered to watch and pulling her mask into place with the other, Lucky walked into the water.

Don't be afraid. She tried to reassure herself that Rudy would never hurt her. On some level she sincerely believed this was true, but an element of doubt lingered in her mind. Maybe she was projecting, sympathizing with Rudy because he was suffering.

Go back. Forget this harebrained idea. Yet she couldn't stop her slow descent. Lucky moved downward, dropping into deeper and deeper water, compelled by a power beyond her control to help Rudy.

Underwater, the volunteer who had been walking Rudy helped Lucky fasten the Velcro-strapped flotation device around the shark. This would stabilize him so she could use both hands to reattach the nearly severed fins. Once the device was in place, the volunteer left the pool in a hurry. Lucky began to walk Rudy, talking to him and sending bursts of bubbles through her air tube.

"If you let me staple your fins on, then you're outtta here." She pointed to the gate with metal bars separating the pool from the sea. Fresh seawater replenished the pool with each tide, bringing with it small fish, but there wasn't enough space between the bars for Rudy to get out. It reminded her of her own experience in prison. Maybe she was projecting, she thought, but she knew she had to do this. She wanted to be the one to throw the lever on the gate and see Rudy swim to freedom.

Lucky took a shallow breath, reminding herself not to alarm Rudy by showing him how nervous she was, and a plume of champagne bubbles drifted to the surface. Inside the bra of her new swimsuit she touched Rudy's tooth—for luck. The suit really wasn't practical for diving, but she loved the way it made her look. She could still recall the expression on Greg's face when he'd noticed it was backless.

"Get your mind where it belongs," she told herself.

Reaching into the pouch at her waist, she took out the institute tag. It was a fluorescent orange disk the size of a quarter, with the name of the institute and the number 1475. Using as much pressure as she dared, she clamped it on his dorsal fin. Rudy flinched, his body snapping to one side, showing more strength than usual.

Lucky inhaled sharply, suddenly aware of how loud and harsh her breathing sounded, then forced herself to slowly exhale, keeping the air bubbles a uniform size. Stay calm, she told herself. Show no fear. Talk to him the way you always do.

"Okay, Rudy, forever after you'll be a number, not a name. If anyone picks you up, you're safe . . . a protected animal."

She didn't add that if his body was found, he would be shipped back to the institute for study. She stopped walking and took the staple gun out of the pouch.

"This isn't going to hurt you. It's going to save your life."

Rudy glared at her with the one eye she could see. It was jet-black, the eye of a fierce predator. She moved with slow, deliberate movements calculated not to alarm him and positioned one fin back where it belonged. Suddenly, her lungs ached and she realized she wasn't breathing. She forced herself to take a stabilizing breath.

"Here goes. Now don't give me any trouble."

Her heart beating lawlessly, Lucky managed to hold the gun steady. She aimed and squeezed hard. Thunk! The noise seemed unusually loud as the staple crunched into his leathery skin. Rudy whipped his head toward her, revealing a vicious set of teeth with one missing tooth.

"See? That didn't hurt one bit," she said, but Rudy did not look convinced.

She waited, expecting his powerful jaws to rip off her arm with one deadly bite. *Get out of here,* screamed the logical side of her brain. *Fast.* But she couldn't desert him, couldn't give up even though her life was in danger.

Unexpectedly, her niggling fear evaporated, and Lucky realized she was bound to this fearsome creature by destiny. They had both been left to die, given one chance in a million to be found alive, yet here they were.

Somehow she sensed that the worst lay ahead for her, that her darkest moment was lurking in the future. For Rudy there would be no tomorrow unless she saved him today. Everyone else—even Greg—had written him off as just another vicious shark, but to her he was a kindred spirit, one who had seen the dark, evil side of man.

Rudy deserved a chance to live. He couldn't help being a shark no more than she could help what she was. Sometimes fate left you without a choice. But he didn't deserve to have his fins sliced off and to be left floating helplessly, slowly bleeding to death.

She had absolutely nothing on this earth she could truly call her own. Her clothes had been bought, and she still owed Greg for them. She didn't have a single possession of her very own. Not even a toothbrush. Everything she had or used belonged to someone else, had been bought by someone else.

She didn't even have a name.

All she had, and the only thing she could give Rudy, was the chance to survive.

"Come on, Rudy, let me help you." Lucky raised the gun again, ignoring Rudy's bared fanglike teeth a scant inch from her wrist. "Let me bring you some luck."

The first thing Greg noticed when he came through the gate into the pool area of the institute was the unnatural quiet. Even the noisy seals weren't barking. Then he noticed the crowd around the shark pool and his brother, a head taller than the rest, standing off to one side. He dashed up beside Cody to confirm his suspicions.

"Aw, shit!" There was Lucky in with the shark with something he could hardly see through the shimmering water. It had to be the staple gun. Naturally, she'd defied him. He yelled to Nomo, who was nearby, "Get her out of there before that shark turns on her."

"Don't worry about Lucky," Nomo said. "She's already got one fin reattached."

"She'll never forgive you if you haul her out now," Cody added in an undertone.

"He could kill her in a second." Greg refused to admit that Cody was right, but he didn't insist that Nomo pull her out.

He was every kind of pissed, and the more he thought about her deliberately defying him, the more furious he became. Though he'd vowed not to lose his temper, it was slipping fast, exposing a raw anger that was new to him even though he'd lived with anger simmering just below the surface for the last two years.

Son of a bitch! He'd saved her life. Posted bail. And what had she done? Turned to Sarah for help, calling in some hotshot attorney and arranging to go on television. He had said that he would help her, that he would find an attorney on the mainland, but she'd spurned his offer.

Then she had teased him, using her body, luring him to the brink, only to announce that she was a "new" person. Okay. He'd gone along with it, believing she deserved a fresh start, touched by the pain of her abuse by her mother.

And, jerk that he was, he'd let her get to him—yet again— with Rudy's tooth. He had thought that she understood the danger but she'd ignored his warnings, sneaking behind his back to do this. If the meeting hadn't broken up early, he would have missed this whole show.

"Thought you might want to know Fenton Bewley's press credentials don't check out." Cody interrupted his thoughts, and Greg shot him a look that bordered on a death threat. "He's too sleazy even for the *National Outrage*. He just a freelancer who sells them articles on occasion. He wrote the Pele's ghost story the *Tattler* is running.''

"Did they pay him for it?"

"Yeah, but not much. I can't believe this story is worth Bewley's time, but he's still hanging around.''

A cheer went up from the crowd. "She's done it," someone yelled. "Rudy's fins are back in place," someone else cried.

The enthusiasm of the crowd was obvious. The thought crossed his mind that this little stunt of Lucky's would probably result in more donations to the institute than would any of his lectures on marine biology. But Greg didn't give a damn about the money. She'd defied him, risking her life.

"Now what's she doing?" Cody wanted to know.

How in hell would I know? She never tells me anything, Greg thought, but refused to admit this to his brother

Nomo had walked over to them, saying, "She's reattached those fins. Now she's taking off the flotation device so Rudy can swim on his own.''

"I didn't know they made flotation devices for sharks," Cody remarked.

Nomo grinned, revealing large, crooked teeth. "They don't. Lucky made it out of life jackets.''

Greg smiled inwardly, still furious with Lucky for risking her life but unable to help feeling proud. And immensely relieved that Rudy hadn't eaten her alive.

The device floated to the surface while Lucky took Rudy under her arm. Bubbles were rising so rapidly that Greg knew she was talking to the shark. The crowd silently waited while she took several turns around the pool. Finally, she let Rudy go and stepped aside to watch him swim. The shark floated in place for a moment, drifting in the pool's current, then sank to the bottom like a dead weight.

"Oh, no," Greg couldn't help saying along with the others. Lucky had tried so hard, had been so clever, and to fail didn't seem fair. Not that he actually believed this would save Rudy.

His fins were too far gone, but if he would at least try to swim, Lucky would feel better.

Naturally, Lucky wouldn't give up. A burst of bubbles erupted on the surface, then another. She was babbling away to the shark. Then she picked him up and walked him to the shallow end of the pool, still talking. She let him go and this time he stayed afloat, moving slowly on his own.

"All riiiiight!!" yelled the crowd.

Rudy picked up speed, and everyone kept cheering. Except Greg. Now the shark was going very fast, with quick darting motions, as if his fins had never been cut. Typical, aggressive shark behavior that preceded a strike. *Get out of that pool before he turns on you.*

Lucky bobbed to the surface just as Greg charged up to the side of the pool. He hauled her out with a quick hoist of his upper body, before the damn shark turned on her. Nomo helped with her air tank while Greg waited, torn between throttling her and hugging her. Water ran down her body, pooling around her feet. With her hair slicked back, she was all eyes and a smile that could melt the polar cap.

Everyone was talking to Lucky, offering congratulations and telling her how brave and smart she was. But she wasn't paying attention to anyone, not even to Dodger licking her hand. Her eyes were on Greg, her smile for him alone. She looked so pleased with herself, glowing with a childlike enthusiasm Greg had lost so long ago that he wondered if he'd ever had it.

"It worked! He's swimming." Lucky threw her arms around him, her face alight with excitement.

In an instant, his shirt was sopping wet. He, Greg Alan Braxton, who was deservedly called a coldhearted bastard, suddenly experienced a secret thrill that penetrated the barrier of his self-control and centered deep in his chest.

He hugged her back, allowing himself to let go of his anger and share her triumph—because she was so thrilled to share it with him.

"I want to open the gate and let Rudy go," Lucky said.

"We better study him for a few days. See how he does."

"We can't do that."

He was still holding her, his face so close to hers that he could see the individual clusters of eyelashes that had been drawn into spikes by the water. He had a good mind to kiss her, right then and there, but they were surrounded by people.

"I promised Rudy that if he would just swim, we'd open the gate so he could get back to his mother."

Man, oh, man, she was a world-class loony tune. Sharks, particularly tiger sharks, didn't have family ties. But now was not the time for another lecture on projecting. There must be some part of Lucky's psyche that was reacting to that traumatic incident with her mother, her only memory from the past.

"Okay," Greg relented. "Let's get you out of those swim fins first."

He knelt down and pulled at the snug-fitting slipper foot, while Lucky put her hand on his shoulder for balance and chatted a hundred miles an hour to the group, telling them how anxious Rudy was to find his mother again. He couldn't afford to get sentimental about Lucky, Greg reminded himself. She was a psychological basket case beyond his help.

As the fin slipped off, he saw the soles of her feet. There were clusters of scars—old from the looks of them—small circles the size of an eraser's tip. How had he missed them that night in the tent? Come to think of it, he'd never looked at the bottom of her feet.

Mommy burr me.

Burn me.

Christ! Her mother must have taken cigarettes to the bottom of her feet. A muscle quivered in his jaw and Greg stared down at her toes, not trusting himself to look up, willing his usual self-control to reassert itself. He couldn't begin to fathom what she must have suffered. Obviously, she'd been abused, tortured.

Had she ever known love?

He'd been "lucky," he decided. Cody had loved him, adored him, actually. No matter how cruel Aunt Sis had been, they'd had each other. Tormented by conflicting emotions, he told himself he hated Cody. But he didn't. When he'd needed love the most, as a child, Cody had been there.

They'd had each other. Greg's sixth sense kicked in, telling him Lucky hadn't been so fortunate. No one had been there for her.

Cody stood by Nomo, watching as his brother pulled off Lucky's swim fins. He'd never thought he would live to see the day his brother would be at some woman's feet. He certainly had a strange look on his face, Cody thought, noticing Greg staring at Lucky's toes. Friggin' weird.

Suddenly, Greg looked up and his gaze met Cody's, disconcerting him so much that Cody almost turned away. Then he realized his brother looked utterly lost, naked anguish etching the harsh planes of his face, revealing all he must have suffered during the last two years.

Transfixed, Cody stared at his brother, recognizing that intimate look. So achingly familiar. Straight from the past, communicating their special bond. And something deeper. The ache in his chest grew more intense with each heavy beat of his heart.

He exhaled a measured breath, not daring to believe that Greg was mouthing the words *I owe you one.*

Cody didn't dare approach Greg, thinking he might have misinterpreted something. Still, he detected a chink in the emotional armor that Greg had so carefully worn since Jessica's death. Why? Cody wondered. What had happened?

"You know," Nomo said, breaking into his thoughts, "there is a shark hovering along the shore. Divers got a look at it yesterday. It's a tiger shark and it doesn't have a clasper."

"Really?" Cody was no expert on marine life, but he knew enough about sharks to know that a clasper was a penis, so this shark was a female.

Arm around Lucky in an uncharacteristically protective manner, Greg guided her to the lever that lifted the gate separating the pool from the bay. Lucky tugged on the lever and it made a creaking sound.

Rudy made a beeline for the opening while the group chanted, "Go, Rudy! Go! You're outta here! *A-a-aloha!! A-a-aloha!*"

Rudy shot through the channel into the bay, a blur of tiger stripes in a wash of clear aquamarine.

"*Aloha*, Rudy! *Aloha!*" yelled the group. "*Aloha!*"

"Look," someone shouted. "there's a shark waiting for Rudy."

"*Lalani kalalea*," Nomo said, using the Hawaiian term for dorsal fins that islanders shouted when sighting a dangerous shark.

Sure enough, an enormous dorsal fin knifed through the waves and hovered around Rudy. Circling. Circling. Circling. Ugly, aggressive behavior that usually preceded a kill.

Then both fins disappeared in a swirl of foam-capped waves. The wind-ruffled water shimmered in the late-afternoon sunshine, whitecaps studding the waves. But there was no sign of the sharks.

Silence fell over the crowd, and Cody moved forward so he could see Greg. He still had his arm around Lucky, but disappointment etched his face. His expression charged with tenderness, Greg pulled Lucky closer, whispering something to her.

"Looks like Rudy's lunch," Nomo told Cody.

"Really?" Cody kept his eyes on his brother, still feeling the afterglow of those special words: *I owe you one.*

"Look! There they are!" screamed one of the volunteers, pointing toward the lava rock breakwater protecting the bay from the open ocean.

"Well, I'll be jiggered," Nomo said. "Rudy is swimming off with that shark."

Chapter 17

"Look at this! Unfuckingbelievable!" The Orchid King's partner waved a fax at him. "What does she think she's doing?"

They were sitting in the office they'd recently set up in the Chinatown warehouse. The Orchid King took the fax and read the *Maui Tattler* article.

"Pele's Ghost Frees Brother," he read the headline out loud. Silently, he scanned the rest of the article, conscious of his partner's questioning gaze. "I find this shark stuff amusing, don't you?"

"Fuck, no!" His partner vaulted to his feet. "If you think that's funny, you have a really sick sense of humor."

"I merely find it amusing that so many people believe those myths." He rocked back in his chair, confident he was concealing his true feelings from the one person who knew him best. "Pele was the goddess of fire and volcanoes. Now I ask you, does it make sense that her brother was a shark?"

His partner glared at him. "You're missing the point. What kind of genius are you? Mensa should revoke your membership. How can you believe what they printed in that rag? Can you see her, of all people, jumping in with a shark and reattaching its fins . . . risking her life?''

"She's a different person now that she's living with Braxton," the king informed him.

"Sure. Fucking him every which way to hell."

The king almost flinched at the raw anger in his partner's voice. What did he expect? He controlled his anger while his partner vented his.

"Want to know something funny?" His partner did not sound the least bit amused. "The Braxton brothers had a big-time fight when Greg Braxton found out his little brother was fucking his wife."

"That so?" the king asked. "Think history will repeat itself?"

"Shit, yes. You know what she's like."

Trouble was, the king didn't know exactly what she was like. He thought he had known, but he'd been wrong. She'd turned on them after they'd helped her.

"Read this." His partner handed him the transcripts of the session with the hypnotist.

It took the king a few minutes to read the information. "So it would seem that she doesn't know who she is and doesn't remember anything about her past."

"Convenient, wouldn't you say?"

Skepticism etched his partner's voice as well as his face, but the king didn't share the man's feelings. He kept seeing a small child at the mercy of an abusive mother. It explained a lot about her personality and made him sad.

"It appears she recalls nothing about the past," the king said. "We won't have to worry about her exposing us, will we?"

"No." His partner plopped down into his chair. "We're safe, and she's stuck there—"

"Unless *Missing!* turns up someone from her past."

The king had always known she was hiding something, lying to them about her past. But he hadn't challenged her or encouraged his partner to question her. He had been too obsessed with her to want to know the truth.

"I say we play the ace," his partner said.

"We're not showing our hand yet. Why should we risk everything? Let her go on *Missing!* See if anyone comes forward to identify her."

"Then we play the ace, right?"

The king laughed, the first genuine belly laugh he'd had since she'd double-crossed him. "Yes, then we play the ace . . . and, remember, the joker's wild."

"Are you comfortable?" Dr. Carlton Summerville asked Lucky.

"Yes, thank you." She swirled the sugarcane swizzle stick through her iced tea and gazed out at the pristine beach with the rows of cabana-chaises facing the water. She'd reluctantly come to the doctor's luxurious suite. "Could we start? Tell me what I can do to help anyone else who has Hoyt-Mellenberger syndrome."

She sounded snippy, but the doctor ignored it. "I've been over your records, and I've seen what the other doctors have concluded. I still want to make my own evaluation."

"I don't want to be hypnotized. You can use Dr. Forenski's report." She had no intention of repeating that harrowing experience.

"I haven't been able to get her report yet. Could you fill me in on the details?"

Lucky told him about the session with the hypnotherapist. She kept assuring herself that she wasn't bothered by what she'd learned. The incident in the closet had happened so long ago, in a life she could no longer remember, that it wasn't true. Sometimes late at night, she'd awaken, near tears.

Never forget. I love you. Where was that person, she wondered. It wasn't her mother. The hypnosis session had proven that much. She wished she could remember the person who'd uttered those comforting words. Too often the raw, aching need to love and to be loved overwhelmed her.

"Knowing your mother abused you is upsetting, isn't it?"

"Yes," she conceded, shifting her attention from the dapper doctor in his suit and conservative tie to the beach, where a windsurfer was skimming across the waves with awesome agility. She did not want to talk about this.

"Posthypnotic suggestions don't last forever," he explained. "That's why hypnotists can't cure chronic overeaters or smokers."

Lucky shrugged it off, truly not knowing if she awoke at night solely because of her troubled past. More likely it was the present. Who could sleep soundly with a man like Greg Braxton down the hall, the door to his room open? The thought of being in his arms was almost too tempting to resist.

"I'm doing just fine," she insisted, tamping down a spurt of anger. Why couldn't she keep her mind off Greg? "Now, tell me what you want to know."

He pulled out a large ringed notebook from a briefcase that looked so shiny, it was difficult to believe it had ever been used. Everything about the man, from his glossy black shoes to his maroon handkerchief nattily tucked into his suit pocket, looked brand-new.

Lucky listened with as much patience as she could muster, verifying that she had her sense of smell, didn't recognize her face in the mirror, couldn't give her name, and a variety of other facts that now bored her.

Dr. Summerville put the notebook away and took out a stack of photographs. "I want you to tell me who these people are. If you don't know a name but the face looks familiar, say so." He hesitated. "Do you know what a placebo is?"

Placebo? Placebo. She could almost feel her brain searching through the maze that was her mind, scrambling for the answer. It suddenly popped out. "It's a fake pill that you give to someone. If it works, it's all in their mind."

He smiled broadly. "Exactly. You must have had an excellent

education. Most people wouldn't know that word unless they'd been to college.''

College. The thought pleased her immensely. Lucky knew Greg had a doctorate, and she wanted to have something in common with him. Too often she floundered, embarrassed, feeling like a mental bantamweight.

''Some of these photos are like placebos. They're pictures of people you couldn't possibly know. We do this to make the test scientifically valid.'' He spread a series of photographs across the coffee table. ''Take your time. Study them carefully. Do you know any of these people?''

She picked up one immediately. ''This is Dr. Hamalae. He treated me when I was brought to the clinic here. He's a really nice man.''

''What about the others?''

She reached for the one of a pretty young woman with clear blue eyes and dark blond hair. ''She looks very familiar, but I don't remember her name. It's on the tip of my tongue, but—'' she halted mid-sentence, realizing what she was saying. ''This has happened to me before. I'm positive I know this person, but I won't be able to tell you her name.''

''Why not?''

''It's like my own name. It's there, but it won't come out no matter how hard I try.''

''Don't worry about it,'' Dr. Summerville said, removing the photo. ''That's typical of Hoyt-Mellenberger.''

''It is?'' For the first time, she almost liked the man. ''I'm not alone?''

''No. Most Hoyt-Mellenberger victims recognize famous faces but often can't put names with them,'' he replied, and she began to feel better. There was a reason certain faces looked familiar. ''That's Diana, Princess of Wales.''

''I know her. She's married to UpChuck—or was. British royalty, right?''

''UpChuck?'' Dr. Summerville laughed. ''Prince Charles? That's a new one, but you're correct.''

"Why would I know his nickname and not recognize her?"

"If you said UpChuck often enough, you'd know it by heart, like memorizing multiplication tables. The key is in the repetition."

"Then why can't I remember my name?"

It was a question that kept nagging at her, recurring with irritating frequency, leaving her frustrated. And angry. There was a wellspring of anger that seemed to build with each passing day. Lucky managed to keep it under control but it was there nevertheless, threatening to explode.

"Not remembering your name makes your case unique. I have absolutely no explanation."

She silently blessed him for not spouting the prostitute-who-used-many-names theory, or the second favorite, the criminal with an alias for every week.

They went through the stack of photos, and Lucky recognized Greg and Nomo but failed to identify a series of famous people, including the president and Elvis.

"Why can't I recognize their faces if I know who they are when you tell me?" she asked.

"Don't worry. It's consistent with Hoyt-Mellenberger. You probably wouldn't know your own mother. She would just look 'familiar.'"

Lucky doubted that she wanted to know her own mother but didn't say so.

"The brain stores information about people in two places. You've heard things, which are stored in one area, and you've read things, which are stored in a completely different place in the brain. With pictures, you're just seeing without any verbal clues. That isn't enough when you have HM."

Lucky liked the doctor better by the minute. He was explaining why so much seemed familiar yet she couldn't always identify it. And it was good to know she wasn't alone. She didn't want to be a freak; she wanted to be like other people.

"You're very fortunate to have retained *any* ability at all to combine the visual image with the stored information."

"What are you talking about?"

"Didn't anyone tell you many Hoyt-Mellenberger patients 'mask'? That means they can't *ever* remember a face—just as if the people around them were wearing masks. Every time you would see me, I would have to say my name. You wouldn't recognize me. Once I told you who I was, you'd remember all about me. But you would have lost the ability to link the visual with the stored information."

Lucky twirled the sugarcane swizzle stick through her iced tea, thinking how very "lucky" she was. What if she couldn't recognize Greg's face and had to have him tell her over and over who he was? How humiliating. There were so many things she hated about her life, feeling as if she had nothing but dignity and pride to shore her up, yet she had much to be thankful for.

She wanted to relearn as much as she could as quickly as possible—to make Greg proud of her. "How long will it take me to relearn the faces of the people I should know, like the president?"

"Learning is dependent on two factors—your intelligence and your interest." He smiled reassuringly. "A man can often tell you the names of every player on a team, while a woman will remember exactly what dress she wore on a date a dozen years earlier."

"You learn what's important to you."

"Precisely. How fast you learn it—meaning how many exposures it takes—depends on your intelligence. In your case, I would guess that you're very intelligent. It'll take two, maybe three exposures to a face, then it will be in your memory bank again. Your relearning time will be minimal."

Lucky rose and strode to the balcony that overlooked the beach. "You don't know what I would give to know my own name. I could go to jail for stealing that car if I can't tell them who I am and why I was driving a stolen vehicle."

* * *

Cody stood in the parking lot outside his office waiting for the FBI agent. Scott Helmer had flown in last night—incognito—and had insisted that they meet outside the building. It was total bullshit, Cody thought, but he went along with it. After all, the Feebies had charisma. It would make a good story to tell the kids in years to come.

"Chief Braxton?"

He turned and found a young punk with dark hair that was close cropped over his ears yet stood straight up across the top of his scalp. He sported a skull and crossbones earring and had a three day beard like a rock star high on a controlled substance.

Cody was about to read him his rights when the punk pulled a Feebie ID out of his wallet. FBI. Christ! Where were his tax dollars going?

"Let's walk this way," the kid said. "I'm Scott Helmer, field agent with the bureau. This is about the unidentified white female whose exhumed remains you sent to our facility in Quantico. We've IDed her."

"Really?" Cody couldn't help being impressed. It had only been a few days. His months of correspondence to police departments nationwide had yielded zilch. "Who is she?"

Helmer stopped under the twin palms guarding the lot, casting slender shadows across the pavement. Heat was rapidly building, even though the morning had hardly begun. "This is confidential—understood?"

It pissed him off to listen to an arrogant kid, but he kept thinking about his brother and how he'd had his arm around Lucky when the shark swam to freedom. Cody would do anything to end this case—now. And get rid of Lucky before it was too late. He didn't want Greg to be hurt again.

"Right. Not one word to anyone."

"Good," Helmer replied. "We're meeting out here until I can sweep your office for bugs—"

"Bugs? Are you kidding?"

Something lethal in Helmer's eyes told him that here was a young but world-weary bastard who just might have seen more of life's dark side than Cody could ever imagine.

"This is serious business. The woman you found was Thelma Overholt, a special investigator for American Express. She was assigned to the unit investigating credit card fraud. Counterfeit cards sting companies for millions each year, but one group's gotten incredibly sophisticated.

"They're able to access the computer records of banks, issue credit cards—even the hard-to-reproduce ones with holograms and photographs of the cardholder. They hit the bank for millions, yet know when they've been discovered and get out. They operate with kick-ass speed, firing phony credit cards around the world overnight. No one's been able to figure out how they're doing it."

Cody had heard of the scam. It was a big problem on the mainland but a minor one in Hawaii. "Is there trouble here?"

Helmer's eyes scanned the lot, stopping for a second on each vehicle, missing nothing. A chill of apprehension waltzed up Cody's spine. The kid was a dozen years younger, sure, but a seasoned pro.

"There hasn't been any problem here. That's why Thelma wasn't identified. She disappeared halfway across the world—in Singapore. That's the golden Mecca of counterfeiting. Used to be jewelry and watches; now it's credit cards and computer chips."

"What was she doing hiking here?"

"Her family said Thelma never hiked. She disappeared without a trace from Singapore. No record of an airline ticket. Her passport was never scanned, showing she left Singapore."

"So? Someone screwed up."

"No way. Remember that kid who got paddled for graffiti? The Singapore government wouldn't back down. They're like real tight asses with crack security. If her passport wasn't scanned, how'd she get out of the country?"

"Beats me," Cody said, though personally he thought some-one could have been bribed. "Was the death accidental?"

As ugly as it was, some small part of Cody wanted to hear the worst. Then he could tie Lucky to a murder. It might be the only way to break the hold she had on his brother.

"Forensics in Quantico will get back to us on the cause of death, but I'm betting it's a homicide. I think that Jane Doe with the missing shoe is the key."

Cody hesitated, measuring Helmer for a moment. "I have a theory."

He leveled his watchful eyes on Cody. "Shoot."

"Lucky—that's what we're calling the Jane Doe—was found on the back side of the island during the worst storm to hit here, short of a hurricane, in decades. I think she was up in one of those shacks that are hidden away in the jungle. She had a fight with her boyfriend, got dressed in a helluva hurry, and didn't notice she had on the wrong shoe. She headed out in the storm and accidentally drove off a cliff."

"It's a possibility," the punk conceded.

"I'm guessing that this boyfriend belongs to the *hui*. You've heard of the Hawaiian mafia?" Cody asked, and Helmer nod-ded. "They're somehow part of this counterfeiting ring."

Helmer nodded, slowly warming to the idea. "They could have kidnapped the investigator and held her at the remote location you're talking about, trying to make her tell them her sources or something. They killed her and dumped her body in the brush."

Cody considered this for a second. "It's quite a climb from the closest road to the point where she was found. It would have taken two of them to carry her."

"The area's full of hikers, right?" Helmer asked, and Cody nodded. "Then they had her wrapped in a tarp or something. And they had to get rid of the body quickly before someone happened along and caught them."

"The shoe must have been lost back at their hideout," Cody

said, on a roll now. "Someone tossed it in the closet, thinking it was Lucky's."

Helmer looked skeptical, the sunlight flashing off his skull and crossbones earring. "That hiker, Thelma Overholt, died more than a year ago. Do you really think the shoe sat in— what's her name?—Lucky's closet all that time without her noticing it and throwing it out or something?"

"Sure. Some of those places back in the jungle barely have running water. They use cisterns and septic tanks. It's pretty primitive. People don't live there year-round except for a few artists and writers."

"Probably smugglers who're stealing exotic parrots and dopers running Maui Wowie are using those hideouts, right?"

"Exactly. They don't keep much in those shacks. A couple of changes of clothes, canned food . . . that's about it. Lucky didn't pay any attention to that shoe until the night she mistakenly put it on."

"You're probably right," the punk grudgingly admitted.

Cody banked a smile, positive he'd figured out how Lucky had come to be wearing a shoe that belonged to a woman who'd died a year earlier. "I say Lucky's involved with someone in the *hui*. That's why he hasn't come forward to identify her. He'd have to explain what he was doing in the jungle."

"Could be," Helmer conceded. "One of the *hui*'s leaders is Tony Traylor."

"I knew it!" Cody slapped his head with the heel of his hand. "Traylor's been way, way too interested in this case. How much do you want to bet Lucky is his girlfriend?"

Chapter 18

"Well, you got your wish."

The heavy dose of sarcasm in Rachel's voice echoed across the pool, where several volunteers were tending the orphaned seal pups. Everyone looked at Greg's research partner. Lucky glanced at Nomo, who had just driven her back from her session with Dr. Summerville. Until this moment she'd felt happier, understanding more about what was wrong with her, than she had since the accident.

"1475 has been spotted," Rachel announced.

Lucky couldn't help smiling, even though Rachel was clearly angry with her. "Rudy's still alive? That's fabulous!"

Rachel's stare drilled into Lucky and she stiffened, aware yet again of how much the woman disliked her. "He chewed through the wire netting at Takanaga's and ate several *opakapaka*."

"*Opakapaka*—fish," Nomo explained, moving closer to Lucky. "Takanaga runs a fish farm."

Farm? Lucky saw fields of corn or sugar cane. She'd have

to ask Nomo later. "Good for Rudy. He must be feeling better. He's hunting again. We couldn't get him to eat anything."

"You're missing the point," Rachel said, her voice as contemptuous as her expression. "The institute depends on the goodwill of these farmers. They supply us with surplus fish at no cost. They're furious because we freed a worthless shark—"

"Rudy was only doing what his instincts told him," interrupted Lucky. "And sharks aren't worthless. They have superior immune systems. They don't get cancer. Scientists are studying them, hoping to find a cure for AIDS. I saw it on the Internet."

Rachel pivoted and walked away, leaving Lucky staring at the back of her khaki blouse. The woman had been so hostile after Rudy had been freed that Lucky rarely ventured upstairs to the office when Rachel was around.

"I didn't mean to cause trouble." She turned to Nomo, saddened by his concerned expression. He was a good friend who always tried to help and never made her feel foolish when she didn't know something.

Nomo led her to a side entrance, where trucks were offloading the day's supply of fresh fish. "You didn't cause the trouble. It was already here. Rachel just didn't want to see it."

"See what?"

Nomo regarded her solemnly, which was unusual because he smiled most of the time. "Greg is never going to love Rachel. She's been patiently waiting since Jessica's death. Rachel came back to the institute just as you freed Rudy. I saw her standing there, watching you and Greg."

"There wasn't anything to see," Lucky said, but she didn't meet Nomo's steady gaze. Something had happened with Greg that day, yet she wasn't certain just what it was. Since then Greg had been gentler with her, more understanding. And he hadn't once mentioned sex or done anything to press her.

"Get outta here. Do you really believe nothing happened?" Nomo asked. "Or are you just saying it because you're uncomfortable discussing this? I can't help you if you don't level with me."

No wonder Nomo was so popular with the volunteers. The older man always seemed to understand each person's problems. "Greg is so special to me . . . I can't begin to tell you how special. I guess people must assume that we're"—Lucky paused, searching for the right word—"having an affair because I'm living with him, but we're not."

If Nomo was surprised by this revelation, he didn't show it, waiting, without judging, for her to continue.

"I don't want to be a cheap hooker, and I don't want to be Pele's ghost. I want to be someone worthy of Greg's respect," she confessed. "Someone like Rachel Convey. Then Greg will—"

"Will what?"

"Care about me . . . truly care about me." She couldn't bring herself to say the word *love,* but Lucky suspected Nomo knew exactly what she was thinking.

"He cares," Nomo said quietly. "Normally, he's up in his office this time of year, compiling research on the whales, getting ready for them to return in the winter. He leaves the seals to the volunteers, but since you've come, he's down here all the time." Nomo offered her his trademark smile, all teeth in a broad, happy face. "And he's not checking on the seals."

"I'd like to believe I'm special to him," Lucky admitted, thinking Greg's sense of duty and their physical attraction accounted for any change in his usual behavior.

"You're special," Nomo assured her. "You don't believe it, that's all. *Lokahi*—spirit. You need to get in touch with your inner spirit again. It'll take time, that's all."

They were walking toward the seal nursery now. A newborn pup had been brought in by a dive boat that morning, and they were going to check on it.

"What was Greg like when you first met him?" Lucky asked, remembering being told that Nomo had already been at the institute for a number of years when Greg had first arrived there.

"Greg had a huge chip on his shoulder back then. And no wonder. His aunt was *lolo*—crazy. She never should have been given custody of those boys. Sis Braxton was a compulsive gambler. Nothing else was important in her life. If those boys opened their mouths, she beat the tar out of them."

"Didn't anyone do anything?"

"We tried to get the boys away from her, but Sis wouldn't give them up." Nomo threw up his hands. "Why? Nobody knew. She never even pretended to want them. She was *lolo*, that's all."

"But they turned out fine. They're both—"

"Damaged," Nomo interjected. "Don't think they're not. When people don't get the love they need as children, they're screwed up as adults, unable to love or accept love. Cody's done better because Sarah has helped him. Greg wasn't so wise in choosing Jessica."

"What was wrong with her?" Lucky asked, remembering Sarah calling the woman a bitch.

Nomo shrugged. "Chronic depression they said, but she seemed like a crazy-maker to me. She was always upset about something. Little things were a big crisis. And she was jealous of anything that took Greg away from her, like the Marine Research Institute or Search and Rescue. Even his brother was a threat."

What was wrong with sharing Greg? Lucky wondered. She would be thrilled to be part of Sarah's family and have relatives who cared about her. Sharing was part of being a family.

Nomo stopped and studied her for a minute, his expression dead serious. "Greg needs you, Lucky. You can make all the difference in his life."

Before Lucky could reply, Greg came racing across the pool area, responding to someone shouting from the nursery. She followed them inside and saw a tiny seal, not more than twenty-four hours old, being cradled in a volunteer's arms.

"I can't get her to suck." The girl brought a baby bottle to the seal's lips, but it turned away. "I've been trying my whole shift, but she refuses to touch the bottle."

"She's in pretty bad shape," Greg said. "If she doesn't eat, she'll die."

"Let me hold her," Lucky offered, and the girl gladly handed her the baby seal.

The pup was the size of a football and couldn't weigh much more. Lucky had never felt anything so soft. Its fur was the color of warm sand, and felt like the nap of fine velvet. The little face gazing up at her had a black button nose and a spray of whiskers like a kitten.

The pup's eyes made Lucky's heart turn over in response. Wide. Unblinking. The color of melted chocolate. Those soulful eyes assessed her, and a shudder passed through the tiny body. Obviously, the seal was terrified of yet another person touching her. A terrifying procession of humans with different faces and different smells must have passed her around since her mother had disappeared. The little creature mewled, a plaintive, broken-hearted sound, as if to say, "You're not my mommy."

"Why don't you give her a name?" Greg asked.

"Abigail," Lucky responded without hesitation, smiling down at the pup, cuddling it but at a loss as to how to help. "It's a big name for such a little mite of a thing, but you'll grow into it."

"Not if she doesn't eat."

"What happened to Abbie's mother?"

Greg frowned, his eyes drawn level beneath dark brows. "A shark ate her. Seals are weak after giving birth and become easy prey for sharks. Usually sharks get the pups, too, but this time a dive boat picked up Abbie."

A suffocating sensation tightened Lucky's throat as she remembered Rudy's razor-sharp teeth. Still, she couldn't imagine her Rudy ripping into a seal. "It wasn't Rudy, little one. It was a *bad* shark."

Greg put his hand on Lucky's shoulder, shaking his head.

"It's Mother Nature at work. Sharks are the ocean's predators. Monk seals like Abbie are endangered, and their biggest enemy is the shark. There's nothing we can do about it."

Lucky gazed down at the little face, the woeful eyes seeming to plead for its mother. But Abbie's mother was dead, and nothing Lucky could do would bring back this baby's mother. With the pad of her thumb, she caressed Abbie's pink belly, circling the stub of the still-soft umbilical cord. The pup let out an exhausted little rush of air that sounded like a sigh, and its lids drooped.

Lucky whispered to Greg, "Maybe she doesn't like the rubber nipple on this bottle."

"We've already tried giving her formula on a sugarcane stick," Nomo called from across the room.

"What about my finger?" Lucky wiggled her pinkie at him.

"Anything's worth a try," Greg said, but he didn't sound encouraged.

Lucky sat at the table with Abbie in her arms while Greg poured the contents of the bottle into a pan. The liquid was warm when Lucky dipped her finger into it. Gently, she touched it to the pup's mouth. Abbie turned her head away, as if to say, "Forget it. You are not my mommy."

"If you don't suck, you're not going to grow into a seal big enough to play with Harpo."

Greg gazed at her as if she'd lost her last marble, then he chuckled. They both laughed, imagining Harpo, a mammoth male, with the tiny creature in Lucky's arms. The unexpected laughter caused Abbie to look around, craning her little neck and opening her mouth. Lucky edged her finger inside.

Abbie gazed up at her with a startled expression. Her little pink petal of a tongue gave a quick, tentative brush. Once. Twice. Lucky was positive she'd never felt anything so soft. So heart-wrenchingly sweet.

"That's my girl. Now try sucking."

She dipped her finger in the formula again and again. A few minutes later, Abbie began to suck and Lucky brought her up closer, cuddling her, giving her warmth. And wishing with all her heart she could bring back Abbie's mother.

"Some people have a natural talent for relating to animals, don't they, Greg?" said Nomo with a broad grin.

Lucky ventured a look into Greg's deep blue eyes, thoroughly pleased with herself.

Greg's expression seemed to mingle pride and tenderness as he put his hand on her arm and gently squeezed. "You're a natural, all right. Some people just have the gift."

She smiled at him, blissfully happy. This was how she wanted to feel about herself ... how she wanted Greg to feel about her. Special. "I like working with animals." Lucky wanted to say how much she enjoyed working with him, but she didn't want to break the spell.

Greg leaned closer, his hand still on her arm. "We're going out to the rookery next week. If you want to come, you can see where Abbie was born."

"I'd love to come." I love being with you, being a part of your life, she silently added.

"There you are!" Rachel was standing at the nursery door. "Greg, I need to talk to you."

The tone of Rachel's voice could have turned the sand to tundra. And the look on her face as she stared at Lucky held nothing but contempt. Greg casually rose, seemingly not bothered by the woman's tone. He left the nursery without another word, and Nomo rolled his eyeballs heavenward.

It took Lucky over two hours to convince the stubborn little Abigail that a bottle was as good as her pinkie, but finally the pup took the bottle. She sucked it dry, then bleated, a whiny sound that caused Nomo to laugh and to assure Lucky that one day the noise would be a full-throated seal's bark.

For the second time since the accident, Lucky experienced a sense of elation she knew was pride. She'd been thrilled when she'd seen Rudy swim away, but somehow this was even more exciting. There was something about a baby, a creature so small and helpless, that tugged at her heart.

A volunteer stuck his head into the nursery and said Greg wanted to see Lucky. She protested, reluctant to leave Abbie, who was dozing between feedings.

"I'll get someone to take over," Nomo told her as he picked up Abbie. "You've been at this too long anyway. I don't want the pup to bond with you and refuse to let anyone else feed her. That happens if we're not careful."

Lucky ascended the stairs to Greg's office, smelling like goat's milk. She had a damp spot on the front of her skirt where Abbie had started to pee before Lucky could get a towel under her. She certainly didn't look like anyone special, but she felt . . . well, almost important.

Since the accident she hadn't a clue what to pray for, in which direction to focus. Each day a new, and usually ugly, revelation about herself came to light, knocking her down again and again. But when she'd set Rudy free, something inside her had gained strength. The future was still bleak, but now she had the courage to face it.

The minute she walked into Greg's office, Lucky sensed something was different. It took a few seconds for it to register. The diplomas and awards hanging at Rachel's workstation were gone, her desk clean. *Oh, no, now what have I done?* Lucky wondered as Dodger trotted up to greet her.

"I'm going to need some help up here," Greg said, his gaze steady.

"Where's Rachel?"

"She had a better job offer back on the mainland."

"She's gone, just like that, without saying goodbye to Nomo or any of the volunteers?"

"I don't think she was that close to anyone."

Except you. And I drove her away when she was the one with the expertise to help you. The familiar heaviness, centered in her chest, returned. Just moments ago she'd been applauding her fortitude, feeling better about herself. *Why did she have to cause Greg so much trouble?*

* * *

Greg could see that Rachel's departure upset Lucky, but it didn't bother him. Lately Rachel had become so prickly and sullen. He had found her increasingly difficult to deal with. Lucky was entirely different. Despite all that had happened to her, Lucky was so full of life and warmth and genuine happiness that he couldn't help responding, feeling more upbeat than he had in years.

"I need you to go through these requisition forms, log them in here." Greg pointed to the black notebook.

"Why don't you just enter it in the computer?"

"I haven't had time to set up a program yet."

Lucky smiled, that adorable, pleased-with-herself grin. "I'll get one going."

Greg started to protest that it would take too long, that things had backed up while he'd been on the mainland with Dodger, but he decided that they could wait. With a new system going, things would be much easier in the future. He had stopped being surprised at Lucky's expertise with the computer. If she could wail on the Web, she could set up a simple program for the institute.

"Let me check something first," she said, switching on the computer.

Her full lower lip was caught between her teeth, the way it always was when she concentrated. It was all he could do not to kiss her. Each time he was with her, the pull was stronger. She was more tempting than Eve in the Garden of Eden. It had taken days, but he'd become accustomed to it. He'd given up fighting, focusing instead on concealing his reaction.

His response to her was no longer merely sexual attraction— if it had ever been that simple—but an emotion much more powerful. What he'd seen with the shark she called Rudy reminded Greg of himself.

Greg had been thirteen when he'd come to the institute. A judge had ordered him to do community service rather than go to the correctional facility that provided workers for the cane fields, which was nothing more than cheap labor. At the institute, he'd met Nomo and a group of sea creatures who had needed him, relied on him. Their plight had given him a sense of purpose.

He wanted to give Lucky what she deserved—a second chance at life. Carrying her up the face of the steep *pali* had been only the beginning, Greg realized now. What she needed was direction, purpose. And she'd found it on her own, with little guidance from him.

In a way he resented her independence, wanting her to rely more on him. It annoyed him when the male volunteers were too quick to help Lucky. Greg found Sarah's helpfulness irritating as well, and he was ashamed to say that he even found Nomo's paternal interest troubling. He needed to back off and he knew it.

So what did he do? The minute Rachel had announced her departure, he decided to move Lucky into the office.

"Okay, I'm ready to get started," Lucky said, breaking into his thoughts.

He tried to concentrate on organizing the data on the humpback whale that Rachel had dumped on his desk shortly after announcing she was leaving. It took the better part of an hour to categorize the information so he could study it later. The phone on his desk rang and he answered it, noticing Lucky was hard at work, with Dodger snoozing at her feet.

"I found out something interesting."

It was Cody, and the sound of his voice failed to bring the usual rush of anger. Since he'd discovered the scars on the soles of Lucky's feet, Greg had remembered how close he'd been to his brother. It had become impossible to muster the hostility that had hovered over him like a dark shadow since the night of the accident.

"Okay, shoot," Greg said, sounding ridiculously happy and liking the feel of it. Really liking it.

Two beats of silence. Greg wondered if he'd taken Cody by

surprise. When he'd mouthed *I owe you one,* it had been obvious from Cody's expression that he had been shocked. The two brothers hadn't had a chance to talk since then.

"Dr. Carlton Summerville is a real doctor," Cody told him, "but he's not with the Wakefield Institute."

Chapter 19

How could going out for dinner feel so much like a date? Greg asked himself as he helped Lucky out of the car at Carelli's Restaurant. For Christ's sake, Lucky had been living with him for almost two weeks. But when he'd asked her to come with him to meet old friends who were vacationing here, he'd felt strange. It had been years since he'd been out on a date. Picking up female tourists, then hopping in the sack, didn't count. "You're going to like it here," he told Lucky as they walked into the seaside bistro. "Great Italian food. Fantastic view of the ocean at sunset."

Lucky didn't say anything, but her excitement showed in her eyes, which looked larger than ever. And greener. She wore a lavender dress with a conservative scoop neckline, which Sarah had bought for Lucky's court appearance. Concealing rather than exposing her soft curves, it made her appear even more alluring.

She wasn't wearing any makeup or jewelry, which would have made most women look plain. Not Lucky. She'd spent enough time in the sun to have a healthy tan, which comple-

mented her natural-looking hairdo. There was something graceful yet determined about the way she moved, reminding him
of a woman who would be at home on the tennis court or on
the back of a horse. His type of woman.

Carelli's was an open-air restaurant shaped like a wedge,
with a narrow entrance that fanned out, giving every table a
spectacular view of the ocean. A languid tropical breeze filtered
through the dining room, ruffling the ferns lining the walls,
while soft music crooned from hidden speakers. Greg put his
hand on Lucky's arm and guided her through the crowded
room.

It was early, but the place was already full of diners who
wanted to watch the sunset. The steady hum of conversation
dropped as they walked by. The women's eyes narrowed, while
the men tracked Lucky as she passed. She missed the sensation
she was causing and gazed at Greg with an expectant, eager-
to-please expression that touched him.

Alan Dunbar spotted them and stood up. A tall man with
thinning coppery hair and intelligent eyes, he motioned them
to a prime table at the front of the restaurant, just a few feet
from the beach. Greg introduced Lucky to Alan and his wife,
Carol, a chunky blonde with a sunburned nose. The Dunbars,
already on their third Mai Tai, didn't seem to notice that he
hadn't mentioned Lucky's last name. Greg smoothed over the
moment by ordering another round of drinks.

"Look at that sunset," Carol said. "There's absolutely nothing like it in Texas."

As far as the eye could see, there was an eternity of blue
sky and even bluer sea. A red-footed booby, its wings tipped
with gold by the setting sun, perched on a boulder at the edge
of the sweeping white sand beach, preening its feathers. Even
Greg, who hated sentimental BS, had to admit there was something romantic about being with a woman you cared about and
watching the sun set.

In a flare of Aztec gold burnished with crimson, the sun
disappeared into the indigo sea. Lucky stared, mesmerized,

IF YOU LOVE READING MORE OF TODAY'S BESTSELLING HISTORICAL ROMANCES.... WE HAVE AN OFFER FOR YOU!

*L*ook inside to see how you can get 4 free historical romances by today's leading romance authors!

4 BOOKS WORTH UP TO $23.96, ABSOLUTELY FREE!

4 BESTSELLING HISTORICAL ROMANCES BY YOUR FAVORITE AUTHORS CAN BE YOURS, FREE!

Kensington Choice, our newest book club now brings you historical romances by your favorite bestselling authors including Janelle Taylor, Shannon Drake, Rosanne Bittner, Jo Beverley, and Georgina Gentry, just to name a few! Each book is filled with passion, adventure and the excitement of bygone times!

To introduce you to this great new club which is part of Zebra Home Subscription Service, we'd like to send you your first 4 bestselling historical romances, absolutely free!   And once you get these 4 free books to savor at home, we'll rush you the next 4 brand-new books at the lowest prices available, as soon as they are published.

The way the club works is that after your initial FREE shipment, you will get our 4 newest bestselling historical romances delivered to your doorstep each month at the preferred subscriber's rate of only $4.20 per book, a savings of up to $7.16 per month (since these titles sell in bookstores for $4.99-$5.99)! All books are sent on a 10-day free examination basis and there is no minimum number of books to buy. (And no charge for shipping.) Plus as a regular subscriber, you'll receive our FREE monthly newsletter, *Zebra/Pinnacle Romance News*, which features author profiles, contests, subscriber benefits, book previews and more!

So start today by returning the FREE BOOK CERTIFICATE provided. We'll send you 4 FREE BOOKS with no further obligation: A FREE gift offering you hours of reading pleasure with no obligation...how can you lose?

We have 4 FREE BOOKS for you
as your introduction to
KENSINGTON CHOICE!
To get your FREE BOOKS, worth
up to $23.96, mail the card below.

FREE BOOK CERTIFICATE

Yes! Please send me 4 Kensington Choice (the best of Zebra and Pinnacle Books) Historical Romances without cost or obligation (worth up to $23.96). As a Kensington Choice subscriber, I will then receive 4 brand-new romances to preview each month for 10 days FREE. I can return any books I decide not to keep and owe nothing. The publisher's prices for Kensington Choice romances range from $4.99-$5.99, but as a preferred subscriber I will get these books for only $4.20 per book or $16.80 for all four titles. There is no minimum number of books to buy and I may cancel my subscription at any time, plus there is no additional charge for postage and handling. No matter what I decide to do, my first 4 books are mine to keep, absolutely FREE!

KF0197

Name _____

Address _____ Apt._____

City_____ State_____ Zip_____

Telephone (_____) _____

Signature _____

(If under 18, parent or guardian must sign)

Subscription subject to acceptance. Terms and prices subject to change.

4 FREE
Historical
Romances

*are waiting
for you to
claim them!*

—◆◆◆—

(worth up to
$23.96)

—◆◆◆—

*See details
inside....*

AFFIX
STAMP
HERE

KENSINGTON CHOICE
Zebra Home Subscription Service, Inc.
120 Brighton Road
P.O.Box 5214
Clifton, NJ 07015-5214

||...|..|..|||....||....||.|.|..|.|..|.|..|..|||.|..|||....|

sucking in her breath with a little sigh. Then she turned to
Greg, gazing into his eyes with an intimacy he found exciting.
Unspoken feelings eddied between them, and he desperately
wished they were alone.

"That's why we vacation here every year," Carol informed
Lucky, breaking the spell of the moment. "You can't beat the
sunsets here."

"Don't let her kid you," Alan said with a wink at Greg.
"We vacation here as a compromise. Carol likes to sit on the
beach and read. I spend the day up in the rain forest."

Greg watched Lucky as she listened intently while Alan told
her about his hobby. Hawaii had hundreds of plants and animals
found nowhere else on earth. The remote archipelago was home
to more than a third of the birds and plants on the endangered
species list. And Alan could tell you about every one. For
hours.

As the waiter was serving their drinks and the sky was
deepening into a dark plum twilight, Greg looked across the
room and noticed Tony Traylor. He was staring with blatant
interest at Lucky. Greg despised the fat son of a bitch. As head
of the joint council, Traylor pretended to be interested in the
working man and the preservation of Hawaii for Hawaiians.
What a crock!

Traylor's real interest was in his pockets. Greg had gone
head-to-head with him over the polluted runoff from the sugarcane field poisoning the offshore reefs. Traylor had sided with
the big-money sugar interests, so the pollution continued, worse
than ever.

"Today we spotted an *'apapane,'*" Alan told them. "That's
a red honeycreeper with a curved beak. He used it to get nectar
out of blossoms like a hummingbird."

"Really?" Greg said, keeping Traylor in his peripheral
vision. "There are damn few of them around these days." He
scooted his chair closer to Lucky. "Only a handful still exist."

"Like the O'o," Lucky said.

"Right!" Alan replied obviously thrilled to find Lucky

shared his interest. Great. Now they were in for it. They wouldn't be able to get Alan off the subject. "You saw an O'o?"

Lucky shook her head, jiggling the dark curls clustered around her face. "No. I wish I had. I heard one, though. Sarah told me about them."

Carol rolled her eyeballs at Greg as if to say, "Here we go again." Greg had known the Dunbars since his days at MIT. The high school sweethearts had married the day after graduation, and they were still in love all these years later, even though they shared few mutual interests. Their successful marriage had made him believe that he and Jessica could have the same type of relationship. How wrong he'd been.

Alan launched into a lecture on Hawaii's vanishing species, and Greg shifted his position slightly to get a better look at Tony Traylor. The cocky little prick was at a table surrounded by *mokes* who lived to act tough. Beside him was a blonde with bleached hair that hung over her shoulders, emphasizing a bust that probably was featured in some plastic surgeon's brochure. Personally, he preferred original equipment. He stole a quick peek at what little could be seen of Lucky's cleavage.

When he looked up, he saw Traylor was eyeing Lucky again. He told himself most of the men were sneaking peeks at her, but Traylor was different. He made no attempt to hide his interest. People didn't recognize Lucky as Pele's ghost. With her hair short and dyed a warm brown, she looked like a different person. But Traylor was studying her intently, and Greg wondered if Cody had told him about Lucky's new look.

Greg watched Traylor put both hands on the table and lever his considerable bulk into a standing position. He lumbered across the crowded restaurant with a bully's attitude and a swagger to match, heading in their direction.

"I'll be right back," Greg said, slipping away from the group that was now listening to the fascinating details of the mating habits of ground nesting birds.

"Braxton, what the fuck are you doing?" Traylor asked when Greg blocked his way.

"Keeping you from bothering my guests." He grabbed Traylor's beefy arm.

"Let go of me, asshole. I want to talk to the bitch who stole my car."

Greg tightened his grip. "Go near her and I'll beat the shit out of you."

"Who gives a flying fuck!" Traylor sneered, his pocked face insolent in the afterglow of the setting sun. "My boys—"

Greg got right in his face, his nose an inch from Traylor's. "I'll have your jaw split in half and your nose planted behind your ears before either of those *mokes* looks up from their beer to see you need help."

The color leached from Traylor's face, then rushed back so quickly that his eyeballs bulged. The bully to end all bullies, Traylor wasn't used to anyone challenging him. He yanked his arm away. "Fuck you, Braxton. You're gonna regret pissing me off."

Greg had no doubt that he would. Traylor was the vengeful type all right, carrying a grudge like Khomeini. But at least he wouldn't upset Lucky tonight.

Back at the table, Greg eased into his seat and took a sip of his drink while he listened to the conversation. They'd progressed to the devastation mongooses had caused by preying on ground nesting birds, almost wiping out entire species. Lucky looked so happy, so animated. Damn, she was sexy.

"You're a—?" she asked Alan, searching for the right word.

"I'm an entomologist."

Greg felt Lucky's hand on his knee and knew she had no idea what that was. He opened his mouth to relieve the pressure, but Carol beat him to it.

"Bugs," Carol said with a laugh. "Alan studies bugs. There are millions to be made in mosquitoes, you know. Billions in killer bees."

"Mosquitoes?" Lucky was puzzled. "Killer bees?"

"Alan works for a research firm in Texas that's producing environmentally safe products to keep mosquitoes and other pests under control."

Lucky nodded at Greg's information, her expressive eyes wide, and Alan was obviously pleased. Few people were impressed with his chosen profession; even Greg found insects boring, but then Alan probably found whale research a major snoozer.

Greg tried to link his fingers through Lucky's but discovered she was clutching Rudy's tooth. Why? he asked himself. Obviously, she had a psychic connection with that damn shark. He glanced up and caught Traylor staring at Lucky again.

"Alan's dying, simply dying, to find his *very* own bug," Carol said, and it was obvious she was getting a little tipsy, so Greg signaled to the waiter that they were ready to order. "That's what he's really doing tromping around the bush, not just ogling birds and going gaga over ferns."

"I don't quite understand," Lucky said tentatively. He could tell she didn't like not knowing things, even something like this that was more of an in-joke.

"If Alan discovers an insect that has never before been cataloged, then it'll be named after him," Greg explained. "Diseases are often named in just the same way." He looked into Lucky's eyes, trying to send a silent message. "If two people find something new, then it's named after both of them." He could see by the shadow flickering across her eyes that Lucky understood he meant Hoyt-Mellenberger syndrome.

"Dunbar's Cockroach. It has a ring to it, don't you think?" Carol giggled and Alan laughed, obviously accustomed to his wife's teasing.

"Greg, what about those two bugs they found in the hiker's hair? Maybe Alan could look at them."

"What bugs? What hiker?"

"Over a year ago, a hiker fell from a trail near the Iao Needle. There were two odd-looking bugs in her hair," Greg told Alan. "The coroner is with the Society to Preserve the

Hawaiian Wildlife Habitat, so he kept them, thinking they were from the rain forest.''

"Nobody recorded them? Where are they? How were they preserved?'' Alan fired one question after another at Greg.

"Nobody recorded them because a few scientists swore they'd already been recorded, but others disagreed.''

"Were the insects sent to the FBI lab along with the hiker's body?'' Lucky asked.

Greg was glad Cody had taken so much time to fill him in on all the details of the case, and he'd discussed them with Lucky. "No. They're at the society headquarters in Lahaina. Why don't you go over there tomorrow and check them out?''

Carol rolled her eyes, but Alan ignored her. "Good idea.''

The waiter gave them menus, and silence fell over the group. Greg saw Traylor and his entourage leaving. The beefy bully caught Greg's eye and paused. Behind Lucky's back, Greg raised his hand and gave Traylor the Italian salute.

"What's *opakapaka?*'' Lucky asked him.

"It's really good. A light pink snapper.'' He guessed by the look on her face she didn't remember what a snapper tasted like. If she'd ever had it.

"I'll try some. If it's good enough for Rudy, I'm sure I'll like it,'' she said, laughter kindling in her eyes.

They said good night to the Dunbars and decided to walk along the beach in front of the restaurant. A familiar shiver of awareness rippled through Lucky, a feeling she'd had most of the evening. She was enjoying Greg's closeness and the occasional jolt of his thigh as it brushed her hip, checking his stride to match hers, his arm around her waist. They'd left their shoes on the restaurant's steps and were walking barefoot along the surf.

Lucky inhaled deeply, thankful yet again that her sense of smell hadn't been destroyed along with her memory. There was nothing like a balmy tropical night, its air fragrant with the scent of the sea and the heavier, sweeter smell of plumeria. A lover's moon had risen slowly during dinner and was now at its zenith, casting light like a handful of silver coins on the water. Bright, scattered stars studded the dark sky doming overhead.

"Now we know why there are no vampires in Italy," Greg said.

Vampires? All that came to mind was a vague image of a black cloak and an incredible set of teeth.

"What's a vampire?" she felt free to ask him. So many questions had come to mind this evening but she'd restrained herself, not wanting to appear stupid in front of his friends. But Greg knew her the way no one else did and realized she had so much to relearn.

"Vampires are just a myth—a fairy tale."

"Like the girl with the hood?"

He chuckled. "Yeah. Like Little Red Riding Hood. In the islands we have stories about the *menehune,* the little people. They're like the leprechauns in Ireland."

Lucky stopped, the warm surf rushing over her toes, curling around them and then retreating, sucking the sand out from beneath her feet. "Ireland. I can visualize it. Near England, right? And they're always fighting?" she asked, and he nodded. "But I can't think what a mena-who looks like or a lepre-chaun."

"Men-ee-who-nee," he enunciated each syllable. "They're small . . . very small people."

A word hovered in her mind; it was a second before she remembered it. "Midgets."

"Smaller than that, actually. Hey, this is a fantasy. They don't exist except in people's minds, but there are lots of stories about them." Greg pointed to the vast expanse of dark water. "See the moonlight on the waves? According to legend, spar-kling water means the *menehunes* are dancing on it."

"How sweet," Lucky commented, but inside she was more than a little disturbed. Not only was there a real world she had to relearn, but a vast imaginary world as well. Was there no end to the things she'd forgotten? "Tell me about the vampire. I'm thinking big teeth here."

"I was trying to make a joke," he explained. "Vampires are supposed to be men with fangs. They pounce on unsuspecting women—usually late at night when they're sleeping—and suck blood from their necks."

"Oh, yuck!" She tried to imagine someone's teeth embedded in her neck but saw Rudy's teeth instead. Lucky hastily slipped her hand into her pocket and touched the shark's tooth. "What do vampires have to do with Italy?"

"Garlic protects you from vampires. You know about garlic?"

"Sure," she said without hesitation. "Every cook knows about garlic, but how does it protect you from vampires?"

"It's just a silly story." Greg seemed to be watching her intently, his gaze focused on her lips. "I was trying to make a joke. There are no vampire myths in Italy because they use so much garlic. It's supposed to ward off vampires. Tonight the pasta had enough garlic in it to kill a pack of vampires, but since we both had some, it doesn't matter if I kiss you."

He lowered his head and, too late, Lucky raised her hands to keep him from kissing her. Her palms hit his chest as his mouth closed over hers and his arms circled her waist. In an instant she was engulfed in heat. His or hers? She couldn't tell.

The warmth of his body was so male, so comforting. She arched against him, opening her mouth to accommodate him and accept the moist thrust of his tongue as it mated with hers. Beneath her hand, still pinned against his torso, his heart thundered. Lower, she felt the jutting hardness against the soft folds of her skirt. Oh, my, she thought. Anticipating.

Breaking the kiss, Greg whispered, "Pretend I'm a vampire."

Lucky recognized the teasing laughter in his voice and almost responded by giggling. Until his lips found the sensitive spot at the curve of her neck. She'd never felt anything quite like this. He nipped, a gentle tap of his teeth, and heat shot through her all the way to her toes, until they curled into the sand.

"There's some truth to this vampire stuff," she murmured.

He stopped kissing her neck and gazed down at her. Unable to help herself, Lucky reached up and unbuttoned his shirt. They were quite a ways from the restaurant now and it was dark except for the full moon, but she could see his tanned chest as she shoved the panels of his shirt aside, aware of him watching her every move.

She longed to put her lips on his bare skin, feel him stiffen, then respond as her lips blazed a trail across those taut muscles. Letting out her breath in a soft rush, Lucky allowed her fingertips to nudge through the springy hair and caress his raised nipples.

A surge of desire like a swift-rising tide, even more potent from all the times she'd resisted temptation, returned full force. Each encounter took more strength of will, wearing her down until they both knew it was only a matter of time.

Having allowed herself this much, she couldn't turn back. She explored the hard contours of his chest. One inch at a time. Returning again and again to those intriguing male nipples and the whisk of hair between them, savoring the virile masculinity of his body.

"Angel," he said, manacling her wandering hand at the wrist. "You want me. Why deny it?"

In her heart she knew he was right, but she refused to admit she was this weak, this easy. Yet she couldn't have pushed him away if her life depended on it. His hand closed over her breast, hot and ruthless like the flare of passion in his eyes.

"We can't keep our hands off each other. Why fight it?"

She didn't answer, but she didn't push his hand away either as his thumb found her taut nipple and caressed it through the thin fabric, making it throb. And beg for more. He lowered his head again, kissing her, pressing his lower body against hers. Hot and hard.

A burst of laughter from somewhere up the beach brought

Lucky to her senses. They were on a public beach, for heaven's sake! Some distant part of her brain told her that if she didn't stop right now, she wouldn't be able to stop. She pulled back, staring at him, trying to catch her breath and wondering what to say.

"Come on, angel. Let's go home and hop in bed."

"No," she mustered the strength to say. "I'm sleeping alone."

He went still, gazing at her with heavy-lidded eyes. "How many times do we have to go through this?"

"I want to be someone special." She tried to explain what she was feeling, but it wasn't coming out right. Working with Abbie today, Lucky had begun to regain some measure of self-esteem. But she wasn't quite there yet. She didn't want to slip back and become a woman who relied on sex to get what she wanted. "I keep seeing that face in the mirror. I don't want to be a tramp with blonde hair. I don't want to behave the way I did that night in the tent."

Greg didn't respond. Instead, he took his time and slowly buttoned his shirt. He was angry with her, and she couldn't blame him. She was angry with herself. This had been a perfect evening, her first date. The beginning of a new life. So what had she done? Ruined it.

He tucked in his shirt. "You are special. I just don't know what it's going to take to convince you."

"I feel better than I've felt . . . since the accident," she said, not adding that today for the first time she'd felt almost—normal. Like a real person, living her own life, not like some freak.

Greg started to walk, still heading down the beach away from the restaurant. Lucky cursed her stupidity. Why did she keep doing this? She couldn't blame him for being angry. Silently, she walked beside him, wondering what she could possibly say to redeem herself.

"How did it go with that doctor? I didn't get a chance to ask you."

"Great," she replied quickly, thankful that he didn't sound angry but realizing that he didn't exactly look like a happy camper either. "I didn't like him at first, but then I warmed up to him."

"Really? Why?"

"He explained a lot of things about Hoyt-Mellenberger that I hadn't understood."

They had reached an outcropping of lava rocks that separated the beach into two sections. Greg leaned against one of the boulders and Lucky stood nearby, but she didn't make the mistake of touching him.

"Some faces I see are familiar, but I can't seem to put a name to them. Now I know why. Some victims can never ever remember a face," she rushed on, describing the condition known as masking. "I'll have to relearn faces like the president and Elvis."

Greg nodded thoughtfully, but she couldn't tell what he was thinking.

"It disturbs me that there are so many things I don't know. Every day there seem to be more and more. I think I was doing better right after the accident. I actually seemed to know more then."

"Not really. Your world was small then, encompassing little more than a hospital room, then the jail. Now you've broadened your experiences, so you're discovering more and more that you'll need to relearn." He leaned over and kissed her forehead, a quick, friendly peck. "Don't worry about it, angel. It'll come with time."

She wanted to share his confidence but couldn't. Some dark, forbidden memory, like an elusive wisp of smoke, drifted through her mind, vanishing before she could get a fix on it. There was something she should remember. Something . . .

"I need to talk to you," Greg said, and Lucky immediately sensed that this was not good news. "There are lots of people who will want to take advantage of you. Be very careful whom you confide in."

"Sarah and Nomo have been wonderful."

"I know, but there are people like Fenton Bewley who only want to make money off your problems. You've read his articles in the *Tattler*. You—"

"I haven't spoken with him. Someone at the institute must have told him—"

"True, but if he tries to talk to you, don't say anything." Greg hesitated, gauging her for a moment. "Don't have anything more to do with Carlton Summerville, either."

"Why?" she asked, alarm bells sounding. "Dr. Summerville helped me. He explained a lot about Hoyt-Mellenberger."

"I know, and I'm glad he made you feel better, but he's not with any research institution. He's not helping people who've suffered head trauma. He's writing a book. It's going to be all about you."

Lucky swallowed hard, trying to hide her shock and disappointment. Why did everyone want to use her? Couldn't they just leave her alone?

Chapter 20

Live Bait's parking lot was full when Cody pulled in, driving the police Bronco. He parked next door at the Clean Rite Laundry, where a constant plume of steam shot into the sky from the round-the-clock shifts washing hotel linen. He jumped the low wall separating the commercial laundry from the bar that attracted the island's lowlifes. *Mokes.* Paradise's version of Hell's Angels. And a handful of good guys, laundry workers sweaty after hours tending steaming vats.

Jesus! Scott Helmer could sure pick meeting places. Cody was dreading seeing the punk from the FBI again. After the call from Greg less than an hour ago, Cody knew he'd screwed up—big time.

Cody shouldered his way through the swinging doors and stopped inside the bar. The joint was dark, the only light coming from the Silver Bullet sign hanging behind the bar. Peanut shells littered the floor beneath square wooden tables covered with red and white checked vinyl tablecloths.

The cork walls had been haphazardly nailed in place. Someone had taken a hot poker and seared a message into the soft wood: "You can't kill a man born to hang." All around the sign customers had tacked up condoms—some new, some designed for horses or bulls, some interesting colors not usually seen in the south forty.

To further enhance Live Bait's ambiance, old Don Ho songs blared from a secondhand jukebox. Overhead a ceiling fan wheezed, circulating air rank with stale beer, cardboard pizza, and bodies in need of a shower. Christ, what he wouldn't give to be on his way home to Sarah.

Cody's eyes adjusted to the lack of light, and he scanned the room jammed with the five o'clock crowd having a few brews before heading home. Despite his uniform, no one looked at him twice. People didn't find the police as intimidating as they did on the mainland because the cops took it easy on tourists. No reason to give paradise a bad rap by harassing visitors. Fair was fair, so they gave the locals the same break. Sometimes he felt like a baby-sitter, not a cop.

Across the room Cody spotted Helmer ordering from a waitress in gold lamé shorts cut so high that her cheeks hung out. Helmer fit right in with the crowd. He looked like a dropout from the mainland who spent his days surfing and did pickup construction work when he fell behind in the rent.

Cody walked over, saying hello to a few men he recognized and smiling at those he didn't. He ordered a Primo, although he figured he would need something stiffer than a beer when Helmer heard what he had to say.

"Your office is bugged," the punk informed Cody before he could lower himself onto the wooden stool opposite the agent.

"You're kidding."

"Nope," Scott assured him. "Nothing at your house or in any of the squad cars, though."

"You were in my house?" Jesus! He hated this, feeling violated somehow.

"Yep." Helmer took a swallow of Red Dog, then pointed

at him with the beer bottle. "Your brother's clean, too. Just the one bug in your office right under the edge of your desk."

"On the side with the visitor's chairs?"

"Exactly. All anyone had to do is walk into your office and stick it there."

Cody remembered the people who'd come about Lucky. Fenton Bewley. That doctor wearing a suit. Tony Traylor. Even the hypnotherapist. Any of them could have planted the bug. "So where's the receiver? If they're listening, someone's recording, right?"

Helmer took a swig of beer. "Who knows? It's a brand-new model with a half-mile range. It could be anywhere in Kahului—even right here. We can't find it, but that's okay. This way we feed them the info we want them to have."

The waitress slammed Cody's Primo onto the table, along with another Red Dog for Helmer and a bowl of crack seed. She sashayed away, wiggling her fanny for the *mokes* at the next table. Cody took a handful of crack seed, the island's version of Trail Mix, and munched on it.

"You haven't told anyone about IDing the hiker, have you?"

Cody shook his head, then downed half the bottle. How was he going to tell this kid that he had screwed up?

"Let's keep it to ourselves until we want whoever's listening to know." Helmer put both palms around the beer bottle and wiped off the condensation. "The producers of *Missing!* are going to run the story on the blonde."

"Really?" Cody perked up. Getting rid of Lucky was his number one priority.

"We talked to them. Told 'em to do it," Helmer said. "Talk about the show in your office for the bug. That way whoever is listening will have something meaningless to hear. The program will air in two weeks."

"That long?" He kicked back the rest of his beer, figuring by then Lucky would be Sarah's best friend and so much a part of his brother's life that nothing short of a nuclear blast could separate them.

"They're only on once a week. It takes a while to produce a show."

Cody tried to signal the waitress for another beer, but she was playing kissy face with a tableful of *mokes* who worked for Tony Traylor. That reminded him: "Anything on Traylor?"

"We're working on it."

The way Helmer shifted on his stool told Cody that he probably had a whole lot on the creep but wasn't going to share it with him.

"Any chance Lucky's one of Traylor's babes?"

Helmer nodded. "Possibly. He's got a thing for cheap blondes with big tits."

"I found out something interesting about that hiker today," Cody began, forcing himself to confess. "When the coroner examined Thelma Overholt, he found two unusual bugs—you know, insects—in her hair."

Helmer shoved the second empty Red Dog aside. "I didn't see that in the report."

"It didn't make it to the report," Cody explained. The kid looked like he'd just been told aliens were running the coroner's office. "Hey, this is paradise. We don't have a full-time coroner. We rotate bodies between the three funeral homes on the island. If anything serious comes up, we ship the body to Honolulu. This looked like an accident—"

"It was no accident." Helmer ground out the words, and Cody couldn't help wondering if the punk would have told him had he not brought up the bugs. "The cause of death was a blow to the head, caused not by the fall, but by a sharp instrument. They're still working on the details. We'll know more later."

"Murder. I knew it." And Lucky was involved. This could be the way to get her out of Greg's life. Link her to a homicide.

"Don't tell anyone. Not a soul, understand?" Helmer said, and Cody mumbled his agreement. "Back to those insects. What about them?"

"Alan Dunbar, he's a friend of my brother's—examined

them this morning. He says that they are rare. I mean, *really* rare. There's only one place on earth with bugs like these—"

"Wait a minute! You didn't send them to Quantico with the body? Why not?"

There was steam coming out of the kid's ears, and Cody couldn't blame him. There was no excuse for something like this. "The bugs weren't sent because they weren't with the evidence. The coroner picked them out of the woman's hair and took them over to the Society to Preserve the Hawaiian Wildlife Habitat thinking they'd come from the rain forest and needed to be cataloged."

"Fucking A! It's a good thing you remembered these bugs."

Now was not the time to admit he hadn't remembered the bugs. He'd told Greg about them just after Lucky had been found, when Cody had been desperately trying to talk to his brother. "Turns out the bugs come from a place called Jinghong. It's in southern China on the Mekong River, just over the border from Laos."

"No way the woman was in Singapore one minute, then China, then here, without purchasing an airline ticket or passing through a passport checkpoint somewhere." Helmer waved to the waitress, putting up two fingers. "I want those bugs. We've got a forensic entomologist at Quantico. Let him examine them."

"Really? An entemologist on staff, huh?"

Helmer looked at him as if Cody's shoe size was larger than his IQ. "Sure. We had several before the budget crunch. Insects can help establish time of death or tell us whether drugs were involved. Often they're the key to knowing if the body was moved."

"Your man can examine the bugs, but he'll find the same thing. Dunbar's the best entomologist in the country. He's literally made millions with bugs."

As usual, money talked, and Scott said, "Southern China? I don't get it."

Cody put both elbows on the table and leaned toward the

kid, relishing the moment. Helmer was baffled. "Here's the *re-e-eally* interesting part. These little critters are found only on one special type of orchid plant."

The waitress delivered their beers and Helmer grabbed his Red Dog, then began rotating the bottle between his palms. You could almost hear the kid's brain crunching the facts. Cody took a long pull before delivering the knockout punch.

"It gets better. This particular orchid wasn't even discovered until a few years ago when China opened up its jungles to Western travelers. It's a rare, endangered species."

"Who knows about this bug thing?"

"Dunbar, my brother, Lucky." Cody thought for a moment. "Dunbar's wife, I guess."

"Shit! Why not put it on the six o'clock news?"

"I told my brother not to—"

"I'm going to have everyone served with a special FBI order to refrain from discussing anything about those insects with anyone."

Cody hadn't heard of the order but didn't doubt that it existed. "Before the American Express investigator arrived here, she must have been in southern China."

"Impossible! Two days before she was found dead here, she met with one of our agents in Singapore. Thelma said she had a hot lead on the credit card counterfeiting ring. They planned to meet the next evening, but she never showed. That wouldn't give her enough time to get to China. There's got to be another explanation for those bugs being in her hair. I want those bugs in an overnight pouch to Quantico. They'll give us an answer."

When Lucky and Greg arrived at the institute the following morning, a man from the FBI's Honolulu office served them with an order not to discuss, communicate in writing, or by any other means with anyone about insects, living or dead, that they might have heard about, seen, or read about that could, in any way, shape, or form, have been involved in a possible still-unsolved police case.

"What does this mean?" Lucky asked Greg when the man left.

"It means what Alan discovered is really important, and they don't want it to leak out."

"I won't say a word," she told him as she went out the door to check on Abbie, Dodger at her heels as he usually was.

Since their interlude on the beach, Greg had kept his distance. He didn't seem angry or cold, but he'd stayed in his office, not checking on Abbie as much. Last night they'd had the Dunbars over for dinner, Greg had made sure not to be alone with her.

As she crossed the pool area and went into the nursery, Lucky reminded herself that this was what she wanted. But was it? She thought she could do this, she honestly did. Of course, she'd anticipated problems. She'd expected Greg to force himself on her yet again, but he hadn't—not really. But just knowing he wanted her and all she had to do was to say the word was so tempting.

She was so confused that she often felt like screaming. Anger would suddenly well up inside her—for no apparent reason—and she had to fight to control it. Don't be angry, she told herself. Things will work out.

She slipped her hand into the pocket of her shorts and touched Rudy's tooth. For luck. Last night Cody had called to say *Missing!* was going to do her story. With any luck someone would identify her, and she could clear her name.

"Wait!" She bent over to pet Dodger. "I won't just clear my name, I'll have a *real* name. I won't be Jane Doe or Lucky anymore."

Dodger gave her a quick lick, studying Lucky with loving eyes, and she was amazed at how happy she felt. It wouldn't be long before she had a past. She stood up and touched the shark's tooth again. *Don't let it be a bad past. Don't let me be the woman in the mirror.*

She had a secret plan. Well, almost no one knew. She had

spent a lot of time talking to the animals. Dodger knew, Rudy knew, and now Abbie knew that if the news about her past wasn't something shameful, she was going to stay right here in Maui and make a new life.

But she wasn't free to start over until she knew the truth.

"Wark! Wark!" Abbie noisily greeted Lucky as they walked into the nursery, clapping her little flippers together, begging to be picked up.

"Okay, okay. Hold on." She reached into the pen and lifted Abbie out. "Whoa! You've gained weight. I'll bet you weigh seven pounds now."

Abbie's soulful eyes blinked twice, and she made little sucking sounds. Cradling the pup in one arm, Lucky took a bottle of goat's milk from the refrigerator and put it in the microwave.

"There." She touched her index finger to Abbie's jet-black nose. "It'll just be a few seconds." Dodger rubbed against her leg, his way of getting her attention. She dropped to her knees, not wanting him to feel left out. "This is Abbie."

Dodger backed up, held his ground, then slowly approached. He sniffed Abbie, nosing around her tiny head, then swiped her with his big tongue. Abbie leaned into the caress, mewling with contentment. Dodger licked her again, this time moving closer.

"Wark! Wark!" cried Abbie.

"Well, I guess you've made a new friend." Lucky petted Dodger, running her hand over his smooth fur.

She loved animals, trusting them more than she did people. And she identified with these two special animals. She was adept on the computer because there was something in her brain that knew what to do, but she enjoyed working with animals even more. If Greg didn't need her help in the office, she would spend all day down here.

Dodger at her feet, Lucky was in the rocker, giving Abbie her bottle and crooning a ballad to her. She heard a noise and looked up to see Sarah and Molly.

"Yucky! Yucky!" squealed Molly, reaching out for Lucky.

"Honey, Lucky's busy. She can't hold you *and* the baby seal."

"Hi, there," Lucky said. "What brings you here?"

Sarah put Molly down and the child toddled off. "I came by to check out your roots. Hmm. Just as I suspected. Your hair is even darker than the color we dyed it. It's the same shade as your eyebrows."

"Does that mean we're going to have to dye it again?"

"No. We can leave it for a few weeks. It won't be noticeable until then."

"Sweetie," Sarah said to Molly, who was inspecting the trash can, "look at the seal. Can you say *seal?*"

Molly ignored her mother, toddling toward Dodger instead. "Doggie. Doggie." She smacked him on the snout, giving him a noisy kiss, and began talking gibberish to him.

"Is everything all right?" Sarah asked. "Are you okay?"

"Sure. Things are great." Lucky wished she could tell Sarah about the strange bugs.

"I keep thinking something's wrong. Cody isn't talking about your case at all. He says things are fine, but I'm concerned."

Lucky was upset, too, Sarah thought as she watched her cuddle the sleeping pup against her breast. "You heard I'm going to be on *Missing!*"

"Yes. Someone out there knows who you are," Sarah said, her hand on Lucky's shoulder, her eyes filled with kindness. "With any luck, they'll call in right after the show."

Lucky wanted to reach for Rudy's tooth and give it a quick good luck rub, but both her hands were full with Abbie.

The Orchid King watched the last of the six-foot-long wooden crates go into the refrigerated air freight container bound for Chicago. His partner had been right: Opening the warehouse in Chinatown had streamlined the business. They no longer had to rely on shipments out of the Orient, where the Asian *tongs* threatened to horn in on the business he'd built. He'd had his fill of dealing with those ruthless gangs.

His partner came up behind him. "Did you see the latest *Maui Tattler?*"

Of course, he'd seen it. He made it a point to read their contact's daily report each morning before he went jogging. It gave him something to mull over. "What did it say now?"

"Pele's ghost and her brother, the shark, both love *opakapaka*. There's a whole page devoted to the shark she saved breaking into a fish farm and gorging on *opakapaka*. That same night she goes out with that creep Braxton and has the same fish."

"You'd think they would have something better to write about. An earthquake or a fire or a murder . . . something."

"You're missing the point."

The king knew exactly what the point was. He just didn't want to discuss it. Not only was the woman he loved living with Braxton, but she was going out with him as well. Making a new life for herself.

"In two weeks she'll be the feature story on *Missing!* Not that it's any surprise," his partner said. "I knew they'd do her story."

"So we wait two weeks and see what the show turns up."

It was a lifetime, but the king didn't say so. Instead, he plucked the most exquisite orchid he'd ever seen from a newly arrived case. Its serrated petals were a delicate violet color, with a deep throat of a slightly darker hue. "See this?"

His partner looked only mildly interested. He didn't share the king's appreciation for orchids. "Yeah."

"They just arrived from the Amazon. The orchids are on the endangered list." He couldn't resist smiling. "Each is worth over a hundred thousand dollars to collectors."

His partner failed to be impressed. Why should he be? They made more than that before sunup every day. Orchids were just a sideline. A front.

The king reached for the switch and turned off the lights in the warehouse.

"What in hell—"

"Look at the orchids now," the king said.

The clusters of orchids glowed softly, emitting an eerie light in the dank darkness of the old warehouse. The king flicked the lights back on and the usual fluorescence filled the building.

"Not only do these orchids glow in the dark, but they're also killers." He was gratified to see his partner was truly impressed now.

The king reached into the crate, gently moving aside the priceless orchids. He lifted out a huge rat by its tail. His partner backed up, clearly repulsed. But then, he never had the guts to do the dirty work.

To kill when necessary.

"This African rat happened to crawl in with the orchids. What do you think killed him?" He swung the rat back and forth like a pendulum. His partner took another step back. "Fumes from the blossoms. They are the most beautiful flowers on earth. Rare. Priceless. Deadly."

His partner retreated yet another step. "Is it safe to breathe near them?"

"Sure. The fumes dissipate in this much air." He slung the rat into a bin of discarded wrappings. "I can hardly *wait* to ice someone again. This is the way to do it. Death by orchid."

Chapter 21

"You what?" Cody stared at Sarah.

"I invited Lucky and Greg here for lunch after church on Sunday."

Cody was amazed. Greg had never been big on church, probably because Aunt Sis had always attended services, insisting they come, too. The old biddy was the hypocrite to end all hypocrites. She'd pray at the top of her lungs, thumping the Bible with a clenched fist, then she'd march them home from church and beat the crap out of them.

"You're sure Greg said he'd come?"

Sarah smiled, obviously pleased with herself, nodding. Cody tried to hide his excitement by kissing her cheek. He hadn't been able to discuss what had happened with Greg the day they released the shark because he hadn't a clue exactly what had happened.

Even now, days later, Cody clung to the memory, reliving the moment, reshaping and redefining it until those four little words were nothing short of a miracle.

I owe you one.

Once they had both used that expression, but they were casual words tossed out easily. Not anymore. Although he couldn't possibly have explained it, even to Sarah, Cody knew something profound had happened.

Now it was more important than ever to get rid of Lucky. Greg was a proud man—some might say stubborn—but Cody preferred to think of his brother as proud. It would humiliate Greg beyond belief if he found out Lucky was Traylor's girl. There was no one Greg despised more than Traylor, blaming him for the pollution destroying the offshore reefs. To have Lucky involved with Traylor in a *hui* murder would be the worst.

And she was involved. Absolutely no question about it. The shoe linked her to the murder committed a year earlier.

"Darling," Sarah said, breaking into his thoughts. She was handing him a bottle of wine to open.

He looked around, noticing for the first time since he'd come home from work that there were candles on the table. "Where are the kids?"

"Mom and Pop have Molly. The twins are on a Boy Scout campout at Big Beach, remember? We pick them up first thing in the morning, and then your job is to make certain their room is clean for Sunday when Greg and Lucky visit."

Cody saluted with the wine bottle. "The house to ourselves—almost heaven."

Sarah leveled those magnificent brown eyes at him, her swath of dark hair streaming over her shoulder. "Heaven will be Sunday after church when I have the family here together again."

He had to swallow hard to get rid of the lump in his throat. Honest to God, Sarah understood him and loved him like no one else ever had. He hated himself for what he'd done to her. He put down the bottle and gathered her into his arms. "I can't tell you how much I love you, Sarah. If there's ever anything I can do—"

"Cody, please help Lucky." The touch of Sarah's hand on

his cheek was almost unbearable in its tenderness. "I know you don't like her, but try to help her."

"I'll do what I can," he hedged. "So much will depend on what *Missing!* turns up."

"Maybe she has a husband and children like ours."

Cody shook his head. "No. If that were true, we'd have a missing persons report on her."

He left it there. Helmer had forbidden him to discuss the case. Cody had explained to Sarah that the FBI was involved and the code of silence had been invoked. Even if he had been at liberty to discuss the situation, he wouldn't have had the heart to tell Sarah that he suspected Lucky was Tony Traylor's girl and that she was up to her cute little ears in a murder.

Greg walked beside Lucky to the second row pew where Cody was saving them seats. The last time he'd been in this church had been for Jessica's funeral. Seemed like a lifetime ago. The hurt and anger he'd struggled to control then had vanished. Some people might have thought time eased the pain, but that wasn't true. Just a few weeks ago he'd been as bitter as he'd been at the funeral.

Lucky had changed everything, he thought, glaring at her. She beamed a smile at him, and he knew that this woman was both a blessing and a curse. She'd brought him back into the land of the living, sure, but she had the potential to hurt him in a way that Jessica never had.

Once he couldn't wait to get rid of Lucky. Now he dreaded having *Missing!* air. There was always the possibility some wild card would turn up and lay claim to her. The unimaginable would happen. Lucky would be taken away from him.

"Good morning," Cody said as they slid into the pew beside him.

Sarah had already taken her place with the choir and the children were in Sunday school, so it was just the three of them, with Lucky in the middle. Greg knew damn well Sarah and Lucky had cooked up this little scheme to get him together with Cody again. He'd only put up a token protest. His experiences with Lucky had shown him how important family was. He missed Sarah and the twins and the baby he'd only recently met. Most of all, he missed his brother.

"The boys have a soccer game this afternoon," Cody told them. "They'd love to have you see them play."

Lucky answered for him. "Sounds like fun, doesn't it, Greg?"

"Sure," he replied, not meeting his brother's eyes. There were bound to be awkward moments like this, when he was uncertain how to respond.

Reverend Tadaku began his sermon with a prayer. Greg bent his head, stealing a quick glance at Lucky. She had her head down, too, her eyes closed. She'd developed an inner strength these last few days. He had to admit he was terribly proud of her, not just of her work with the animals, but also of the way she accepted her situation without complaining, trying to relearn things as quickly as possible.

"Sinners . . . sinners, avoid temptation!" Reverend Tadaku's tremolo shook the dust off the rafters, no doubt awakening the dead in the nearby graveyard. "Repent now . . . or suffer the eternal fires of hell."

As the reverend lectured them on ways to avoid temptation in a world with a moral compass that had gone haywire, Greg caught Cody looking at him. Greg smiled at his brother, and Cody grinned back. Cody always did have the damnedest smile.

From the choir box to the right of the pulpit, Sarah smiled at Greg. He winked at her, acknowledging that he knew she was behind this. Greg had always liked Sarah, even when she'd been nothing more than a pain in the ass little kid who followed them around like a puppy.

It was a few years before their hormones kicked in and every boy in school noticed Sarah. Of course, she had had eyes only for Cody. With unwavering devotion, she'd loved him since she had been a young girl. And she'd stood by him even when he'd publicly humiliated her. What more could a man ask of a woman?

The choir stood and the congregation rose along with them to sing "Amazing Grace." Greg knew better than to do anything more than mouth the words. When he sang in the shower, Dodger would usually hide in the other room.

The organ struck a note that swelled through the small church, and the choir burst into song. Lucky's voice rang out just as a shaft of radiant sunlight hit their pew. Rainbows of light sparkled from the leaded glass window, splashing them with a palette or color as clear and true as her voice. Along with the finest sopranos in the choir, she sang, her voice rich yet delicate.

"I once was lo-o-o-st . . ." She hit the high note and held it. Perfectly. Lucky angled her body to face him, her eyes meeting his, filled with anguish that her voice didn't betray. There was a loneliness, too, a raw pain Greg instantly recognized, having felt it so often himself.

Her fingers curled around his and she squeezed slightly, still singing. "I once was lo-o-o-st . . . but now I'm found."

His throat tightened and he let his gaze drop to the base of her throat. A strong pulse throbbed, her graceful neck arching as she sang from the heart. "A-ma-zing Grace . . . how sweet the sound that saved a wretch like me-e-e." Lucky smiled again, appealing to his innermost feelings. "I once was lost but now I'm found."

Her lilting voice reached toward the heavens, holding the final note with astonishing ease. Her eyes never left his, and Greg was only dimly aware that she was the only one singing now. It was a highly charged moment, intensified by dozens of people staring at them even though Lucky seemed oblivious to it all.

Found. The word echoed through his head, even after the sound died away and people began to return their hymnals to the racks. Greg clasped Lucky's hand, reveling in the shared moment and the sense of intimacy the song had unexpectedly brought.

He understood what she was trying to tell him: The accident had changed her forever, damaging her mind, altering her life. But day by day, one little step at a time, she was finding herself. And she gave him credit for helping her.

The congregation took their seats again. Gazing into Greg's eyes, seeking his soul, Lucky whispered, "Thank you for everything."

Reverend Tadaku was concluding the ceremony before it dawned on Greg that Lucky had known "Amazing Grace" by heart. She had to have sung it enough times to record it in her brain. Weird. She knew a religious hymn, yet she'd shown no sign of knowing any of the popular tunes played on the radio.

A gourmet cook who sang like an angel and surfed through cyberspace. Definitely not the profile of a two-bit hooker. There had to be another explanation—and it was probably the key to why she hadn't been identified. It wasn't the first time he'd had this thought, but he kept returning to the night he'd found her and thought she was a tramp.

She had looked the part. Acted the part.

Okay, she'd changed. Head trauma often caused personality changes. What had she been like before? Maybe it didn't matter. If *Missing!* didn't turn up anything, Lucky would be free to start over and be whoever she wanted to be.

The minute the service was finished, Reverend Tadaku rushed up to them. He hastily shook Greg's hand, then turned to Lucky. "You belong in our choir. I've never heard such a voice."

"Really?" Lucky was clearly baffled but pleased as well.

"They practice on Wednesday nights," Cody offered.

"You can drive my car," Greg said. "I can ride the Harley."

Lucky shook her head, her soft curls swaying. "No. I can't drive your car."

"You don't know how to drive?" the minister asked, just as several other members of the congregation came up to tell Lucky that she had a beautiful voice.

Cody pulled Greg aside. "We're not picking up any DMV

fingerprints on her. I just received the last of the hand-checks done by the smaller states last night. No matches anywhere. Hand-checks aren't as accurate as computer scans, so I thought maybe someone missed Lucky's prints. But there weren't any prints to miss if she never applied for a driver's license."

"True," Greg agreed, then he told his brother about the computer and Lucky's ability to cook. "Something's wrong here. We're missing a piece of the puzzle."

Cody didn't look convinced. "Strange, Lucky claims she can't drive. Jesus H. Christ, I ask you, how stupid does she think we are? She drove that car off the cliff."

Greg shrugged, too disturbed to discuss it. He had to ask Lucky.

Greg and Lucky walked out to the car while Cody and Sarah herded their brood into Sarah's minivan, agreeing to meet at Cody's house. Dodger was waiting in the shade of the nearby eucalyptus tree. He spotted them and trotted over.

Once they were on the road, Greg continued to ask himself why she'd lied. Cody was right; she had been driving on the night he'd found her. So why pull this? "You never mentioned you couldn't drive."

"I can drive," Lucky assured him. "I just can't drive this type of car." She pointed to the gear shift. "I can drive an—"

"Automatic transmission."

"That's right. Is it hard to learn to shift?"

"Nah." He pulled over to the side of the road, relieved to hear her explanation. "Change places with me. I'll show you how."

It took at least a dozen tries before Lucky came close to getting the hang of it. By then, Greg was sure the transmission was shot. But he wasn't one bit angry. How could he be? She tried so damn hard and was so earnest about everything.

Her shifting was still jerky when they pulled into Cody's drive and saw that the family was already there. Lucky threw the car into reverse, grinding the gears before she managed to get it into park and turn off the ignition.

"Thanks," she said, smiling at him. "Now I'll be able to drive to choir practice."

Lucky behind the wheel. Now there was a scary thought.

She touched his arm. "I meant what I said back there. I once was lost but now I'm found. I can feel it. I'm found. Everything is going to be all right."

Found. A crucial part of himself that he'd never quite known was lost had been found the night he'd discovered Lucky. And Greg knew without a doubt that his life would never be the same.

Lucky softly hummed "Amazing Grace" as they walked into the house, Dodger at their heels. He should have been happy that she believed things were working out. But he wasn't. Some elusive thought niggled at the back of his mind but he couldn't quite bring it into focus. He didn't have a chance to concentrate on it. The second he came through the door, the twins barreled into him.

"Uncle Greg, Uncle Greg!"

Two years. Too damn long. Why had he been such a stubborn son of a bitch? Jason and Trevor were half grown. Without him. Greg hugged first one, then the other, cursing himself.

"Come here." Trevor grabbed his arm. "I have this awesome catcher's mitt."

Greg looked over his shoulder and saw Lucky disappearing into the kitchen, where he could hear Sarah and Cody talking. He followed the boys to their room, which was suspiciously clean. He bet that if he opened the closet, a mountain of junk would tumble out. He'd been their age once; he still remembered the tricks.

Greg marveled over the brand-new and obviously expensive baseball mitts the boys showed him, recalling when he and Cody had been this age. They had shared a mitt the coach had scrounged up somewhere because Aunt Sis wouldn't buy them a damn thing. Their mitt was so old and worn that his hand stung each time he'd caught a really hard hit.

"How are your grades?"

"Mostly B's," Trevor replied without hesitation. "Some C's. Good enough to make the team."

"Mine are real good," Jason admitted.

Greg read between the lines. Jason had straight A's just as Greg had had at the same age. Trevor was like Cody, more interested in sports. Greg had almost wasted a Godgiven talent—his intelligence—just to spite Aunt Sis. He'd gotten into so much trouble that he never would have gone to college if that judge hadn't sent him to volunteer at the institute.

The twins insisted he come down to the corral to see the colt, who had been born earlier that year. Greg leaned against the fence rail and watched the boys coax the shy colt into letting them put a halter on him. Yes siree. Cody had given his sons the life he and his brother had always wanted.

Greg reached down and petted Dodger, thinking about those nights when they would whisper back and forth, careful not to awaken Aunt Sis. They fantasized about how life would have been if their parents had lived. They'd have new baseball mitts and sneakers without holes. A dog for sure and maybe a cat. Definitely horses. Mom would bake them cookies and her special chicken pot pie. And Dad would attend every ball game, cursing the ref's bad calls.

Cody had made their dreams come true for his boys. The Braxtons didn't have much extra cash. Greg could tell from the state of the house and the barn that could stand a new roof. But the kids had everything they needed. Especially love.

"Take it easy. Let Max get used to you." Cody had come up behind Greg and Dodger and was calling instructions to the twins, who were still attempting to put a halter on the skittish colt.

"They're great kids," Greg said as Cody joined him at the fence.

Cody put his foot on the bottom rail, his eyes still on the boys. "No one could ask for better kids . . . or a better family."

Greg had told himself it didn't matter that the past was just that—ancient history—but he had to know. "You have everything any man could want. Wonderful kids. A drop-dead gorgeous wife. How could you risk losing them?"

His brother turned to him, and Greg gazed into the blue eyes that were so like his own. Cody's dark brows drew together, intensifying the agonized expression on his face. For a moment he said nothing, the air filled with the twins' happy chatter.

"I wish I could give you a reason. Sarah deserves an explanation, too," Cody answered, a faint tremor in his voice. "I've asked myself the same question a thousand times or more. Close as I can come is that I've been with Sarah ever since I can remember. Maybe I should have dated more when I had the chance. Jessica was always coming on to me. One day I gave in to temptation."

A flash of wild anger ripped through Greg. The old bitterness was back, startling in its intensity. He opened his mouth to lash out—

"Dad," yelled Jason. "We did it, Dad." The twins had the halter on the colt.

"Lead him to the far end of the pasture, then back to us," Cody directed the boys, keeping them away.

Greg watched the twins, some of his anger evaporating when he remembered all Cody had given his sons. "Okay, okay, I can understand temptation. But your own brother's wife. What did I ever do to you?"

"Absolutely nothing. You'd been the best brother in the world. I wish I could give you a reason, but I don't have one." Cody cleared his throat, looking away for a moment. "Would it help to know it only happened once. The night of the accident I told Jessica I had made a terrible mistake and had no intention of repeating it."

"That's supposed to make me feel better?"

"I'm sorry, Greg. The last thing I ever wanted to do was to

hurt Sarah or you. I don't know why I did it, I honestly don't. I can't change the past." Cody spoke with quiet but desperate honesty. "I can only say I'm truly sorry."

No chance this piss-poor explanation satisfied Greg, but he reminded himself that they had once been more than brothers. They'd been best friends, each supplying for the other what had been stolen from them when their parents had died—love. Mistakes were mistakes. Shit happened. He wanted to be happy, to be family again.

Greg put his hand on Cody's shoulder. "Let's forget it, okay?"

Cody hesitated a moment, watching his boys, who were coming closer. "About the accident. Jessica was driving, you know."

Christ! How could he forget? Even now he could see her beautiful, mangled body. Cody had been thrown clear, which saved his life.

"She deliberately drove the car over the embankment. Just before she hit the accelerator, she said life wasn't worth living."

A suffocating sensation tightened Greg's throat as he struggled to comprehend what Cody had just said. He stood there, staring at the fence post. He'd thought the accident had been just that—an accident. Until this second he'd never known that Jessica had deliberately tried to kill them both.

My God, he'd almost lost Cody. And he hadn't known it. Losing Jessica had been bad enough, but if Cody had died . . . Christ, what would he have done?

"Jessica was really screwed up." Cody's tone was gentle, his voice low. "You couldn't have helped her."

A strange heaviness centered in Greg's chest and it took him several seconds to control himself. "I don't know what I would have done if I'd lost you."

Cody bear-hugged him and Greg clutched his brother, holding him as tight as he could. As they embraced, Greg let go of his anger and of the past he could never change. Think of the future, he told himself.

"Are we okay now?" Cody asked.

"Yeah, we're okay." He wanted to tell Cody about Lucky's scarred feet and what he'd felt that day when she'd freed the shark, but Greg was afraid he would break down if he talked too much. "Thanks for being there. You know, when we were kids . . . and now."

"Take Max around again," Cody called to the twins, who were approaching. Then he turned to Greg, his expression even more concerned. "Look . . . about Lucky. I'm afraid she's like Jessica—"

"She's confused because she doesn't know who she is. Hell, she has a special medical condition—"

"True, but I think you should prepare yourself for the possibility that she's committed a crime . . . maybe even something very serious. I don't want her to come between us."

Chapter 22

Cody looked across the crowded dining room table at Lucky, who was spoon-feeding Molly apple sauce. He prayed he was right: *Lucky wasn't going to come between them.*

Lucky and Sarah had prepared a feast, and it was clear the two were becoming fast friends. Sure enough, the woman was worming her way into the family's heart. If she turned out to be Traylor's girlfriend—or worse—he'd have to be the one to lock her up. Then break the news to Greg and Sarah.

"Wednesday night while we're at choir practice, you guys should take the kids for pizza, don't you think?" Sarah asked Cody.

"Sure." He darted a quick look at his brother. Greg had been quiet during dinner. Cody suspected he was still a little shaken after learning the whole truth about the accident that had very nearly killed him.

"Greg taught me how to drive his car," Lucky said. "Now I can get to choir practice on my own."

"He taught you to drive in one lesson . . . amazing!" Cody's suspicious tone drew a sharp look from Sarah. What did she expect? Lucky was a bald-faced liar. It took more than one quick lesson to learn to drive.

"I never said I couldn't drive. I just couldn't use a gear shift," Lucky explained, her tone level.

Cody gave her credit for looking him right in the eye. She didn't like him any more than he liked her. Greg vaulted to his feet, knocking his chair backward. He looked at Lucky as if she'd just bitten him.

"What's the matter?" Cody picked up Greg's chair.

"Come on." Greg motioned for Cody to follow him. "We'll meet you all at the game."

"What about dessert?" Sarah protested. "I made *haupia*. Coconut pudding is Greg's favorite."

"Thanks. We'll eat ours later," Greg called over his shoulder.

"What's the matter?" Cody asked as Greg rushed him through the front door.

Greg didn't respond. Instead, he headed for his car, and Cody was forced to follow. Dodger loped along beside them. They jumped into the car, and Greg was almost out of the driveway before Cody could close his door.

"What's going on?" Cody asked as the car barreled down the country lane.

"With Hoyt-Mellenberger syndrome, whatever you make a conscious effort to learn stays with you. Like a foreign language. What you've done over and over stays with you. Like—"

"Knowing the words to 'Amazing Grace,' right?"

"Right. Lucky's better on the Internet than Bill Gates. She must have logged on hundreds, if not thousands, of times." Greg braked for a mongoose, who darted across the road and disappeared into a bank of ferns. "Lucky can drive a car. She's not terribly good at it, but she can drive."

Cody couldn't understand where this was going or why Greg was driving hell-bent for leather toward Kihei, when they could be eating *haupia*, but he let his brother talk. Personally, he wondered about just how real Lucky's memory loss was.

Totally infatuated with her, Greg believed every word, buying into a condition so rare that even the experts couldn't agree on the diagnosis.

"Is the police impound lot still behind Hoho's Gas and Tow?" Greg asked.

"Yeah. Why? Is that where we're going?"

"The car Lucky was driving had a stick shift. I remember distinctly because her shirt caught on it when I pulled her out. She couldn't have been driving that car because she doesn't know how."

Now that depended on whether you believed Lucky couldn't remember the past, but Cody kept his mouth shut. It was obvious Greg had gone for the blonde's story. Just see how this plays out, Cody told himself. He didn't want to have another fight with his brother.

"If she wasn't driving the car, who was? And why do you want to see it?"

Greg shrugged his shoulders, bringing his car to a stop behind a busful of Japanese tourists. They were standing along the side of the road, garlands of cameras around their necks, snapping pictures of the sugarcane stalks.

"Lucky was behind the wheel—at least that's where I found her—but someone else must have been driving. Where was he? Unless a person was a mountain climber, no one could have made it up that *pali*. The cliff was just too steep."

"Do you think someone pushed that car off the cliff? That's impossible. You would have seen or heard something."

"Not necessarily. It was an unusual storm. When was the last time we had thunder and lightning on the islands? The crash might not have made enough noise to be heard above the storm." Greg pulled into Hoho's Gas and Tow, driving past the garage to the impound lot behind the shop.

"There's another possibility. The car could already have been there when Dodger and I arrived. We couldn't see the ravine from where we were. If Dodger hadn't found Lucky, it might have been days before anyone came along."

The lunch Cody had devoured—so happy to have his brother at his side again—became a load of cement in his stomach. This case was getting worse by the minute. And he had the terrible feeling he'd screwed up again.

"I never actually saw the stolen car," Cody confessed. "My guys showed me the license number, so I knew the Toyota had been stolen from one of Traylor's agencies. There was no reason to look at it. They'd checked it and found nothing."

Greg shot him a withering glance but didn't say a word. Cody climbed out of the car, mumbling something about getting the key. Tendrils of moist heat rose from the blacktop as he headed to the office. He was drenched in sweat, but it wasn't from the searing sun. He could only imagine what Scott Helmer would say. Why hadn't he at least looked at the car instead of trusting his men to report to him?

"Two men had to be involved," Greg said when Cody returned with the keys.

Two men, Cody thought. That's exactly the way Scott Helmer had analyzed the case. Christ! Greg was smart. He unlocked the gate and they went into the lot, with Dodger strutting along beside them. They picked their way around dozens of junked cars and several tour buses.

"One man drove Lucky to that *pali*. Together they pushed the stolen car off the cliff, then drove away in the other car."

"It's the only thing that makes sense," Cody agreed. "There was a storm warning. No one would have tried to hike out of such a remote spot, knowing a killer storm was on the way."

Cody opened the door to the white compact, his hand protected by a paper towel from Hoho's restroom. "We might want to dust the car for prints."

Greg had been right; it was a stick shift. Cody was looking under the front seat, praying his men hadn't missed anything important, when he heard Dodger whining frantically. He jerked upright, bumping his head against the door frame. The dog was behind the car, pointing like a retriever at the trunk.

"Open the trunk," Greg directed, grimacing.

The sickening feeling in Cody's gut became real pain. He walked to the back of the car and inserted the key in the lock. The trunk popped open with a whoosh, and Cody forced himself to look.

"Oh, shit!" Greg reached forward.

"Don't touch a thing," Cody warned.

The Orchid King stared at the computer screen, not really seeing the myriad lines of numbers and codes. Gateways and ports and secret passwords were changed constantly for security, but he didn't have much trouble figuring out the bank's new codes. Once he had been proud of his ability to breach even the tightest security. Nothing much seemed to make him happy these days, however.

"Did you see the latest report from our source?" his partner asked.

"Yeah," the king replied. How could he forget it?

"What do you think?"

The king swung his chair sideways to face his partner at the adjacent terminal. "She's making herself a new life. Attending church. Can you believe it?"

"Unfuckingbelievable! She wouldn't be caught dead in church."

The king managed a chuckle. "Maybe with that weird syndrome, you're born again and find religion."

"It's not funny." His partner sprang to his feet and paced the small office. "It's hard to be patient."

"We have only one week until *Missing!* airs. If that doesn't turn up something, we'll make our move."

"The bug in the police chief's office recorded some info about Lucky's story appearing on TV, but that's all." His partner dropped into the chair beside him. "Don't you think that's suspicious? The police are supposed to be working on this case."

From a grunt beat officer to the head of the FBI's Violent

Criminals Apprehension Program, there was no one in law
enforcement whom the king respected. How could they catch
him? They hadn't even figured out that a crime had been committed. "They're too lazy to really work on this case. You've
seen the transcripts of the office conversations. Drunk and
disorderly conduct cases. Some jerk accuses another fisherman
of stealing his marlin. Petty criminals. Petty crime. Petty
minds."

"Something's wrong, but I don't know what it is," Lucky
confided to Nomo the day following the lunch at Sarah's house.

They were in the nursery and she was giving Abbie a bottle
while Dodger lay at her feet. Nomo sat beside her listening
with the patience and understanding that she'd come to expect
from the older man.

"Just as we were finishing lunch, Greg jumped up and
dragged Cody off somewhere. So Sarah and I took the boys to
their game. Greg showed up halfway through and said Cody
had to fly to Honolulu." Lucky pulled the empty bottle from
Abbie's mouth. "Greg took everyone for ice cream after the
game but he was so quiet, as if he was sad . . . or something."

Nomo nodded thoughtfully. "He was like that a lot when
he was having problems with Jessica. Greg doesn't communicate as well as he should. Sometimes he just needs time to
think."

Lucky leaned down and placed the sleeping seal pup beside
Dodger. The dog nuzzled Abbie, then curled protectively
around her. Lucky petted Dodger, thinking this was the sweetest
sight she'd ever seen. The huge chocolate-colored dog and the
tiny seal pup with ivory fur.

"*Nani*—beautiful," Nomo said, tilting his head toward
Dodger and Abbie. He touched Lucky's arm and smiled the
toothy grin that had become so familiar. "You did a good thing
getting Cody and Greg together again."

"Sarah did it. I just—"

Nomo shook his head. "Greg did it to please you. I've known him since he was a kid. Next to Cody, no one knows Greg better than I do. He's falling in love with you—in spite of himself."

"Then why does he keep a picture of his wife on his desk? After what she did to him, I just can't understand it."

Nomo's tanned face became even more animated. "I asked him that about a year ago. Greg said he kept the picture out to remind himself not to get involved with women. They weren't worth the trouble. Looks like he's changed his mind, though."

Lucky would give anything if this were true. Yes, Greg was helping her, meaning he was involved in a way. But she wanted more from him. She couldn't voice her feelings out loud, yet she suspected both Sarah and Nomo knew: Lucky wanted Greg to love her, and she wanted to be worthy of his love.

"Nomo!" One of the volunteers rushed into the nursery, out of breath. "We just caught a creep with his camera hiding behind the oleanders."

"Fenton Bewley. What a sleazeball. I'll bet he's trying to get more pictures for another column in the *Tattler.*"

"We ran him off," the volunteer said with a proud smile.

"Good work," Lucky told him, and she meant it. The group at the institute had rallied around her, as protective of her as Dodger was of Abbie. In a way they were her extended family, and their caring attitude brought tears to her eyes. She reached in her pocket and touched Rudy's tooth.

That night when they were at home, Greg remained silent. Sometimes Lucky thought he was gazing at her oddly, seeming to be studying her, but then he would quickly look away.

"Let's take Dodger for a walk along the shore," she suggested after dinner.

"You go," he said. "I'm expecting Cody to call."

"Is Cody still in Honolulu?" Lucky had spoken with Sarah

that afternoon. Cody had called but hadn't told Sarah why he'd left so suddenly or when he planned to return.

"He's still there."

Greg didn't offer any further information, and something about his expression warned her not to pry. Lucky was halfway down the hall when the telephone rang. She waited, hoping it was Cody. Maybe after he'd spoken with his brother, Greg would change his mind about going for a walk.

Greg's voice was low, but she caught the words: "I just don't know how I'm going to break the news to her."

Lucky fought to control the spasmodic trembling, convinced this was the worst news possible. She was going back to jail.

Chapter 23

Lucky listened to the heavy thunk of the receiver and knew Greg had hung up. She inhaled a calming breath and told herself she was stronger now. *You can face this.* But she waited a few seconds, thinking about the institute and how happy she'd been there. She didn't want to go back to jail, not now, not when her life was getting back on track again.

"Lucky." Greg's voice reverberated through the quiet house.

She walked slowly into the living room, reluctant to hear the news but knowing that delaying wouldn't change anything. Dodger trotted out of the shadows and licked her fingertips, almost as if he knew what she was going through. Lucky brushed his silky head with her palm.

Greg had his balled fists jammed into the pockets of his cutoffs. He looked so disturbed that it was all she could do not to walk over and put both arms around him, even though she would soon be the one to need comforting.

"Lucky, sit down. I need to talk to you."

Suddenly, she was conscious of being nearly naked, clad only in the skimpy one-piece bathing suit that was entirely backless. Not that clothes really helped, but being so exposed intensified her feeling of vulnerability. Lucky slowly eased down onto the sofa, braced for the worst. Dodger settled at her feet while Greg sat beside her, his expression concerned.

"Okay, shoot," Lucky said, in a vain attempt to sound nonchalant.

"I don't know where to begin . . . exactly."

She rubbed her hand twice against the side of her suit before she realized she was automatically reaching for her pocket to touch Rudy's "lucky" tooth. "Start at the beginning."

Greg reached over and took her hand. The gesture was compassionate, gentle, yet somehow alarming. Lucky did her best to ignore the nervous flutter in her chest. "The stolen car you were in the night I found you had a stick shift."

It took a moment for his words to register. "It did? How could I have driven it? I know off-the-wall things like how to butterfly, but I didn't know how to shift until you taught me."

Greg kept those intense blue eyes leveled on her, and they seemed frighteningly sad. Finally, he spoke. "You weren't behind the wheel that night."

"I was the passenger? But the morning after you found me, you told me no one else was in the car."

"That's right. There wasn't anyone in the car."

From his grim expression, she knew there must have been another passenger. "Someone was thrown from the car. Why did you wait so long to tell me? Did they just find the body?"

He hesitated, measuring her for a moment.

Something was really wrong here, yet she had no idea what it was. Greg knew about her problems and realized she didn't always have enough information in the right parts of her brain to solve these puzzles. Why didn't he just come right out and tell her?

Greg squeezed her hand gently and pulled her a little closer before he continued. "There wasn't anyone else in the car . . . just you."

He kept drawing her closer and closer, until her thigh was flush against his and his arm was wrapped around her bare shoulder. There was something disturbing about his behavior. It was a protective gesture, like Dodger curling around Abbie, yet it alarmed her.

"I was the only one in the car, but I can't drive that kind of car." A sudden chill of apprehension waltzed across the back of her neck, then across her bare flesh, leaving goose bumps in its wake. "It doesn't make any sense."

After two beats of silence, he explained. "Cody and I think that somebody—probably two people—drove you to that remote site." He hesitated, tightening his grip on her. "They put the car in gear and pushed it over the cliff."

"No!" The word automatically erupted from her, but the look in Greg's eyes and the steadying pressure of his arm assured Lucky it was true. "There must be another explanation. Why would anyone try"—she could hardly get out the words—"try to kill me?"

Greg moved closer and pressed his lips to her forehead, holding them there for a long moment. "I don't know. We can only guess. Maybe you saw something or knew something that someone considered dangerous. They tried to kill you."

Tried to kill you. Tried to kill you. Tried to kill you. The words echoed through her head, ricocheting with increasing velocity, the effect on her shattering. "Oh, my God, if you and Dodger hadn't come along—"

She didn't have the strength to say the words: *I would have died.* Of course, from that first morning, she'd known that she'd cheated death. But this was different; now she realized she'd almost been murdered.

Their eyes met as he tenderly hugged her, but there was something chilling in his expression. Warning spasms of alarm shot through her, leaving her a hairbreadth away from sheer panic. Lucky mustered the courage to whisper, "Tell me the rest."

* * *

Greg gazed into those matchless green eyes, filled with such intense emotion that he literally could not speak. A glazed expression of utter despair had spread across Lucky's features. How could he tell her something that might destroy her courage, her spirit?

He held her snugly against his chest. His hand slid down her bare back, gently stroking, trying to comfort her. She buried her face against his throat, and her soft curves molded to the contours of his torso. They sat that way for a few minutes, until the silence became oppressive.

"What is it you aren't telling me? How is it they just now discovered someone tried to kill me?" She'd fired the questions at him, expecting answers, her eyes sharp and assessing.

He had no choice but to tell her the whole truth. "I realized you hadn't been driving because I had to teach you to use a stick shift. It was at the back of my mind the whole time I was teaching you, but it didn't register until we were finishing lunch."

"Why didn't you mention it then? Why leave? Did this have something to do with Cody going to Honolulu?"

"I wanted to look at the car to see how badly it was damaged. That night, between the storm and finding you, I didn't pay much attention to the car. It sailed off the *pali* but didn't roll. So you didn't have terrible cuts and bruises. You had nothing more than a minor wound on the back of your skull, a strange place considering—"

"Someone hit me on the back of the head."

He nodded. "Yes. People don't willingly let someone push them off a cliff. Cody and I think you were probably knocked unconscious somewhere else. There were two of them and they dressed you in a hurry, not noticing your shoes didn't match."

Lucky snuggled closer to Greg, and he could see the fear in her eyes. "What makes you think there were two of them?"

He launched into a lengthy explanation about the storm and

another car to take the killers back into town. He was stalling, anxious to avoid telling her about the trunk. But finally, he ran out of things to say.

"When we were looking at the car at the impound lot, Dodger began whining the way he did the night I found you in the closet." The words were coming out in a breathless rush, and Greg told himself to slow down. "Cody opened the trunk. Inside was a black scarf with several long, curly blonde hairs on it."

"Mine?" she whispered, her eyes widening as the truth dawned on her.

"Yes. Under the scarf was a spot of blood the size of a half-dollar. Cody removed the lining and flew to Honolulu with it. There's a sophisticated crime analysis lab there. He called just now and confirmed that it was your blood."

He felt the shudder pass through her, but Lucky's expression never changed. "They put me in the trunk?"

Her words had the hollow ring of disbelief to them. He would have given everything he ever had, or hoped to have, not to be forced to tell her the rest of this. "The minute Dodger came up to the car, he began to whine. Your scent must have been very strong, because the lid was shut and the rubber seal wasn't damaged in the accident. You must have been locked in the trunk quite some time. Hours, maybe longer, to leave a scent that Dodger could detect before we even opened the trunk."

Her eyes widened with horror and she let out a heart-wrenching gasp. He put both arms around her and clasped her to him, mentally searching for the right thing to say. But the truth was so ugly that nothing could soften it.

"Remember I told you how you were babbling that night in the tent?"

"Yes. I kept saying something about making you love me, right?"

"You said those words clearly. You were mumbling other words that I couldn't quite understand. I thought you were saying something about thrills. It fit in with the way you were dressed and the way you were acting." His breath caught in his throat the way it had when Cody had opened that damn trunk. He had to force himself to go on. "Now I understand you were saying *'Don't kill me.'* . . . You were begging for your life."

Her trembling arms circled his neck and she clung to him. It was a silent reminder of all she'd suffered. The hell she'd endured. An ache lodged deep in his chest and he wished he could do something to comfort her, to change the past.

"Am I in danger now?"

"No," Greg assured her. "If they wanted to kill you, they've had plenty of opportunity. I'm positive that losing your memory saved you."

"They could be around, though, watching me." Her voice had dropped to a low, hushed whisper.

"Cody and I don't think so. Your picture has been in every island paper dozens of times. The Pele's ghost brouhaha has been a blessing in disguise. It's given your story lots of attention, yet no one recognizes you. I think whoever did this to you is long gone. But, just in case, Cody's on this full time. When he finds them, I'm going to tear them apart with my bare hands."

And he meant it. He never imagined he would feel this way. He'd lived his life to save animals and people. Now he was filled with a rage that was raw, primitive. Nothing would please him more than to take apart these killers with his bare hands, to make them suffer for what they'd done to Lucky.

"There is some good news. The DA is dropping the charges."

"Thank God," Lucky said, her tone odd. "The good news is I didn't steal the car. The bad news is I was almost murdered."

She began to giggle, the sound reverberating through her trembling body, escalating into laughter. The noise built, becoming increasingly louder, until he realized it was hysterical laughter. And she couldn't stop.

Chapter 24

Lucky's laughter slowly died as Greg put his hands on her shoulders and gently shook her. Smothering a sob, she jumped up and raced out the door into the darkness. The night air was warm and sultry, with the usual tang of the sea and the scent of tropical flowers. She stood on the grass, her eyes on the ribbon of moonlight on the water, and gulped in deep, calming breaths.

Someone had tried to murder her.

Who could hate her that much? Tears clouded her vision, blurring the star-filled night. An inexplicable feeling swept through her. Fear, she realized, imagining what she couldn't remember. She'd begged for her life, trying to bargain with her body. She'd been desperate—desperate beyond comprehension.

Trembling, she stared at the water, physically reacting to the horror of the revelation. Moisture sheened her body, making the balmy air feel cool against her skin, and she knew she was perspiring unnaturally. She must have been terrified that night, she thought. Had she been sweating then and shaking with fear the way she was now? They'd tossed her into the trunk of a car. She couldn't imagine anyone doing something so cruel.

"I won't let anything happen to you."

Lucky turned, realizing that Greg had followed her and was standing at her side. Dodger was nearby, his head cocked, gazing at her forlornly. She stared at him, remembering the greyhound's tragedy. A washout on the race circuit, Dodger had been dumped in the Everglades, left to die. A kindred spirit.

Lucky dropped to her knees, then sat on the grass. She reached for Dodger and he willingly came into her arms. "We're so lucky."

Greg sat beside her and put his warm hand on her arm. "No. You two aren't just lucky. You're both survivors. The will to live, the courage to face a new, uncertain future, sets you apart."

She ran her fingers over Dodger's smooth head, trailing downward to the chrome badge on his collar. His first life had been as a race dog; his second was search and rescue. Her second life was just beginning at the institute, helping stricken animals. But what of her previous life? What had she done to make someone want to kill her?

Facing Greg, she said, "Do you know what worries me the most? I might be the terrible blonde I saw in the mirror. She looked mean and hard, like a woman who'd done something bad enough to make someone want to kill her. I don't want to be someone like that. I want to be a truly good person, someone who helps others."

His steady gaze was compassionate. "You're not a bad person. You're very talented. Think of all the things you do well. You're a whiz on the computer. You sing sweeter than an angel. You could get a job as a chef. And most of all, you have the empathy essential to work with animals. You're not a bad person."

"I pray you're right." Her voice broke miserably.

"I know I am. When you go on *Missing!* someone will come

forward and you'll find out all about your past. I promise you, it'll be something that will make you proud."

Lucky wished she could believe him, but she had the unsettling feeling that the woman in the mirror was really her. Mean-spirited and difficult. Someone people wanted to kill.

He took her face in his hand and held it gently. "You're the best thing that's ever happened to me." His gaze never wavered, making his heartfelt words even more sincere. "I'm crazy about you."

Those were the words she'd longed to hear. *Crazy about you.* But after what she'd learned tonight, Lucky was so overcome by emotion that she couldn't respond.

"Don't be afraid," he said. "The worst is behind you. Remember what Dr. Forenski said: This is a chance to start over."

"I liked the doctor. She made me feel better."

"Know what makes me feel better when I'm upset?"

Lucky swallowed to rid herself of the lump that lingered in her throat. "What?"

"I sit right here and watch the ocean." Greg pointed to the starlit sea lulling quietly in the cove a few feet beyond the rocks. "There's something timeless and healing in knowing you're a small speck in a larger, bolder part of nature's grand scheme.

"A million years ago Haleakala exploded, blasting lava into the sea, creating this island. It took tens of thousands of years for plants to take root in the barren rock, transforming the island year by year, inch by inch, into a lush, tropical paradise. When I look out on the sea and realize that I'm only here for a brief period of time—a blip on nature's timetable—it makes me feel humble. And fortunate to be a part of something larger than myself."

He'd put it so simply, so beautifully. Her composure, already as fragile as an eggshell, threatened to shatter into a thousand pieces that would manifest themselves in more hysterical laughter. Or worse, uncontrollable tears. She chose to nod, accepting his sage comments without speaking. Edging closer to Greg, Lucky sought the shelter of his arms.

Her head fit perfectly into the hollow between his shoulder and his neck. She rested there, breathing in his masculine scent and taking comfort in the strong arms holding her as she gazed at the surf. Her whole being seemed to be filled with the need to be close to another person. She needed Greg.

"I'm crazy about you," he whispered, repeating what he'd said earlier.

"What if I'm a bad person?"

He didn't hesitate. "What you *were* doesn't matter. What you *are* now counts the most. That's the person I know." He gently kissed the nape of her neck, a warm, too brief touch of his lips. "The person I'm crazy about."

Lucky had no idea how long they sat, bodies entwined, watching the moonlight sparkle on the sea. Little by little, she felt better, and she told herself that the past was behind her. Whatever she'd done—or been—couldn't hurt her now. She had a new life with someone who thought she was special. That's what counted.

She was the one to turn to him and offer her lips. For a long moment she felt as if she were floating, her pulse skittering alarmingly even though all he'd done was brush his mouth across hers in a brief kiss. She clung to him with a desperation that came from within, forcing him to really kiss her.

His lips were so masculine, so reassuring in their possessiveness, that she gratefully surrendered to him. *I once was lost but now I'm found.* The words of the hymn echoed through her head as her lips parted and his tongue found hers. Twisting in his arms and arching slightly, Lucky tried to get even closer as his hands swept down her bare back to her waist.

His tongue gently explored the cavern of her mouth. This was so different from the other times he'd kissed her. So sweet. From a man who was usually so tough.

She lay back on the warm grass, bringing him with her. She'd been alone too long; she needed to be a part of someone.

An emotional anchor, she told herself, meant a physical commitment.

Pulling away from her, Greg gazed into her eyes. "Angel, are you sure . . . ?"

"I'm positive."

She'd unleashed a dragon. The tenderness was still there, apparent in his kiss and the controlled way he held his body against hers, but underlying it all was latent aggressiveness that was reassuringly masculine. And protective.

"I need you," she whispered into his ear.

He moved his mouth over hers, devouring its softness, then nibbled at her earlobe. "I'm here. Count on it."

His lips recaptured hers, more insistent this time. She had a burning desire, an aching need to become part of this man. She reveled in the sweetness of his kisses as they trailed a moist path down her shoulder to the high neckline of the swimsuit. *Yes, oh, yes,* she thought. *This is so right. Why had she been fighting it?*

He angled himself across her body so she didn't have to take the full brunt of his weight. Having him hold her was one thing—being under him was quite another. She couldn't move for a second, the sensation was that exquisite. That erotic.

Pressed against the grass, its fragrant scent wafting up from the velvety carpet, she inhaled the smell of the soap he'd used. Above her a thousand winking stars smiled down on them, and she felt so very lucky to be alive, here, with someone so special.

The strap of her suit had slipped off her shoulder and Greg pulled it lower yet, easing it downward an inch at a time until the fullness of her breast was exposed to the moonlight. And his unwavering gaze. He lowered his head, gently kissing her breast.

Arms around his neck, Lucky tugged at his head, urging him to show less restraint, yet realizing he was being sensitive to the disturbing news she'd heard earlier. But right now she didn't want to focus on what horrors she might have endured—and not remembered. Now she needed an affirmation of life.

And she truly couldn't remember feeling more alive. More passionate.

Suddenly, one of his legs was between hers, nudging its way upward with astonishing sensuality. She gasped, "Oh, yes!"

Her hands found their way under his shirt and were now digging hard into his bare skin. She quaked beneath him, mindlessly trying to get closer.

"Are you okay?" His voice was rough with desire.

Her inner thighs were warm, urging her to offer herself to him with astonishing passion. Had she ever felt this way before? She didn't know, didn't bother to consider the question for more than a second. There was only the present. This moment. This man.

"Don't stop," she urged, shifting beneath him, feeling his hardness pressing against her leg.

Greg levered himself upward, balancing on his forearms, his breath whispering over her fevered body. She yanked on the tail of his shirt, and he got the message, shrugging out of it and tossing it aside. The crisp hair on his chest tickled her uplifted palms, sending another shiver of delight through her.

"Oh, Greg, why did I wait so long?"

"I haven't a clue."

He hesitated, hovering over her, his eyes reflecting the light of a lover's moon. Her hands sought his chest, lingering over the taut nubs of his nipples, running her thumbs over the rigid peaks. His breath instantly became more rapid and his eyes narrowed as he lowered his upper body down on hers. Sharp and insistent the urge to taste him, not just feel him, compelled her to run the tip of her tongue across his skin.

The taste was slightly salty yet sweet. A promise of delights she couldn't imagine even though her body insisted she would adore every second. Emitting a breathless sigh, she skimmed across his chest, raising her hands to his strong shoulders. Lingering there. His pupils widened in the moonlight, becoming dark orbs banded by slim hoops of silver-blue.

A surge of feminine pride swept through her. She wasn't the

only one totally aroused. "Darling," she whispered, using a word she'd wanted to say for so long.

She roved across the hard planes of his chest, exploring lower and lower until she reached the waistband of his shorts. Her hands stole under the fabric to caress his bare skin.

He yanked her hands from under his shorts. "It takes two to tango," he whispered.

One breast was already exposed, now the other was bared to the starlit sky. She didn't have to look down to know her nipples were tight, reflecting her desire. His head dipped low as he took a taut nipple between his lips.

She arched beneath him, moaning at the hot pleasure of his tongue on her breast. Yet her body continued to strain upward, welcoming his intimate caress, silently begging for more. The searing pressure of his hand on the other breast, cupping and gently squeezing was almost unbearably erotic.

"You know what I need," he said, his voice rough with passion matching her own. "I've waited far too long."

She didn't hesitate, thrusting her body upward, maintaining contact with his. "So have I. Much too long."

With one swift movement, he covered her completely, his knees between her thighs, nudging insistently, making room for him. His callused thumb stroked the nipple that was still moist from his kiss, rolling it between his fingers. She urged his head lower until his mouth was on her other breast, sucking with such pressure that her head spun.

She wanted him—and no one else—forever.

And he wanted her. The hot, thick proof of his desire was already branding her, pressing against the apex of her thighs. Yet his eyes delivered another message, telling her this was more than just passion in his eyes. Much more.

The bathing suit was off her body in an instant. Down around her hips, then skimming across her thighs, before disappearing over the tips of her toes. Greg tossed it aside and Dodger caught it. Now she was naked beneath the light of the most beautiful moon she had ever seen. A lover's moon.

It didn't feel the least bit awkward to be exposed to Greg's gaze. Not at all. He'd already seen her, been in bed with her. And he knew her better than anyone. Lucky smiled up at him, inviting him to kiss her again. She shuddered as an aching hunger invaded every corner of her body.

"The waiting's over," he said, nudging her with the iron-hard evidence of his desire. "We've danced around this long enough."

"Waltzed," she whispered. "We were slowly waltzing in circles."

His lips covered hers and he kissed her, his tongue a hot, deep caress that mimicked the movements of his groin against hers. Then he edged lower and lower. His tongue flicked lazily down the slope of her chest, and she found herself praying he'd kiss her breasts again. But he swept past her nipples, edging lower, still kissing, but moving downward until he reached the smooth plane of her lower abdomen.

There he stopped, raising his head and gazing up at her. With a growl deep in his throat, Greg lowered his head. And she thought this would be a repeat performance of the last time they'd been in bed.

How wrong she was. In an instant, he'd flicked his tongue over her most sensitive, private areas. She closed her eyes, dizzy with pleasure. He'd done this to her before, but this time she responded much more quickly. Because she remembered, she thought with a thrill of delight. You remembered, so you anticipated.

This was something she'd never forget. A truly unforgettable man.

He reared back, unzipping his fly and shoving down his shorts with amazing quickness. He hovered over her, so male, so fully aroused that she couldn't help but feel proud of herself for having inspired such passion.

He lowered his body, the hot tip of his erection nuzzling her bare flesh. She grabbed his waist, pulling him closer and closer. She was dizzy with anticipation, the stars overhead whirling in a velvet-black vortex. Why had she waited so long to make love to him?

She was aching with need, and willing, so willing, that she thrust her hips upward. His hand eased between their bodies, finding the sweet spot and tracing the sensitive skin with an experienced finger. She heard herself panting, waiting in anticipation . . . waiting.

He eased one finger deep inside her, and she cried out with pleasure. Smiling faintly, he slowly withdrew the finger, bringing with it moist heat. Then he twined two fingers together and slipped into her again. Harder and deeper. She clung to him, her nails embedded in the muscles of his back as his fingers rasped with bittersweetness against the most intimate part of her body, bringing a heady rush of breathless passion.

"Greg, oh, Greg. Don't stop."

He swore, half under his breath, muttering something about hell freezing over. Nudging the hot tip of his erection against her, he slowly parted the moist folds, entering her by degrees. Lucky raked her fingernails across his bare back, unable to stop herself. Greg shoved forward then, breaching her soft opening. In one swift movement, he buried himself to the hilt, then stopped, clutching her to him, the hard contours of his body dominating hers.

"Lucky, you have no idea . . ."

She couldn't concentrate on what he was saying. The searing hardness of him inside her was so erotic, so arousing. She responded instinctively, churning her hips beneath his. Hips hammering, pounding against her relentlessly, he drove into her. And she rose, meeting each thrust with eager passion.

Lucky heard him groan, instinctively knowing he'd climaxed. White-hot heat speared through her body, bringing her innermost muscles satisfying relief. Beneath her hands his body pulsed, trembling with spent desire. She closed her eyes, vaguely aware of her body sheathed with moisture, yet sated.

She stroked his hair, whispering, "I'm crazy about you, too."

* * *

Cody sat at one of Live Bait's tables eating a slice of pizza that looked like the bottom of his shoe and tasted just about as appetizing. It was lunchtime, and the joint was filled with laundry workers noisily consuming pizza and kicking back a few brews before the whistle blew for the next shift. Across from Cody sat Scott Helmer, picking anchovies off his pizza.

"It's turning out to be quite a case, huh?" Scott commented.

It had been two days since the lab in Honolulu had matched the blood sample on the trunk liner with blood taken from Lucky when she was in the hospital. Helmer had gone ballistic when he found out the liner hadn't been flown directly to the FBI's Investigative Support Unit in Quantico, where the exhumed remains of the hiker were being analyzed. Cody had done it on purpose, wanting to give Greg an answer as quickly as possible.

Again he experienced the same gut-wrenching sensation that had hit him when he opened that trunk. He imagined Lucky being stuffed into the trunk, the lid slamming down, leaving her trapped in utter darkness. A cold knot formed in his stomach. Had she been conscious when she was in the trunk? Had she known she was going to die?

All this time he'd been down on Lucky, determined to get rid of her, but now he deeply regretted having treated her so harshly. He was going to make it up to her by doing the best he could to catch the men who'd tried to kill her. His money was on Tony Traylor. Now if he could just prove it.

"Let me get this straight." Helmer licked the grease off his index finger. "Tomorrow morning the DA is announcing that he's dropping the case against the Jane Doe, and this whole trunk business will be reported in the local rag sheet."

"Lucky has every right to know the truth and clear her name."

"Yeah . . . well, it would have been a real help to keep the case under wraps for a while and see what we could turn up."

Cody clutched the Primo bottle with both hands to keep himself from bashing the callous jerk. "I already started talking about the trunk in my office so the bug would pick it up. It might make whoever's listening suspicious if I didn't, then it came out in the *Tattler*."

"Well, that's the first thing you've done right."

The heat rose across the back of Cody's neck. "I explained why I hadn't inspected the car's trunk. Even if I had, I might not have realized that little brown spot was blood. It was the dog who clued us in."

"Jeez-us! Good thing someone's on the ball."

"I know what I'm doing. I spent four years with the LAPD."

The punk hooted. "That's supposed to impress me?"

Cody lost it. He leaned across the small table and grabbed Helmer by the ear, twisting the silver skull and crossbones earring until the undercover agent winced. "Look, you cocky little shit, stop treating me like I'm some dumb fuck." He released the punk's ear. "I want to know what's going on with this case. I've got a vested interest in it."

Helmer gingerly rubbed his earlobe. "Your brother, right? He's involved big time with . . . Lucky."

"Yeah," Cody admitted, another stab of guilt knifing through him. He hadn't been fair to Lucky. He should have abided by the innocent-until-proven-guilty theory. Instead, he'd assumed she was a criminal and had treated her like one. He bit into a slice of pizza, cursing himself.

Helmer waved two fingers at the waitress, signaling for more beer. "You're still sworn to secrecy. This case is much bigger than attempted murder. I overnighted the trunk liner from the lab in Honolulu to Quantico. They put a rush on their analysis. Microscopic traces of Thelma Overholt's blood were on the liner, too."

The pizza hadn't quite hit Cody's stomach. It stalled halfway down as he imagined two terrified women—a year apart—in the same trunk. What kind of criminals were they dealing with? "The car was stolen several days before the hiker's body was discovered. Lucky was wearing Thelma's shoe. The two crimes are linked, but how?''

Helmer spoke in a very low voice, even though no one could hear them above the Don Ho ballad blaring from the rickety jukebox. ''Don't breathe a word of this to anyone. The orchids are the key. Your brother's friend was right. Those bugs really were from plants grown only in southern China.''

Helmer paused to let the waitress plop their beers down on the table and sashay off. ''Examination of the trunk liner revealed part of a dried orchid petal. I forget the name, but it was some rare, endangered species from the rain forest right here on Maui.''

Cody gulped his beer, excited to be part of an interesting, complicated case for a change. Not only were the orchids the missing link, but this was a detail known only to the killer or killers. Such facts were often deliberately kept from the public in order to eliminate suspects or nuts who confessed to every crime just to get their picture on the six o'clock news.

''Smugglers are stripping the rain forest of rare orchids. There isn't enough manpower to keep an eye on them.'' Cody swigged his beer again, thinking. ''Of course, orchids and Maui Wowie grow side by side. Could be a drug deal gone sour. I really suspect Traylor.''

''Maybe,'' Helmer said, not sounding convinced. ''I checked with headquarters. A promising source claimed to have information on the credit card scam. The source was supposed to get back to us with proof. That information could tell us more about what Thelma was on to before she was murdered. It might help us make the connection between the two women.''

''I don't trust secret informants,'' Cody told him. From his brief stint with the LAPD, he knew just how unreliable they could be. ''Most of them would sell their mother for a few bucks to buy drugs.''

''True,'' Helmer conceded. ''Secret sources are nothing but trouble. This one hasn't contacted us again, so it probably doesn't matter.''

Secret sources. Tony Traylor. Orchids. Friggin' weird, Cody thought.

"There's one other thing," Helmer said, his eyes darting around the room. The whistle had just sounded for the afternoon shift, and Live Bait was nearly deserted. "I got the final report on the hiker's death. The cause was a blow to the back of the head . . . by the exact same instrument that was used on Lucky."

"Shit!" Cody slammed his bottle down on the wood table, his stomach churning. Thank God, he was sworn to secrecy. He couldn't tell Sarah this. She'd cried, sobbing for almost an hour when he'd told her about Lucky being the victim of cold-blooded killers who'd thought nothing of stuffing her in a trunk.

"Both crimes were the same thing. An icing."

Icing. The word alone sent a chill through Cody, accompanied by a stab of fear. The *hui* was notorious for ridding itself of troublesome people in a way that appeared not to be murder. Accidents and suicide were favorites of the Hawaiian gang. Profits from tourism were the gang's lifeblood. Murder and paradise simply did not mix. No way was Hawaii going to become Florida—a tourist's nightmare—so the *hui* iced people. And they were buried without a police investigation.

The icing. The orchids. Tony Traylor. Cody bet they were all linked. What he wouldn't give to solve this case, to make Sarah and Greg happy. All right, he'd feel less guilty about the way he'd treated Lucky, too. But in the back of his mind he realized that just because they had tried to ice Lucky didn't mean she wasn't somehow involved in some type of criminal activity.

Chapter 25

"I'm going to kill that fucking dog!" yelled the Orchid King's partner. "If it hadn't been for him, no one would have known we tried to ice her. Now they'll tie us to that bitch from American Express."

The 800 number blared across the screen, signaling the end of *Missing!* The Orchid King switched off the television. The program had been astonishingly accurate . . . up to a point. The actress portraying Lucky hadn't done her justice.

And they had no idea what she really looked like. The picture they'd shown of her had been taken the day she'd been brought to the hospital. She had looked like death with big hair. Blonde hair.

"Calm down," he said to his partner. "Nothing can link us to those icings."

"Unfuckingbelievable! You're not worried."

The king turned away to inspect a crystal vase with a rare lady slipper orchid in muted tones of mauve. "I'm not in the least bit concerned about the police. I'm more worried that someone from her past will turn up."

"But the FBI has the American Express agent's remains."

The king examined the delicate veins of deep amethyst running through the orchid's petals like a fine cobweb. "So? They haven't come up with anything, or the bug would have told us about it. Thelma Overholt was six feet under for two years. That means major decomposition. Plus she was embalmed—all her body fluids were removed. It doesn't leave them a lot to work with."

"I don't like it. I don't like the *feel* of this."

"I prefer the privacy that using a computer gives us," the king agreed. "We can probe into everyone's closet and yank out the dirty linen without them knowing we've been there. That's why I don't like paying people to plant bugs and send us tapes, but sometimes it can't be helped."

The dirty linen comment he'd just made gave the king an idea. Computers ruled the world for sure. He'd tapped into numerous data banks and erased one woman's entire existence because she'd crossed him. Why not fuck up Braxton? Alter his credit rating or max out his charge cards. Come to think of it, the prick didn't have any charge cards. What type of man went through life without a Visa?

The kind of man who deserved to suffer.

Greg checked his watch and saw that it had been exactly nineteen minutes since he'd last gone down to check on Lucky. Seemed like hours. He couldn't help himself. He wanted to be with her, not preparing the log for the yearly journey to Niihau Island to count the monk seals and give the males their shots.

It had been an agonizingly long three weeks since *Missing!* had been shown. The episode had generated hundreds of tips. Lucky had been spotted in more places than Elvis. From Vermont to Arizona, people claimed to have known Lucky. None of the leads had panned out. Thank you, God.

The phone rang and he picked it up, hoping it wasn't the bank again. Some idiot had made a mistake and the money he'd deposited hadn't been credited to his account. He'd bounced checks from one end of the island to the other.

It was Cody. "Yo, Greg. How's it going?"

"Great," he responded, but every muscle in his body tensed. He kept waiting for the ax to fall, for Cody to tell him that someone was going to take Lucky away from him. "Hear anything on Lucky?"

"Nope. Not a damn thing. The FBI's checked out all of the promising leads already. They're just running through the other stuff now. They say after this much time, it's unlikely they'll find anything. It's totally weird. You'd think that someone would recognize Lucky."

"What about your investigation? Any idea who tried to kill her?"

"I'm still working on it."

Cody sounded discouraged, but Greg didn't question him further. He knew the FBI was working with Cody, forbidding him to discuss any details. He reached for the stack of unopened mail and began sorting through it as they talked.

"We're taking the boat out to the rookery on Niihau tomorrow," Greg said, tossing aside yet another announcement that he was a grand sweepstakes winner. "Time to count the monk seals and give the males their shots."

"Shots?"

Greg had forgotten the program had gone into effect when he hadn't been speaking to Cody. "Yeah, it's a new thing. They developed it over at the U of H. We give the males a shot to lower their testosterone."

"Jeez-us! Don't come near me with that stuff. Why are you doing that?"

Actually, the way he'd been behaving around Lucky, Greg figured he should give himself at least a dozen shots. "There are so few females left—another was just eaten by a shark— that the males mob females in heat. By the time they're through, she's either crushed or severely injured. Either way she dies, meaning there are still fewer females, so the mobbing gets worse with each season. We've made the males less aggressive by lowering their testosterone levels. More females are surviving.''

"Sounds like gang rape to me."

Greg couldn't disagree. "It's the instinct to survive. Monk seals never behaved like this when there were enough females."

"Be careful out there. Don't those males weigh a quarter of a ton or more?"

"Yeah, and they can be mean." He added a bill for Abbie's goat's milk to the stack of unpaid bills. The next one looked strange, and Greg ripped it open while Cody told him about the twins' next soccer game "Shit!"

"What's wrong?"

"Cody, you won't believe this. They're going to repossess my car. They're totally screwed up. I made the payment on time. I have the canceled check."

"Those things happen. I'm always getting late notices." Cody laughed. "I deserve 'em. I'm always juggling bills."

"It's weird. My bank account shows overdrawn even though there's plenty of money in there, and I have the deposit slips to prove it."

After two beats of silence, Cody said, "Coincidence, that's all. Look, I gotta go. Call me when you come back from Niihau."

"Right. I owe you one."

I owe you one. Cody was still smiling when he drove up to Mama's Fish House to meet Scott Helmer. It felt great to be talking to Greg again. What he wouldn't give to discuss the case with him. This need for secrecy was a bitch.

He spotted the Toyota that Helmer had rented and knew the agent was waiting for him down on the rocks. Stiff winds buffeted the horseshoe cove, making it a favorite with windsurfers. Riding colorful boards with clear vinyl sails trimmed in fluorescent pinks, greens, and purples, the kids flew across the white-capped water, delighting the tourists chowing down at Mama's. Some of the surfers could actually do backward flips with their boards.

"It's a wonder they don't break their necks," Cody said to Helmer as he came up beside the agent, who was sitting on a boulder watching. He eased himself down on a nearby rock as a sand crab scuttled away.

"Crazy kids." Helmer pushed his sunglasses to the top of his head, facing Cody. "Where'd you get the name of that shrink who hypnotized Lucky?"

"I contacted a buddy at U of H in Honolulu. He put it on the Internet, and Dr. Forenski contacted me. Why?"

"She was in your office, right?"

Cody suspected where the punk was going with this. "Is she the one who planted the bug?"

"Yeah. She's holed up in a condo not far from your office, transcribing tapes recorded by the bug."

Cody stood up and walked over a few feet to the tide pool. "One of my men picked her up. She was supposed to go directly to the clinic, but she had him drive her by my office. Said she wanted my 'impression' of Lucky on the day she was brought in. I should have smelled a rat, but I didn't. She had excellent credentials. She seemed like a nice old lady."

"There's nothing wrong with her credentials. She's a first-rate hypnotherapist in Honolulu. Someone got to her. They're paying her a fortune to sit around here."

"Who?" He returned to the rock, truly excited. This could be the break they needed.

"Dr. Forenski's cooperating, but she doesn't know who hired her. She agreed to treat Lucky, then someone contacted her on the phone. It was so much money that she went for it. Question is, how did they know to contact her?"

"The computer. They're monitoring on-line services." Then a flash of insight hit him. "They're screwing with my brother right now."

"What do you mean?"

The silver skull and crossbones earring in Helmer's ear winked in the bright sunlight as Cody explained. When he finished, there was grudging admiration in the punk's eyes.

"You're probably right. I'll get our experts on it. I'll bet it ties to the credit card scam. Someone's able to breach the bank's security systems. That's how they know which accounts to use and when to get out before we catch them."

"What about Traylor? Anything on him? I still think he's tied to this."

"I'm working on it, but it looks like he's running a little Maui Wowie, that's all."

Clearly, trafficking marijuana didn't rank high on the agent's priority list. Who could blame him? The agency was strapped for cash, and major drugs were coming in from Mexico and South America. But Cody cared. This was his island; his family lived here. He promised himself he'd get Traylor.

"Is it okay to tell Lucky that the wound on her head matches the one on Thelma Overholt? She has a right to know the same person who tried to kill her murdered the hiker."

"Shit, no! We're close to cracking this case. Don't blow it."

Cody hated keeping something this important from Lucky. And Greg.

Greg managed to work for a few hours, then he went down to the pool, anxious to see Lucky. She'd been through an experience so horrible it defied the imagination. The fact that she couldn't remember the experience made it even more terrifying. What had happened to her in those hours before the car was pushed off the cliff? *I can make you love me.* She'd been desperate, willing to do anything to save her life.

What else had they done to her?

Again, the urge to kill overwhelmed him. If he ever learned who had made her suffer, he doubted he could control himself. Yet Lucky seemed to have accepted her fate. If revenge was on her mind, she hadn't mentioned it to him. Instead, she concentrated on building a new life. Her courage and spirit gave her a power and a depth that made other women he'd known seem weak.

"*Aikane,* you gotta see this."

Hearing Nomo call him buddy in a happier tone than normal, Greg ducked around the oleander hedge and into the seals' area.

"She's a natural," Nomo told him as he pointed to Lucky, who was in the pool.

"*Hele, hele,*" she called in Hawaiian for Abbie to come on. The pup was on the ramp leading into the water, but having none of it. "It's okay, sweetie. Come here. *Hele.*"

Lucky's hair was wet and slicked back, which emphasized her green eyes. Everything about her called to him. Once it had been just her body. He still adored every inch, from the scarred soles to the small scar on the back of her head, but what drew him to her now was a much deeper emotion.

Lucky waved at him, then called, "Dodger, show Abbie what to do."

Dodger pranced over to the ramp and nuzzled the timid pup. Taking tiny steps, the dog inched down the ramp, with Abbie at his heels, mincing along. They reached the water and Dodger plunged in, swimming rather than dog-paddling, not splashing at all. The pup flopped into the water, flippers slapping frantically, her eyes wild with fright.

Nomo shook his head. "That's what happens when you don't know you're a seal. Abbie's bonded with Lucky and Dodger, not with the other seals. We're trying to get her back on track developmentally."

"*Pono!*" Careful cried Lucky. "Watch me!" She sliced her arms through the water, pretending to be a seal.

It was the most ridiculous, comical sight he'd seen since he'd watched the reruns of *Spanky and Our Gang* while Aunt Sis had been out playing poker. Slapstick comedy. But it was working. Little Abbie seemed to take courage, bobbing up and down like a furry cork, fluttering her flippers and sending a skein of water droplets toward the sunny sky.

Dodger hovered nearby, treading water. Suddenly, Abbie got the hang of it and stopped the frantic splashing. Her flippers glided through the water, propelling her forward effortlessly.

"*Akamai 'oe,*" Lucky told Abbie.

"You're so smart," Greg translated, looking at Nomo. "You're teaching Lucky a lot of Hawaiian."

The big man shrugged, grinning even more than usual. "She wants to live here. We don't want people thinking she's a tourist, do we?"

Greg watched the threesome swim to the deep end of the lagoon-shaped pool and back. Lucky was executing a flawless breaststroke, careful not to kick up any water, which might frighten the pup.

"She'd make a wonderful mother," Nomo commented.

Greg didn't admit the older man had read his mind.

Chapter 26

The Orchid King closed the door to the special refrigeration vault that had just been installed in the Chinatown warehouse. "Perfect. Houdini himself couldn't get out of this chamber—or into it."

"I don't know why you're worried about those damn orchids," his partner said. "Who would want to steal them?"

"You'd be surprised what some collectors will do to get their hands on a rare species like these."

"How are you going to go into that vault with those orchids giving off poisonous fumes?"

The king pointed to the special switch on the outside of the refrigerated chamber. "I have a ventilation switch to keep the air from the outside circulating, so fumes don't build up. But if we ever need to kill someone, just lock them in here"—he flicked the switch with a grin—"then turn off the ventilator."

His partner looked ill. Clearly, the man who'd once been as close as his brother was losing his guts—if he'd ever had any. Did he have the balls to make the next move in this game?

"How long does it take for someone to die in there?"

The king chuckled, imagining Greg Braxton in the vault with a cache of beautiful, but lethal, orchids. Gasping for every breath.

"You die slowly ... very slowly. The fumes paralyze your lungs." The king laughed again. "But while you're dying, it feels as if your lungs are on fire. Want to know the best part? The authorities won't know what the hell killed you. It's a poison so rare that they haven't developed a test to detect it. The perfect icing."

"Number 68," Greg called out to Lucky as they trooped across the sandy beach on Niihau, counting the monk seals.

Lucky checked off the enormous male, who was wearing a green tag. It meant he'd been tagged over a dozen years ago when they'd started. An old dude, Greg thought, as Nomo held the seal's head while Greg quickly injected him with the testosterone depressant.

"*Pono!*" Careful! Nomo yelled as the seal pivoted, showing surprising agility. The animal blasted out a noise that sounded like an elephant roaring.

Greg jumped aside. "We're outta here!"

Barefoot and wearing the provocative black one-piece suit, Lucky walked beside him. Damn, she was sexy. But she didn't seem to realize it, too caught up in the experience to pay any attention to the way she looked. From a nearby rock, a red-footed booby whistled and fluttered its black wings, catching her attention.

"Everything here sounds so ... different," Lucky commented, and Greg imagined her green eyes were wide beneath her sunglasses. "No city noises at all."

True, he thought. The dozens of seals made a variety of sounds, from foghorn snorts to snuffling to the high-pitched cries of the young pups cavorting in the surf. The adults were molting, shedding their coats, which made them itchy and grumpy, and thus more noisy than usual.

A counterpoint to their cacophony was the chatter of the terns and frigates patrolling the shore in search of fish. As always, the background music was the rhythmic rush of the surf on the shore. Lucky was right: Civilization was far away, and he wished it would stay there.

Lucky linked her arm through his, clutching the institute's notebook to her chest with her other arm. "When will we be bringing Abbie here?"

They waded into the warm water, heading for the dinghy that would take them back to the *Atlantis.* The *Boston Whaler* was anchored inside the reef, bobbing in the waist-deep water.

"When Abbie's able to catch her own food, we'll tag her and release her here. The count's up, but they still desperately need females."

Greg gave Lucky a boost into the *Whaler.* She smiled, the delighted smile that never failed to captivate him. There was nothing he'd like better than to kiss her right then and there, but Nomo was with them, now heaving his considerable bulk into the dinghy.

They were back at the *Atlantis,* which was anchored beyond the reef, in a matter of minutes, leaving the private island, the haven for monk seals, behind. Nomo volunteered to take the helm while Greg went into the cabin below with Lucky. To check the tallies. Yeah, right.

The last thing on his mind was the seal count. All day he'd resisted the urge to haul Lucky into his arms and make love to her on the sugar-white sand. Be professional, he'd told himself. You have work to do. Now his job was complete, and his body reminded him of what he wanted every time he looked at Lucky.

"I'm going to hop in the shower," Lucky said, stripping off her suit.

She was across the small cabin and in the stall before he had his trunks off. Freeing his erection, he grunted, then kicked the wet suit aside. The physical tension in his body, his constant need for this woman would once have disturbed him. Not anymore. He accepted it, welcoming it.

"We both can't fit in here," Lucky protested when he opened the shower door.

"Wanna bet?" He slid the door shut behind him.

There was just enough room between their bodies for the water to sluice over them, washing away the salt and gritty sand. In places there wasn't any room. Lucky's full breasts pillowed against his chest. His hard sex nudged her thighs.

She'd already rinsed off, her hair was slicked back with beads of water clinging to the curls and to her lashes. One tantalizing drop of moisture clung to the curve of her upper lip. Rivulets of water flowed over her breasts, arrowing down the flat plane of her belly to the dark cluster of curls.

"You're a mess," she said, sparks of laughter in her eyes. "I'd better take care of you myself."

Greg widened his stance to counter the slight sway of the boat while Lucky removed the bottle of biodegradable soap from the shelf. She squirted it over his torso, then ran her hands across his chest, lathering him. The smooth gliding of her fingers sent a shudder through him and his groin throbbed in response. Lucky grinned at him, moving provocatively against his burgeoning erection. Her palm traced the contours of his chest with agonizing slowness.

"Maybe I should do your back." she said with feigned innocence. "It's probably filthy."

"Forget it. Just keep going lower. That's where the problem is."

"What problem?"

One of her dark eyebrows was tilted upward, teasing him. But her hand kept moving south. She soaped his stomach, her thumb circling his belly button in a way Greg found unexpectedly arousing. His groin muscles contracted as she slowly inched lower, taking her damn sweet time. Torturing him on purpose.

"My stars! *What* is this?" she asked, brushing a soap-slick fingertip over his penis. "Didn't we make love last night—and again this morning? I think you need a shot of that testosterone depressant yourself."

"I wasn't this horny before you came along."

Lucky threw up her hands, sending soap bubbles into the air. "You're saying this is my fault."

"Damn right."

He grabbed her hand and guided it to his cock, which was hot and achingly hard now. He swallowed, his throat tight. She soaped him, sliding her small hand along the hard shaft, squeezing, squeezing, squeezing. Letting go, she moved lower still, cupping his balls in her soapy palm, lifting them.

"Christ!"

"Is this a religious experience?" she asked.

"Damn right."

"You're cursing a lot for someone expecting salvation."

He grinned, noting the tell tale signs that she was just as aroused as he. The rapid tempo of the pulse, throbbing at the base of her throat. The dilated pupils, reducing those magnificent green irises to a thin orb of color. The way she arched toward him, unconsciously offering herself to him.

Her fingers feathered through the thicket of hair around his cock. He nuzzled her thigh with the hot tip of his erection. She ignored it, playing like some damn kid with the bubbles on his belly.

"Time's up," he said, pushing her against the shower wall. "My turn."

His hand was between her thighs in a second. Her skin was wet from the shower. And slick. She arched into his hand, her arms around his neck, pulling him closer. He eased one finger inside her and her muscles tightened around him.

Lucky moaned, then whispered, "Hurry up."

"You're not rushing me, angel."

He kissed her, his tongue mating with hers as his thumb found her most sensitive spot, caressing it. She went up on tiptoe, swaying against him, her nails biting into his shoulders.

A pulsating tide of raw desire shot through him, making every part of his body taut, begging for release. He murmured something about how crazy he was about her, how he couldn't get enough of her.

Greg guided himself into her, burrowing between the soft folds, trying to be gentle. But it was impossible. Lucky brought out his most primitive instincts. He pushed hard, stretching her until she raked her nails down his back. He cupped her bottom with both hands and brought her upward so she could wrap her legs around his waist. The new position allowed him to plunge a bit deeper, so deep now that she moaned.

"Am I hurting you?"

Her eyes were black now, without a hint of green. "A little . . . but it feels great. Don't stop."

He sucked in his breath, striving to pace himself. Instead, his lungs filled with hot, moist air. "Aw, hell. I'm ready to come."

"Hurry up," she whispered, and he moved back and forth, feeling her taut inner muscles clench around him. "Harder."

He thrust into her, pounding his thick shaft into the moist heat of her body. She met each stroke with an upward push. He was out of control now. Hell, they both were. It took all his willpower to last the next few minutes, until he felt the first quavering of orgasm shake her body. Then he let himself go, hammering into her one final time just as a white-hot bolt of bittersweet release shot through him.

He reared backward, so savage was his body's reaction, hitting his skull against the showerhead. For a second he didn't move. He stood there, Lucky still in his arms, letting the water flow over his face.

"Darling," Lucky whispered.

He opened his eyes, realizing she was pulling away. Not wanting this to end, he held on to her for a moment. Then he let his still-turgid cock slip out and quickly rinsed off. He wanted to say something. All he did was act like an animal around her, rutting at every opportunity. Craving down and dirty sex.

Back in the cabin, they dressed in silence. What was she thinking? he wondered. She had on shorts and a "Save the Whales" T-shirt, and was reaching for the counter where she'd put Rudy's tooth, when he stopped her.

"I have a hard time saying what I'm thinking," he told her. "What goes on between us isn't just sex—not to me, anyway. I care about you very much." He gazed into those green eyes and told her the honest truth. "I love you."

"Do you?" she whispered. "I was hoping you did. I'm so happy with you ... with my life."

Okay, she was happy. Did she love him? "How do you feel about me?"

Tears welled up in her eyes, but she rapidly blinked them away. "I love you. I can't imagine ever loving anyone else."

He bear-hugged her, then realized he was holding her too tight and loosened his grip. "I want to share my whole life with you. I want you at my side this winter when the whales return with their calves. I want you with me when we return to count the seals next summer. I want—"

"I want you, too," she cut him off.

Greg smiled, then grinned even more at her enthusiastic expression. "I've been waiting to see what *Missing!* would turn up. It would be easier if we knew your legal name. As it is, you don't exist. But I've been checking on it, and there are things we can do to get you a new name. You'll need one for the marriage license."

Her features became even more animated. "I told Dr. Forenski I wanted to be Lucky Braxton. Now I want it more than anything."

With pulse-pounding certainty, Greg knew he would never love anyone the way he loved Lucky.

* * *

It was late afternoon when the *Atlantis* returned to the wharf, having left before daybreak. Greg spotted Cody and Sarah standing on the dock. There was no reason why they shouldn't meet them; they often did things together. But Cody hadn't mentioned it.

Greg helped Nomo tie up the *Atlantis,* alarm bells ringing inside his head. Lucky waved happily to Sarah and jumped onto the dock. Cody and Sarah walked toward them, their expressions solemn. Greg stood beside Lucky, braced for the worst.

"The hot line for *Missing!* turned up something," Cody said.

Greg glanced at Lucky and watched as the smile was wiped off her face. She anxiously looked at Sarah, then at him. He slipped his arm around her, silently praying.

"Lucky, there isn't any easy way to tell you this." Cody sucked in his breath. "Your husband's here."

A wild flash of anger ripped through Greg. His worst nightmare had just come true. "Her husband!" he shouted. "Where the hell has he been?"

Lucky looked shell-shocked. She was staring at her left hand, at her ring finger. "I wasn't wearing a wedding ring."

"You'd taken off your wedding ring." Cody looked directly into Greg's eyes. "Brad Wagner never reported Lucky missing because he assumed she was having a fling somewhere."

"He thought she'd come home when she was ready," Sarah added. "The way she had before."

A fling? Greg didn't believe it. Then he recalled the night he'd found her. Evidently, she and her husband had problems with their relationship. Lucky was a different woman now. Okay, they could get a divorce. It happened all the time.

"Wagner. Wagner," Lucky repeated, testing the name. "What's—"

"Kelly," Sarah answered. "You're Kelly Anne Wagner. Isn't that a beautiful name?"

"Kelly Wagner." Lucky grinned at him, her green eyes filled

with excitement. She grabbed Greg's hand and squeezed. "I know my name now! I'm Kelly Anne Wagner."

Cody and Sarah didn't look as thrilled as Lucky. Actually, they seemed troubled, and the ray of hope Greg had experienced when thinking about the divorce evaporated.

"Are you sure this Wagner guy is really her husband?"

Cody nodded. "The FBI checked him out. Brad flew in this morning. He's over at the Four Seasons."

"Where does he live? I mean, where did I live?"

"You're from Honolulu," Sarah said. "You live in the ritzy Kahala area near Diamond Head."

"Wait a minute! Something's fishy here," Greg said. "You checked her prints with the DMV in Honolulu and came up with nothing."

Cody nodded, his expression grim. "True. Lu—Kelly doesn't have a driver's license. She doesn't need one. She has a full-time chauffeur and limo. The ring she took off is a diamond as big as a doorknob."

Greg could see that Lucky wasn't impressed by the money. He knew her well enough now to believe she'd stay with him even if it meant giving up a fairy-tale existence. She'd said she loved him, and she'd meant it. His arm was still around her; he couldn't resist giving her a little squeeze.

"Why did he wait so long after *Missing!* aired to come for me?"

"He didn't see the program," Cody explained. "It seems you have a maid who's in this country illegally from the Philippines. She saw the show but was afraid to call in. She waited until Brad returned from a business trip and told him."

"Does he have any idea who tried to kill her?" Greg asked.

Cody shook his head. "Apparently, Kelly had left some time ago. He didn't know where she went or who she was with."

The nagging feeling in the back of Greg's mind refused to go away. "What kind of guy is he besides rich?"

Cody quickly looked at Sarah. "Brad seems like a nice guy. Average height. Sandy hair. Likable."

Bitter jealousy raged through Greg. Brad Wagner had lived with Lucky. Greg didn't want anyone else to have touched her. She was his—his alone. It was an irrational feeling, he told himself. She had a past, and there was bound to be a man in it. But he still hated the man.

"Brad's made a fortune with designer beef," Sarah added.

Brad? Did everyone have to be so damn chummy with this jerk?

"What's designer beef?" Lucky asked.

"It's meat from cows who are specially bred so that their bodies have less fat. It's sold in upscale markets and trendy restaurants," Sarah informed her.

Lucky nervously moistened her lips, gazing up at him. "You understand, I have to meet this man. He'll know about my past. He's probably just here to see that I'm all right."

Greg expelled a sigh of relief that ruffled the damp hair across his forehead. Lucky saw the situation the way he did. The tightness in his throat eased a bit, and he put his hand on her shoulder. "Of course, you have to talk to him."

"I need to explain in person that I want to stay here," Lucky said. "If I left without telling him where I was going, our relationship must have been in trouble. I doubt that he'll care." She turned to Sarah with a smile. "Greg and I want to get married. I would like to have a family."

She loved him and wanted to marry him. Hell, they hadn't discussed a family yet, but he was ready. More than ready. He loved her; he wanted to start a new life. Now they could wipe the slate clean and begin again.

Sarah and Cody exchanged a look that Greg couldn't quite decipher. Sarah stepped forward, her expression concerned. "Lucky, you already have a family. Brad brought your daughter, Julie, with him."

Chapter 27

A daughter. Everything inside Lucky went cold and still. In all the scenarios she had envisioned—and there had been hundreds—she'd never imagined a child. She'd assumed she would have sensed being a mother.

A suffocating wave of self-hatred engulfed her. Not only did she have a child, but apparently she had deserted her daughter. Why? What possible explanation could there be for leaving a child? Lucky had the awful feeling that her worst fears had come true. She was a terrible selfish person, not a good mother like Sarah, who'd done everything to hold her family together.

"How old is my daughter?" She choked out the words.

"Four," Sarah responded. "Julie looks just like you. Beautiful brown hair and deep green eyes."

Lucky trembled, but the pressure of Greg's hand on the small of her back steadied her. *A fling.* She recalled Cody's words with a sharp pang of humiliation. Her husband hadn't reported her missing because he assumed she was off having a fling and would return. What kind of person left a child for a fling?

The woman in the mirror.

They were in Cody's Bronco now, driving to the hotel where her family was waiting. The oppressive silence was broken only by occasional transmissions from the police radio.

"I can't imagine leaving my child," she said to Greg, then looked at Sarah. "Did Brad say what had happened?"

"No." Sarah shook her head. "He just said you two had been having problems."

"You would never have left—"

"Don't be hard on yourself," Greg interrupted Lucky. "You don't have any of the facts. Wait until you talk to this man."

They drove into the palm-lined courtyard of the Four Seasons. Two doormen rushed up to the car, followed by a hostess with a colorful *lei* around her neck. Trembling, Lucky stepped out of the car, consumed by self-doubt. What would she say to her young daughter? If only she knew more about what had happened.

"I'll go in with you," Greg offered.

Lucky hesitated for several seconds, finally mustering the courage to say, "No. I have to do this myself. Please wait for me."

"We'll be in the bar overlooking the beach," Sarah said.

Cody gave Lucky the suite number, then guided Sarah toward the beach. Greg hung back, staying beside Lucky. She knew he wanted to speak with her privately.

"I have to see this man—my husband." She put her hand on his arm. "I must find out why I left my daughter. Please understand."

He brought her hand up to his lips and kissed her palm. It was a gentle kiss, yet it conveyed his inner strength. His love.

"Of course, I understand. You have a child. That changes everything. What it doesn't change is the way I feel about you. I love you."

"I know, and I truly love you."

He nodded, then slowly walked away. Lucky struggled with the uncertainty of the situation. She loved Greg—of that she was completely certain—but what of her past life? Had she once loved Brad Wagner the way she now loved Greg? Impossible. She could have never loved anyone this much.

Yet the man she was about to meet had married her and had given the most precious gift—a child. But it was a life she could no longer remember. She had a new life now, and she was so happy.

The elevator door slid silently open, and the beige marble foyer of the hotel's concierge level stood before her in all its opulence. Lucky tentatively stepped onto the cool surface, and a man rushed up to her. She managed to mumble the suite number, and the concierge ushered her down a lushly carpeted corridor to the suite occupied by her family.

Her family. The thought sent a shudder of disbelief through her. Somehow she'd never thought of herself as part of a family. She had been certain that she would have known she had a child. But she'd been wrong.

Lucky began walking faster, confused, panic just a hairbreadth away. Her pulse had accelerated and a sheen of moisture cloaked the back of her neck. She felt disoriented and hot all over, the way she had felt that first morning when she'd awakened to a strange orange sky.

The concierge stopped outside the suite where her husband and daughter waited. He knocked, and the sound seemed unusually loud in the elegant hallway. For a moment Lucky wished Greg were with her, but she inhaled a calming breath and told herself that this was her life, her family. She had to deal with this alone.

The door swung open and Lucky breathed a sigh of relief. A maid in a pristine uniform answered the knock.

"This is Mrs. Wagner," said the concierge.

Mrs. Wagner. The words had a strange, unnatural ring to them. She'd never thought of herself as anyone but Lucky Braxton. But that title was nothing more than an illusion. She was married to another man and had a young child.

The concierge left and the maid ushered her into the spacious room. Off to one side was a small round dining table overlooking the beach and the setting sun. A young girl sat there on a booster chair, eating, opposite a man with sandy hair and deep-set eyes. He looked very familiar.

"Kelly? Is that you?" He jumped to his feet but didn't come closer.

The child turned, spoon in hand, and faced her. Oh, my God, Lucky said to herself. That's exactly how I looked when I was four—straight brown hair in a rich shade of chestnut and vibrant green eyes.

"Brad?" Lucky forced herself to say, facing the man who was her husband.

"Are you okay? They told me you'd been in an *accident*." He rolled his eyes and she understood the facts about what really happened had been kept from the child.

Brad Wagner's hazel eyes surveyed her with concern. He was a slim man of medium height, with a long-distance runner's build. His sandy hair brushed the top of his forehead in loose, wavy curls.

There wasn't anything about him that would have made her look twice had she passed him in the supermarket. Certainly, he didn't resemble the virile Greg Braxton. But she instantly saw why Sarah had liked Brad. He had a down-to-earth quality that stood out despite the luxury suite.

"Mommy?" Julie scooted out of the booster chair. "Mommy, what happened to yore hair?"

Yore, not *your,* made Lucky smile. A child, an innocent child, still learning to pronounce words properly. Lucky's heart floundered in her chest, then sank to her feet at the love and wonder shining from her daughter's eyes.

The young girl looked familiar, but that was all. She didn't remember anything about Julie. Until this moment, the enormity of what she'd lost when her memory vanished hadn't really registered. Now Lucky was heartsick, wishing she could remember Julie as a tiny baby with just a tuft of dark hair instead of the deep bangs and longer hair of a child.

"Mommy got a haircut," Lucky said, conscious of Brad staring. "Do you like it?"

Julie rushed over to her father and grabbed his leg with both arms, obviously confused and in need of reassurance from him. Brad Wagner's hand touched his daughter's dark hair. It was a natural gesture, instantly conveying a close, loving relationship. It made Lucky feel even more guilty. Where did she fit in?

"Julie's a little frightened," Brad explained.

Lucky dropped to her knees, recalling what Greg had told her about frightened animals. Get low; meet them on eye level. *"Hele, hele,"* she said, her voice soft. "Come on. Come to Mommy."

Julie's green eyes widened and she walked forward, her steps slow and tentative. "Mommy?" She took a few more steps toward Lucky's outreached arms. "Where did you go?"

"It doesn't matter. I'm back now," Lucky replied, just as her daughter came within arm's length. Every fiber of her being longed to cradle the child to her breast.

Julie smiled and catapulted herself into Lucky's embrace. Her little arms circled Lucky's neck and she kissed her on the cheek. Lucky kissed her daughter, first on one cheek, then on the other. She hugged the little girl to her bosom and closed her eyes.

A few seconds passed and she opened them. Tears sheened her vision, and her throat was so tight she could barely swallow.

"Don't cry, Mommy." Julie brushed away a tear. "A kiss will make you betta'." She kissed the rise of Lucky's cheek with her sweet lips, concern in her eyes.

Unable to speak, Lucky cuddled her daughter. She experienced a swell of intense emotion, instantly recognizing it was love. This child was her flesh and blood. An innocent. The best part of her.

"Julie, finish your dinner," Brad instructed. "Mommy's going to be just fine."

Lucky released Julie, and the child scampered over to the

table. Brad put out his hand to Lucky, helping her stand. She rose and looked into his eyes, too overcome with emotion to speak.

He guided her to the table, asking, "Do you want something to eat?"

Lucky shook her head, blinking back tears. The last thing she wanted was food. She wanted to watch her daughter eat what appeared to be a cut-up piece of chicken. Who had taught her to hold a fork?

Suddenly, all the things she would never remember were overwhelming. Her first glimpse of her newborn baby. Julie's first step. Julie's first word. Memories other mothers cherished. *Gone forever.*

She had convinced herself the past didn't matter. She had been making a new life for herself. But she realized she'd done it thinking her own past was ugly and frightening. She'd been afraid she was a prostitute, not a mother.

But the past did matter. Lucky watched Julie, thinking of events she no longer recalled. Again her heart ached for the precious moments she would never remember—memories of her daughter.

Lucky was conscious of Brad staring at her, and she mustered a smile. There were so many questions she longed to ask about their relationship and why she'd left. But now with Julie happily eating, stabbing each piece of chicken with her fork, was not the time. They needed to be alone.

"Honey, eat your vegetables," Brad told Julie.

She speared one pea with her fork and slowly brought it to her mouth. Lucky couldn't help smiling. Julie hates peas, she thought, just like most children. What else doesn't she like? What else have I forgotten?

"Does she have to eat those peas?" Lucky asked. "She doesn't like them. Maybe we could get carrots. Do you like carrots?"

Julie looked at Lucky as if she were crazy. Then she gazed uncertainly at her father.

Brad was staring hard at Lucky. "You always insist she eat what comes on her plate. You don't want a pampered princess."

"Oh." Obviously, they were wealthy. Perhaps the child was in danger of being overindulged. "Maybe this once Julie could skip the peas."

A bewildered expression crossed Brad's face, then vanished. He smiled at her and she realized this was the first time he'd smiled. It was an easygoing smile that seemed to suit him perfectly. She couldn't help smiling back.

Lucky watched Julie attack the rest of the chicken, one piece at a time. The child put down her fork with a thunk and reached for her glass of milk, knocking it over. The milk sloshed across the plate, swamping the chicken and peas.

Wide-eyed, Julie stared at Lucky, clamping her small hands over her ears. A second later, she burst into tears. Lucky jumped up and grabbed the sobbing child.

"Sweetie, it was an accident. It's all right. We'll get you another milk."

Julie wailed even louder, her hands still on her ears. What was wrong with her? It was only milk. Brad quickly took Julie from Lucky's arms, telling the child it was all right. She gradually stopped crying while Brad rocked her in his arms.

"What's wrong?" Lucky asked him.

"You always yell at her if she spills something or accidentally breaks something," he replied, a censuring note in his voice.

"I do?" A wave of revulsion swept through her. What kind of mother had she been? She wanted to be a loving mother like Sarah. "I'm sorry. I—I . . . " She didn't know what to say.

Julie blinked, her wet lashes spiked around her green eyes. "Tell me, Mommy, tell me."

"Tell you what, sweetie?" She touched Julie's moist cheek. "Mommy's been in an accident. She forgets things. You'll have to help her." This brought a smile to Julie's face. "What do you want me to say?"

"Nebber forget. I love you."

All the air whooshed out of Lucky's lungs in a loud gasp. Oh, my God. *Never forget. I love you.* She was such a self-centered person. All this time she'd imagined some wonderful man passionately uttering those words. Instead, they'd been an apology for a hair-trigger temper.

"Sometimes you overreact," Brad said kindly. "You're angry and you scream at Julie, but then you cool off. You always tell her you love her afterward."

Weak with self-loathing, her lips trembled as she tried to smile reassuringly at her daughter. "Mommy's sorry that she's screamed at you in the past. I'm not going to do it anymore. I promise."

Wide-eyed, Julie gazed at her. "I love you, Mommy."

Tears blurred Lucky's vision for the second time in a matter of minutes. Obviously, she'd yelled at this child enough times that Julie anticipated her mother's rage. Yet the little girl still loved her.

"I love you, Julie. Please believe me. I'm not going to scream at you."

A strange look crossed Brad's face. "I'm going to put Julie down for a short nap. Then we'll talk."

"Mommy, will you be here when I wake up?"

"Of course."

"Don't go bye-bye anymore, Mommy."

Brad whisked Julie out of the room before Lucky could respond. What would she have said? She was so confused. She loved her daughter; she loved Greg. She longed to assure Julie that they would never be separated again.

But was it true? She didn't want to turn her back on the man she loved, yet she couldn't imagine leaving Julie, either. Surely there was a solution to this mess.

Staring out at the beach and the setting sun, Lucky thought about all the times she had felt her temper flare. But she had managed to control it. What kind of person had she been not to control herself around a child?

The woman in the mirror.

All this time she'd held out hope that the hard, mean-spirited woman in the mirror wasn't her. She'd told herself she'd been trying a new hairstyle. She looked mean because she was afraid. But none of those excuses were true. She was the woman in the mirror. A bitch.

I hate myself. I hate myself. I hate myself.

"I'm leaving for Honolulu tonight on the ten o'clock plane." Brad had come up beside her. "It'll be less disruptive to Julie if she can go to school tomorrow as usual."

"What about me?" Lucky whispered, stricken with guilt.

Brad cleared his throat, then shrugged awkwardly. This was difficult for him, she realized. Not only had she been mean to her child, but she had caused this man unimaginable heartache.

"What about you? I don't know what you want. I have to do what's best for Julie."

"I want what's best for her, too," Lucky said, on the verge of tears again. "I don't want her hurt."

Brad reached into his pocket and pulled out a stunning ring with a diamond the size of her thumb, the kind of gaudy bauble she associated with tourists.

"If you put on this ring and come home again, I want it to be for good. I can't allow you to tear Julie apart again. When you walked out, she cried for days. You're hot-tempered and yell at her too often, but you're her mother. She adores you."

In his voice she heard anguish, not just for his daughter, but for himself. She'd hurt this man terribly, yet he was willing to take her back and give their marriage another chance. On his own, he might not have done it. But he truly loved his daughter.

Could she go back to him when she loved someone else? For Julie's sake, she wanted to. But Greg was a wonderful man. He deserved more than this.

"What happened, Brad? Why did I leave you?"

Again he shrugged, and she realized this was a habit of his. "I wish I knew, Kelly. You married me for my money. I accepted that. You wanted a child in the worst way. But once

Julie was born, you hadn't a clue about how to be a good mother. One day you packed a few things, took off your ring and left.''

His hazel eyes were earnest and filled with emotion. Another sharp pain beneath her breastbone caused her to inhale sharply. Yes, she loved Greg with all her heart and owed him so much. Her very life. But this man was her husband, a good man who loved their daughter.

"Don't you think you owe it to Julie to give our marriage another chance?" he asked.

For a long moment Lucky thought about Greg and the love she'd found. Then her daughter's adorable voice echoed in her brain: *I love you, Mommy. Don't go bye-bye anymore, Mommy.* She'd done so many things in this life that were wrong. Adding to the list would be reprehensible.

Her only alternative was to get a divorce and share custody. What would that do to Julie? The child would be ping-ponged between two different homes at a time when the solidarity of a family was all-important. Lucky remembered how Sarah had sacrificed, suffering the humiliation of Cody's betrayal to keep her family together. It had worked out for them.

Good mothers did what was best for the family. Obviously, she'd spent much of her life doing what she pleased. Julie's happiness hadn't been important. But she wasn't that selfish woman anymore. Before she could change her mind, she put out her hand. Brad smiled, a delighted boyish grin. He slipped the ring on her finger.

A perfect fit.

Chapter 28

Greg sat in the terrace bar, a fourth Stoli in his hand, listening to Sarah chatter. He knew she was trying to distract him, but it wasn't working. Neither was the booze. He was slowly sinking into a black pit from which there would be no escape. A child. The one thing that could take Lucky away from him.

He stared into his drink, trying to think of some way to keep Lucky with him. He told himself there had been problems in the marriage. She'd left Brad Wagner once. Lucky couldn't possibly love that man the way she loved him. But he kept seeing the look on Lucky's face when she had learned about her daughter.

"There they are," Cody said, standing up.

Greg saw the young girl in Lucky's arms. Thumb in her mouth, her eyelids at half-mast, partially concealing her green eyes. Even from a distance, Julie was the image of her mother. She should be our daughter, Greg thought, a heart-wrenching longing tearing at him.

Until this moment, he hadn't realized how much he wanted

children. Lucky's children. That was their destiny, he had told himself, but reality was another man's child in her arms.

He noticed the ring on Lucky's finger, shining like a beacon on a moonless night. Aw, hell. He felt as if someone had planted a knockout punch squarely in his gut.

"She's wearing her wedding ring," Sarah whispered. "Lucky must be going home with him."

Wearing her wedding ring. The words cycloned through his brain until he could barely move, barely breathe. *Her wedding ring.* That fact became a throbbing, burning ache deep in his soul. As they came closer, Lucky's gaze sought his, and Greg saw the light had vanished from her eyes, the animation replaced by a chilling seriousness.

He sensed her silently begging him to forgive her. Numb, yet aching with the desperate need to reclaim the woman he loved, Greg waited. He was standing now, although he couldn't remember leaving his chair, his fist clenched so tight his fingers hurt.

Greg barely heard Lucky making introductions. His eyes were riveted on Brad Wagner. He was so ordinary looking that it was hard to imagine him with Lucky. What could she have seen in a wimp like him?

"I want to thank you all for helping Kelly," Brad said with unquestionable sincerity. "She told me what special friends you are."

"We were glad to help," Sarah spoke up, easing the awkward moment.

Brad turned to Greg. "You saved Kelly's life. There are no words to express how I feel."

There were words to express how Greg felt. He hated this bastard. He wanted to put his hands around the son of a bitch's neck and squeeze until he dropped dead.

"I want to pay you back for the clothes and—"

"Forget it." The words came out as if he were chewing tin foil.

"Brad is taking the ten o'clock flight home. Julie needs to

be in preschool tomorrow morning,'' Lucky said, the words coming out very slowly. She paused and looked away. "I'm . . . going with them.''

Jesus H. Christ! She didn't even look at him when she said it. Greg growled deep in his throat, a low sound of utter frustration and barely concealed rage that no one else could hear. Cody noticed, though, and shot a warning glance at him.

Julie piped up, saying, "My teacher is Mrs. Natku. I'm in pre-school.''

"You live in Honolulu.'' Sarah again tried to ease the tension, speaking to Lucky. "That's less than half an hour away by plane. We can still see each other.''

"Yeah, we won't lose touch.'' Cody's words sounded uncharacteristically awkward. He didn't look at Greg either.

"I want to get my things and say goodbye to a few people,'' Lucky told Cody. "Could you get me to the airport in time for the flight?''

"Sure. No prob—''

"Mommy, Mommy, don't leave me,'' Julie cried, throwing her little arms around Lucky's neck.

"I'll be back. I promise.'' She hugged the child, kissing her cheek. "I'll never leave you again.''

I'll never leave you again. Greg's heart did a back flip. This wasn't a nightmare; it was hell on earth. He marched out to the Bronco, Cody at his side. Greg wished he had the fortitude to once again fall back on his pride, the way he had after learning about Cody's affair with Jessica. But this time the wound was too deep, the pain too sharp to pretend he didn't give a damn.

Behind them walked Lucky and Sarah, speaking in voices too low to hear. Once they arrived at the car, Greg climbed in front with Cody. If he sat in back with Lucky, he'd beg her to change her mind. And it wouldn't do a damn bit of good.

Dreams. That's all he'd had. Nothing more. The logical side of his brain had anticipated this moment, dreaded it. But nothing had prepared him for the agonizing reality of losing her. The feeling of utter hopelessness.

Lucky asked to go to the institute to say goodbye. They rode in gloomy silence, broken only by staccato bursts of chatter from the police radio. Even Sarah realized it was a lost cause and stopped talking.

Cody pulled to a stop in front of the institute. "Lucky, we're going home now. Greg will drive you to the airport."

"This is goodbye, then," Lucky said. "Thank you, Cody."

"We'll see each other again," Sarah promised. "You're not very far away."

"Please understand if you don't hear from me," Lucky responded, the threat of tears in her voice. "Brad wants me to concentrate on rebuilding our marriage. He believes I won't be happy if I'm thinking about my time here."

Shit! Not only was the son of a bitch taking her away, but they weren't even going to hear from her. Obviously, Wagner realized Lucky's heart was here, and the only way to really get her back was to cut all her ties.

"We understand." Sarah told her softly. "We're here if you need us."

Greg climbed out of the car without saying a word to Cody. He knew his brother had deliberately left him alone with Lucky. He waited while Lucky and Sarah kissed goodbye, then they walked into the institute.

"Get outta here. Why are you two back?" Nomo asked as they entered the nursery, where he was giving Abbie a bottle.

The smile on the older man's face vanished when Lucky whispered, "I'm leaving tonight. I'm going home."

"Her husband's come for her," Greg explained, bitterness underscoring every word. "She has a young daughter who needs her."

Nomo put Abbie down and hugged Lucky. Over her shoulder the older man gazed at Greg, his eyes revealing his surprise. "I'm gonna miss you, *loa*. You were perfect for this work."

"My daughter needs me. Julie's just four and—"

"Hey, I know you wouldn't leave unless you thought it was the right thing to do. But that doesn't mean I'm not gonna miss you."

Miss her? An understatement. Greg's entire being ached so much for Lucky that it hurt to look at her. What would the pain be like later, when she walked out of his life forever and he never saw her again?

"Nomo, thank you for teaching me Hawaiian . . . for showing me how to work with the animals. I've loved every minute of my time here. . . ." Lucky's voice dropped lower and lower, until she was whispering the words.

"Don't be sad," Nomo told her, his voice cracking. "Treasure the memories. You can come visit us."

"That won't be for a long time. I have to straighten out my life first."

"Wark! Wark!" cried Abbie.

Lucky picked up the pup, cradling her to her breast. Greg met Nomo's eyes. This was as close to tears as he'd ever seen his friend.

"Abbie, sweetheart, I have to go," Lucky said. "You know I wouldn't leave you if I didn't have to. I want you to be a good little girl—for me. Promise to mind Nomo. Let him teach you how to catch fish."

Nomo wiped his eyes with the back of his hand.

"I won't be there to see it, but you're going home again, like me," Lucky continued. "They'll take you back to Niihau, where your family is. I wish I could be there to see you swim off with the other seals."

"I'll take a picture and send it to you." Nomo could hardly get the words out. The naked emotion in his voice echoed Greg's. Christ! How was he going to live without her?

"Oh, yes, please take a picture." She kissed Abbie's soft head and the pup mewled contentedly. "I wish I could be there."

"We'd better get going," Greg said. He couldn't take much more of this.

Lucky handed Nomo the pup, then stood on tiptoe and kissed the older man's cheek. "Take care of her for me. Teach her all she needs to know to make it out there on her own. I'll say a prayer for her every night."

Tears in her eyes, Lucky left the nursery. Greg walked beside her, wishing there were something he could say or do to make her stay. The futility of the situation frustrated him. There was no stronger bond on earth than that of a mother and child.

"Could Dodger come to the airport with us?"

"Sure, he's around here somewhere."

"Dodger! Dodger," Lucky called, and the greyhound bounded out of the darkness.

Lucky remained silent during the short drive to the airport. From the back of the car Dodger hung his head over the top of her seat, his muzzle resting on her shoulder almost as if he understood her agony. Did Greg? He had yet to say one word since they'd gotten in the car.

He pulled into the parking lot at the airport and turned off the engine. This was it, she thought, the moment she never imagined would come. It was over; time to say goodbye. But how do you thank someone who saved your life, then taught you how to love?

They all got out of the car and stood there. Lucky gulped in a deep breath of night air and gazed upward at the starry sky. Wobbling light came from a slice of the moon hidden off and on by wisps of clouds.

Lucky dropped to her knees, thinking it would be easier to say goodbye to Dodger first. His soulful eyes watched her as she stroked his silky head, pleading with her to stay.

"I want you to be a good boy, Dodger. Mind Greg, and look after Abbie for me. She's going to need you now. You curl around her so she can fall asleep, but think of me. I'll always be with you in spirit."

Dodger licked her hand and gave a low whine.

"Be careful doing search and rescue. I don't want anything to happen to you."

This time Dodger licked her cheek. Lucky was conscious of Greg watching her, but she wasn't ready to deal with him yet.

"Thank you for finding me. You have such a great nose. I'd be dead now if it weren't for you. I would never know I had a daughter. I want you to come visit her one day. I'm going to tell her all about you, understand?"

Dodger cocked his head to one side almost as if he comprehended what she was saying.

"I'll miss you so much. I'll think about you all the time." She put her arms around him, hugging him the way she had that day in Kmart, needing his strength because her own was ebbing rapidly. How could she leave Greg?

You have no choice. Julie needs her mother. You promised never to leave her.

She slowly rose and turned to Greg. "You know I have to go, don't you?"

"No, I don't. You were having problems in your marriage. You don't have to go back to him." He swept her, weightless, into his arms. "I love you. Stay with me."

"What would you think of me if I deserted my daughter?"

"You can share custody . . . or something. There are lots of children around these days with divorced parents."

His words were low, suffused with pain and bitterness. Lucky touched his cheek with her hand, letting her fingertips trace the emerging stubble. This was the last time she'd marvel at the firmness of his jaw and the rapid growth of his dark beard. Her hand lingered on his cheek until she mustered the courage to speak.

"You, more than most people, know how important a mother's love is. I can't leave my child."

"Maybe you could get custody—"

"No. Brad loves her, and Julie loves him. You should see them together."

He put his hands on her shoulders, the tenderness in his gaze heartrending. Lucky knew beyond a doubt that he loved her. And she would always love him. Her obligation was to Brad and her daughter, but her heart would always belong to this man.

"Don't you understand? I owe it to Julie to give the marriage another try," she said, and he tightened his grip on her shoulders. "Remember me telling you about my greatest fear?"

"Yeah. You were worried that you were the woman in the mirror."

"I *am* that woman. I asked Brad what had gone wrong. He said I married him for his money, didn't take care of Julie—"

"I don't believe that."

"Darling, I wish it was a bald-faced lie, but it's not. Julie spilled her milk, then began to cry because she expected me to yell at her. Oh, Lord, it broke my heart to find out the truth about myself. But I have to face it. I wasn't a good mother."

"You're a wonderful person. I've been with you long enough to know."

Greg lifted one hand and cupped her chin. Lucky kissed his palm, savoring the warmth and strength of his hand. She only wished she were worthy of him. But she'd done the unthinkable. She'd deserted her child.

Guilt, along with a desperate desire to make things right for her daughter, to be a better mother this time, surged through Lucky. It gave her the strength she needed.

"No, Greg. I was a selfish person. I went off 'to find myself' and left a husband and daughter behind. I'm sure there's so much more that I don't know. Julie couldn't fall asleep in a strange place, so she came out and interrupted us before Brad told me everything."

"I don't believe it."

"That's because you love me."

"You're damn right I love you."

In his eyes she saw all the love any woman could ever want. An undying love she didn't deserve. "I love you, too. You know that."

"But you're going to leave me."

"I wish things were different, darling. Every child needs a mother. I have to at least try—for Julie's sake."

Lucky stared into those marine-blue eyes that were so like the sea he loved, compelling and constantly changing. His dark brows furrowed above them, the way they always did when he concentrated. His black hair fell across his brow and lifted slightly in the light breeze, just the way it had the first time she saw him.

Closing her eyes for a moment, Lucky wished that God had granted her a longer stay. She thought back over the weeks. Across every memory was the image of one man. There were so many things she wanted to tell him. Things she'd intended to share but had put off until tomorrow. Now she was out of time. For them, there would be no more tomorrows.

"How am I going to get along without you?" Greg asked.

She opened her eyes, then replied, "You're the strongest man I know. You'll get over me."

He rested his temple against hers. "No, I won't. Not ever."

"Please help me. I can't be strong for both of us. You know I have to go."

He pulled away, rocking back on his heels. For a moment he stared at the crescent moon riding low over Haleakala.

"I'm afraid," she confided. "I'm going into a whole new world again. Without you, without your strength. I don't want to fail Julie, but I'm afraid I will somehow."

He put his arms around her again, his lips very close to hers. "You won't, angel. I wish you would, so I could have you back. But I know you—the person you are now. You had the courage to get in the pool to save a killer shark. You persuaded Abbie to eat. You'll do just fine with Julie . . . and her father."

His words were reassuring, spoken quietly in a voice steeped with love. Lucky put her head against the solid wall of his chest, wanting to hear the steady beat of his heart one last time. *Thunk-thunk. Thunk-thunk.* Oh, how comforting the sound had been on the motorcycle ride that first day. And in the middle of the night when she'd awaken. She would slide over and put her head on his chest. This was the last time she would listen to the heart that loved her.

"Lucky," he whispered, and she could tell he was on the verge of tears, "if it doesn't work out for any reason, I'm here. Don't even think twice. Just come home." His voice broke. "Promise me."

"I promise." She pulled back, knowing that if she didn't leave right then she would never be able to go. "It's time. I can't miss the plane."

"Kiss me goodbye." He bent down, brushing his lips against hers as his hands roamed across her back, down her waist, then dropped to her bottom, as if he were saying farewell to every inch of her body. She clung to him, her tongue mating with his one last time, knowing that this would be their final kiss.

Somehow, Lucky found the strength to pull away. She turned and ran toward the terminal, swiping at the tears with the back of her hand. She didn't look back. She knew that in the darkness stood a man and a dog. Watching her. Loving her.

Chapter 29

After the short flight to Honolulu, a chauffeur-driven limousine met them at the curb. It was a long, glistening white limo that Lucky associated with the luxury hotels on Maui. Remembering Sarah and her brood in a minivan, it seemed inconceivable that a family of three needed such a big car.

"You're going to have to help me relearn things," she whispered to Brad once they were inside, with Julie sleeping in her father's arms.

"Of course. We'll take it one step at a time." His eyes were gentle and understanding.

Part of her wished he was a brute—someone she could hate. But he wasn't. If he'd noticed her teary eyes at the airport, he'd been sensitive enough not to mention it. Julie had fallen asleep on the plane, giving her the opportunity to explain about Hoyt-Mellenberger syndrome. She'd found Brad Wagner sympathetic and a good listener.

"This looks . . . familiar," she said. A tiara of lights glittered along a golden shore. "There's a mountain like Haleakala nearby, isn't there?"

Brad smiled indulgently. "Yes, beyond the hotel strip along Waikiki Beach is Diamond Head. It's not as tall as Haleakala. It's shaped like the prow of a battleship."

So familiar. Unlike Maui, Honolulu was a place she knew. If she let her brain go into its automatic pilot mode, she could find her way around. The thought comforted her, and she realized that her own home would be familiar, too. At least, on this level, the situation wasn't as intimidating as she'd anticipated.

The limo entered a residential neighborhood with enormous houses showcased by the artsy kind of lighting she'd seen at Maui's posh hotels. Most homes were behind ornate gates, but as they passed, Lucky glimpsed lushly planted grounds. Many of the houses had unusual blue tile roofs that gleamed in the moonlight.

The limo paused outside a set of wrought iron gates flanked by royal palms. The driver, whose name was Raul, pulled out a small box and clicked it. The gates swung open and they drove into a stunning cobblestone courtyard with a big lion spouting water from its mouth into a pool at its feet. Lights, strategically placed to create a dramatic effect, spotlighted the fountain and the rough trunks of pygmy palms with bright crimson flowers at their bases.

She sensed Brad gazing at her expectantly. "It's lovely."

A uniformed maid greeted them while the chauffeur took Brad's bag. Lucky had taken nothing but her purse when she left Maui. Walking through the towering doors, she entered a dramatic marble foyer. Beyond was an enormous living room with high vaulted ceilings and wide-open terra-cotta walls, extending the living area outdoors to a beautiful lanai with a spectacular pool that resembled a mountain lagoon.

"Where are the windows?" she asked.

"The glass slides into the walls. We leave it inside unless there's a storm."

"Mommy?" Julie woke up, looking at Lucky from her father's arms.

"I'm right here, sweetie." She reached for her daughter, and the child came eagerly into her arms. Lucky's heart swelled with tenderness.

"Let's get her into bed." Brad led them to a sweeping staircase that spiraled up to the second floor.

"Everything is black or white," Lucky commented, thinking out loud.

"It was your choice," Brad said, with a trace of bitterness in his voice. "This house was your dream. You worked with the decorator. I was too busy."

Sheesh! She didn't really care for so much black and white. Everything about this place expressed luxury and wealth beyond comprehension. Lucky couldn't imagine living here. No wonder Brad seemed to resent her choice of decor.

The maid appeared in a doorway with pink bunny pajamas in her hand. She reached for Julie, but Lucky wanted to put her daughter to bed.

Brad watched her struggle to get Julie out of her sundress and into the jammies with the bunnies on the feet. "You never help Julie dress. That's what we have a maid for."

"I'm different now. I want to spend time with my daughter." She kissed the child's soft cheek.

"Mommy, would you tell me a story?"

By the tentative sound of Julie's voice, Lucky knew she hadn't taken the time to tuck her daughter in and read to her. "Sure, but first let's say our prayers."

"Prayers?" Julie repeated, as if it were a foreign word.

Lucky hesitated, remembering Sarah praying with her children. Well, maybe the awful mother she'd been didn't know enough to pray. "Put your hands together like this." She watched as Julie's little hands came together. "Then bow your head and tell God what you're thankful for. I'll do it tonight, and tomorrow night it'll be your turn.

"Most Holy Father, thank you for bringing our family together again. Bless us and guide us and give us the strength to build a life together." She suddenly remembered her promise to Abbie. "And Father, could you please watch over little Abbie?" Silently, she added a prayer for Greg. "Amen."

Lucky looked up and caught Brad's eye. Apparently, the last thing he'd expected was to see her praying.

"Who is Abbie?" Julie wanted to know.

Lucky briefly explained, then said, "Now let me tell you a bedtime story about Rudy—the wonder shark."

"No, Cinderella. I want *Cinderella*."

"Mommy doesn't know that story," she acknowledged, and Julie gawked at her, amazed. The child stuck her thumb in her mouth and listened to Rudy's story. They hadn't even gotten to the part about reattaching the fins when Lucky realized her daughter was asleep.

She and Brad tiptoed out of the room and down the hall. Oh, God, where were they going? Did they share a room? So much had gone on tonight that she hadn't anticipated this problem. Please, no. I can't. Not ever.

Lucky reached into her pocket to touch Rudy's tooth. It wasn't there! She must have left it on the *Atlantis*. Calm down, she told herself. You're not out of luck. Everything's okay.

"This is your room, Kelly." Two beats of awkward silence. "I'm down the hall if you need me."

She hesitated a second, then decided to go with her instincts. "I don't want to be Kelly. She wasn't a nice person. Do you think you could call me Lucky?"

"I suppose." He sounded uncertain but he smiled.

The maid came out of her room. "I've turned down your bed, madam. There are vases of fresh flowers where you like them. Will there be anything else?"

Lucky shook her head, then waited until the maid walked away. "I don't think I'll get much sleep tonight. Is there a photograph album of my family I could look at?" she asked. "Tomorrow you could tell me about them."

"There are pictures of you and Julie in an album downstairs," Brad said. "I'll bring it up. But there aren't any pictures of your family that I know of."

"Are my parents or grandparents alive?"

Brad shook his head. "No. Your parents were divorced and you lost track of your father's side of the family. Your mother died before you moved here. I think you have distant cousins in Iowa, but I'm not sure."

Brad left to get the album and Lucky stood there, staring at the long corridor. *I once was lost but now I'm found.* How wrong she'd been. She was more lost than ever now. A strange house. A strange man. No relatives to tell her about her past.

Disheartened, Lucky walked into the bedroom, which turned out to be a suite. The room was a study in white silks, some of the textures as smooth as the white marble floor beneath her feet. The other fabrics were nubby raw silks. It was stunning in a dramatic, high-fashioned way that made her feel uncomfortable.

In the black marble bathroom she discovered a sunken tub the size of one of the seal's pools. She caught sight of her reflection in the mirrored wall. Dusky brown curls with dark roots haloed a slightly sunburned face. She still wore the khaki shorts and "Save the Whales" T-shirt that she'd put on before dawn.

Worse than something the cat dragged in. That's what Sarah said about her boys after they played soccer. Well, that's what she looked like now. "You don't belong in this palace."

"Get used to it," her reflection replied. "This is your life. Your daughter is sleeping down the hall. You promised never to leave her."

Lucky found a closet the size of Greg's home. It was filled with double-tiered rows of blouses and skirts. Behind glass doors were racks of shoes. A special case held floor-length gowns by the dozen. She stood in the center of the room, awed and baffled. Who needed so many clothes? And why were the price tags still on most of them?

"Here's the album," Brad said, startling her.

Lucky turned and saw that he'd come up behind her. In his hand was a black silk album with a gold *W* on the cover. She took it from him and asked, "Why are most of these clothes new?"

"You love to shop," Brad replied without hesitating. "You spend most of your day shopping or going to the beauty parlor or working out with your personal trainer."

For a moment she was speechless, then she remembered the woman in the mirror. She had yelled at her daughter for no reason. Why was it surprising that she had led a decadent life? "Those days are over. I'm going to—" She stopped abruptly. "What am I going to do?"

He smiled the indulgent smile that was so familiar. "It's late. Let's deal with it in the morning."

Brad left, and Lucky took the album and sat on the chaise in her bathroom. The pictures chronicled her daughter's life from birth to a preschool photo taken recently. Again Lucky was saddened by all she'd missed, the precious milestones in her daughter's early life.

The pictures of herself were startling. Yes, it was the woman in the mirror, except her hair wasn't blonde. It was shoulder length and ruler straight. Why would she bleach and perm such lovely hair?

There was a certain edge to the person she had once been. It was reflected in every shot, even in the picture taken at the hospital with her newborn daughter. She radiated vanity and self-absorption in a subtle way. Lucky knew men must have considered her beautiful. She had the same dramatic quality that this house had. A larger-than-life, unattainable aloofness. It reminded her of the trophy wife that Sarah had once pointed out.

She snapped the album shut, ashamed and disgusted. How had she become the woman in the mirror? Tomorrow she'd ask Brad more about her past. There had to be something she was missing.

Lucky padded barefoot across the cool marble floor and out onto the balcony. Below were the lushly landscaped grounds and beyond them a crescent-shaped beach, its sand glowing like a pearl in the moonlight.

Gazing up at the sliver of a moon, she remembered its light etching the masculine planes of Greg's face as they'd shared their last kiss. He was so near, less than a half hour away. What was he doing right now? Did he miss her? Was he able to sleep?

Her eyes on the star-filled sky, Lucky recalled the moonlit nights she'd shared with Greg. So much love. So little time together. Every moment had been special. At least she had those memories to give her strength and courage.

She imagined Greg standing in the dark parking lot the last time she had seen him. Oh, Lord. She couldn't imagine what life had in store for her . . . a life without Greg.

"Good night, my darling. I love you with all my heart."

The first smudges of a crimson dawn stole over the horizon, firing the gray underbellies of the rain-swollen clouds with amber light. Greg knew this was just the harbinger of yet another tropical storm. It would blow over the island, vanishing before most tourists hit the beach.

Lucky had left over twelve hours ago, but he hadn't gone home. Why should he? The empty house was a specter, an echo of the past. A reminder of what they'd shared, what he'd hoped was their future.

Stealthy fingers of golden sunlight filtered through the palm fronds at the institute, the branches fluttering in the dawn breeze as Greg went into the nursery. Nomo had spent the night there, coaxing little Abbie to eat. His attempts had been futile, however. From the moment Lucky had left the pup's spirit vanished, and the seal refused to eat.

"We're going to lose her," Nomo said.

"Put her down and let her sleep. Maybe you'll have better luck later."

Abbie was too big now for the makeshift crib, so Nomo put

her on the concrete floor. Dodger, who had been at Greg's heels, trotted over to the pup and nuzzled her. Abbie emitted an exhausted mew that reminded Greg of the contented sound the pup had made against Lucky's breast. Abbie curled into a fetal position, her tiny flippers fanning out in front of her as if she were praying. In one fluid motion, Dodger sank to the floor and lay down, surrounding the pup with his slim body.

At least they have each other, Greg thought. Dodger had spent the hours since Lucky had left waiting by the door. Expecting her to return.

"I'm going to put a bottle between Dodger's legs," Nomo said. "Maybe Abbie will take it."

"It's worth a try," Greg agreed, but he doubted it would work. Monk seals were notorious for refusing to nurse when their mothers died. "Why don't you go home and get some rest?"

"I'm not leaving you," Nomo insisted, his voice charged with emotion.

Something clicked in Greg's mind. Years ago as a troubled teenager, he'd come to the institute. Nomo had shown a special interest in him, nurturing his love of animals, encouraging him to go to the mainland and get a first-class education as a marine biologist.

All these years he'd thought of Nomo as his mentor, sure, but nothing more. Now the truth hit Greg: Nomo was a surrogate father. Greg had flourished due to his love and support.

But he'd never properly thanked him. Greg put his arm around the older man, a person who loved animals as much as he did, someone who worked harder than anyone to help others. Greg hadn't a clue what to say. He just kept his arm around Nomo and they stood there watching Dodger try to convince Abbie to take the bottle.

Finally, Abbie took a few pathetic sucks of goat's milk. Exhausted, Greg left Nomo in the nursery, somewhat hopeful the pup would survive.

He returned to his office and sat there, staring at the

paperwork, thinking about Lucky. Reliving every moment they'd shared. Greg realized he had lost track of time, when a knock startled him. The bright, harsh light of the new day flooded his room with dazzling sunshine, and Cody walked in, his expression serious.

"I went by your house but you weren't there. I called your home number. It channeled into a 900 number with a phone sex message."

It took a minute for his brother's words to register. "Get real!"

"It's true. I called the phone company. It's some computer glitch. They're trying to straighten it out."

Greg let out a world-weary sigh. "Phone sex, what next?"

"Aikane!" Buddy! yelled Nomo, rushing into the room, interrupting them. "Look at this!"

Nomo held a paper in his hand. "Lucky didn't sign her name when she accepted delivery of the goat's milk. She wrote *C-311* in the signature space. What's that supposed to mean?"

"I don't know," Greg said. "People sign their names so often that they automatically do it—without thinking what they're writing. I always thought that Lucky would say or write her real name, yet she never did. People had all sorts of weird explanations why she never knew her name. But I have no idea why she would use a number."

"I'll bet I know," Cody said, his expression grim.

Greg stared at his brother, unable to imagine what he was talking about.

"She was in prison," Cody said quietly. "All she had was a number. I'll bet she was prisoner number 311 in cell block C."

Chapter 30

The Orchid King checked the corner of his computer screen to see how much time had elapsed. Two hours and fourteen minutes. Probably not long enough to cause death, he thought. He rocked back in his chair and studied the ceiling.

"Let's see what else I can do to make Greg Braxton's life hell."

He'd already screwed up his bank account. It would take Braxton years to reestablish his credit rating. His phone calls had been rerouted to the most explicit phone sex enterprise around, which was one of the king's more novel ideas. At first he'd intended to disconnect his telephone, but phone sex was more fun.

"Now it's time to actually repossess his car."

The king was talking out loud to himself, but he didn't care. There was no one around except the alley cat, and the filthy little beast couldn't hear him. He accessed the data bank holding the paper on Braxton's car, electronically altering the information to trigger a repossession order.

The king chuckled. "The repo man cometh."

This was more fun than he'd expected. Not only was he the Orchid King, but he was also king of the information superhighway. They'd been running a phony credit card scam for years, hacking into bank's data bases. But this was more exciting. Because it was personal.

"The IRS is next. Let's say Braxton owes half a million in back taxes." The king roared, totally pleased with himself. Every hacker knew IRS files were ridiculously easy to break into.

He could shut down an airline if he wanted to. The phone company. An entire city. Terrorists with bombs were chicken shit. He could cause a technological Chernobyl with a modem and a keyboard. Fucking up Braxton's life was a piece of cake.

Thoroughly pleased with himself, he checked the time again. Two hours and twenty minutes. Was the cat dead yet? It had taken over three hours for the poisonous fumes in the orchid vault to kill the last cat. This time he had put more of the deadly orchids in the chamber to speed up the process.

"Two hours. A man has to die in two hours."

No one came into the warehouse except for the deliverymen who brought the orchids. Hidden in the bottom of the orchid crates were the counterfeit credit cards from Singapore. He and his partner repackaged them, then shipped them out, not trusting anyone else to do it. The fewer people involved, the less chance there was of being discovered.

Every few hours the deliverymen came for a pickup or left containers. The Orchid King had to be able to kill someone with those orchid fumes and pack the body in a crate of orchids in under two hours, or risk someone seeing the dead body.

The king walked into the warehouse and switched on the ventilator in the chamber. Considering the orchids he'd added, the alley cat he'd enticed with a bit of fresh albacore was probably in catnap heaven. True, a cat wasn't a man, but he couldn't very well experiment on real people.

There was a dog he'd like to get his hands on, though.

He swung open the steel door to the vault. He'd had the

chamber built like a brick shit house. Once you were in there, you weren't getting out. The perfect icing, he thought with a chuckle.

"Here, kitty, kitty," he called when he didn't see the cat.

It must have gone behind the plants and died. He carefully pulled back several orchids. Nothing. He moved aside another, reminding himself to hurry. Fumes had built up, and he couldn't chance damaging his lungs.

"Ye-e-ow!" The cat flew out of nowhere, claws bared, snarling.

"What the fuck!" The king jumped back, but not before the cat caught him on the underside of his forearm. Its claw snagged the tender skin, ripping it open. Blood streamed out as he kicked at the fleeing cat. It darted past him and charged out the door.

The Orchid King realized his lungs were starting to burn and he was feeling light-headed. The ventilation system hadn't been on long enough to draw out all the deadly fumes. Blood dripping from his arm, he stumbled out the door and slammed it shut behind him.

"It's going to take more fucking orchids than I anticipated to ice him."

Cody found Scott Helmer outside Makawao, watching the *panielos*. The cowboys were roping calves and branding them, the scent of singed hide filling the tropical air.

"Always wanted to be a cowboy," Helmer remarked. "But I grew up in the city. I don't even know how to ride."

"What are you doing here?"

"I'm meeting a source at the Road Kill Bar and Grill in an hour."

"I need your help," Cody said. It took him a few minutes to tell the undercover agent about the situation with Lucky. "Could you find out if she was in prison?"

"With one phone call," Helmer assured him. "You're a lot smarter than I thought. I think you solved this puzzle. Lucky was a prisoner in a smaller state. A three-digit prisoner number means there were less than a thousand inmates in that facility when she was incarcerated. A large state would have a bigger number."

"She has a four-year-old daughter. So it had to have been over five years ago that she was in prison."

Helmer shook his head, his skull and crossbones earring sparkling in the sunlight. "Not necessarily. Remember the serial killer, Ted Bundy? He fathered a child while he was in prison. That's conjugal visits for you."

"You checked out Brad Wagner. Was there any record of his wife being in prison?"

"Nope. The group in Quantico is still checking on him. Let's see what comes of this lead. She probably did time for some petty crime and never told her husband."

"That's exactly what I think, The dude's a little nerdy, but rich. She didn't tell him she was an ex-con."

"I did get some interesting information on Thelma Overholt. The final report came in on the cause of death." The only people around were the *panielos* doing the branding, but Helmer lowered his voice. "She was dead at least two days before she was tossed off that hiking trail. We figure she was killed in Singapore. Her body was shipped here because no one would think to look for her in Hawaii."

"That's why the airlines didn't show her traveling and why her passport wasn't scanned in Singapore," Cody commented. "But how in hell do you get a dead body halfway across the world?"

Helmer smiled, his cocky punk's grin. "In one of those long wooden crates that they use to ship orchids. They send them in refrigerated containers. Perfect for a body. There isn't any smell."

"That's how the bugs from the orchids got in the woman's hair. She wasn't in southern China, she was in the container hidden under a bunch of orchids."

"Exactly what we figured."

"I guess it blows my theory about how Lucky got Thelma's shoe."

"Not necessarily," Helmer said. "They flew the body here, but I doubt they opened it where anyone could see what was inside. They took the container somewhere, and the shoe fell out. Instead of throwing it away, they kept it. A year later, Lucky comes along and puts on the shoe."

Cody watched the *panielos* brand a runt of a calf. "You should be able to trace the orchids through air freight shipments, right?"

"We're working on it. The orchids are the key."

The second morning in her new home, Lucky made the macadamia nut pancakes that Greg liked so much. Brad liked them, though she suspected he preferred the fresh fruit and granola he usually ate. But Julie only picked at them, then attempted to drown her pancakes in syrup.

"Wang's nose is out of joint," Brad said. "He was hired to do the cooking because you insisted that you never wanted to cook another meal as long as you lived. Now you're taking over."

His tone was gentle, and she smiled at him to let him know she wasn't upset. He'd been great the past two days, giving her space.

"Yeah," Julie chimed in. "Wang makes the best peanut butter and jelly sandwiches."

Lucky accepted the backhanded reprimand from her very intelligent four-year-old daughter. Yesterday morning, her first day back, Lucky had sent Julie off to preschool with a turkey sandwich. It came back uneaten.

"I like to cook," Lucky insisted. "Maybe we don't need Wang."

Brad put down his fork. "Let's see how long you stay interested in cooking. A first-rate chef like Wang is hard to find."

Lucky looked away, a rush of unreasonable anger pushing

against the walls of her chest. The demon—her temper—was rearing its ugly head again. She had a second chance at life; this time she was going to control her temper. Brad had every right to doubt her. She would just have to prove him wrong.

"It's time for you to go, pumpkin," Brad told Julie.

Lucky stood up, saying, "I'll walk you to the car, sweetie. Remember, when you come home we're going to the aquarium."

At the door, Malia, the maid, handed Julie her Barbie lunch box. It slipped, hitting the marble floor and popping open. The contents of a container of orange juice spilled across the white marble. Julie threw her little hands over her ears, and Malia drew back. Lucky realized they both expected her to get angry.

Lucky dropped to her knees and hugged the child. "It's okay, Julie. It was an accident. Malia will get you another juice."

Julie took her hands off her ears. "Yore not mad?"

"No, sweetie, I'm not. Mommy's sorry if she's been angry with you in the past. Can you forgive me?"

Julie responded by kissing her cheek. It was a tentative little peck, and Lucky realized her daughter hadn't kissed her often. She had so much to make up for. Hugging Julie, she kissed her daughter's cheek.

"Instead of going to the aquarium this afternoon, maybe we could go and pick out a puppy. Wouldn't you like to have a dog?"

"Could we, Mommy? Could we?"

"Sure," Lucky agreed, glancing up. Brad had walked into the entry behind Malia, who'd returned with another juice.

"You hate dogs. When you were a child a dog attacked you. Are you sure you want one?"

Julie's little face crumpled at her father's question. Lucky quickly hugged her and smiled reassuringly.

"You know, I'm glad I don't remember that. Children need pets. Maybe we'll get a cat, too."

Lucky walked her daughter out to the courtyard, where Raul

was waiting with the limo. Julie tugged on her hand, and Lucky bent down so her daughter could whisper in her ear. She seemed to whisper to her more often than necessary. Lucky decided this was just an excuse to get close to the mother who in the past had been so cold.

"Mommy, could you drive me to school like the other mothers?"

It hadn't occurred to Lucky that arriving at preschool each day in a stretch limo would set her daughter apart, making her feel awkward. "You bet. It may take a while because I don't have a car. I'll ask Daddy to get us one."

Julie kissed her yet again. "I love you, Mommy."

"You know I love you. I'll be waiting here when you get home."

She watched the limo pass through the gates, then turned to see Brad coming out of the house. He would hop in his jet-black Porsche and take off for his office, leaving her alone in this mausoleum of a house.

"Brad, do we need a limo?"

He looked startled. "You really have changed. You're the one who wanted the limo."

"I'm thinking about a minivan so I can haul around kids who eat jelly sandwiches."

"Really? Well, sure." He hesitated a moment. "You know, you might want Sebastian to look at your hair. There's a business thing tomorrow night . . . a cocktail party. I want you to come with me."

She wasn't really up to meeting people yet. Like an ugly duckling dropped into a pool filled with swans, Lucky had no idea how to act around Brad's friends, who were undoubtedly wealthy and sophisticated. But she couldn't disappoint him. He'd been so great about everything.

He hadn't touched her. Thank God. She wondered if this was strange. Had they stopped sleeping together long ago? Was that why they had separate bedrooms? Lucky wasn't sure what to think about this, and there was no one she could ask.

Climbing the marble staircase, she thought about Greg. How she missed him. Trying to fit into Brad's life, a life that seemed so foreign, wasn't as easy as she'd anticipated.

"You've got to try harder," she whispered to herself. "You promised Julie."

Upstairs, she surveyed the closet for something to wear. The wardrobe from hell. Everything the woman in the mirror had chosen either had necklines that tickled her navel or was one size too small. And most of the clothes were black or white. She'd determined this yesterday morning when she'd tried to find something to wear.

She checked the address book she'd discovered in the nightstand. Sebastian was not listed, and she hadn't asked his last name. Thumbing the pages to see if she could find him, Lucky again noticed how few friends she had. Brad had confirmed this yesterday, saying she was close to her hairdresser, her manicurist, and her personal trainer.

She hadn't known what a personal trainer was until Brad had explained: He comes to your house with weights and makes you work out. Amazing. She was so rich she could afford to pay someone to make her sweat.

Forget the trainer. She wasn't wasting money like that. Think of all the institute could do with the money she'd thrown around.

"No, don't think about Abbie and Nomo . . . and Greg," she whispered to herself. "You have to make a new life."

She heard the limo returning and rushed downstairs. "Take me to the hairdresser," Lucky told Raul as he was getting out of the car.

Raul didn't question her. He just opened the door with a flourish and she climbed in. They drove through the city, where T-shirt vendors lined the sidewalks and tourists with lobster-red sunburns snapped up the bargains. Everything looked vaguely familiar, although she couldn't have named a single street.

The limo glided to a stop in front of a salon with a high-tech chrome sign that read CACHE. Raul opened the door and she stepped out.

As deferential as Raul had been, the receptionist hadn't noticed the limousine. The woman glared at Lucky as if she were something she wouldn't want to step on in the dark. Lucky asked for Sebastian and was coldly informed that he had no appointments open for weeks. She began to leave but stopped suddenly, reminding herself of all she'd been through. And survived. This uppity receptionist wasn't going to get the best of her.

"Tell him Mrs. Wagner is here."

The woman's mouth quirked and she squinted at Lucky. "Oh, my God. I didn't recognize you!" She jumped up and dashed around a glass-block partition into the salon.

Seconds later, a young man with a ponytail the size of a pencil eraser rushed out. He wore two matching diamonds of about two carats each. One pierced his ear; the other gleamed from his left nostril. Instantly, Lucky realized she knew him. Like Brad, this man's face was very familiar. He halted the moment he saw her, his deep brown eyes widening.

"My stars! *What* did you do to your hair?"

Before she could answer, he sashayed up to her and kissed the air beside each cheek, smacking loudly. "Never mind. Sebastian will make it all better."

He guided her into the salon, where there were enough ferns to stock a hothouse. Lucky sat in the chair, realizing the place seemed familiar. Sebastian, too, was someone she knew, even though she hadn't recognized his name. Thumping the end of a rattail comb against the diamond in his nose, he studied her from every angle.

"I read in the paper about what happened," he said. "Someone tried to kill you and now you don't remember a thing about the past."

"That's true," Lucky replied, thinking that this man was gay. She didn't care; she instinctively liked and trusted him.

He inspected her hair, running it through his fingers. "It looks like you used a cheap home perm. Why? You had such dynamite hair."

"I bleached it blonde. If you saw *Missing!* there was a picture—"

"I did see that episode and I thought the woman's eyes looked familiar, but I didn't recognize you. Honey, your own mother wouldn't have known you from that picture. You were always so proud of your hair. It was thick and dark and sexy. I never dreamed you would do anything so drastic as bleaching and perming it. My stars, what were you thinking?"

"I have no idea. Can you do something with my hair? There's a party tomorrow night—"

"Now don't go ballistic on me. I'm going to suggest cutting off this overpermed hair and going short—" he put his hand on his hip and jiggled "—but sophisticated."

"Do I go ballistic often?" Oh, Lord, what did she do? Yell at everyone?

"We get along fine, but you have been known to pitch a hissy fit now and then."

"I see," she said quietly. It was the same story over and over. She had been a self-centered bitch. "Do whatever you need to. Make me presentable, but see if you can keep that little scar on the back of my head hidden."

He turned her over to a slim Hawaiian girl who washed her hair, then led her back to Sebastian's chair. He started snipping away. "*Hakuna matata.* Not to worry. You'll knock 'em dead at the party."

"Are we close? I mean, Brad says I don't have many friends. No women friends at all."

"You don't like to be around women. You told me you'd had enough of them." His gaze met hers in the mirror. "I was your best friend. You accepted me even though I'm gay."

"Tell me about myself. Brad doesn't know much about my past. He said I came here a little over five years ago. He hired me to do some word processing for him. Do you know where I lived before or anything about my family?"

"No. You said you'd worked as a temp in Denver—or was

it Chicago? Your parents are dead. I think you have distant relatives in the Midwest. That's about all you ever told me.''

"Didn't you find that strange?"

"No. You were always aloof—above it all. Very private.''

"I was selfish and mean to my daughter.''

He whirled the chair around so they were facing each other. "You love your daughter. I met you before you became pregnant. You wanted Julie in the worst way. But you haven't the patience to be a good mother.''

"Now I do. I'm different.''

She explained to this man, who appeared to be her only friend, how Hoyt-Mellenberger worked. He listened attentively, seeming to be very sympathetic. In a way he reminded her of Sarah, someone who naturally related to others.

"When I left, did I tell you where I was going or anything?''

"I thought you were in LA buying clothes. You went several times a year. You gave me a small shopping bag the last day I saw you. I would have brought it today, but you didn't call ahead.''

A chill of apprehension skipped across the back of her neck. Greg believed she'd known something or had seen something that made the killers target her. This could be the key. "What was in the shopping bag?''

Sebastian shrugged. "Not much. It's a small bag with two envelopes in it. I didn't look closely. I think it's clippings of dresses you liked. You always asked my opinion about clothes and gave me pictures to look at.''

Great! This man was responsible for the provocative wardrobe that was almost exclusively white or black.

"Do you want me to bring the bag to your house?''

"No. I'll come by here tomorrow and get it.''

"Remember—'' He whacked his forehead with the palm of his hand. "I keep forgetting you don't remember these things. I leave at noon for the Big Island. I'm in the salon in the new Four Seasons there until Thursday each week. Come by

Thursday. I'll bring the bag with me and decide if this is a dress you *must* have.''

Knowing what a selfish bitch she'd been in her previous life, there was probably nothing worrisome in the envelopes. They probably contained nothing more interesting than a picture of yet another black or white dress. Still, Lucky couldn't help reaching into the pocket of her sundress to touch the tooth that wasn't there.

Chapter 31

Mommy, Harry's a studmuffin.

Lucky swam the length of the cove, giggling as she recalled what her daughter had said during breakfast. Lucky had met Harry—the studmuffin—yesterday afternoon. He'd heard she was back in town and had dropped by to "tone" her thighs. Sheesh! Was there no end to the self-indulgence? Who needed a personal trainer? She'd tone her own thighs, thank you very much, by swimming.

She backstroked across the cove, then flipped over to butter-fly. In the distance she saw the Waikiki skyline, sunlight glittering off the high-rise hotels. Walking onto the beach from the public access path between the estates was a man. He was too far away to see who he was, but something about him reminded her of Greg.

"Stop it!" she said out loud. Everywhere she went, she kept expecting to see Greg. She loved him so much that she was driving herself crazy.

Then she saw the dog following the man. Dodger. She swam toward shore, pure joy bubbling through her. For a moment she indulged herself, pretending they were back on Maui. Greg was coming down to the water the way he often did when she went swimming. Tail wagging, Dodger plunged into the surf to greet her—the way he always did.

"Good boy."

She stood up, water sluicing off her, and patted his head, lovingly stroking his silky fur. He bounded onto the sand where Greg was waiting. Greg smiled at her, but his riveting eyes scoured her body. His expression told her that he didn't approve of her skimpy bikini. She had exactly thirty-three swimsuits, many of them with the price tags still on. All of them bikinis. This was the most conservative of the lot.

"Hi," she said, picking up the towel she'd left on the beach. She longed to throw her arms around him, but if she did she would never let him go. "Are you here with Dodger for S and R training or something?"

"No, I had to use Dodger to get on the plane, though. My bank account's so screwed up that I couldn't get money for an airline ticket. Aloha Air flies S and R teams for free, so I took Dodger to the airport with me. They thought we were on official business and flew us here for free."

"Do you need money? I can run up to the house and—"

"Nah. Cody gave me some cash. I'm going to spend the night with Claude Winston from the U of H. He's the doctor who developed the testosterone depressant we're using on the monk seals."

"Oh." Lucky couldn't help feeling disappointed that he hadn't come just to see her. "Business brought you here."

"No. I came to talk to you." He pushed his sunglasses to the top of his head. Uh-oh. She knew that serious look.

"Abbie? Something's happened to her," she said, but he shook his head. "Rudy?" Again he shook his head, putting his hand on her arm. "Sarah or the kids?"

"It's about you. Is there somewhere we can talk?"

Filled with anxiety, Lucky led him to the grove of date palms nearby. Out of the corner of her eye, she watched him as they walked up to the rocks beneath the trees. He seemed on edge and tense in a way that she'd never seen him.

Under the shady palms, she plopped down on a sea-worn boulder with a flat surface like a small bench. Greg sat beside her and Dodger settled down at their feet, peering up adoringly at Lucky.

"Tell me what's wrong."

He reached for her hand, his strong fingers curling around her palm. "Does the number C-311 mean anything to you?"

She considered the question for a minute, thinking that the number sounded vaguely familiar, but she couldn't place it. "No, not really."

"The day before Brad came for you, several shipments arrived at the institute and you signed for them with the number C-311. The number must have just popped into your head and you jotted it down the way someone who regularly signs his name would."

"That's just what the doctors said I would do. But why would I write down a number instead of a name?"

He squeezed her hand, his expression compassionate. "You were in prison. They used numbers instead of names."

Lucky gasped out loud. The woman in the mirror was a bad person, true, but had she done something so horrible that they'd put her in jail? "How do you know?"

"The FBI traced the number. Cody called the warden in a Montana prison. I was on the other line, so I spoke with him, too. We even talked with the prison psychologist about you."

The truth twisted inside her, forming a cold knot of disgust in the pit of her stomach. It was bad enough to discover she really was the woman in the mirror, a bitch of a mother, and a totally self-indulgent person. But to have actually committed a crime seemed inconceivable.

"What had I done?"

He put his arm around her bare shoulders. "You were only eleven days past your seventeenth birthday, which made you an adult in the eyes of the judicial system. You were with your boyfriend, and he robbed a convenience store. You were out in the getaway car when he shot the store clerk . . . and killed him.''

Lucky stared at him, his words echoing through her muddled brain. Murder. She'd been involved in killing someone. Anger mushroomed inside her, making her want to scream that it wasn't true. She struggled to control herself, tightening each muscle until she was rigid.

He drew her to him, and in his eyes she saw love and understanding. No matter what she'd done this man loved her. Lucky allowed her body to relax, snuggling against him for comfort.

"How could I have done something like that?"

"You claimed you didn't know he was going to rob the store, but you were sentenced to twenty-two years as an accessory to murder. You served ten years and a few months."

She pulled out of his arms and stared in disbelief at the waves tumbling onto the golden shore. She'd spent a third of her life behind bars. Incredible. Shuddering, Lucky recalled the short time she'd spent in the Maui jail. Behind the bars, she had experienced a sense of being subhuman, reduced to nothingness.

A number. Yes, even though she hadn't been able to remember her time in jail in Montana, she'd felt that nothingness, that sense of being just a number. Not a person. It had been frightening and humiliating. A sensation of intense sickness and desolation swept through her.

Maybe having no memory was a blessing. The few days she'd spent in jail had been hell on earth. Lucky didn't want to remember the ten long years behind bars. Yet she couldn't help wondering about the person she'd been—and what had led to a life in prison.

"What else did they tell you?" she asked quietly.

"Dr. Carmichael, the psychologist, knew a lot about you. She took quite an interest in your case."

"Did she know if I have family somewhere?"

"No, not unless they're distant relatives. Your father didn't marry your mother. There's no record of who he was."

"My mother's dead, isn't she?" Lucky asked, remembering what Brad had told her about her family.

"Yes, your mother died in an automobile accident when you were six." Greg visibly braced himself. "You were placed in a foster home. You couldn't say one word."

"I couldn't talk?" Unimaginable. At two, Sarah's daughter was talking. At four, Julie chatted up a storm, saying Harry was a studmuffin. "Why?"

"I don't think we'll ever know for sure. Apparently, you were so traumatized that you were afraid to talk. Remember, you thought your name was Shut Up. Every time you tried to say something, your mother must have yelled at you to shut your mouth. Judging from the scars on your feet, she burned you with a cigarette."

Guilt arced through Lucky, making her disgusted with herself. "Oh, God. I did the same thing. I screamed at Julie. I told you—"

"You weren't as bad as your mother. Did Brad say you ever hit Julie?"

"No, but—"

"Our earliest years are the most impressionable ones. You had a horrible experience, yet like many abused children you duplicated the pattern of behavior you'd seen. You were trying to fight it. You lost your temper but you never hit Julie."

"You're right. After I'd yell, I'd tell her that I loved her." Lucky ran her fingers through her short hair, furious with herself. "Talk about confusing a child . . ."

"You're not losing your temper anymore, that's what's important."

She shuddered, the undeniable and dreadful truth making her hate herself. Still, she wanted to know everything about this terrible person. "What else did you find out?"

"Your first foster mother was a very kind, religious person. She took you in, believing you were mentally retarded because you couldn't talk. She tried to work with you. She had some success, but you still didn't speak. One day in church, you began to sing.''

''That must be why I knew 'Amazing Grace,' '' she said softly, her heart aching because she couldn't remember this wonderful woman who'd lovingly helped an abused child. Lucky imagined someone like Sarah, a person who cherished her family and loved them with all her heart.

''Your singing gave her hope, and she continued to work with you. Finally, you did speak. She put you in school and worked hard to help you catch up. Never having been in school, you were two grades behind. Your life might have been very different had this woman lived.''

''She died? How sad. I wish I could talk to her. I'd love to thank her.''

''The reports Dr. Carmichael had said she was older, widowed. She died of a stroke, and after that you went into a series of foster homes. Dr. Carmichael didn't have the details beyond the social services reports, but your grades went down. You found your tongue—and your temper. You got into fights. You hung out with a bad crowd.''

''I must have done something good. I was on the swim team, wasn't I? Did I win any races?''

Greg paused, as if weighing his next words carefully. ''You were on the swim team—the prison swim team.''

How would she ever be able to explain this to Julie? she wondered. True, she wouldn't have to tell her until she was old enough to understand, but still, she'd been so bad. Who would want a mother like this?

''Dr. Carmichael worked with you on your temper, but you still fought with the other prisoners and the guards. They put you in solitary confinement several times. You were a lone wolf who didn't make friends. For the first five years you worked in the kitchen.''

''That must be the reason we have a chef. Brad said I hated

cooking. I remember how to cook because I'd done so much of it. But I don't remember hating it.''

Greg smiled at her, more than a trace of sadness in his eyes. ''You studied hard and did so well that you were chosen for a special computer training class. You were exceptionally talented. The warden personally selected you to be one of the workers to convert the prison records to the new computer system.''

''Finally, I did something right.''

He gave her a quick hug, chuckling. ''Not exactly. You were so clever that you deleted any mention of yourself from the prison records. Nothing—not even a fingerprint—exists in their data bank. They IDed you from the picture. Your eyes gave you away, because you'd had long brown hair when you'd been in prison.''

''All the pictures Brad has show me with long hair. I went to Sebastian—he's my hairdresser. He couldn't believe that I had permed and bleached my hair. I guess I was really vain about my hair. Why would I bleach it?''

''I don't know,'' Greg replied, brushing her damp hair. ''It's really short now. All the curl is gone. You look like a pixie with huge green eyes.''

''Sebastian said to let it grow out and become healthy again. I don't know. I may just keep it short. I don't want to be *anything* like I was.''

''I can understand how you feel.'' He kissed the tip of her nose, and she wished she was worthy of the love she saw in his tender gaze. ''I'll always love you—long hair or short.''

Lucky looked away; she couldn't go through this again. Saying goodbye once had been hard enough. ''I still can't understand why I couldn't remember my name. Even if I'd used a number for ten years, I used Kelly since leaving prison.''

''There's a good reason.'' His voice was calm, his gaze unwavering. ''The name on your birth certificate was Abigail Sue Reston.''

"Abigail? That name just popped into my head when you asked me to give Abbie a name."

"I know. It was in your head because it was your legal name. Your foster mother gave you another name. She called you Rudy-Anne."

"Really?" Lucky took in a quick breath of utter astonishment. "When I was underwater with the shark, I thought his name was Rudy. But it was my brain telling me my own name, wasn't it?"

"Apparently, that's what happened. You've had a lot of names—starting with Shut Up. One of the reports that Dr. Carmichael had from school says you used the nickname Dusty when you were in high school. No wonder you didn't know your name."

"I moved here and made up a new name, didn't I?"

"Yes. You met someone through the Internet. You came to Hawaii to take a job as a computer programmer—at least that's what was in the parole report. Dr. Carmichael thought you were a real hard case, but you'd been rehabilitated. She said you kept telling everyone you would die before you'd ever go to jail again."

Lucky thought for a moment, recalling how little Brad knew about her. "I never told anyone here about my past. I didn't want anyone to know. I'm *positive* the psychologist is right. I never wanted to go to jail again."

"Who can blame you for not telling anyone? A criminal record is hard for some people to accept. Dr. Carmichael said you were determined to marry a rich man and live like a princess." He gazed at the mansion she now called home, pausing a moment. "You got your wish."

No, I didn't, she wanted to scream. I want to live in a cottage by the sea with you and Julie. And your baby.

"I'm going to make up for all I've done wrong. I'm not the woman in the mirror. I'm worse. A total bitch. I—"

He touched his finger to her lips. "I came to tell you all this myself because I know how upset you've been, thinking you're a bad person." He bracketed her face with his hands, forcing her to look at him. She saw so much love and anguish that it brought tears to her eyes. "Lucky, don't blame yourself. You never had a chance. Don't hate yourself.

"What you experienced is typical of what happens to many abused children. The abused child becomes the troubled teenager, who then grows into a young adult who runs into trouble with the law."

"Not always," she argued. "Many abused children don't end up in jail."

"True," he conceded, "but if you look at the statistics, the majority of criminals came from abusive backgrounds or highly dysfunctional families."

"I refuse to make excuses for myself. I take responsibility for what I did—even though I don't remember doing it. I've paid my debt to society." Swallowing the sob rising in her throat, she realized he was smiling at her, love—and acceptance—in his eyes.

"That's my girl," Greg said, heartfelt tenderness in his voice. "I knew you wouldn't look for excuses. Think of this as an opportunity most people never get. That blow to your head changed your personality."

"It certainly did. Not only was my daughter afraid of me, but everyone else seemed to be expecting—what did Sebastian call it?—a hissy fit. I must have been a prima donna with a temper. How does an abused child become a self-centered, first-class bitch?"

"Your inner personality dictates what you become. You can cave in and be a weak, timid person, or you can fight. I don't think we'll ever know the whole story, but you chose to fight."

"I was mean and self-centered."

"You had faults. Everybody does. Now you have a second chance to be whatever you wish."

"It took a major head injury to make me a likable person and a good mother." She shook her head in disgust. "I'm going to make you proud of me."

"I'm already proud of you. I'll always be proud of you, angel."

An ache lodged deep in her chest when she realized that Greg knew everything about her—and still loved her. What she felt for him went beyond love into some uncharted realm of her soul.

"I want you to promise me that you'll try hard to make your marriage work. You deserve—"

"Don't you love me anymore?" Lucky asked, aware of how desperately she needed him.

"Of course, I love you. Two years ago when Jessica died, I would have bet anything that I would never endure pain like that again. Wrong. Losing you has been a thousand times worse. I can't keep seeing you. I'm just torturing myself." He lightly kissed the tip of her nose. "You deserve to have a wonderful life. Julie's a great kid, and Brad seems like a nice guy. Forget me. Give your marriage a real chance."

She choked back a sob, knowing he was right. As long as Greg was in the picture, her marriage was doomed. "I'll never forget you. No matter where I go or what I do, I'll always love you. Had things been different—"

"Don't say it. Things aren't *different*. You have a daughter and a husband." He reached into his pocket. "I brought you something. You probably don't want it. Undoubtedly, you have a safe full of jewels."

Greg handed her Rudy's tooth. It was dangling from a fine gold chain.

"Oh, thank you. Thank you. I'll wear it all the time. I know it sounds silly, but I do feel it brings me luck." She put it on and the tooth hung just above her breasts. "I'm so lucky—lucky you found me. You've given me the greatest gift of all, the ability to know true love."

He pulled her into his arms and she relaxed, sinking into his welcoming embrace. His eyes were usually a searing blue, but now there was nothing in them except a profound sadness that nearly destroyed her. He loved her and had helped her through the worst crisis of her life. What did he get in return? Heartache.

His lips met hers for a sweet kiss filled with the pain of parting. His tongue touched hers for one last time. Strong arms that had carried her up the cliff cradled her in a final embrace. Vibrant blue eyes that had gazed at her so often with love and understanding looked into hers, silently telegraphing the anguish he was feeling.

"Goodbye, Lucky. Be happy."

Greg released her, then clicked his fingers. Dodger hopped up, gazing expectantly at Lucky. They walked down the beach to the access path. Dodger kept looking over his shoulder, baffled that Lucky wasn't coming.

"Goodbye, my love," she whispered after they'd disappeared from sight. "Have a wonderful life."

Chapter 32

Lucky walked into the party beside Brad and quickly scanned the small group to see if anyone looked familiar. No one's face triggered a response, but then maybe she hadn't met these people. This was a business affair.

Everyone looked chic and sophisticated. Rich. She glanced at the diamond sparkling on her finger, a stab of guilt buried in her chest. The institute scraped by, getting donations where they could. When she was more comfortable with Brad, she was going to ask him to make a contribution. Almost as if he knew that she was thinking about him, he reached for her hand and gave it a quick squeeze.

"Thanks so much for the Suburban," she whispered as they walked across the lanai to the bar.

"You can exchange it for another color, you know."

Lucky smiled at Brad, thinking how lucky she was to have him. She had walked back from the beach to find he'd come home early. He'd bought her a car to drive Julie to school. Minutes later, Julie had returned from preschool and had been thrilled with the car. They'd taken it for a drive around the island, getting home just in time to change for the party. They hadn't had a moment alone so she hadn't told Brad about her past. She owed him the truth. The woman in the mirror might have deceived him, but she wasn't that person anymore.

Brad paused to greet a couple and introduce Lucky. She made herself sound upbeat and happy. Still, she couldn't help gazing out at the beach. They were two doors down from where they lived, the distance so close they'd used the footpath rather than drive. This mansion was directly in front of the grove of date palms where she'd said goodbye to Greg.

"Welcome back," said a familiar voice from behind her.

She turned and faced a handsome man, instantly realizing that she knew him even though her brain wouldn't supply his name. Tall with close-cropped blond hair and intense brown eyes, the man smiled at her, canting one eyebrow slightly, a gesture that seemed very familiar.

Lucky was wearing the most conservative cocktail dress she owned, a white halter-top creation. It nipped in at the waist and skimmed her hips, falling in wispy folds of sheer silk to her knees. The only jewelry she wore was Rudy's tooth. The man's eyes went right to the tooth dangling above her cleavage.

"Remember me? Judd Fremont," he said, his eyes meeting hers again. "Interesting piece of jewelry."

"It's a shark's tooth," she explained, uncomfortable that Brad had moved away to talk to another man. "It's good luck, like a rabbit's paw."

"Rabbit's foot," Judd corrected her, then snapped his fingers at a passing waiter. "Bring a glass of Cristal for Kelly."

The way he gave the order and the intensity in his eyes told her that he was a powerful man, someone who expected to be obeyed. She wondered how "Kelly" had dealt with this man. "Call me Lucky," she told him.

Suddenly, his eyes became flat and as unreadable as a stone, but his words were kind. "I guess after all you've been through, the name Lucky suits you better than Kelly."

"What's Cristal?" she asked, feeling uneasy.

"Your favorite drink—expensive French champagne. I always keep a case in the wine vault for you."

Inwardly, Lucky groaned, but smiled politely because he looked immensely pleased with himself—or something. "Were we good friends . . . before?"

He leaned so close she could smell an expensive men's cologne, whispering in her ear, "Very, very close . . . friends."

Sourness invaded the pit of her stomach. Was he implying they'd had an affair? Judd smiled, a slow knowing smile, arching one brow again. That was *exactly* what he meant.

"I don't remember anything about the past."

"So Brad tells me."

Though quietly spoken, there was a hint of something in his voice she couldn't quite define. Lucky had the distinct impression he expected to resume their relationship—whatever it had been. The waiter arrived with a flute of champagne. She took it and politely sipped, the bubbles rising off the top, tickling her nose.

"Excuse me," she said, mustering a smile. "Brad promised to introduce me to all his friends."

Lucky hurried to Brad's side and he introduced her to everyone. She noticed they avoided discussing her brush with death, but they all knew about it. Once Brad had brought her home, her story had been front-page news. Although people didn't question Lucky about her experience, she caught several of them looking at her oddly.

"I just love your necklace!" exclaimed a plump blonde with a neck like a shar-pei and bright blue eyes. "If you're wearing it, I'm sure it's the latest."

"It's a one-of-a-kind piece," Lucky replied, then decided she sounded haughty. Evidently, this woman knew her—even though she didn't seem familiar—and recalled her passion for clothes and jewelry. "What I mean is, this is a tooth from a shark I helped save."

The blonde's jaw dropped, making her neck wrinkle even more. "Really?"

Pele's ghost had been headline news in Maui, but obviously Honolulu was too sophisticated for island lore to be turned into front-page news. Lucky had probably been relegated to a single column beside the obituaries until they discovered she was Brad Wagner's wife.

"I wear it to remember Rudy." *And the man who loved me enough to give me up.*

The blonde took a step back, and Lucky thought she might actually run.

"Do I know you?" Lucky asked quickly. "Some people look familiar, but I don't remember their names."

"My hair was brown like yours, so you probably don't recognize me. I'm Mitzy Morgan. Not that you ever paid any attention to me," she said with more than a trace of sarcasm. "You never had anything to do with women."

Because I'd spent ten long years surrounded by women. But she couldn't remember that episode of her life, and now she needed a friend like Sarah. "I'm sorry if I was rude to you in the past. I don't remember what I said or did to offend you, but please forgive me."

"We-ll, we-ll," stammered Mitzy. "You didn't do anything exactly. You just never said more than hello. I never saw you except when Judd had a party like this."

Time to make a friend, Lucky thought. "Would you like to have lunch one day next week? Julie comes home at one-thirty, so we'd need to eat on the early side."

Mitzy beamed. "Sure, I'd love to."

"Do you have children?" Lucky asked.

"Three. That's why my waistline went south on me."

"Good." Lucky shook her head. "I mean, it's good that you have children. I need some advice about raising my daughter."

Clearly, Mitzy Morgan was astonished—and delighted—that Lucky was consulting her. They spoke at length about the various problems of raising young children. Mitzy wasn't as insightful as Sarah, but she genuinely loved her children and gave Lucky some helpful tips: Expect children to come home from school with words like *studmuffin*. They learn outrageous things from the older children. Keep them from watching MTV as long as possible.

Lucky was just feeling comfortable when they went into dinner. Judd Fremont had an open-air style house with an enormous dining room that led onto a lanai with a lagoon, where three white swans were serenely floating, barely rippling the placid water. Brad escorted her to a place card that read "Kelly," and she sat down at a table so long it could have doubled for an airplane runway.

Mitzy, Judd, and Brad were seated too far away for Lucky to be part of their conversations. The people around her were discussing local politics. She tried telling them about the institute's work with the monk seals and the whales, hoping these wealthy people could be parted from their money for a worthy cause. It didn't work.

By the time dessert and coffee had been served, Lucky wondered if solitary confinement could be much worse. No doubt it was, but this wasn't her idea of fun. She gazed wistfully at the grove of date palms down at the shore. In her mind she could still see Greg's face as he spoke about her imprisonment. He had been so loving, so understanding. Tears sprang to Lucky's eyes. Was she ever going to get over him?

"Excuse me," she said, getting up. She headed down the hall to fix her lipstick. She'd had so much time on her hands that she'd been watching talk shows, learning a lady should always excuse herself from the table and never apply lipstick in public. It sounded like a silly rule, but it gave her an excuse to get away.

Mitzy joined her. "Which way to the little girl's room?"

"There's one right down the hall on the left. I'll use the bathroom upstairs."

Lucky was upstairs in the bathroom doing the silly lipstick thing when something dawned on her. She had given Mitzy directions, then found this bathroom. She hadn't known her way around her own home, yet in this mansion that could double for a hotel, she knew how to find the bathrooms.

If you've done something over and over, you remember it. Like logging onto the computer. She must have been in this house a lot. Something wasn't right here. She rushed out of the door, intending to get Brad alone and ask him, and almost bumped into Judd Fremont.

"Judd, I knew how to find this bathroom." She pointed down the wide hall lined with tree ferns and soft lights artistically highlighting the alcoves built into the walls. "There's an office down there. Why do I know all this when I almost had to leave a trail of bread crumbs, like Hansel and Gretel, to find my way around my own house?"

Judd chuckled, his dark eyes alight with humor. "You've been reading fairy tales to Julie, I see." His brow canted slightly. "This house should be familiar. You and Brad lived here while they built your house."

"Oh, that explains it." Lucky was relieved yet still troubled. It was Judd, she decided. The man gave her the willies. Had he followed her upstairs?

They were walking down the hall now, and he was telling her something about the special lighting in the house. He stopped in front of a mirrored alcove, showcasing an unusual plant in an exquisite container. The coral-colored plant had a single blossom the size of a football. It had three petals in soft coral, the color deepening to a vivid crimson in the throat of the flower.

"It's new," Judd told her with unmistakable pride. "It's a rare, endangered species from the Amazon rain forest."

"What is it?" The flower didn't look like anything she'd ever seen.

"This is the largest orchid known to exist. It's got a ten-syllable zoological name, but collectors call it Orinoco Sunrise because the first plant was discovered on the banks of the Orinoco River. Now there are only a few left."

"Who took it out of the rain forest? That's illegal," she

said, remembering all Alan Dunbar had told her about the harmful stripping of Hawaii's rain forest.

"I bought it from another collector." Judd's tone could have frozen lava. "They're cutting down the Amazon rain forest so rapidly that these beauties will be gone forever—without collectors like me to save them."

"I don't remember that much about the Amazon. But I know that Hawaii's rain forest is being stripped of its rare orchids. I heard about it when I was on Maui. There's no excuse for it. The government is doing everything it can to preserve our rain forest."

Judd smiled slightly. "Well, I'll be. You've turned into an environmentalist."

"I want to preserve the earth's treasures, like the plants and animals, for Julie."

"Naturally, you do," he said, leading her down the hall. "I couldn't agree more. At some point, the Brazilians will stop cutting down their rain forest. When they do, collectors can give them orchids to replant."

He stopped in front of another alcove. Here was another plant, in yet another container, that must be priceless. This orchid was an unusual shade of blue, and it had multiple blossoms with serrated edges like Rudy's tooth.

"Watch this," Judd told her as he reached for the light switch.

The hall became pitch black, with only faint light coming from the far end where the stairs were. In the darkness the orchid's petals glowed slightly, giving off a faint blue-white light.

"Wow! How does that work?"

Judd had moved closer. Lucky could smell his cologne again, and she edged away. If they'd been intimate in the past, she wasn't repeating her mistakes, one of which had obviously been Judd.

"This beauty comes from Zaire—another nation that does nothing to protect its rain forest. The phosphorus in the soil combines with the plant's own chemicals, so that it glows in the dark.'' He'd moved closer again, and she felt the heat of his body. "Don't inhale. It gives off a poisonous gas."

Lucky reached for the wall, her fingers searching until she found the light switch. Flipping on the lights, she said, "I don't smell anything."

Judd smiled at her, the twinkle back in his eyes. "It's practically odorless. I built a special chamber just for them. It has a ventilation system to keep the poisonous fumes from building up, otherwise somebody could wander in there and die."

"Really?" she said, studying him. Judd was tan, with a well-toned body. Not a workingman's hard body, like Greg's, but Judd had a physique. He probably had a personal trainer like Harry, the studmuffin. Judd reached out to lovingly touch one of the deadly orchid's petals, and she saw the livid cut on his arm.

"What happened? How did you cut yourself?"

He looked at his arm as if he'd just noticed it, then smiled at her. Something in his expression made the fine hairs across the back of her neck stand at attention. How could she ever have been friends with this man?

"A cat scratched me. I'd befriended this stray who hung around the warehouse where Brad and I have our office."

"What warehouse?" Brad had told her he had an office downtown, but he'd never mentioned a warehouse.

"One of the businesses in which we're partners is orchid importing and exporting. When you came to Hawaii, you came to work for us right here in my home. Now we have our office downtown in a Chinatown warehouse. It's easier."

"I thought Brad was in designer beef."

"We've invested in a number of companies. With America on a rampage against fat, designer beef is a real winner."

There seemed to be a lot Brad hadn't told her. But then, she was guilty of not telling him about herself. He'd given her space and time to adjust. No doubt, he'd soon tell her all this himself.

"I interrupted you. What about the cat who scratched you?"

He smiled that disturbing smile again, then said, "It accidentally wandered into the vault where I keep these blue orchids. I looked for it everywhere, then decided it had slipped out. Hours later, I opened the door to the vault. The poor thing was panic-stricken and it scratched me. After all that time with those poisonous fumes, it should have been dead, but it wasn't. It really gouged me."

"Is the cat all right?"

His eyes were fired by a strange inner light, and he waited half a beat too long before answering. "No. It's very sad, but the poor little thing got only a few feet before it collapsed and died. I rushed it to the vet but—"

Anger and alarm rippled down her spine. That was *not* what had happened. Lucky didn't know what exactly had tipped her, but she was positive Judd was lying. Why? She touched Rudy's tooth.

Get out of here, her brain screamed.

"I've got to find Brad."

She rushed down the hall and took the stairs two at a time. Instead of returning to the dining room, she dashed out onto the lanai. Her heart was hammering against her breastbone, her breath coming in ragged spurts. Sweat gushed from her pores. What was wrong with her?

Lucky sucked in deep, calming breaths of the balmy tropical air. What had triggered such an intense reaction? She loved animals, true, but the death of a kitty she'd never even seen shouldn't cause such an intense physical reaction. As her breathing returned to normal, she recalled several things Dr. Summerville had told her.

Of the five senses, smell occupied the largest space in the brain. That's why smells rekindled more memories, which were more vivid than the memories stored by the other senses. At the time these facts had seemed like meaningless trivia. But now she appreciated what she'd learned.

Dr. Summerville had insisted there was one more, very

important, sense—the sixth sense. Intuition. Her intuition had just kicked in, Lucky decided. Something else the doctor had told her came to mind. Fear. Scientists had actually located the spot in the brain where fear was centered. That part of her brain was completely intact.

Was the fear center in her brain trying to warn her by triggering her sixth sense? Someone had tried to kill her, and she was instinctively afraid of Judd Fremont. Maybe the two weren't connected, but her gut instinct said they were.

"Mrs. Wagner, there you are. Your housekeeper is on the phone."

"Julie," she cried, rushing after the maid.

"It's probably nothing," Malia said when Lucky came to the phone, "but Julie has an upset stomach."

"Tell her that Mommy is coming home right now."

The Orchid King turned out the light in his bedroom and gazed out at the private strip of beach known as the Gold Coast.

She was back. After *Missing!* hadn't produced anyone who could identify her, they'd played the ace—Julie—and gotten Kelly away from Greg Braxton. It had taken him time to convince Brad, who'd insisted bringing Kelly back was only inviting trouble.

But she wasn't Kelly anymore, flaunting her tight ass and big tits. Judd liked this new woman who was all eyes now, her hair short and sassy-looking. There was a certain shyness to her that he found immensely appealing.

"This time, she's all mine," he said out loud.

This new woman was into motherhood, a lady worthy of having his children. Gone was the smart-mouthed, self-centered but sexy-as-hell woman he'd fallen in love with. She was still drop-dead smart, though. She'd picked up on something when he'd told her about the cat.

Big fucking deal. So he'd kicked the cat to death. The filthy little beast deserved it. He would probably have a scar on his arm.

"Lucky," he whispered in the darkness. "This time you belong to me. No one else but me."

Judd reluctantly admitted he'd made a mistake. He'd met Lucky on the Internet. It had been love in cyberspace, and he'd invited her to come to Honolulu and work for him. When she arrived, Lucky proved to be even sexier and more interesting in person than she had on-line. But he held back, waiting for Kelly to understand that he was the man for her. Then Brad had stepped in.

"Stepped in? Fuck no! Kelly pounced on him—for his money."

Judd had gone on a two-week orchid expedition. Nothing exciting—just your basic jungle stripping. When he returned, they were married. Next thing he knew, Kelly was pregnant.

He had told himself that he'd get over her. After all, she was married to his best friend. But time hadn't changed anything.

"I want her as much now as I did then. Tonight I laid the groundwork. She thinks we had an affair. A lie, but that'll make it easier to get close to her."

He stared at the water for a moment, finalizing the plan he'd been thinking about for days.

"You know what you have to do now."

It wasn't going to be easy to lure Brad into the chamber. His partner knew how deadly the orchids were, but he'd think of something. Then he'd have to kill Greg Braxton, because with Brad gone, Lucky would run to that prick.

He'd been at the house watching through high-powered binoculars as Lucky took her usual early morning swim. Even now he could feel how painful his erection had been. Watching. Imagining her beneath him.

His hand slipped beneath the waistband of his pants, finding his swollen cock just the way he had that morning. This time, however, pleasure came with a few swift strokes.

This morning his cock had wilted like an orchid in the searing sun the minute he'd spotted Braxton and that fucking dog strolling onto the sandy cove Judd had always thought of as his beach. He had trained the binoculars on Lucky and Braxton as they'd talked. Lucky thought she loved the bastard.

No doubt about it. He would have to kill two people. First Brad, then Greg Braxton. And make it look like an icing—an accident.

Chapter 33

Cody parked the Bronco in the Traylor car rental lot, thinking about Greg. He'd called last night from Claude Winston's home in Honolulu. Greg had told Lucky about her past and said she was okay with it. Well, why not? A princess with a cute kid and a rich husband had a tough life, right?

He knew he wasn't being fair to Lucky. She'd suffered more than anyone he'd ever met, but now his brother was going through hell, loving a woman he couldn't have. At least they were close again. Maybe having a family around would help Greg, but Cody had his doubts.

Cody walked into Tony Traylor's office reluctantly. The jerk had been calling him for several days, but Cody had avoided him. He'd been too involved in tracking down the warden and the prison shrink who had worked with Lucky. Knowing Traylor was involved in the Maui Wowie drug trafficking made Cody furious. He could hardly wait to arrest Traylor's fat ass.

"Where the fuck have you been?" Traylor bellowed the second Cody came through the door.

''I've been busy doing my job,'' Cody replied, a mean edge to his voice.

Traylor jerked his head toward the office door and one of the two *mokes* who always hung around him closed it. Uh-oh. Now what?

''I want one of those secret source agreements,'' Traylor said. ''I tell you something. Use it, but don't tell anyone where you got your information.''

The fat weasel had gotten wind of Helmer's investigation. This must have something to do with blaming his drug trafficking on someone else. The fact that this man was an elected politician, head of the joint council governing Maui, made Cody sick.

''I can't cut any deals. Only the DA has the authority to do that.''

''If you don't give me your word, I'm not telling you shit.''

The creep's vocabulary was limited to four-letter words. Cody had given up swearing when the twins began parroting such words. Okay, okay. So once in a while he slipped. Cody reached for the doorknob. ''Suit yourself.''

''I figured you'd want to help your brother.''

Cody spun around. ''What are you talking about? Why would you care about helping Greg?''

''I hate the motherfucker, but I've got an image to protect. Your brother blabbing that I'm responsible for pollution destroying the reef is hurting my reputation. I'm gonna help him, then you persuade him to keep his mouth shut.''

There wasn't a power on earth who could silence Greg when it came to environmental issues, but Cody merely nodded. Traylor had him curious.

Tony pulled out a copy of the *Tattler*. It was the latest issue, with a front-page picture of Lucky getting on the plane with her family. PELE'S GHOST DISAPPEARS. The banner headline and the close-up picture—courtesy of Fenton Bewley—captivated the islanders. Just like the legend, Lucky had disappeared as unexpectedly as she had appeared.

"This here article says her husband didn't know what happened to her. He hadn't seen her in months. That's a fuckin' lie. We saw 'im right here, didn't we, boys?"

Like mimes, the *mokes* nodded silently. For a second, Cody thought his heart had stopped beating. "No way. The FBI checked Brad Wagner's story."

"Fuck the FBI. About three months ago, we were up in the rain forest hunting wild pigs, weren't we, boys?"

Again the *mokes* nodded but didn't speak.

"I mean, we were way the hell back there. We came to a trail head and there was this car. We saw them but they never saw us, 'cause the jungle's so thick around there. We saw two men and this woman—Pele's ghost. She was sitting in the backseat starin' out of the open window like she was on something. Right, boys?"

More silent nods from the "boys." Cody's heart was thumping now, and he was sweating as if he'd run a marathon. Two men. It had taken two men to dump the hiker's body. The same with Lucky.

"You know, I kept thinkin' I knew the bitch. Those eyes. They're hard to forget. But I didn't put it together until I saw the man's picture. Brad Wagner was with Pele's ghost. He and another guy were loading orchids into the trunk of a car."

Orchids. The key to the case. With the back of his hand, Cody swiped at the sweat coating his brow.

"I didn't recognize Pele's ghost because her hair was long and dark. Straighter than a stick. Next day she drives off some damn *pali* with bleached blonde hair all curly. Fuckin' weird."

"Yeah, fuckin' weird," said one of the *mokes*. "They had Tony's stolen car but we didn't know it."

Traylor zapped the *moke* who dared to speak with a killer frown. "I got hundreds of fuckin' cars. I don't have their license plates memorized. It had been missing a year. I didn't even think about it bein' my car."

Cody didn't say a word. He was out the door in a second. Oh, Christ, no. Brad seemed like such a nice guy. Even Sarah liked him, and she usually had good instincts about people. But they'd been wrong. He was certain that they'd handed Lucky over to the man who'd tried to murder her.

It took two hours for him to locate Greg in Honolulu. Cody had first alerted Helmer, who was stunned by the news, but there wasn't anything the authorities could do. They didn't have any evidence of a crime other than Tony's confidential story. There was no chance of getting Traylor to talk.

Tony would never admit to anyone that he'd been in the rain forest. Cody didn't buy the pig hunt story. They were running Maui Wowie. That's why Traylor wanted this kept quiet. After all, next year was an election year.

"Look, I know you're pissed big time," Cody told Greg over the phone. "The FBI's working on it. Helmer called the Honolulu office. This is the break we needed. We can't send in the police without some evidence."

"I'm getting Lucky out of there."

"Be careful. Brad Wagner has killed once—that we know of. There's another man out there working with him. We don't know who he is. Could be the chauffeur Brad mentioned. Could be anyone. They won't hesitate to kill you if you get in their way."

"I'm going over to her house right now."

"Good idea," Cody agreed. "Tell her in person, but be sure no one overhears you. That would put you both in danger. Right now Brad must be feeling secure. I can't believe he had the nerve to come get Lucky. He could have just left her here."

"No. Brad loves her too much. She must have seen or heard something she doesn't remember. I can't imagine any other reason he would try to kill her, then want her back."

"You're probably right," Cody said, cold sweat running down his back. "I wish I was there to help you. Be careful."

"Right. I owe you one."

"Sebastian is on the telephone," Malia whispered to Lucky. "He says it's urgent."

Lucky tiptoed out of Julie's room. She'd spent the night beside her daughter's bed. The doctor had been right. It was just an upset stomach, and once Julie went to sleep, the child hadn't had another episode. But Lucky had kept her home from school and now Julie was napping.

"You've got to come down here," Sebastian told her when she took his call.

"I can't. Julie's home—"

"You have to," Sebastian insisted, sounding frantic. "I just looked in the shopping bag you gave me. I should have opened it right away. My stars, I'm such a twit. I'd come to you but I'm double booked as it is. Trust me, you're going to want to see this."

"I could leave Julie with Malia, I suppose."

Telling the maid she'd be right back, Lucky took her new blue Suburban to Cache. She couldn't imagine what could be in the bag. Sebastian had said it was a small bag. It couldn't be anything that terrible, could it?

She was still a little shaken about the panic attack she'd had at the party. Judd Fremont was trouble with a capital *T*. Something was really wrong here. She would have discussed it with Brad, but he came in late from the party and went right to bed after checking on Julie, saying he had a breakfast meeting in the morning. Lucky hadn't minded because she didn't want to leave Julie's side. Now, though, she wished she had talked to Brad.

Sebastian was in the middle of something he called a weave. Strands of the woman's hair were wrapped in strips of tin foil, but he left his customer and hustled Lucky into his office.

"Here it is." He grabbed a small shopping bag off a desk. "You said to keep this for you. I didn't open it until last night. My stars, I saw the two envelopes, but I just thought they were pictures of dresses. You were always showing me outfits you wanted to buy."

He pulled a white envelope from the bag and handed it to

her. Lucky recognized her own handwriting. The note inside puzzled her, though.

> *Sebastian, I'm hearing the night marchers. If anything happens to me, mail this immediately.*

"The night marchers must have been the ones who tried to kill me. Who are they? Is Judd Fremont involved with them?"

Sebastian shook his head. "The night marchers are part of island lore. Superstitious people think that if you hear footsteps at night when you're trying to sleep, it's ghosts of Hawaiian warriors marching to sea the way they did in ancient times. It means that someone is going to die—usually the person who hears the night marchers."

Lucky hesitated, astonished to discover this man must have been her closest friend. She trusted him, but not her husband.

"I must have known I was in trouble. Did I tell you anything about it?"

"No. I would have mailed this if I'd known."

He pulled a small manila envelope out of the bag. It was addressed to Ned Adams, Special Investigator at the Federal Bureau of Investigation.

"What would I have to send to the FBI?" Lucky ripped open the envelope and found a small plastic case. Inside were two computer disks.

Sebastian pointed to the computer on the desk. "You'd better see what's on them."

Lucky sat at the desk, suddenly realizing the office seemed eerily familiar, like Judd's house. She knew there was a drawer with office supplies and the bottom drawer would have a bag of Hershey Kisses in it. "Have I been in here a lot?"

"You bet. You set up my inventory system. Now I know exactly how much of everything to order. I keep track of my operators' salaries, write checks, and all because you said I was a dinosaur. And you were right. My life is so much easier."

He gave her a quick pat on the shoulder. "Get to work. I've got to finish Mrs. Doram."

Lucky logged onto the computer, the password HAIR popping into her mind immediately. The first disk tracked orchid shipments. Most of them came out of Singapore and went to places all over the country. Seemed harmless, but there must be some criminal activity involved or she wouldn't have feared for her life and wanted this sent to the FBI.

Orchids meant Judd Fremont. And her own husband. She froze, fingers splayed across the keyboard, and stared at the screen. Surely the father of her child hadn't tried to kill her.

Unquestionably, Brad loved Julie and was a good father. He seemed so kind, so understanding. But did that make him a good man—or a man adept at hiding his innermost feelings? Beware of what's too good to be true, came a warning from some distant part of her brain.

With shaking fingers, she changed disks and scanned the next one. It was a series of numeric codes that made absolutely no sense to her. There wasn't one single word on the disk, just an odd assortment of numbers.

Lucky put the two disks back in the plastic case and dropped it into her purse. Common sense told her that Brad and Judd knew exactly what these disks meant. The information was valuable enough for them to kill her over it. She picked up the telephone and called the FBI facility in Quantico, Virginia, where the package had been addressed.

It was late back there and no one was on duty who could help her. She insisted on getting Ned Adams's home telephone number, but they refused to give it to her. They took her name and the shop number and said Ned Adams would call her.

"What was on the disks?" Sebastian came into the office as Lucky was hanging up.

"Nothing that made any sense to me. I called the FBI. They're supposed to call me here." She took a deep breath and gazed at the man she'd trusted to help her. "Be honest with me. What was my relationship with Brad and Judd like? Did I tell you anything about them?''

Sebastian sat in the chair next to the desk. ''We were very close friends, but you weren't very open about your past or your private life.''

''Did I love Brad?''

''You said Brad was nice but a total bore, yet he was rich and gave you anything you wanted. You did say you originally wanted to marry Judd, but when you went to work for them, you liked Brad better. I think he was easier for you to manipulate.''

''I sound like such a bitch. How could anyone stand me?''

''You were—are—fun. You loved to tell jokes and stories. You always knew the latest, trendiest restaurant or boutique. You were smart and sexy. Men instantly liked you.''

''Did I have an affair with Judd Fremont?'' Lucky held her breath, praying he would say no.

Sebastian smiled, shaking his head. ''No. The creep was crazy about you and you knew it. You flirted with him, mercilessly teasing him. That's all. But if you would have given him half a chance, he would have hopped in the sack with you.''

She gazed at her friend for a moment. ''Do you think Judd and Brad would try to kill me?''

All the color leached from his tanned face. ''What would make you think that?''

''One of the disks is a shipping report or something on orchids. They import them. Judd collects rare, endangered orchids, which are probably stolen. Someone tried to kill me. The orchids must be the key.''

''I don't know. Judd and Brad are creepy and strange. The two of them are so close. You all lived in one house until you insisted on building your own.'' Sebastian shrugged. ''But would they try to kill you? I wouldn't put anything past Judd.''

The phone rang and Lucky picked it up. Ned Adams was on the line. Sebastian slipped out of the room, leaving her alone.

"You said this was urgent." Five time zones away, Ned Adams sounded exhausted and short-tempered.

"Don't you know me? I must have contacted you before."

"About what?"

"I don't remember," Lucky responded without thinking. Oh, boy, she sounded like a total nut. "Your address was on a package I was sending you."

"Look, lady, I'm tired. When you remember what it was—"

"I have two computer disks here. One is some sort of record of orchid shipments from Singapore—"

"Hey, wait a minute. You called me before, but you refused to tell me your name. You said you'd been in prison once and had no intention of going to jail again. You claimed to have information on a credit card scam."

She didn't remember anything about this. "How are orchids and credit cards related? I don't get it."

Four beats of silence, then, "You just left Maui, didn't you?"

"Yes, I—"

"Son of a bitch! *You're* the woman in the car they pushed off a cliff, aren't you?"

"You know about my case? Hasn't the FBI been investigating it for some time?" Lucky asked, remembering that Cody had contacted them when he couldn't identify her.

"Damn straight, I've been in on this case. You were wearing the shoe that matched the one on the agent from American Express. She'd been investigating a credit card scam in Singapore." He let out a long sigh. "I had no idea you were the woman who contacted me about the credit card scheme."

Lucky's blood coursed through her veins, chilling every inch of her body and leaving her feeling weak. Singapore. Orchids. Her worst fears confirmed. Brad had tried to kill her. Oh, please, no, not Julie's father.

"Tell me again what you've got on those disks." Now Ned Adams sounded totally awake.

"I don't know. It's a lot of routing information or something, showing shipments out of Singapore."

"Great! It will tell us who is distributing the counterfeit credit cards."

"Really? Are they shipping them in boxes of orchids?"

"Absolutely. The boxes probably have a false bottom, which conceals the cards. We could shut down the operation right now, but without the distribution list, the scam will just go on."

Lucky could almost see the smile on his face, but she was so heartsick she could hardly speak. The father of her child. A cold-blooded killer.

"What's on the other disk?"

"I have no idea. It's a jumble of numbers—"

"And strange-looking symbols?"

"Exactly. Have you seen it?"

"Holy shit! You've got an encryption breaker."

Realizing the man who'd fathered her child had tried to kill her had hit her like a knockout punch. Lucky could barely ask, "What's that?"

"It's a software program designed by a sophisticated hacker—who's nothing more than a common criminal—to crack the intricate codes banks use to protect their computer systems. Crack the code the way these counterfeiters have, and you're into the bank's confidential records. You know their credit card sequence numbers and all sorts of technical information, which allows you to manufacture phony cards."

"Oh," she whispered into the receiver, wishing Greg were at her side. He'd seen her through the worst. He could help her now.

"Do you have those disks in your possession?" Ned asked.

"Yes. Should I send them to you?"

"Hell, no! I want you to call our field office in Honolulu. One of our agents will meet you. Give him the disks, then get out of there."

Lucky listened while he explained the blow that had nearly killed her matched the wound on the American Express agent.

As he filled her in on other details, anger coursed through her. White-hot fury, a remnant of the woman in the mirror.

Julie's earliest years, the memories other mothers had to treasure, had been stolen from her. While some people might say Lucky had been blessed not to remember the terrible times in her life, she didn't agree. She wanted to remember so she could understand herself. But thanks to Judd and Brad, she would never have the chance.

Blind anger obliterated everything else. She barely heard what Ned was telling her. She wanted revenge with a savage intensity that made her tremble.

"They tried to kill you once," Ned insisted. "This time you're a dead woman. Get out of there."

Chapter 34

Greg managed to squeeze a bit of information out of Lucky's housekeeper. He learned Lucky had received an emergency phone call from Sebastian at the Cache salon in the pricey Ala Moana district. Greg drove there, Dodger at his side, using Claude Winston's car.

Lucky wasn't at the swank salon, but she'd told Sebastian about Greg and the hairdresser willingly talked about her. With growing alarm, Greg listened to the ponytailed man with diamonds twinkling from his ear and left nostril explain how he found the disks Lucky had entrusted to him—finally. Greg balled his fists to resist the urge to deck him. If Sebastian spent less time mincing around in patent leather sandals and more time paying attention to important things, he would have contacted the FBI and Lucky wouldn't be in danger.

"What do you mean you found a gun for her?" Greg asked Sebastian.

"After Lucky spoke with the FBI, she sat there"—Sebastian pointed to the chair at the desk—"and asked if I had a gun. I knew she was afraid. Who wouldn't be? Judd and Brad had tried to kill her. So I went next door and borrowed Dixon's gun for her.''

Sebastian shook his head as he told Greg all about the credit card scam. ''Ned Adams told her to contact the local FBI office. I wanted her to go to them right away, but she ran out without saying exactly what she was doing. I think she went home to get Julie.''

Greg raced back to the Gold Coast but Lucky wasn't there. He called the FBI field office and found out that they were expecting her call but hadn't heard from her yet.

Lucky had asked for a gun.

Greg remembered the way Lucky's temper would flare. With pride, he recalled her determination to save Rudy. Lucky hadn't wanted a gun because she was afraid. She'd gone to confront Brad and Judd.

Would she do something that foolish? You bet. This was the woman who jumped in the pool with the type of shark famous for attacking people.

Greg got the address of the warehouse from the maid and climbed into the borrowed car, talking to Dodger. ''Damn it! Don't let her do anything stupid. Let's hope we're not too late.''

Lucky paused outside the Chinatown warehouse and told herself to calm down, but the anger simmering inside her refused to listen. Instead, it intensified, telling her that she knew how to use the gun in her purse. Where or when she'd learned, she couldn't be sure. Lucky touched Rudy's tooth for luck, then slipped inside the warehouse.

It was dimly lit, but she could see crates lining the wall. Each was stamped FLOWERS—FRAGILE. Orchids and phony credit cards. At least the woman in the mirror had learned her lesson. She hadn't wanted to be sent back to jail. Obviously, she had planned on turning in Judd and Brad when she discovered they were crooks.

At the rear of the building was a brightly lit office where Brad and Judd were working on computers, their backs to her. Brad had told her that all he needed was a computer to do his work. He didn't even have a secretary. It had seemed odd at the time, but now she knew why. They didn't want to risk anyone discovering what they were doing.

Next to the glassed-in office was a strange-looking metal chamber with a thermostat on the door and a ventilation switch. Judd's deadly orchids, Lucky thought as she passed the unit.

Brad jumped up the second she opened the door. "Lucky, what are you doing here?"

"I wanted to ask you both a few questions," she said, her tone reflecting the fury that nothing could temper.

"Hey, you sound upset," Judd remarked, rising from his chair.

Upset? Get real. She was mad as hell, ready to kill.

"Honey, what's the matter?" Brad asked, coming closer.

Lucky pulled the gun out of her purse, stopping him dead in his tracks. He took a step backward and looked at Judd.

Judd's stance was casual as he leaned back against the desk and surveyed Lucky as if she were an interesting, rare orchid, not a woman with a loaded gun in her hand. "I think the lady wants some answers."

She aimed the gun at Brad, saying, "Did you hit me over the head? Did you really want to murder the mother of your child?"

"Hey, I don't know where you got such a crazy idea," Brad protested.

"Oh, please, don't insult me. As soon as I get my answers, I'm calling the police. After all I've been through, I want to have the pleasure of seeing you both hauled away in handcuffs."

Brad whirled around to face Judd. "I told you we should have left her with Braxton."

"Shut up! She can't kill us both before we get the gun away from her."

"Yeah? Right!" Brad gripped the edge of the desk, his knuckles white.

"I won't hesitate to kill you unless I get the answers I want. Which one of you actually hit me over the head? He gets the first bullet."

"Judd did it." Brad sank into the chair. "You stumbled upon our counterfeiting scheme. You'd been living with us for years and never knew how we really made our money."

"Then you got nosy." Judd studied Lucky, canting one eyebrow in that irritating way of his. "I had no choice but to kill you."

"Why was I wearing a dead woman's shoe?"

"It was a mistake. We lured you to a shack in the rain forest by pretending to be after some exotic orchids. There we drugged you and forced you to bleach and perm your hair."

Lucky listened to Brad, who willingly gave the details, hoping to save his own hide. She imagined herself in those final hours. A hard, self-centered person, but a woman who did love her child and was struggling to be a good mother despite her past. A woman who had been to prison once and had learned her lesson.

What had it been like, knowing she was going to die? Even though she'd been drugged, if she had enough presence of mind to give herself a home permanent and bleach her hair, Lucky had known death was only hours away.

She must have been panicked, struggling to think of a way of escaping, a way to save her life. And Julie, oh, Julie. She must have been terrified that this monster, who looked so meek, was going to raise her daughter.

"You were out cold when we dressed you," Judd told her without even a hint of remorse in his voice. "We made you up to look like a dollar-a-trick whore, then we each put on a shoe. Brad's so stupid. He hadn't thrown away Thelma's shoe. It was still in the closet. Brad got so rattled that he put it on you by mistake."

So she'd been out cold when they'd put her into the trunk

of the car. Lucky imagined the night of terror—death just minutes away. At least she hadn't been awake when she was in the trunk.

"The woman you killed in Singapore had a family, a right to a life. Maybe she had a child she loved as dearly as I love Julie. Did you ever think of that?"

Suddenly, a grin split Judd's face and he lifted one brow. The chill of fear prickled across her scalp. Julie. The chink in her emotional armor. The woman in the mirror would have killed them, but Lucky would not. She was a different person now. She was bluffing and Judd realized it when she spoke about Julie.

"You know, Brad," Judd said, his tone so casual they might have been discussing the latest in PC software, "I think we should put Lucky in the vault with the deadly orchids, switch off the ventilator, and let her die."

"She's going to kill us," Brad said, a distinct quaver in his voice.

"No, she's not." Judd grinned. "She's thinking of Julie. How would she explain killing Julie's father?"

"Self-defense," Lucky said quickly, but her tone wasn't as forceful as it had been a moment ago.

She opened her mouth to tell them to put their hands in the air. Judd pounced, grabbing her arm and yanking hard. The gun fell to the floor, and he shoved her down on top of it.

"You bitch! To think I loved you and brought you home again."

Judd planted his knee in the small of her back. Beneath her stomach she felt the sharp edges of the gun. Her fingers clutched at Rudy's tooth and prayed for luck.

Greg used the car phone to call the FBI. He spoke with the field agent who was expecting Lucky's call. Greg gave him the address of the warehouse just as he drove into Chinatown, and the agent promised to get there as quickly as possible.

"Why not call the police?" Greg asked him.

"They're a little iffy. I don't want anyone to tip off the credit card crooks. They're pretty slick. They may have an informant on the police force."

Greg drove down a narrow street flanked by tall, narrow buildings. Chinatown had sprung up overnight—built with the cheapest materials—to accommodate the Chinese who'd been shanghaied to work in the sugar cane fields during the last century. The buildings had Chinese characters instead of names or numbers. He hoped the FBI agent was familiar with the area, Greg thought, thankful that Search and Rescue had trained here.

"That must be her car," he told Dodger. "It still has the dealer's paper license plates on it."

Greg double-parked beside Lucky's Suburban. Jumping out of the car, Dodger at his heels, he inhaled the foul odor of garbage baking in the afternoon sun. Dodger's nose quivered, and Greg knew he detected a trace of opium drifting in the air, blowing their direction from the red-light district two blocks away. This was just about as far from the tourists' vision of paradise as anyone could get.

And the perfect place to hide an illegal operation.

This could have been Hong Kong or San Francisco's Chinatown. A jumble of buildings with laundry hanging from the balconies and the sing-song cadence of Asians yelling to each other through the warren of alleylike streets dominated this world. A place where no questions were asked.

Greg couldn't read the Chinese characters and couldn't decide which of the several large buildings might be International Orchid Importing. There were no shops on this particular stretch of the street, and he had no time to waste asking questions. Even if he did, he doubted many of the people spoke anything but Chinese.

"Okay, boy," he told Dodger, whirling one finger in the air. "Find Lucky."

Dodger wasn't trained to follow a scent like a bloodhound, but the dog had become so attached to Lucky and knew her scent so well that Dodger understood. Taking measured steps, nose in the air, the dog pranced down the street.

There were no parking places. Cars were parked against the sides of the ramshackle buildings. He figured Lucky had parked as close as she could get to the warehouse. They were almost to the end of the block now. Dodger stopped, pointed with one paw raised, and whined.

Greg patted him on the head. "Good work, Dodger."

The building didn't look large enough to be a warehouse, but in Chinatown looks could be deceiving. He eased the door open, then glanced over his shoulder, hoping to see the FBI. The only car in sight was an ancient Toyota belching smoke from its exhaust. Hell if he was waiting. Minutes could make the difference between life and death for Lucky.

Inside the warehouse was pitch dark except for two flares of blue-white light coming from the back. He hesitated a moment, putting his hand down to pet Dodger while his eyes became accustomed to the dark. Slowly, he began to see that the warehouse was larger than it appeared. Crates like coffins lined the sides of the building.

Greg dropped to his knees, the hot, tight vise of fear cinching around his chest. Why weren't there any lights on? What had they done to her this time?

"Find Lucky," he whispered to Dodger.

He gripped Dodger's collar and let the dog slowly lead him to the back of the warehouse. As they came closer, he realized that the small flares of light were actually computer screens, but the rest of the office was in total darkness. Dodger veered away from the office area toward what appeared to be a workstation. He ventured around a tall stack of cartons.

And ran into the barrel of a gun.

Chapter 35

Aw, shit! He'd walked right into a trap. He should have waited for the FBI agents, Greg thought, cursing himself. He released Dodger's collar as the gun prodded his chest. It was too dark to see the person, who was concealed behind the packing cartons.

Dodger whined, his tail thumping against Greg's leg. The sound echoed through the silent warehouse like a cannon volley. The barrel of the gun disappeared.

"Dodger? Greg?"

Relief shot through every inch of his body, leaving him breathless. *She was alive!* Thank God. "Lucky! Are you all right?"

"I'm fine," she said, but she didn't sound fine. She didn't sound like herself at all.

He reached for her, groping in the darkness. She came into his arms, the gun against her chest with the barrel pointing at her chin. Greg gently took it from her and guided her out from behind the cartons.

"What happened?" he asked. "What are you doing back there in the dark?"

"Waiting," she told him, her voice so low that he had to lean down to hear her. "I turned off the lights . . . to think. I always think better in the dark."

He knew this was a throwback to the only memory of the past that she'd managed to retain. A bitter, cruel memory of a mother who'd proved to be the mother from hell. Greg hugged Lucky to his side, silently promising he'd make things right for her in the future.

"Did you come looking for Brad and Judd?" he asked as they approached the shafts of light emanating from the computers.

Her head brushed his shoulder as she nodded.

"You were smart not to confront them. Who knows what they might do." He was downplaying it, of course. He knew exactly what the bastards would do. "Tell me where the light switch is."

She turned, his arm still around her, and led him to a spot outside the glass-enclosed office. He flipped the switch, then stared at her, stunned. Dodger whined again, moving closer to Greg.

Blood coated one side of Lucky's face, running down the side of her neck. In her left hand she was clutching something. Blood dripped from between her fingers, splattering her dress and shoes.

Aw, hell! Something terrible had happened to her. Again. "Lucky, what's in your hand?"

She stared at him, her face pale, her eyes icy and unresponsive. Slowly, she lifted her fist and opened her hand. It took a second for him to recognize what she was holding. Rudy's tooth.

"Did you know that in ancient times Hawaiians made all their weapons from shark's teeth?" she asked, speaking in a monotone. "They didn't have metal until Captain Cook arrived."

She was scaring him now, the way she had that night in the

tent. He put his hands on her shoulders and gently shook her. "Lucky, this isn't the time for a history lesson. Tell me what happened."

She swallowed twice, her nostrils flaring slightly. "Do you love me?"

"I love you more than I ever thought possible." He pulled her into his arms and kissed the top of her head. "I'll love you forever."

She pulled back and gazed at him with those magnificent green eyes. "No matter what I've done? Even if I've killed someone?"

He almost flinched at her words, and at the anger that underscored them. The gun. The bloody tooth. Had she killed someone? The magnitude of his own emotions hit him hard, and he spoke from the heart. "If you've killed someone, I'll still love you. I'll stand by you. But I can't imagine you hurting anyone."

She offered him a suggestion of a smile. "I came here because I had to know what happened that night. Why was I wearing the shoe of a woman who'd died a year earlier? You didn't meet Brad's partner, Judd. He's a monster. He told me what he'd done without a hint of regret. He admitted forcing me to perm and bleach my hair."

"So no one would recognize you."

"Exactly. And Judd's the one who actually tried to kill me."

But Brad was in on it, Greg thought. His gut instinct had been correct, not based merely on jealousy. He'd hated the son of a bitch on sight.

"I was unconscious and they dressed me, putting on one of the shoes by mistake." She looked over her shoulder at the large metal vault. "Judd knew I was bluffing when I said I was going to shoot. He jumped me and knocked the gun out of my hand. The revolver was under me. I couldn't reach it unless he got off me. I jabbed him in the eye with Rudy's tooth."

"Good thinking," Greg said, looking around, wondering where the bastards were. The metal chamber, of course.

Lucky ran her fingertip over the serrated edge of Rudy's tooth. "The jagged edge really slashed Judd's cheek."

"That's where all the blood came from," he noted, relieved.

"No. I shot Brad in the foot," Lucky announced with unmistakable pride. "Then they knew I meant business. I herded them over there into the orchid vault and turned off the ventilator."

His heart swelled with love—and pride. She'd given them a dose of their own medicine. "Why did you turn off the ventilator? I don't get it."

"The orchids produce deadly fumes. Brad and Judd are in there right now with minor wounds. But their lungs are burning and their eyes are watering. They know I'm a new person, but some of the old toughness is still there. By now they think I've left them to die."

"But you haven't. You've called the police."

"You're right. I just called the local FBI office, then turned off the lights to pull myself together. When you came in, I thought it was one of their buddies, or I wouldn't have pulled the gun on you," she explained. "I want Brad and Judd to really believe they are going to die. I want them to know what it feels like."

"I'm so damn proud of you. Thank God, you're all right." Greg gathered her in his arms and gently rocked her. "I love you so much."

"I love you, too. I missed you every minute. If it hadn't been for Julie—"

"Woof!" A sharp bark from Dodger interrupted them.

"Couldn't be," Greg muttered. Yet knowing Dodger had proven to be an infallible S and R dog, he realized it was a signal. Dodger was pointing toward the orchid vault.

"What is it?" Lucky asked, then she understood. "Oh, no! What have I done? I didn't mean to kill either of them."

"How long have they been in there?"

Lucky checked her watch. "Ten minutes. Judd said it takes much longer than that to kill someone."

"Someone's dead in there, but don't worry. You did the right thing. You called the authorities."

"The FBI should have been here by now. If they'd come sooner, no one would have died."

Greg grabbed the gun off the table. "It's hard to find this place unless you know your way around Chinatown. Open the vault and we'll see what happened. Maybe one of them is still alive."

They approached the metal chamber with Dodger at their heels. Greg had the gun trained on the door.

"Please, God," Lucky prayed out loud. "Don't let Brad be dead. I don't want to be responsible for killing Julie's father."

She released the lever on the steel door. Greg kept the gun pointed at the opening, not knowing what to expect. Out staggered a man he'd never seen. It had to be Judd Fremont, because his cheek was gouged and bloody. The man stumbled across the floor, clutching his throat and gasping for air.

"Oh, my God!" Lucky cried. "Brad must be dead. I didn't mean to kill him. Honest. I just wanted to teach him a lesson, then let justice take its sweet time with him."

She started to move into the chamber, but Greg stopped her. "Stay here. Keep the gun on him and don't hesitate to shoot."

The orchid-filled vault was a disaster. Orchid plants had been knocked over, many delicate blossoms crushed. In the back Brad Wagner was sprawled across the floor. His death had been neither easy nor quick.

Greg left him for the authorities and returned to Lucky's side. "It's okay, angel. You didn't kill him. His partner strangled him."

Lucky stared at Greg in disbelief as he took the gun from her. "Why?"

Judd Fremont had recovered somewhat and was sitting up

now, taking deep and ragged breaths. He managed to lift one eyebrow as if to say they were incredibly stupid. A few seconds later, he spoke. "There's only so much air in there. Not enough for both of us. I knew you'd call the police. But when so much time went by, I had no choice—"

"Open up!" yelled a male voice. "FBI."

Greg shook his head. "The door's open. Come on in."

They turned Judd over to the two field agents, who immediately called the local authorities to remove Brad's body. Greg guided Lucky outside into the bright sunlight, where they waited to give their statements.

"I didn't want Brad to die," Lucky said, the threat of tears in her voice.

He put his arm around her, wondering how he could love someone so much and how he could make up for all she'd suffered. "Look, it's for the best. Would you want Julie to see her father on death row for murder?"

"No, but . . . she loves him. How am I going to tell her that he's dead?"

"I'll come with you. We'll bring her to Maui and you'll stay with Sarah. Being around other children will help."

"Yes, Sarah will know what to do."

"Julie's very young. It'll be easier on her now than if she were older."

Lucky gazed up at him, nodding. "Are you? Are we? . . ."

"Going to be together?" he finished, and she nodded. "I'm never letting you go. Do you know what I thought the first time I saw Julie?"

Lucky shook her head. "What?"

"That I should have been her father. It hurt so much that I wasn't," he said, still remembering how devastated he'd felt when he'd seen the little girl. "It'll take time to work through this mess and for Julie to accept me."

"We can do it. I know we can," Lucky told him. "I love you so much."

Dodger whined and licked her hand.

"I love you, too, Dodger," Lucky said, patting his head. "And you're going to help us with Julie, aren't you?"

Dodger wagged his tail enthusiastically as Greg pulled Lucky into his arms. "I'm never letting you go. I love you too much."

Epilogue

Six Months Later

The *Atlantis* sailed across the channel toward Niihau. Lucky stood on the bow with Sarah at her side and gazed at the private island, home to the monk seals.

"The trial's over," Sarah said quietly, even though the children were at the back of the boat with Cody and Greg. "It went much faster than I expected."

"True," Lucky agreed, "but my testimony seemed to last two lifetimes."

Sarah touched her arm, her dark brown eyes sympathetic. "I know it was difficult for you, but Judd Fremont got what he deserved."

"Now that the trial's over, I can get on with my life. We're planning a small wedding next month," Lucky announced with a smile, happy to be able to tell Sarah their plans. "Greg's selling his place on the beach. With the money, we'll be able to buy a home like yours in the up-country. Julie's determined to have her own pony and get a cat to keep Dodger company."

"She and that dog are inseparable," Sarah said. "He sleeps beside her bed and follows her around everywhere."

"She's adjusted much better than I expected. Dodger helped, and you and your family have been wonderful to her."

The breeze fluttered Sarah's dark hair, flinging it over her shoulder. "In time, Julie will love Greg as much as he loves her."

"I know." Lucky smiled, closing her eyes for a moment and blessing Greg for all he'd done to make a new life for them. "I love my life. I'm happy now."

"Sometimes good things come from our worst nightmares," Sarah said. "God never closes a door without opening a window."

They rode in silence, leaning over the bow rail, keeping watch for a shark named Rudy. He'd been sighted by divers the week before. Lucky wanted to see him again, to see how big he'd grown. And to thank him for providing the lucky, lifesaving tooth.

The water was crystal clear, and below she could see the dark shadows of the reef and a school of yellow clown fishes with the distinctive black rings around their eyes. No Rudy. No sharks at all, and Lucky decided this would not be the best time to encounter a shark. Today they were releasing Abbie, setting her free off the Niihau shore to join the other monk seals.

"Mommy," yelled Julie as the boat slowed at the reef protecting the island. "We're ready."

"Coming," Lucky called. She glanced up at Nomo, who was at the helm on the deck above them. He gave her the thumbs-up sign.

In the fishing cockpit, Abbie was surrounded by the twins, Cody, and Greg. Nearby played Molly and Julie in orange life jackets. Dodger hovered around the young girls, his eyes watchful. Abbie was much larger now, no longer a pup but a full-grown seal weighing more than a hundred pounds. Nomo and Lucky had shown her how to fish, although Julie was convinced she'd been the one who'd taught Abbie.

"Wark! Wark!" barked Abbie, the way she always did when Lucky appeared.

Lucky glanced at Greg, loving him. He beamed one of his reassuring smiles. Saying goodbye to Abbie was going to be much harder than releasing Rudy.

The boat slowed and Nomo dropped the anchor, the chain thunking as it fell into the water. He reversed the engines, allowing the anchor to take hold in the soft sand below the surface. He cut off the engines and the boat bobbed, swaying with the current.

Lucky smiled, realizing the rocking deck didn't faze Julie. In the few months they'd been here, she'd discovered her sea legs. Julie and Molly were squatting over a bucket that contained a starfish they'd found and planned to return to its home with the denizens of the deep.

A sailfish swam by, its fanlike dorsal fin skimming along the surface of the azure-blue water, catching everyone's attention. Lucky took the opportunity to drop to her knees and have a last word with Abbie. She fondly petted the seal's smooth coat as Abbie looked at her with adoring eyes.

"Remember everything Nomo and I taught you about fishing. Keep an eye out for sharks, and if you see Rudy, tell him to keep his teeth to himself."

Abbie cocked her head and gazed at Lucky with soulful eyes. Lucky ran her palm over the seal's sleek back, thinking again how much she'd grown. But she'd always be "her" Abbie, a tiny, orphaned pup. Without a mother.

"This is it. I have to say goodbye. You'll be back where you belong—with your relatives. They need you." Lucky grinned, conscious of Greg watching her but knowing he'd understand why she was talking to a seal. "Think of it. Every woman's dream. One female to fifty males. You'll have your pick. Just don't let them mob you. Select one of the strongest males so the others won't bother you."

Greg swung open the cockpit door and the water lapped against the opening. "We're ready. Okay, Abbie. Go for it."

"Go for it! Go for it!" chanted the twins.

"Go, go! Go, go," cried the little girls, while Cody and Sarah looked on.

Abbie didn't seem the least bit inclined to go for anything. She looked beseechingly up at Lucky as if to ask, *Do I have to?*

"You'll be okay, sweetie," she said, her voice choked with emotion. Would she be okay? Would she survive the year until they returned to count the seals and give the males their shots? There were no guarantees.

"Go on, Abbie. Go on," Lucky pleaded. "This is home—where you belong. Know that I love you and my thoughts are with you . . . always."

Abbie scooted toward the opening, then stopped, looking over her shoulder at Lucky. Everyone was silent. Only the gulls circling overhead and the thump of the water against the hull of the boat broke the stillness.

"Go on, Abbie. I'll be back for you next year. I'll bet that by then you'll have a pup of your own."

Abbie couldn't have understood what she meant, but the seal plunged into the water. She pivoted in place and barked, "Wark! Wark! Wark!"

At Lucky's side Dodger whined, and she reached down to fondle his ears, tears blurring her vision. Greg moved beside her, his strong arm circling her the way it had so many times. Abbie shot one final look at Lucky, then disappeared beneath the waves.

"*Aloha! Aloha!*" bellowed Nomo, and the children joined him, chanting goodbye. "*Aloha! Aloha!*"

"Abbie will be okay," Greg whispered into the wispy hair growing around Lucky's ears. "You'll see her next year."

Lucky turned to Greg, grateful to find Sarah and Cody helping the girls return the starfish to his home. Julie was talking to the starfish, giving it instructions about watching out for bigger, meaner starfish.

"Lucky," he said. "Don't be upset. This is what we do. Returning animals to their native habitat is never without risk, but Abbie is going to make it. She's like you—a survivor."

An ache lodged deep in her chest as she turned to Greg, thinking how happy she was to be alive . . . to have her daughter and a new life. "I wouldn't be alive without you. . . ."

"No, you made *me* feel alive again. I loved you instinctively without knowing why. But then, you quickly showed me why."

She touched his brow where his dark hair fell. "I love you, darling. More than I can ever say."

"We're together. That's what's important. We're building a life together with Julie."

Her lips found his, and he cradled her in his arms the way he had so many times. Lucky quivered at the sweet tenderness of his kiss. An amazing sense of completeness swept through her. This man was her destiny, and even though she'd gone through hell to get here, she had no regrets.

I once was lost but now I'm found.

SPECIAL PREVIEW!

Turn the page for a look at
Meryl Sawyer's newest novel . . .

THE HIDEAWAY

Available from Zebra Books
Fall 1997

The wolf was at the door—literally.

Claire Holt unlocked the rear entrance to The Rising Sun gallery and saw the dog peering through the front door. She paused, her nerves responding on an instinctive, primitive level. She adored dogs, but this one frightened her.

Lobo was a hybrid, part shepherd, part timber wolf. His lush, silver-gray coat glistened in the sunlight. He had an aloof, almost regal bearing worthy of the show ring. Yet his eyes had the sinister, predatory glint of a natural-born killer.

Along with the wolf-dog, came someone even more dangerous—his master. Her gallery was several steps below street level. At this angle, all she could see was the dog—and long, steely-muscled legs clad in faded denim.

"It's all right, Lucy," Claire told her own dog.

The golden retriever hadn't spotted Lobo, or she would have hidden. Lucy was frightened of most dogs, especially of large dogs capable of killing. She wagged her tail, looking up at Claire as if to ask why they were so late in opening the gallery.

Last night. The words shuddered through Claire with frightening intensity. It was nothing short of a miracle that she was here after what had happened. She was not up to facing Sheriff Zachary Coulter and his wolf-dog, Lobo.

A powerful fist pummeled the front door. A two-legged wolf if there ever was one, Zach Coulter had been the town's bad boy when she'd been growing up. Now he was sporting a badge. Unbelievable.

"I'm coming. I'm coming."

Claire knew exactly why the sheriff was here, and she would be thrilled to say she had no idea what had happened to Bam Stegner's bear. She unlocked the door and swung it open. "Good morning, sheriff."

Zach Coulter had one powerful shoulder braced against the doorjamb, his long, booted legs crossed at the ankles. He was taller up close, but then six-two in a Stetson and sharkskin cowboy boots seemed even taller to someone who was stretching it to make five-five. This close he seemed larger, more powerful than she remembered.

The black Stetson cast a dark shadow across his face, emphasizing his square, uncompromising jawline. He thumbed back the hat and revealed deep blue eyes trimmed with dense lashes the same shade as his gloss-black hair. Those eyes gave him a smoldering sensuality some women found appealing.

Claire thought he was just plain cocky. He didn't wear a badge or carry a gun. Why bother? No one in his right mind would cross a hell-raiser who was even tougher now than he'd been in his youth. Just the sight of him brought back a memory she'd spent years trying to forget, and she had to force herself to look him in the eye.

"Real late, aren't you?" He sauntered into the gallery, his dog beside him. "Your sign says you open at eleven. It's past noon."

She adjusted the silver and turquoise clasp that secured her long, blonde hair at the nape of her neck. Usually, it tumbled to her shoulders in waves that defied a brush, but she'd been in too much of a hurry to fool with it. She hadn't bothered with makeup either. Not that she cared what Zach Coulter thought.

"I was running behind this morning. Are you interested in buying a painting or perhaps a bronze?" she said with a straight face, positive the only thing he considered art was a centerfold.

"Nope." He removed the black Stetson and tossed it like a Frisbee. It sailed across the gallery and landed on Wild Horse, her best bronze, as if the statue were a cheap hat rack.

"Just make yourself at home."

The cool air in the room developed a thickness, an intensity. The taut silence was underscored by the click-click of the dogs' paws on the buffed wood floor as they ambled off, leaving them alone. The sheriff's dominating, masculine presence radiated a certain intimidating ruthlessness. If Zach Coulter hadn't been the law, he would have been running from the law.

"It must have been a hell of a night." His lips quirked into a knowing smile.

"My private life is none of your business."

He reached into the pocket of Levi's that had been washed so many times they were more gray than blue. How he managed to jam his hand into jeans so tight, let alone get something out of the pocket, was one of life's unexplainable mysteries.

He withdrew a swatch of black silk no larger than an eye patch and dangled it in front of her nose. "Lose something?"

It took a split second for Claire to realize those were her panties, and she knew *exactly* where she'd lost them. "Why on earth would you think they're mine?"

How had Zach Coulter, of all people, gotten them? She had searched frantically, but had been unable to find them. Why hadn't she checked more thoroughly? When Bam Stegner reported his bear had been stolen, Zach must have gone out to The Hideaway and looked around, finding the panties. But why would he think they belonged to her?

Zach hooked his thumbs in the waistband of the skimpy bikinis, stretching them out to full size, and held them up to her silver concho belt. His grin made her want to smack him. "Your size exactly."

"Is there a point to this?" Claire asked, reluctant to tell an outright lie and say the panties weren't hers.

Zach's marine-blue eyes swept from the tip of her head down her stone-washed denim dress to the toes of her moccasins in a heartbeat, seeming to see right through to the sexy panties that matched the ones in his hand.

"Last night at The Hideaway—"

"You bitch!" Bam Stegner burst through the door, slamming it so hard a prize-winning basket woven from yucca, bear grass, and rare devil's claw crashed from its pedestal to the wooden floor. "Where'n hell is my bear?"

Three hundred pounds of enraged bully with jowls like saddlebags glared at her. Bam's bare chest was partially covered by a red leather vest, but it didn't conceal a gut that slopped over a skull and crossbones belt buckle. Or the tattoo of a snake winding up his beefy arm to stick its forked tongue out at her from the top of his shoulder.

Bam Stegner owned the Hogs and Heifers nightclub and the adobe bungalows next door known as The Hideaway. Although he didn't look it, he was one of the richest men in Taos. Most of his money came from illegal activities. He'd done time in prison, but these days he was too slick to get caught.

"What bear?" Claire asked, justifiably proud of her calm tone.

Bam stomped toward her, the spurs on his boots clinking, his huge fists flexing as if he intended to strangle her. "Don't play dumb with me."

"I don't have your bear. Look around." She waved her hand in the direction of the two dogs at the far end of the gallery. "Go out to my place. Check it out."

Bam grabbed her arm, his dirty nails biting into her bare skin. "Look, bitch—"

"Let her go." Zach's voice was low, yet as sharp as a new razor.

Bam released her but still stood menacingly close, his body odor so foul that she wanted to take a bath in lye. She stood her ground, glancing back at him.

"Arrest her ass," Bam told the sheriff. "Throw her in jail until she tells where Khadafi is."

"Isn't he over in Iraq where he's supposed to be?" she asked, unable to resist taunting him.

Bam lunged toward her. Zach's powerful arm shot out with the deadly swiftness of a rattlesnake and halted Bam mid-stride. "Get out, Stegner."

The devil himself wouldn't have argued when Zach used that tone of voice. Bam swaggered to the door, his anger echoing through the room with each spur-clanging step that left clods of mud on the polished floor.

"If I don't get Khadafi back, you're gonna pay, bitch."

"Stegner," Zach's voice boomed through the gallery. "Don't threaten her. If anything happens to Claire, I'm coming after you."

Bam slammed the door so hard that only a miracle kept the glass from shattering. Relief hit Claire like a tidal wave, leaving her knees weak. She'd known Stegner would be furious, but she had never anticipated he would try to attack her in broad daylight. She knew she should be grateful to Zach, but her pride—and the past—kept her silent.

"You're brain dead." Zach cupped her chin with his hand. "Why did you deliberately provoke Stegner? He'll be after you now."

She shrugged, pretending she wasn't concerned, which was difficult because his strong fingers distracted her. "I've got a gun here and another at home."

"Leave Stegner to me," Zach said, his thumb making a slow sweep across her lower lip. And back again.

The suggestive gesture and the sensuality in his blue eyes, kicked up her pulse a notch. It wasn't hard to understand why he'd earned a reputation as the town stud. Women threw themselves at Zach Coulter. Well, she wasn't that stupid.

"You're going to take care of Bam Stegner the way you took care of Khadafi?"

If looks could have killed, she'd be pushing up daisies. "Keeping a pet bear is not against the law."

"Khadafi wasn't a 'pet' and you know it." Her voice kept rising with every word despite her best efforts to temper it. "Bam named him Khadafi so men would think they were macho when he staged fights with the bear. Bam had the bear's teeth and claws pulled out, so he couldn't fight back. Now, I ask you, is that fair?"

"Bear baiting isn't illegal in this state. The bear is personal property. No matter how just the cause—stealing him *is* against the law."

"I did not steal Khadafi," she said with total honesty. "Search the gallery. Search my home. Search me."

"Now you're talking," he said, his eyes taking a leisurely tour of her body, starting with her hair and slowly dropping to her lips. His gaze lingered there an uncomfortably long time before detouring to her breasts. "This might just require a strip search," he said with a grin that canted to one side in a way some women would have found adorable.

The thought of his large hands on her did ridiculous things to Claire's heart rate, which infuriated her. She resented the familiar way he'd touched her a minute ago. No doubt, he was experiencing a hormonal overload that made him manhandle anything in a skirt. Forget this skirt.

"Get your mind out of the gutter. I'm dead serious. I did not steal the bear. I have no idea where it is."

He moved closer and she resisted the urge to step back. "I'm not bothering to look for Khadafi. I've got a bigger problem than Stegner's bear. Somebody blew out Duncan Morrell's brains last night at The Hideaway."

The news hit Claire like a knockout punch. Her breath stalled in her lungs, and for a moment the killer headache vanished. "Duncan Morrell is dead?" she muttered. "Who did it?"

"Stegner claims you did. Morrell had stolen your most profitable artist, right?"

"I didn't have a contract with Nevada. He was free to go to another gallery," she explained, aware of the bitterness etching every syllable, but unable to soften her tone. She'd discovered Nevada and nurtured his talent, only to have Duncan lure him away. "I despised Morrell, but I didn't kill him."

"Okay," Zach said, leaning so close she couldn't miss the trace of citrus aftershave or the challenging glint in his eye. "I believe you, but your panties were found in the bungalow next to where Morrell was killed—along with your wallet."

"My wallet?" She vaguely remembered dropping her purse in that dark room last night. Had her wallet fallen out? The air siphoned from her lungs in a dizzying rush. Her panties *and* her wallet. She couldn't be that unlucky, could she?

About the Author

Winner of the *Romantic Times* Lifetime Achievement Award for Romantic Suspense and Contemporary Romance, Meryl Sawyer has also been honored with the *Romantic Times* Reviewer's Choice Award for Romantic Suspense and the Georgia Romance Writer's Maggie Award for Contemporary Romance. She is a world traveler who has spent time in exotic locations from North Africa to China.

Her home is in Southern California, where she resides with her husband, three golden retrievers, three wild squirrels, and a yard full of peanut-eating blue jays.